The Emperor of Gondwanaland

and Other Stories

To Cathy, Mario & Zach, with love. Paul

The Emperor of Gondwanaland

and Other Stories

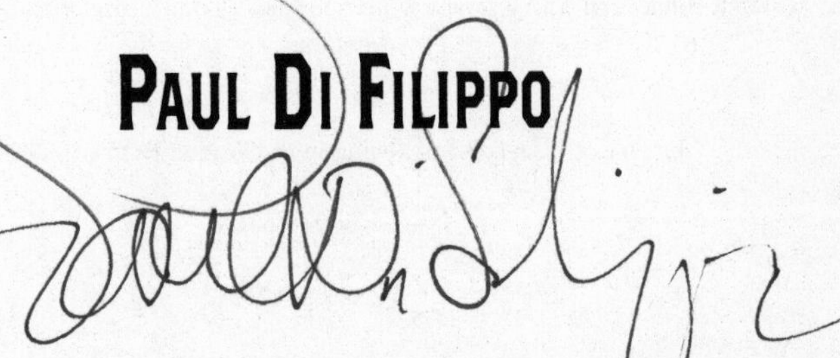

Paul Di Filippo

Thunder's Mouth Press
New York

THE EMPEROR OF GONDWANALAND AND OTHER STORIES

Published by
Thunder's Mouth Press
An Imprint of Avalon Publishing Group Inc.
245 West 17th St., 11th Floor
New York, NY 10011

Copyright Acknowledgments: "Anselmo Merino" first appeared in *New Pathways,* 1986. "My Adventures with the SPCA" first appeared in *Shock Waves 1.1,* 1996. "The Emperor of Gondwanaland" first appeared in *Interzone,* 2005. "Your Gold Teeth, Pt. 2" first appeared in *Aberrations,* 1996. "Beyond Mao" first appeared in *Postscripts,* 2005. "Observable Things" first appeared in *Conqueror Fantastic,* 2004. "Clouds and Cold Fires" first appeared in *Live Without a Net,* 2003. "Ailoura" first appeared in *Once Upon a Galaxy,* 2002. "Time Travel Blasphemies 1 & 2" first appeared in *Proud Flesh,* 1994. "Pulp Alibis" first appeared in *Schegge d'America,* 1998. "Science Fiction" first appeared in *Witpunk,* 2003. "The Curious Inventions of Mr. H." first appeared in *Electric Velocipede,* 2003. "Shake It to the West" first appeared in *Space and Time,* 1995. "Sisyphus and the Stranger" first appeared in *Bifrost,* 2004. "A Monument to Afterthought Unveiled" first appeared in *Interzone,* 2003. "Bare Market" first appeared in *Interzone,* 2003. "And the Dish Ran Away with the Spoon" first appeared in *Sci Fiction,* 2003. "Up!" is previously unpublished.

Library of Congress Cataloging-in-Publication Data is available.

ISBN 1-56025-665-6

9 8 7 6 5 4 3 2 1

Book design by Jamie McNeely

Printed in Canada
Distributed by Publishers Group West

To Deborah, who has seen everything

And to John Oakes:
ten years of making it up as we go along

Contents

Introduction

Every prior collection of mine has had an organizing theme behind it. *The Steampunk Trilogy* featured SF based on the Victorian era, while *Ribofunk* presented a vision of a biology-centered future. *Fractal Paisleys* was a collection of my allegedly humorous stories, as was *Neutrino Drag*, an encore. My "hardcore" science fiction ended up in *Babylon Sisters*, while my excursions into fantasy found a home in *Little Doors. Lost Pages* presented the alternate lives of famous authors. Finally, every story in *Strange Trades* explored the concept of working for a living.

In short, I have shown myself to be an author who likes tidy, homogenous packages of fiction. Rather like a person who prefers to eat an entire quart of vanilla ice cream at one sitting, rather than indulge in a heterogeneous three-scoop sundae.

I think there are some distinct advantages to books that reflect a thematic unity. The stories build on each other—especially if they're actually linked by characters and incidents, as in *Ribofunk*—and they convey a coherent slant on existence.

But there're disadvantages as well. The stories might begin to seem at best too much of a good thing or at worst repetitive. By the time you swallow that last spoon of vanilla ice cream, you're longing for a hint of chocolate.

Hence this collection you hold in your hands. My first non-themed volume of short stories. Actually, the book does have a theme: inclusivity. Here is a sampling of everything I do, all the different modes I work in, available in one place. Eighteen stories that have never seen the light of day since their first appearances. Fantastical, realistic, surrealistic, speculative—this book's a regular foot-long banana-split, with three kinds of sauce, nuts, cherries, whipped cream, and at least one flavor of ice cream you're guaranteed to love.

I'm reminded of a character in a John Barth novel. This fellow vowed to be forever unpredictable in his behavior. But then he realized a paradox: total unpredictability was *a predictable pattern*! Therefore, he decided to violate his rule of total unpredictability in only one category: what he ate for breakfast. He would eat the same thing every day. Thus, this mote of predictability in his sea of unpredictability would preserve the true randomness of his lifestyle from being predictably unpredictable.

This book is my link of unpredictability in my chain of thematic predictableness.

Does your head hurt yet? Mine certainly does!

I

Periauricular Dampness

When I quit my day job in 1982 to embark on the career of a freelance writer, I drew up a little chart. I wrote down the names of all the extant SF zines and planned how often I would sell a story to each one. I figured that if I could place just one story per month among them, I'd have it made, earning about half the money I had been reaping as a programmer. Enough to live modestly on.

Emboldened by Ray Bradbury's exhortation to fledgling writers to write a thousand words per day, thus composing one story per week, I figured I had plenty of room for learning-curve failures. Hell, only one story out of four had to be good enough to sell.

During the course of that first year, I wrote nearly fifty stories, lovingly assigning a number to each one (a tyro's practice that, I was recently pleased to learn, Robert Silverberg shared in the early years of his career). I amassed over a quarter of a million words of fiction.

And I didn't sell a single story.

Eventually, when my savings ran out, I had to get another day job. But I kept writing. And I must've gotten better at it, thanks to Bradbury's formula, since I finally did begin to place a story here and there.

But sell a story per month? Not even Robert Reed or Michael Swanwick or James Patrick Kelly—writers at the height of their craft—do that nowadays.

Wet behind the ears? I guess you could say that.

Once I began selling fiction, I turned back to the stories that hadn't sold. Now, in most cases, I could see why. But there was a single piece from the tail end of that run that seemed to have merit. Maybe it was different from the others because it was based on a template I had stolen from a master. Having read Melville's "Benito Cereno," I conceived of the notion of science-fictionalizing Herman Melville's sea saga. I shook the dust off "Anselmo Merino" and found it a home in a small-press zine, the late lamented New Pathways. *If there was any money involved, I can't recall, but it couldn't have been much. Still, I felt proud to see this in print. Editor Michael Adkisson, wherever you are: thanks again!*

ANSELMO MERINO

BEING A TRUE AND ACCURATE RENDERING OF THE ENCOUNTER BETWEEN THE SHIPS *GOLDEN COCKEREL* AND *MELVILLE*, OFF ENCANTADA ISLAND, AUGUST 24TH, 901 P.S.

All this happened many years ago.

For a period of my life, the events I am about to narrate—for the hundredth time, and yet, in a way, for the first—dominated my thoughts. Then, for a brace of decades, they troubled me little, if at all. Now, however, in my retirement, as I sit in the high tower of my lonely house in Tirso Town, watching the sea by day and night, the strange and disturbing happenings that occupied barely twelve hours of my life recur vividly and portentously, as if fraught with more meaning than I can legitimately and consciously assign them.

So of them, at last, I will write.

I. We Sight the Distressed Ship

My vessel, the *Melville,* was anchored some hundred meters off Encantada Island, a crescent-shaped parcel of land claimed neither by the Union nor the Aristarchy, lying in mid-ocean between Ordesto and Carambriole, some five degrees below the Equator. From where my schooner rocked gently on the pellucid waters of the bay, I had an excellent view of a golden beach, and the *Melville's* cutter grounded there. Beyond the beach, in a dense wall, began the satinwood trees, their silver boles tall and bare of branches and foliage, save for a tuft of feathery green at the very top of each.

From the island drifted faintly to me the brittle hum of the lasers wielded by my men, and the intermittent thump of a tree striking the earth. In an hour or so, the trundlebots would emerge from the woods, each bearing the massy, lustrous heart of a satinwood tree, excised almost surgically by my trained foresters. The bots would load the logs into the cutter. From each tree we took a piece averaging four meters in length and a fraction of the tree's original diameter. Those shining, red-brown cores, cut into boards and finished to a moiré-like sheen, would pay the costs of the entire voyage, with a handsome profit left for every crew member. Wasteful, in a way, to kill such splendid trees and use so little of them. Yet they did no good to the non-existent inhabitants of Encantada Island, and we were careful to harvest judiciously, the trees being our livelihood.

This last load would fill the *Melville*'s hold, and we would then depart for our home port of Tirso Town, capital of the Transmontane Union.

The sun beamed down—very hot, but not cruel—as I stood at the rail, eyeing the land. I was grateful for the lack of clouds, knowing that the banks of faceted solarcells atop the fore and aft deckhouses would be gathering energy aplenty. Overhead, in the rigging of the *Melville*'s twin masts, the sailbots scuttled like spiders, anticipatory of our leave-taking.

The allotted time passed. Breezes stroked my brow. On the sandy shore the trundlebots appeared, laden with Paean's bounty. The entire complement of the *Melville*—myself naturally excluded—followed: four foresters and my first mate, Runcie Belgrano. The robots deposited their loads and entered the cutter, followed by the men. The slim craft put off soundlessly, powered by its small electric motor. How often, when becalmed in the doldrums, had I wished the *Melville* herself might possess larger versions of such motors. But our solarcells could never accumulate enough energy to feed such brutes, and so, Paean being a world poor in fossil and radioactive fuels, we were forced to rely on wind and sun.

And not a bad pair to put one's faith in, for the most part, I always held.

The cutter arrowed across the calm surface of the sea. I began to discern more clearly the familiar faces of my crew, notably the fat, bristled cheeks of Belgrano. It struck me suddenly that contrary to all prior usage, the men did not gaze longingly on the *Melville* and her comforts, but beyond her, out to sea.

I turned with a sense of irrational foreboding.

I had often heard of a ship "limping" into port. Never had I fully appreciated the figure of speech until that moment, being a rather prosaic and unimaginative sort of man, not given to flights of fancy, nor extravagance in words or deeds. Yet the ship that approached us now, and which so riveted the attention of my men, did somehow evoke a human's sore-footed gait, crawling almost in fits and starts.

Like the *Melville*, the ship was a double-masted schooner forty or so meters in length, with clean and fluid lines. There, however, all resemblance ended. Where the *Melville* was trig and polished, scoured and caulked, this newcomer was in disrepair and foul shape. Her sails were in tatters, and devoid of bots. The solarcells atop her deckhouses were smashed, functioning as useless collectors of rain-water. I saw charred scorches on her rails, as if lightning or lasers had bitten there. Her whole aura was one of neglect and desuetude. No living figures did I mark on board, either.

Small wonder my men were so captivated, it was such an unex-pected and disreputable sight.

The cutter had by now pulled alongside the *Melville*. I had in the instant made up my mind what to do regarding the uncanny ship, and so leaned over to shout my orders.

"All bots: Come aboard with the cargo and stow it. Jenckes, Topps, Allen, and Strathmore: You also disembark. Mate Belgrano and I shall visit this stranger. Hold yourselves ready should we need you in any way."

Each trundlebot, clasping a piece of satinwood with two of its arms, ascended the hanging netting up the ship's side using its other two limbs. They headed for the aft cargo hatch, where they would deposit the satinwood and then tap the flow from the solar-cells. Jenckes, Topps, Allen, and Strathmore came aboard in their wake and made off to the galley, to refresh themselves after their work ashore.

I descended the netting, Mate Belgrano steadying the cutter against the *Melville*'s flanks.

In the cutter, I received from Belgrano his usual deferential nod, which I had long since ceased attempting to dissuade him of. Years ago, when Belgrano had first shipped under me, that gesture had rankled, seeming not in keeping with the egalitarian spirit of the Union as I conceived it; more the servile mark of acquiescence an Aristarch might demand. But after a time I realized it was only the old salt's way of acknowledging the trust he placed in my command. Although he had five years over my forty-nine at the time, he treated me as one incredibly superior to him, and I could not but be suitably flattered.

"So, Captain Sanspeur," he said in his hoarse growl, as he shoved off from the *Melville* before starting the motor up, "what do you make of this derelict? Think you we might find something worth salvaging?"

"Much remains to be seen," I said, as if I knew more than in fact I did. Actually, the appearance here of the lame vessel, so far off normal sea lanes, was an enigma to me.

Slowly, as if some unseen force impeded the cutter's progress, we approached the gaunt and haggard ship.

II. Aboard the *Golden Cockerel*, and Her Captain

As Belgrano steered in his assured way nearer and nearer the barely drifting ship, which seemed to have lost the current that had carried her so far, I scanned her bow, looking for her name. Several scores of meters away, I described the name in flaking red paint: *Golden Cockerel*. I knew then, from the style of lettering, that the ship hailed from the Aristarchy.

Why she neglected to fly that country's flag, I could not guess, unless it had been destroyed like her sails.

Also, at this distance I noticed the movement of figures on the ship's listing deck. So then: this was to be no salvage mission, but one of succor and rescue. I was grateful that the *Melville* held a surplus of food and fresh water (for I had replenished both on Encantada), with which to allay their sufferings.

Every minute our boat drew closer, I expected the rails to fill with the eager faces of the survivors I had glimpsed. The spaces at the starboard rail remained empty, however, as if no one noted or cared about our approach.

Finally we were bobbing close against the ship's battered hull. No ladder was in sight. Belgrano silently returned my gaze, as if to ask, "What next?"

"Drop the anchor, Master Belgrano," I said, and he heaved it overboard, paying out the line through his roughened hands. In the clear waters of the bay, we could watch our metal grapple sink for many a fathom, until it went where we could not follow.

"Ahoy, the *Cockerel,*" I shouted. "Toss us a line."

I expected no response from the incurious ship, and so started a bit when a thick hawser flew from nowhere and thwacked against the hull.

Old as Belgrano and I were, we still retained a spryness of limb many a younger man might envy. It was an easy task to ascend the rope.

Aboard the *Cockerel,* there was so much to see at first—and so many of the sights exceedingly jarring—that I hardly know now where to begin to describe what greeted my eyes. Let me start—arbitrarily, for I cannot recollect after so many years the exact order in which I apprehended things—with the ship herself.

I have mentioned the shattered solarcells and the charred woodwork, visible from afar. Fresh evidence of the *Cockerel's* sorry state was a scarred deck littered with trash: fruit peels, rags, empty bottles, several robot corpses, and, incredibly, pages from the ship's log. The aft deckhouse had several panels missing from its walls. Coils of rope lay in tangles.

Altogether, a most unholy mess. The skipper had to be dead—lost at sea—or insane for such a state to exist.

Simultaneously, I was taken with the figure of the man who had thrown us a line. A short and scrawny fellow, with a beak of a nose and a sharp chin, he wore a soiled knitted ecclesiastical shawl atop a ripped embroidered purple shirt. Purple pantaloons ballooned on his skinny legs. I recognized him as a Sanctus.

Five hundred years ago, the Aristarchy had colonized Paean. As their name implied, they had been severe critics of everything about their home world, including its religion. They had come to Paean, the first humans, to implement their curious and stringent beliefs. The Aristarchs brought with them underclasses to do their bidding. Their religicos bore the title of Sanctus.

On the continent of Carambriole, the Aristarchy flourished alone for two centuries. Then new settlers appeared in orbit, my ancestors among them, and claimed Ordesto, the eastern continent. From this second wave of colonists the Transmontane Union arose.

At the present, there was little commerce between our two cultures. Relations were marked by a coldness that stopped short of belligerence.

All this history mattered little to me at the time, in the face of the chaos around me.

Yet I include it here to indicate how my feelings of unease were compounded by facing this alien ambassador of a hidden land.

The withered man bobbed his head and torso, his hands clasped together in supplication. I gripped his shoulders and straightened him up.

"Stand erect, man," I said. "We're here to help, not plunder. I am Captain Josiah Sanspeur of the *Melville*, out of Tirso Town. I take it your ship is captainless."

His reedy voice sung out as if reciting liturgy. "Oh no, good sir, such is not our situation. We have a most fine and excellent captain, only occupied with pressing matters now is he. Our situation is more dire than mere loss of captain. You see—"

The head of the Sanctus had been constantly swiveling on his crane-like neck as he talked, while his pop-eyes stared here and there for I knew not what. His speech was cut short by the arrival of what he had obviously been fearing.

A Fanzoy walked into view.

The Fanzoii were the native race of Paean. They lived only on Carambriole. I had never seen one before.

Tall and willowy, the Fanzoy was clothed in a billowing off-white robe, sleeveless, with a square-cut yoke of intricate patterns. The Fanzoy's flesh could be observed on its arms and neck and bare feet, as well as its face. It was a subdued orange, like the color of a peach or burra-fruit, and had a velvety nap, not unappealing. The Fanzoy's lips were somewhat prehensile, its eyes a stunning violet.

It regarded us in what I took to be an unmenacing manner, yet the Sanctus was completely unnerved.

"I, I—" he faltered. Then, abandoning all pretense of calm, he turned and fled.

Belgrano and I watched him scurry off in amazement. With no human left to speak to, we approached the Fanzoy.

"Where is the captain?" I asked.

It eyed me stoically, curled its unnatural lip almost into a roll, and departed wordlessly. Had it even understood?

I decided to try the aft deckhouse, where traditionally, at least on Union ships, the captain's quarters would be.

At this point more Fanzoii, two or three dozen, appeared, seemingly springing up from the very planks. All were similarly hipless and possessed of deep amethyst eyes. I could not distinguish between sexes or individuals. Their velvet-flocked faces bore no obvious expression of ill will.

Yet they carried at their sides wooden dowels like clubs.

Belgrano and I hastened to the deckhouse, the Fanzoii following several paces behind, en masse. I confess my heart was racing a bit faster than was its wont. At the rear superstructure, the door hung closed on one hinge. I knocked, and also called out.

"Hallo, captain of the *Cockerel!* This is Captain Sanspeur of the *Melville*. Are you there?"

The Fanzoii ringed us at a small distance. I had no hint as to what their next move might be.

I heard the door opening. I swung about.

A man emerged, closely trailed by a Fanzoy.

"Back, you rabble," he called forcefully, gesturing languidly with one slim hand, which did much to mute the sternness of his command. "These are friends, not pirates. Can't you fools see anything? Get back to your duties."

At his words, the Fanzoii dispersed. However, ten or twelve took up sitting positions in a rubber-limbed fashion not far away, their truncheons resting across their laps.

I had time now to study the captain and his companion.

The man was of medium height, slender and wiry, in his mid-thirties. His face was wan and pinched, its olive skin drawn, like that of a hedonist whose pleasures have betrayed him, or a man used to comfort whom life had treated unwontedly harshly of a sudden. His black hair was cut short. His long mustachios were waxed and pointed. I smelled the pomade's scent. His dress was of faded elegance. His manner was refined, yet indolent.

The Fanzoy had all the qualities of its kind: the eyes, the skin, the long graceful limbs. Yet I thought to detect a play of keen intelligence on its somewhat angular features, a kind of alert inquisitiveness not evident in the others, which set it apart.

The man who had saved us extended a hand that bore several begemmed rings. "Captain Sanspeur," he said in a weary and lax voice totally unlike that which he had assumed to dismiss the Fanzoii, and yet which I took for some reason to be his normal tone, "I am Captain Anselmo Merino of the *Golden Cockerel*, out of Saint Ursula. Welcome aboard. We have much to discuss."

As I shook Captain Merino's bland hand, I marveled at his disingenuous understatement of the situation, and wondered what could possibly follow.

III. Proposals and Rejections

I expected Captain Merino to exercise common courtesy by inviting us into his cabin. Instead, he carefully closed the door—through which I had gotten only a glimpse of shadowy interior—and turned his aesthete's countenance toward us.

The Fanzoy that had emerged with him remained close by.

"I can't tell you how glad I am to see another human face," said Merino in a drained and languorous voice that totally belied any excitement. "As you can see, my ship has suffered disaster—a most unsettling tragedy. Perhaps you can better gauge the extent of it—and more readily appreciate my tale—if we conduct a promenade about the ship as we converse."

Merino's cavalier attitude—which I could only assume was a brave, if somewhat pompous, attempt to put up an unconcerned front—modified my fears that had arisen when the Fanzoii seemed ready to attack us. If this perfumed popinjay felt safe among his alien crew, then I could have nothing to fear.

"Very well," I replied. "Let us talk freely, as one captain to another. I confess there is much about your ship and its status that I find puzzling and improper." I turned to my first mate. "Mate Belgrano, station yourself by the rail above the cutter—to make sure she does not loose anchor and drift."

In truth, I had no expectation of that happening. My real aim was twofold: to prevent any of the Fanzoii from appropriating the cutter, and to be with Merino alone, without subordinates, so that he would perhaps speak more directly.

Belgrano left, somewhat uneasily. I had faith in his abilities to hold off idle Fanzoii, or, failing that, to remove the cutter from their reach. I waited for Merino to dismiss his pet Fanzoy, which continued to hover close by him like an apricot-colored specter.

Merino only sized me up with an open and minute disbelief, as if he could have wished I had done otherwise than send Belgrano away. He pivoted on one booted heel and strode off, leaving me to catch up.

The Fanzoy never left him.

Merino began talking almost before I drew abreast of him. He did not catch my eyes, but stared straight ahead, ignoring both myself and the shoddy mishmash of trash at his feet. His manner belonged to one who recounted a much-rehearsed story that had been leeched of meaning. Yet as his talk progressed, he became a bit more fervid and uneasy, as if he could not repress all he must be feeling.

"We sailed from Saint Ursula over a year ago, on a voyage that was to take three months. My crew was a good and capable one, ten men and the standard complement of bots. Our ship was sweet and swift. Yet witness the once-proud *Cockerel* now: derelict and without destination."

I could well believe that the ship had had a year's worth of neglect. "You shipped with ten men, yet I saw only one."

Merino waggled his hand negligently in the air. "You mean our Sanctus, Purslen Monteagle. *Faugh!* I had not even counted him, else it were eleven. He is supercargo, which the Aristarchy bids me haul, as every one of its ships must. No, not one of the ten remains"—he paused unnaturally—"alive. Nine were swept overboard in one of the fiercest storms I have ever experienced, along with many bots.

Not a month out of port were we when it came upon us. The surviving man—my first mate, who was also my beloved cousin—took a great hurt and died shortly thereafter. With our sails rent and our cells staved in, we have drifted since, at the whim of the currents and the winds. Monteagle and I have been living off the victuals stored for eleven, yet even these are almost gone."

The account seemed credible to me. Merino struck me as an indecisive and artificial captain, who could easily lose his crew through incompetent orders.

"This is your first command, I take it," said I.

Bristling, he turned to impale me with his dark eyes. "Why do you say so? Am I so obviously and contemptibly inept?"

I recalled the stern pride of the Aristarchs, which had caused them to consider themselves superior to those others on their long-ago home-world, and which no doubt operated to this day. I tried to placate the unstable man.

"No, no, it is just that you are young. In the Union, a man is often close to my age before he attains his first command."

Merino relaxed somewhat. "Perhaps I am too young. I had sailed much before this voyage, but only for pleasure, up and down our coast. My uncle, a high Aristarch, chose me for this mission. It is a government voyage I was on."

Merino seemed like the weather, shifting and unpredictable, a man of many extravagant moods. Now he grew the most excited I had yet seen him.

"If you could help me complete my mission, the Aristarchy will reward you generously. You will have my undying gratitude as well."

I was about to ask the central question that I had been withholding all this time: How did the Fanzoii figure in this bizarre affair? But I wished to ask it out of earshot of Merino's pet Fanzoy, which tagged along still, sharp-eared and alert.

Merino must have intercepted my intent study of his familiar. His quick elation subsided to dourness. He said, "You may say whatever you wish in front of Tess. I call her by the closest approximation I can make to her true name. She understands our speech, but cannot reproduce it, and so nothing will be repeated."

I observed then the queerest look pass between the man and the alien. It was a gaze compounded equally of desire, hatred, repugnance, and fatal attraction. I hope never to see its like again.

"All right," I said. "I will be blunt. Why do the Fanzoii roam the ship, armed and dangerous? Why are they aboard at all? Was it some mad attempt by the Aristarchy to turn them into sailors? I have heard they are intractable."

"You speak to the point," Merino said, squeezing his chin, "and I can do no less. The Fanzoii were my cargo. Now they are my crew. I asked you before to help me complete my original mission. I doubt that such a thing could be done now."

Perplexed and not a little frustrated, I said, "How were they your cargo?"

Merino sighed. "You do not have the Fanzoii to contend with on Ordesto, and can perhaps afford to be moralistic about what I shall tell you. Please restrain yourself. We of the Aristarchy are not so lucky, due to the twist of fate that inclined us to settle on Carambriole, and our plight could easily be yours. In any case, the Fanzoii occupy much choice land that our growing country needs. They are reluctant to be assimilated. Coexistence is proving impossible, as we expand. I was taking the first load of Fanzoii to the Nameless Continent, to plant a colony there."

Paean has but three continents. The Nameless Continent stretches from the South Pole north for some forty degrees. Only its extreme northern edge is livable.

"But could they survive there?" I said. "Is it what they are used to?"

Shrugging, Merino replied, "Such questions were not thought to be germane. Our plan was simply to remove all the Fanzoii there and forget about them, so Carambriole could be free. However, with my crew lost, I was forced by practical considerations to free the Fanzoii from belowdecks, for their aid. Tess here has been a remarkable go-between, almost my second-in-command. The rest of the Fanzoii have proved themselves"—he shuddered briefly—"eminently capable at whatever they turn their hands to."

The man's mission seemed both mad and bad, not something that I wished to aid him with. "It is impossible for you to cling to this hulk any longer. Come aboard the *Melville* with me, you and the Sanctus. We will find room for the Fanzoii somewhere in the hold.

With good winds, southern Carambriole is only three weeks away. Your troubles will be over as soon as you land. Let others try the voyage again, if they will."

Merino parted his sensualist's lips, and for a moment I was convinced he wanted—longed—to accept. Then the indigo eyes of the Fanzoy—Tess—seemed almost to spark, its upper lip fluting in that obscene fashion. A visible twinge went through Merino, whose back was to the native.

"No, I am afraid that is impossible. You must do whatever you can to refit my ship, so I may continue. Spare sails, cells, bots—whatever you can lend."

I balked. "It seems like helping to send you to your doom. The Fanzoii are not experienced. You yourself are debilitated by your woes."

Merino assumed a sudden absurd gaiety, clapping a hand on my shoulder. "We are prattling out here under the blazing sun like savages. This is not the treatment I should be extending to a guest—nay, a rescuer. Let's adjourn to my cabin for a meal—it's past noon—and discuss things further."

I considered. It seemed allowable. I might learn more if Merino felt more relaxed.

"Done. Provided we can send my man Belgrano something at his watch."

"Certainly," said Merino. "Come with me."

We reversed our course. As we were passing a large plastic water butt, full of a stagnant algae soup, I chanced to see the crouching figure of Purslen Monteagle behind it. Merino did not notice him, his eyes focused rather on some private landscape.

The Sanctus, knowing he had my attention, worked his wrinkled lips silently, over and over again, mouthing a single word which I at last interpreted as a name.

"Sadler."

IV. A Meal, and Its Consequences

Back in front of the aft deckhouse we encountered the twelve seated Fanzoii. Their demeanor was obscure and unfathomable.

Still in the positions we had left them in—ophidian limbs neatly coiled, truncheons laid across the valleys of their robes—they emanated a curious sensation of mental communion with each other, for all that their ianthine eyes followed our movements precisely.

Merino ignored—or truly failed—to see them.

The Fanzoy named Tess exchanged, I thought, a brief glance with her kin.

The captain of the *Cockerel* laid his bejeweled fingers on the door handle to his cabin. I noticed the smashed security keypad above the handle, and wondered how the storm had done that damage.

"You must," said Merino, "excuse the condition of my cabin. At home, I was overused to servants, I fear, and have consequently never gotten accustomed to tidying up after myself. And with the trouble and all . . ."

I dismissed his concerns—as always, seeking to make myself agreeable to him, and so bring down the barrier I felt he was maintaining between us. "I am not overnice," I said. "Life at sea is not for the fastidious. A moderate cleanliness suffices."

"Not for the fastidious," he mused somberly. "How true."

He swung the invalid door open and we entered.

Besmudged windows excluded much light. My eyes were some time in adjusting. Merino failed to turn on any luminescents, and only then did the ship's complete lack of power hit home. Suddenly, I had a vivid image of Merino sitting in this stuffy cave on a black night, his ship drifting helplessly, the insidious Tess his only companion. I experienced a deep sympathy for the man, tinged with revulsion.

My eyes could see at last. If I had thought the deck full of detritus, it had only just prepared me for Merino's quarters.

More logbook pages lay like a snowy blanket. Organic rubbish bred unhealthy odors. Two large wooden chairs flanked an intricately carved table, whose top was heaped with miscellaneous objects: a broken clock, a ceremonial dagger, glasses, a bottle of yellow wine, redolent cigar stubs. A bunk bore dirty, sweat-reeking sheets in a tangle. A door led inward to what I surmised was a private galley or head.

"Take a seat," said Merino debonairly, as if hosting me in a lavish palace.

Incredulously, I swept debris from a chair and sat. As I did, I noticed two other objects in the room. One was a wall-mounted glass-fronted case, with a useless lock, bearing on racks a score or more of laser pistols. The other was a tall, sheet-draped figure in a corner. From its shrouded lines, I had sworn it were a man, had it not been so stiff and immobile. Perhaps it was some religious effigy, and I thought it best not to mention it.

Not so with the weapons, however, the presence of which made me skittish.

"Why do you carry so many arms?" I asked, nodding toward the case.

Merino, seating himself, said, "It was felt that we should have them against the Fanzoii, should they escape. But you can see how needless such precautions were."

Tess remained standing, seemingly awaiting orders. Merino at last deigned to acknowledge her, speaking directly to her for the first time in my hearing. I listened closely for what his tone of voice might reveal.

"Tess," he said equably, "please serve us a meal."

Nothing. Master to slave, equal to equal, captor to captive—any or all of these might have been inferred.

Tess departed through the second door, and soon the noise of clanking pots and pans filtered out.

"Now," said Merino, "out of that brutal sun, with a glass of good wine to hand, we may truly talk." He lifted the broad-based flask full of amber wine and poured us each a glass. "You must praise such an excellent vintage. It's from my estate back home. I bless the day I thought to ship several cases of it. Truth be told, I believe sometimes it's all that has seen me through this crisis."

I sipped my wine after Merino sipped his. "Very palatable," I said. "But you should not give the wine overmuch credit. Surely the inner qualities of a man count for far more. Fortitude, endurance, courage, wit."

Merino's false ebullience disappeared. "Perhaps you are right. Yet when those fail a man, the consolations of wine are not to be spurned."

Merino drained his glass and poured another. Aromas of cooking wafted out the open galley door.

"This bouquet reminds me of my home," Merino said dreamily. "The dark woods, the bright, cloud-swept lawns, the lavish rooms of Truro . . ." His bronze-olive face grew animated. He stroked his oily mustache. Without preamble, as we sat in the gloom, he launched into a rambling discourse on his distant home.

I had only to listen and nod, and used the interval to study the enigmatic captain. He struck me as whimsical and capricious, by turns mordant and blithe, a poorly balanced fellow, who knew not his own mind. I felt then that his trouble was that he had no code to live by, was rudderless in the ethical sea, despite the imposed strictures of the Aristarchy. I, who have always prided myself on living by a certain code (whose tenets need not be described here), thought this to be the ultimate moral abyss.

What I did not consider at the time was the possibility that Merino had had a code—but that it had broken down of its inherent inconsistencies or limitations, leaving him despairing and deracinated.

The man chattered on, his black eyes liquidly refulgent, seeming to trap all the small light there was. What I gathered from his talk was that his old life had been one of leisure and only ceremonial duties, carefree and pleasure-centered.

Not the best preparation for the mission he had been sent on.

At last Tess entered with our meal: canned beef, heated, with boiled potatoes in which I later found a dead worm.

Her entrance completely transformed Merino. His pathetic panache vanished, and he fell mostly silent, drinking even more heavily.

As I ate, I studied the Fanzoy.

She—I had accepted Merino's assertion of her sex—sat on the bunk while we picked at our meal. Her supple arms hung lightly, with her hands folded in her lap. Her soft skin, with its nap the color of certain pale-orange roses, was pleasant to look upon. Her unreadable face bore down on Merino continuously. I noticed he could not meet her eyes.

I asked to send half my meal to Belgrano. Tess passed the plate out the door to another Fanzoy, waiting instantly there.

Eventually the wine began to tell on Merino. He had drunk an enormous quantity, opening another bottle brought from under the bunk. I was barely on my second glass.

I thought that now was perhaps the best time to mention the name that had seemed so important to Sanctus Monteagle. Perhaps Merino's unimprisoned lips would let slip something.

"Did you have," I inquired offhandedly, "a crewman by the name of Sadler?"

Merino shot to his feet, his face livid. "Goddamn you for a sneaking spy! How came you by the name of Sadler?"

I had expected nothing so fierce. Luckily, I had had the foresight to prepare a story to shield the Sanctus.

"I glimpsed it on a strewn page from your own miskept log. Why take it so meanly?"

Merino sat again, passing a trembling hand across his sweaty brow. Tess had never stirred. "Forgive me. It is only that—I thought—No matter. Yes, there was one Sadler aboard. Sadler Merino, my cousin and first mate, whom I mentioned before. A bold and worthy man, better by far than I. But he is no more. Would he had gone overboard with the rest, instead of dying as he did!"

Merino refilled his glass, which had tipped when he jumped up, adding its yellow river to the mess. I thought he had to forcibly stop his eyes from going to the veiled statue in the corner. Maybe some old touch of religious feeling he sought to deny was upon him.

Now all meanness, Merino barked an order at the Fanzoy.

"Tess, you bloody snake! Clear these dishes away!"

What happened next was uncanny.

Tess arose and approached Merino. When she was less than half a meter away, the captain began to stand, unwillingly, like an automaton, as if his muscles were under another's control. When he was upright, his arm swung in a similar fashion. At the end of its arc, it touched the Fanzoy's cheek.

He stroked Tess's face once or twice in a horrible mechanical parody of affection.

Tess broke the tableau. She gathered the plates and walked away. Merino collapsed sobbing into his seat.

I averted my face.

After a time, he ceased weeping. All his hostility had turned now to solicitude. Which emotion was the real one? Or were both?

"You must return to your ship, to begin ferrying us supplies. Let me escort you to the rail."

He stood. Apparently on impulse, he buckled the short scabbard and dagger lying before him onto his belt.

Tess emerged inescapably to accompany us.

We left the tenebrous cabin for the brilliant sunlight.

V. Return to the *Melville,* and the Unexpected

To step outdoors was to be reborn.

Never had I so appreciated the tropic breezes, the balmy light, the spumy air. The dark cabin seemed now like a grave, and I marveled that I had escaped.

How much more keenly must Merino have felt it, after inhabiting the cabin for a year.

I could see that in the hours I had been with Merino, our two ships had drifted closer together. Now only seventy meters or so separated the two vessels, one so clean and wholesomely gay, the other unkempt and exhaling an almost visible miasma of doom.

Merino, Tess, and I walked toward the rail where sturdy old Belgrano kept his post, a bluff watchdog if ever there was one.

A light pattering behind me caused me to turn.

Eighty Fanzoii or more—what I took to be the full number aboard—now followed us at a discreet distance. Their buff robes and peachy flesh made them seem like a pale wall mottled with skyrr-lichen which was toppling endlessly toward us. Their inexpressive faces were more alarming at the time than the ugliest masks of human hatred.

In their midst, through a gap, I thought to glimpse poor Purslen Monteagle, herded like a lone sheep among wolves. His face exhibited an agonized alarm; his mouth worked, yet no sound emerged.

My heart went out to the inoffensive man. I almost stopped to demand that Merino extricate him from the tangle of Fanzoii. Yet how could I justly interfere? The *Cockerel* was Merino's command, no matter how shabbily he had performed so far. How would I react if he began to give orders aboard my ship? No, I had no say here.

Perhaps if I had known it was the last time I would see the Sanctus alive, I might have acted differently.

We reached Belgrano.

"Anything to report, Master Belgrano?" I queried.

"Nary a thing, captain," he replied, looking relieved at my long-delayed reappearance. His face bore an expression that said that if I had asked for his opinion of the *Cockerel* and her captain, he would be glad to disburden himself of a few choice words.

"Very good." I turned to Merino. "Perhaps I can yet persuade you to abandon this mad scheme of continuing to the Nameless Land. You yourself mentioned that you cannot regard the Fanzoii as cargo any longer. Is it that they have expressed a wish to go there?"

Intense emotions flickered across Merino's saturnine face. "No, they're not cargo, and yet—we must go on sailing. It seems it will be forever. If only—but it cannot be. You must help as best you can."

His jumbled speech seemed the sign of an increasing tumult in his weary brain. Surely he would die ignobly not long after we parted, by his own hand or by Fate's.

"I have tried all I can to make you see sense. Failing that, I cannot deny you any materials I can legitimately spare without endangering my own ship. We will warp our two vessels together, and thus make loading easier. My first gift will be an anchor for your wayward craft."

I gripped Belgrano's shoulder. "Let's be off."

My mate descended first. I had one leg over the rail when Merino shouted.

"Wait! I must go with you. If only to be off this ship for a minute."

I regarded him searchingly from my awkward position, striving to detect any ulterior motive. He continued to beseech me silently. I deemed him truthful at last in wishing only a change of scenery, however small.

"Follow me, then," I said.

Once in the cutter, I looked up.

Merino descended the rope with weak limbs.

Tess came after him

I almost urged Belgrano to pull the cutter away, rather than have the Fanzoy set foot in it. Yet that would have left Merino dangling literally at the end of his rope. I doubted he could make it back up in his ineffectual fashion. Would the Fanzoii on the deck help him? Maybe, and maybe not. I could not leave him in such a strait.

I let Merino and Tess enter the cutter, despite my irrational loathing of the native.

"Master Belgrano." I ordered, "take us back to the *Melville*."

We motored off smoothly.

I felt my heart lightening as we neared my ship and left Merino's behind. The glum and high-strung captain of the *Cockerel* failed to match my spirits however. He seemed abstracted and lost, buried in private speculations.

We reached the *Melville*'s port side, whence we had departed hours ago—hours that loomed as years. I grabbed the wet netting lying athwart the hull. I was in good spirits again, my usual self.

"Come aboard, Captain Merino," I declaimed, "and let me return your hospitality. Bring Tess too." (As if they could ever have been separated this side of death!) "I'll have my mate run a line back to your ship and we'll begin the warping. You can step back aboard her when we're done."

Merino looked longingly at my vessel, returning the curious gaze of my men gathered at the rail. "I—I can't," he said. "I can't come aboard. Thank you, though. Thank you."

This I liked little. Yet who could account for the whims of an unstable mind?

"In that case, I'll ascend and toss down the line. Mate Belgrano will stay with you."

I wasn't about to lose my cutter at this stage, if Merino took it in his head to abscond.

Up the netting I scrambled, and was soon on deck. How welcome it felt! The first thing I noticed was my men's shocked faces, as when they had first sighted the drifting hulk. Events seemed to be repeating themselves in an endless cycle.

I looked back to the cutter.

Merino had come unsteadily to his feet in the rocking dinghy. His dagger was unsheathed and upraised. Belgrano was still rooted to his seat in amazement, but in the process of shifting to stand. Tess was sitting calmly.

The dagger began its plunge toward the Fanzoy's breast.

It was arrested in midair, Merino's hand caught fast in some invisible grip.

Things happened with baffling speed. Belgrano stood and moved on the Fanzoy. Either unable or unwilling to stop him as she had stopped Merino, she resorted to physical means, striking him an unexpected and massive blow across his thighs from her seated position. He toppled backwards and overboard.

Merino's dagger began to reverse its course, heading slowly toward his own heart.

His face was frozen in a rictus of fear.

Tess was immobile and dispassionate.

I glanced frantically around on the deck. The tree-cutting lasers lay where the men had first dropped them upon coming aboard, not stowed because of the strange happenings.

A slovenly failure I would certainly have upbraided them for. But now—what an unexpected blessing!

I snatched one up, rested its snout on the rail.

Before Merino could bury his blade in his own heart, I had driven a beam of light through the Fanzoy's chest.

She died soundlessly.

Merino collapsed over the gunwale, his head dangling just over the waves.

VI. The Slaughter, and Its Aftermath

Now the sun was falling in the west, as we fished Belgrano—unhurt—out of the water, and brought him and the unconscious Merino aboard.

The corpse of Tess we heaved into the uncomplaining water, watching it sink like an unattached anchor out of sight.

Once we were all aboard the *Melville*, we turned naturally toward the *Cockerel*. It had drifted closer to us in the meantime.

All the Fanzoii were clustered silently at the rail. They still seemed nonthreatening.

Suddenly a human scream filled the air. I knew it instinctively for the death cry of the Sanctus. A shudder went through my crew.

The scream served to awaken Merino, who got unsteadily to his feet. He passed a shaky hand across his wracked features, as if brushing unseen cobwebs away. I was at a loss what to do, and awaited Merino's insights into the situation. Clearly the Fanzoii were murderers and brigands and had to be stopped. But how?

Merino stumbled to the rail and rested his hands upon it. He looked toward the *Cockerel*, like Lazarus at his vacated tomb.

There was a parting of the ranks of the quiet Fanzoii. Two individuals walked forward with the sheeted statue from Merino's cabin.

So now they were planning to taunt Merino with sacrilege, I thought.

Merino blanched as if drained of blood.

The Fanzoii whisked off the sheet.

A man—clearly of flesh and blood—was revealed. He began to jig and prance and wave his arms, in a grotesque and obscene parody of a tarantella.

Merino spoke in a voice empty of all emotion, as if from beyond death. "It is my cousin Sadler. He is no longer truly alive." He turned imploring eyes on me and his voice rose in a shriek. "My God, sink that ship of devils and end his misery!"

With that he collapsed onto the deck once more.

I have said previously that I have always tried to live by a certain code. One tenet of that code was never to attack a helpless foe. For all the grief the Fanzoii had caused, I could not bring myself to fire upon them. What I would have done had they not escalated the battle I do not know. Perhaps tried to capture them unharmed, and so have doomed myself and all those who relied on me.

As it was, the *Cockerel*'s laser pistols suddenly appeared in the hands of the Fanzoii.

One shot the dancing Sadler through the head.

The rest began firing on us.

The beams were not meant for such long-range work. Yet one freak shot scorched the hand of Topps, the meekest among us.

A deep and furious rage came upon me then, and I shouted, "Up with our own lasers, lads, and hole the bastards below the waterline!"

The men fell to with a will. Four beams—much more powerful

than those of the pistols—concentrated on one spot, causing the water to steam and boil.

Soon the beams ate through the hull. The *Cockerel* canted thirty degrees and began to sink.

Fanzoii jumped into the water. Some started to swim our way.

Then did I violate my own code irreparably. I have never fully trusted myself since.

With a thickness in my throat I said, "Fire on any who approach —to kill."

The men complied.

When the carnage was over—and there were never any screams or cries, only the hiss of the beams biting—my men and I felt as one, that we would retch and never stop.

Our only casualties were Belgrano's bruised limbs and Topps's burned skin. Both took painkillers and proclaimed themselves well.

We winched the cutter aboard, and set sail from the tainted bay.

If any Fanzoii escaped to Encantada Island and there prospered, I cannot say. I have never been back after that fateful voyage.

Night fell. Merino regained consciousness in my cabin, on the bunk where we had laid him. After he took a meager meal, he remained seated at my table, myself opposite him, in a reprise with variations of our earlier encounter.

How different those two sessions seemed at that moment! My bright and well-appointed quarters contrasted immensely with that dank and unhealthy cave of his that now lay beneath the waves. Security and goodwill flourished here, in place of danger and suspicion. Yet a whiff of the *Cockerel's* malaise lingered, seemingly immune to being exorcised.

Merino sat with a gray blanket wrapped around his hunched shoulders. He sipped now and again at a small tumbler of medicinal brandy. He had not spoken during his meal, and I had not forced him.

Now, however, without prompting, he began to tell me the true story of his voyage, holding my eyes with his own tormented ones.

"There was no storm," he commenced. "Or rather, there was a storm, but it came later, after the real damage had already been done.

"We sailed from Saint Ursula as I told you: ten men, the Sanctus, and myself, with the Fanzoii as our cargo, our goal the Nameless

Land, where we indeed hoped to plant a colony. Was there ever a more misguided venture, with a less capable fool in charge?

"I was truly ill-fit for the rigors of months at sea. At home I had whatever I fancied. At sea I was cast back on my own resources. They proved limited indeed. Books held no interest for me, nor did the petty details of managing the ship and crew. I began to chafe under the dull monotony of the trip. The sameness of the food, the company, the sights.

"One daily sight was that of the Fanzoii taking their exercise on deck. Sadler had advised me to let them rot in the hold, but I contended that they were our charges, and could hardly function as colonists if mistreated. So we let them come up five at a time under guard, to take light and air.

"After a while, I began to notice one Fanzoy in particular. You will hardly need to be told that it was Tess. She seemed more vibrant than rest, almost human. And then there was her sinuous way of carrying herself, which gradually grew more and more attractive to me."

Here Merino coughed, sipped his brandy, and resumed speaking.

"I have always been a womanizer, I fear. It was so easy to indulge, in my privileged position. There were always women—of my own class or lower—who were willing to satisfy my lusts.

"On the voyage, there were none. And it was maddening.

"I resisted the evil urge to sleep with the Fanzoy Tess as long as I could. Perhaps you, or another strong soul, would never have succumbed. I can only recount what I did—did deliberately, but with no foreknowledge of the consequences, I swear.

"One night I had my men act as bawds and fetch the Fanzoy to my cabin. They obeyed, but eyed me with disgust. They left us alone.

"Not to mince words, I took the alien carnally, upon the very bunk she sat on so mockingly while you were there.

"She did not resist at all.

"It was like yet unlike sex with a human woman. I will say no more than that. What is crucial is what happened after.

"I found myself bonded psychically to the Fanzoy."

Merino assumed a contemplative air for a second, as if he had long considered this part of his gruesome experiences in a detached way, insofar as it applied to his whole culture.

"We know so little about them, having ignored them all these centuries of our uneasy coexistence. Apparently, from what I later learned, the Fanzoii—highly telepathic among themselves—mate but once, and for life, forging a special mental link between couples.

"Among Fanzoii, the bond is a two-way union between equals.

"Between a human and a Fanzoy, it is a chain binding slave and master.

"I was now subject to Tess's compulsions. Although I could fight them for a time, I always caved in. She proved that during the first night. Also, a vague conceptual link sprang up between us. Tess could easily project her thoughts to me, but had trouble reading mine.

"I was forced to keep Tess in my cabin all the next day. The men spoke of it behind my back, uneasy and afraid. When the next night came, Tess had me free all her comrades from belowdecks, promising that my men would not be hurt.

"But there was instant carnage. The Fanzoii broke open the armory and lasered all my men, save for Sadler and the Sanctus, who hid in the galley.

"One man—I know not who—had the presence of mind before being hunted down to wreck the solarcells and command many of the robots to hurl themselves overboard.

"When dawn broke the *Cockerel* was a bloody abattoir, under complete control of the Fanzoii.

"With their savagery dissipated, the Fanzoii let Sadler and Purslen live. But they wanted them under their control. So another Fanzoy female raped Sadler. When they stripped Purslen they found him to be a capon. They almost killed him outright, but he begged so piteously they relented, deeming him harmless, which he proved indeed to be.

"Three days later the storm truly came upon us. Without men or bots, we sustained the damage you saw.

"In the storm, Sadler received a concussion from a falling spar. He never awoke from it, and would normally have died, I believe, save for the bond with the Fanzoy female. She kept his autonomic nervous system functioning. They used him like a toy, as you saw. He was held rigid, barely breathing, under the sheet in my cabin, as you sat unknowing, not two meters away."

Merino's tale of horror made my stomach and mind revolt. Yet I longed to hear it through to its end. As I watched the shriveled man speak, clearly a husk of his former elegant self, the same mix of pity and repugnance I had felt for him earlier swept over me.

"The next months were a torpid living hell. The Fanzoii, as I understood through the thoughts of Tess, longed to return to Carambriole, or, failing that, to make landfall elsewhere. Many times they were so frustrated by their situation that Monteagle and I were nearly put to death.

"But always they saved us to be their go-betweens, should we ever sight another ship.

"And then you hailed us.

"When you and your mate came aboard, you nearly died. Outside my cabin, the Fanzoii were ready to set upon you, despite their prior plans. Through Tess, I saved your lives. I convinced her that we could get all we wanted through subterfuge, and that if we killed you it would alert your ship, which would sail away.

"The rest you know. I emerged and made my show of commanding those who commanded me. Then fell to me the task of convincing you of our innocent need. Every second you were on the *Cockerel*, death hovered at your back, should you so much as breathe suspicion of the true state of affairs.

"Only my play-acting kept you and your mate—and possibly the rest of your crew—from death. Or from becoming living puppets.

"When you proposed to warp our two ships together, the Fanzoii rejoiced. They planned to swarm aboard in seconds and take over the *Melville*. The best you could have expected was to be cast adrift in my wreck.

"I knew I had to do something. I begged to come with you. Tess silently assented, believing me sapped of my will. Luckily she could not see the whole shape of my thoughts.

"It worked out as you witnessed. God be thanked it did. If only Monteagle might also have been saved. If only none of this had happened!"

Merino drained his glass. I wordlessly refilled it. He sat unspeaking.

Here then was the man I had labeled in my mind a coward and a spineless fop. Weak in the face of his unnatural lusts he might have been—but which of us has not some hidden master he bows down to will-lessly? Coward? Fop? How would I have endured his fate?

"I will take you home," I said at last.

"If only you could," said Merino, and gazed ceilingward with a shiver.

VII. A Partial Transcript

Seventeen years passed between the time I watched the despondent Anselmo Merino, a borrowed suit of my clothes hanging loosely on him, walk down the gangplank of my detoured ship and onto the dock at Saint Ursula, and the time I next heard of him.

Much happened, of course, in those years. I returned to Tirso Town, a continent away, where I sold my last load of satinwood for more than I had expected when I embarked. There I paid off my men and found quite to my surprise that all my taste for being a free trader was gone, leaving a film of ashes in my mouth. It was as if something vital had been sapped from me off Encantada Island, never to be replenished.

I became a shipper of other men's goods, an easy and undemanding profession. Gradually I recovered my old spirits, but was never wholly as I had been.

One day, after the interval of time mentioned above, I found myself supervising the loading of some crates. Trundlebots were streaming aboard like ants when one malfunctioned and plunged back several meters down to the stone quay with its box. Robot and crate smashed with a sickening sound.

In the process of cleaning up the debris I noticed that the pottery in the crate had been wrapped in old and yellowed newspaper. Idly, I examined a sheet.

Its masthead read *The Saint Ursula Daily Gleaner*. The date was several months after Merino had disembarked.

I gathered up all the sheets I could find and returned to my cabin.

There I read—with, strangely, no feeling of surprise, as if I had always known that I would some day learn of this—a partial transcript of the trial of Anselmo Merino, on charges of dereliction of duty, gross misconduct, and bestiality.

The possible sentence specified that the prisoner be remanded to the Holy Inquisitors for undescribed punitive measures, should he be judged guilty.

I here re-transcribe what I believe is the most relevant—and revelatory—section of the fragment, in an effort to further illuminate that odd and flawed, yet compelling, man, Anselmo Merino, with whose life mine had the fortune—whether good or ill, I still cannot say—to become inextricably entangled, and whom I yet brood on constantly.

His fate the fragment failed to reveal.

I dare to hope they found him innocent, or deemed mercy applicable and pardoned him.

Testimony Given in the Trial of Aristarch Anselmo Merino, in the Matter of the Loss of His Ship, the *Golden Cockerel,* and the Miscarriage of His Mission. 6 January 902 Post Scattering

JUDGE: Quiet in the court! There must be a decorous silence, however repugnant the testimony becomes, or the court will be cleared! Fine. See that it is maintained. Prosecutor, you may proceed.

PROSECUTOR: Thank you, Your Honor. Let me recapitulate, Aristarch Merino. You do not deny having carnal relations with one of the Fanzoii you were transporting?

MERINO: No.

PROSECUTOR: Nor do you deny that said relations, by chaining your will to that of the alien referred to hereafter as "Tess," were ultimately responsible for the deaths of your entire crew and the total failure of your mission?

MERINO: No, I do not deny that.

PROSECUTOR: Can you suggest any reason why the court should see your actions as anything other than arrogant self-indulgence that resulted in the most dishonorable tragedy in the Aristarchy's history? How can your actions fail to besmirch all Aristarchs by implication, in the eyes of the lower classes? How can we be lenient with you, and not appear to condone your deeds?

MERINO: [*After a pause*] I cannot by any means justify what I did. And it would be reprehensible to lay the blame on those above me, who chose an imperfect tool for their task. I can only express my sincerest sorrow for the men I doomed, and wish that they had had a better captain. As for the taint I placed on the Aristarchy, I hereby affirm that I alone am culpable. I heartily wish that events had not transpired as they did. Yet who can undo the past? I only caution all those involved in similar ventures in the future, who might be quick to pass judgment on me, to examine their own souls and hearts and ask if they too might not fail when put to the test.

JUDGE: Refrain from instructing us in morality, Aristarch Merino. You are hardly in a position to do so.

MERINO: I realize that, your Honor. I only sought to point out the possibility that others might act as I found myself acting, should the Aristarchy persist in this misguided scheme.

JUDGE: I, for one, find such an imputation baseless and arrogant. And your attempt to shape policy is itself misguided. In fact, your whole attitude during this trial has struck me as overbearing and lacking in contrition.

MERINO: I repeat my deepest regrets for the suffering I have caused.

JUDGE: Protestations of sorrow are easy to make, yet truly felt perhaps only under the hands of the Inquisitors.

MERINO: [*Silent*]

PROSECUTOR: Do you have anything further to say in your defense?

MERINO: No.

JUDGE: The jury will now adjourn.

II

Adventures of a Restless Mind

We've all heard the famous adage about the fox knowing many small things, and the hedgehog knowing one big thing. It seems to me that this truism applies to writers more so than to those in other professions.

There are writers who focus on the same material from book to book, digging deeper and deeper into seemingly inexhaustible motherlodes of theme and topic. Then there are writers who feel the need to prospect across vast literary Alaskas, hungry for new horizons and possible riches in anyplace other than where they've already been.

It should be obvious to anyone who's read my stuff that I'm one of the latter. A fox on the move, a butterfly or industrious bee, zipping from flower to flower. I like to think such constant change keeps me flexible and fresh, makes me widen the tunnel vision we all inevitably develop.

So here in this section, you'll see me dabbling in realism, fabulism, ribofunk, horsepowerpunk, and what might be called "galactic core values."

I might not have struck gold yet, but I keep looking.

My, my, how times do change! Once, not so very long ago in a more innocent age, the notion of "monkey-wrenching" or "culture-jamming" seemed like good, clean fun. A stolid, stable, somnolent society can always use a few jesters to speed up its pulse and awaken the stupefied masses to thoughts of alternatives to their daily grind. But in a world where society teeters on the brink of collapse (or is perceived to be so teetering), due to enemies within and without, where the majority of citizens are scared stiff and a premium is placed on not rocking the boat, the actions which earlier had been considered tolerable buffoonery now look like sheer sedition. After 9/11, every yippie became a terrorist by default. But perhaps you can let your freak flag fly high once more for just the space of a few pages . . .

My Adventures with the SPCA

I screwed on the stolen plates, while Fiona used bungee cords to mount the PA system speakers on the Toyota's roof, next to the illuminated Domino's Pizza sign we had lifted from an unattended delivery car. Burr had his head under the hood.

Standing, I brushed grit off the knees of my jeans.

"Are we ready?"

Fiona twanged the bungee cords. "Snug as a plug in a jug." Tonight for some reason she was smiling. It looked good on her, and I felt sad she couldn't do it more often.

Burr emerged from beneath the hood and slammed it shut.

"All wired," he said, brushing black curls away from his eyes.

Tonight for some reason Burr was scowling. It looked lousy on him, and I was glad he didn't do it more often.

"What about the leaflets?" I said.

"Shit!" said Burr. "Almost forgot. I'll get 'em."

I watched Burr go inside our house. Then I turned to Fiona.

"Everything all right?"

"Yeah, fine."

"Sure?"

"Oh, quit worrying about me. I'm great. If you must know, Burr tried grabbing my ass a few minutes ago in the kitchen."

"That's just Burr. Don't let it get in the way of our job."

"Oh, I won't."

I still didn't understand something. "Why are you smiling?"

"I'm picturing his face when he looked down and saw the knife."

"Woof!"

Burr came out with the box from Kinko's. "All set!"

We clambered into the car. I was driving, and Burr was beside me in front, mic already nervously in hand. Fiona held the open box of leaflets in her lap. It had cost an extra penny apiece to get them folded, but was well worth it for the professional look.

"Take the freeway?"

"It's a little too light out yet," Burr said. "We don't want to make it easy for people to remember our faces. Let's go crosstown."

"Good thinking."

No one said much on the ride. It was a nice summer night, but we were all busy thinking about what could go wrong.

Burr tried whistling the *Mission Impossible* theme song once, but gave up when it fell flat.

The south side of the city was Burnout Town, trickle-down economics at its finest: vacant lots littered with trash; old rows of dismal project housing; fortified stores; a lone Salvation Army outpost; human wreckage almost indistinguishable from the inanimate junk. All that was missing to make it look like the worst Brazilian favela was a flock of circling buzzards, vigilante-strung corpses on the few remaining light poles, and a burning garbage dump.

Suspicious and indifferent black and Hispanic faces watched us from corners, stoops, and windows. Although Domino's was only half a mile away, on the edge of the devastation, their drivers seldom ventured in this direction.

"Better start," said Burr nervously. "Before they decide we look like a can of government surplus meat waiting to be opened."

"That's really unfair and judgmental," Fiona said.

"Don't get on my case now, you and your frigid bleeding heart—"

"Forget it," I said. "Let's just do it."

Burr flicked on the PA. He coughed a couple of times, and it came out sounding like God's bronchitis. He turned down the volume, then began his rap.

"Free pizza! Help celebrate our anniversary! Free pizza for the first thousand people! Grab a flier! Use the coupon! Free pizza right now!"

Fiona started tossing fliers from the car. The people already on the street snatched them from midair or piled on them like football players. Men, women, and kids were pouring out of the buildings.

The fliers looked really pro. Burr had typeset them on our Mac, using scanned Domino's illos. The pizza joint's address was in twelve-point bold.

At the bottom, in minuscule type, a line read: "Sponsored in part by the SPCA."

There had been a quaver in Burr's voice. But now that he saw how successful his spiel was, he got cocky.

"Extra pepperoni! Double cheese! Anchovies and pineapples!"

"Hey, cool it, man . . ."

We drove up and down through the neighborhood until all the fliers were gone. Then we made a big circle back toward Domino's.

Parking a dozen blocks away, we switched plates, dismounted the sign and speakers, and trashed them in a Dumpster.

"Hate to waste good equipment like that—" said Burr.

"They're incriminating. And besides, we won't be needing them again. No repeating ourselves, remember?"

We started to walk toward Domino's. Four blocks away, we could hear the angry crowd noise.

"I'm a little scared," Fiona said.

"Nothing to be scared of. Believe me, no one got a good look at us. They were too busy diving for coupons."

Sirens started to wail, plainly converging on the disturbance.

We couldn't get any closer than a hundred yards to the Domino's. It was surrounded by a solid mass of people, and the people were ringed by squad cars, their lights painting the scene a patriotic red, white, and blue.

A chant began to swell.

"Pizza! Pizza! Motherfuckin' pizza!"

I approached a cop. He dropped his hand to his gun instinctively, then recovered himself.

"What's happening, officer?" I said in my best concerned Young Republican voice.

"Some kinda crazy publicity stunt that went cock-eyed." His walkie-talkie crackled. "'Scuse me."

I eavesdropped on his conversation. Apparently, every Domino's in the city had been enlisted to deal with the crisis. All orders in progress had been diverted to the scene of the incipient riot. Ovens were being crammed with pizza after hastily assembled pizza to satisfy the crowd. Extra tomato sauce and mozzarella had been requisitioned from as far away as Boston. All speed limits and traffic laws had been temporarily waived for the courageous drivers.

I walked back to Fiona and Burr.

"Ladies and gentlemen, we have ignition."

Perhaps a little unwisely, considering the cops, we gave each other high-five salutes. But we couldn't help it, and they were too busy to notice.

"Let's get home," said Burr. "I'm starving."

"There's nothing in the fridge," Fiona reminded us. "Takeout?"

"Chinese? Or pizza?" said Fiona reflexively.

And that's when we lost it, laughing through tears so hard that we could hardly find the car.

The Society for Poetically Creative Anarchy was born in a laundromat, while our grass-greened workclothes were in the spin cycle.

That's where Burr and I met Fiona.

Burr and I had grown up together. We went through elementary school, high school, and three years of college as buddies, reading the same comics, the same science fiction, the same boho philosophers, the same semiotic jarheads. When we both ran out of intellectual steam and tuition money at the same time—that year they axed the Pell grants—we dropped out together and started a landscaping business with a used Ford Ranger and some old tools and mowers given to us by Burr's uncle Karl, who wanted to retire.

The work was hard but the money was decent, and we were our

own bosses. We even had a few months off in midwinter, when we collected unemployment.

We were pretty much content to glide along as we were doing. But even though we were pretty comfortable, we still liked to bullshit about how fucked-up society was.

We were metaphysical malcontents, our brains warped by too much Edward Abbey and secondhand Bakunin, but lacking any clear goals.

That day in the laundromat we were talking about this book called *The Abolition of Work*.

I guess we got pretty loud and excitable. The next thing we knew, this woman was standing over us.

She wore a backwards baseball cap, overalls with one strap dangling across a thermal undershirt, and the inevitable Doc Martens. She had red hair shorter than mine, too much purple lipstick, and six studs in one ear, each one a different fake gem.

A pin on her bib said: ANARCHY WON'T WORK? THAT'S AN INDICTMENT OF WORK, NOT ANARCHY.

Her voice was roughened by smoke and drink. "Have you guys read Hakim Bey?"

"Who?"

She told us about this mysterious Arab and his theory of "poetic anarchy." It sounded intriguing.

So we read him.

Burr and I started hanging out with Fiona. We found out a little about her.

She worked a phone-sex line, and hated it. But she couldn't stand any other job, either. She shared a crummy apartment with a junkie girlfriend on welfare. And somewhere back in her past, she must've been really hurt by some guy.

This part we more or less deduced by her determined stoniness to advances from either of us.

Her life was like a Lou Reed outtake. Easy to poke fun at. Except that it was all too real for her.

A few months after we met Fiona, Uncle Karl died of a heart attack.

So much for retirement.

We were amazed as hell to learn he had willed his old house to Burr, along with a few thousand dollars.

Fiona helped us move our junk in the Ranger.

When we had carried in the last box, it somehow didn't surprise me when Burr said, "Now we'll go for your stuff."

"Okay," said Fiona.

That night, over dinner, Fiona said, "You know, we're pretty lucky. A roof over our heads, food, money . . . Let's have a toast to Uncle Karl!"

We clinked our glasses, full of cheap jug wine.

"We'd be pretty irresponsible," Fiona continued solemnly, "if we didn't take advantage of our good fortune." Burr smiled as if he knew exactly what she meant. I realized with a start that I kinda did, too.

"Meaning . . . ?"

"Meaning that the time for talk is over. Now it's time for action."

"Poetic?" Burr said.

"Creative?" I asked.

"Anarchistic!" Fiona replied.

I pulled up in front of an unmarked steel door at the rear of the mall and put the Toyota in park, leaving the engine running. Odors of french fries and plastic clothing seeped in.

I turned to look at Fiona. She was sitting primly in the passenger seat, knees together, clutching a patent-leather purse in her lap by its gold chain. Sodium light lit her from overhead. I burst out laughing.

Fiona wore a teased and frosted wig. Her face was made up so she looked like Tammy Faye Bakker's slightly more sophisticated sister. A frilly blouse, madras skirt, opaque pantyhose, and pumps completed her outfit.

"Who's your husband again?"

Fiona's rough voice had somehow been transformed into that of a pampered suburban hausfrau. All that phone sex, I guessed.

"Councilman Danvers. And he's going to be so worried unless we find little Jennifer right now!"

Her voice had escalated into a kind of peremptory hysteria on the final phrase, and I found myself utterly convinced, even though I had helped write the script.

"Great. Buy us half an hour, and then we'll pick you up right here."

Fiona locked gazes with me then, only her pirate eyes familiar in her strange face. "Don't forget me in there," she urged in her normal rasp.

I was taken aback by her intensity. I couldn't think of what to say, so I reached for her hand.

The mall door opened, and someone hissed.

"Okay, you guys—hurry!"

The weird moment ended. Fiona jacked open the car door and hustled inside the mall. Burr took her place.

"No one will see her come in without little Jenny," Burr chortled. "There's nothing down that corridor but the rest rooms, and that'll be her excuse out."

I was kind of irritated that Burr had chosen just then to break up whatever might have been about to happen between Fiona and me, even as I told myself I shouldn't be. "I know all that, man. We've been over the plan a hundred times."

Burr looked hurt. "Hey, chill out. I'm as nervous as you, for Christ's sake."

"Let's get to it, then."

I drove around to the front of the mall. The immense parking lot was three quarters full. Saturday night at Consumerville. Nail painting and arcade action, digitized portrait T-shirts that read WORLD'S GREATEST DAD. Slurpees, burgers, and six screens of Hollywood entertainment. Who'd ever want to leave?

Tonight we'd find out.

We spotted the security guard's Suzuki Samurai parked in the shadows near the closed bank branch. Almost as soon as I killed our engine, he wheeled off toward the mall.

The search for missing little Jennifer was on. I could almost hear Fiona's desperate supplications.

Burr and I emerged. We each wore zippered belly-packs containing fifty tubes of Krazy Glue, their tips already presnipped and recapped. Now we took out one apiece.

Burr held his up like a sword. "For Duty and Humanity!"

"Duty and Humanity!"

We took up our positions on opposite sides of the random first car, Burr on the left and me on the right.

Like some bizarre precision skating duo, we inserted our tube tips into the car's keyholes and squeezed.

"All right!" exclaimed Burr.

"No time for gloating. Five seconds per car, remember?"

"Gotcha."

We started trotting, sneakers digging into the tarmac.

Finger the keyhole, insert, squeeze. Jog, jog, jog. Finger, insert, squeeze. Jog, jog, jog

Our first tubes sufficed for twenty cars, all in a little over a minute and a half. We wouldn't quite finish the fifty tubes in the time allotted, unless we picked up the pace.

"Are you game for speeding things up?"

"Lead on, MacDuffer!"

We began to seriously haul some ass.

After about the two hundredth car, Burr began to chant a eulogy for the dead with every hit.

"Inner cities! Downtown theaters! Vanished wetlands!"

I joined in. "Country roads! Independent bookstores! Public transit!"

"Clean air! Mom 'n' pop markets! Pushcart vendors!"

We had to quit chanting as we began to breathe harder. We were squirting locks shut about every three seconds. Security was still nowhere in sight. Hardly any mall patrons had emerged either. They were probably all gawping at Fiona's simulated distress.

At a bit under the halfway mark by our watches we reversed direction, heading back toward the Toyota, down another aisle.

"Shit! A keypad!"

"Cement the fucking wipers!"

We arrived back at our car almost breathless.

"We crack a thousand?"

"Think so. C'mon, Fiona'll be waiting." We pulled up outside the emergency exit. "—four, three, two, one!"

No Fiona.

A minute crawled by like a slug on 'ludes.

Burr began to mutter. "C'mon, c'mon, c'mon, you beautiful crazy bitch. Don't blow it—"

The door burst open, and Fiona dashed out.

I peeled out as soon as she had one leg and half her body in the car.

Beneath the absurd makeup, her face was pale. "They sent a lady cop to the john with me. I had to slug her."

"With what?"

Fiona cracked her purse. Inside was a brick.

"Remember Shepherd's Department Store, down on Main? They knocked it down last year—?"

"Way to go, girl!"

All the local stations had remote crews at the mall for the eleven o'clock news. The mayor of Malltown was ranting about harsh justice for the perpetrators of this "outrage against all decent consumers." Approximately fifteen hundred very fussy and irate people were stranded. Every tow truck in the state was lined up to haul their useless vehicles away. Cops earning copious overtime juggled the wreckers with the incoming rescuers: family members in second cars, as well as several hastily commissioned school buses for those without extra wheels. The mall management had coerced several restaurants into dispensing free refreshments to quell the indignant bitching. Liability suits were expected to total several millions.

Fiona wiggled her sore toes atop the hassock, her face pink from scrubbing. She raised a glass to the television.

"Shop till you drop, folks!"

The SPCA lay low for a few weeks after that.

Not that we were totally inactive. Just that our activities were a tad less high-profile.

One day we ambled down to the courthouse. The sun was bright as a brass button, the wind scented with maritime odors off the bay. Our bellies were full of sausage sandwiches and draft beer, and it was a wonderful day to be alive.

We strolled through the parking lot reserved for judges. Burr had a notebook and a pencil out. For every Saab, BMW, Mercedes, and Volvo in a judge's space, he copied down the tags and specs.

Almost finished, we were approached by an antiquated rent-a-cop.

"Hey, what're you guys doing?"

"This is our cousin from France, sir. Fiona, say hello to the nice man."

"*Bonjour.*"

"She's a bit simple. Her hobby is collecting license plate numbers from around the world, and we were just providing a few local samples for her. Tell the man 'Thank you,' dear."

"*Mangez merde, cochon.*"

"Well, okay, I guess."

Our friend Mister Jimmy worked at the registry. From him, we got the names of the judges and their phone numbers. Then we took out a classified ad for each car, identical except for model specs:

> 1991 Volvo, red, automatic, low-mileage, one owner. Must sell cheap & quick to finance messy divorce. Call 555-2222, days or nights till 1 A.M.

The newspaper—a monopolistic, jingoistic tyrant—ended up settling out of court for several thousand dollars per judge. A wise move, considering.

We bought a fax machine and a directory of public fax numbers. Several deserving corporations—GE, Dow, Martin Marietta, the usual suspects—received continuous-loop transmissions overnight via "borrowed" phone lines. The images we sent varied, from starving kids to war-torn cities. A fine use of corporate toner and paper.

This reminded Burr of something he had read, about automatic dialers. You can tie up a whole exchange for days with one. It makes thousands of calls per day, to listed and unlisted numbers alike, mindlessly cycling through all possible combinations.

With a part of Uncle Karl's inheritance we purchased such a machine and paid the rent on a studio apartment for a month.

Using a fake name, we had the phone company install a line. The message we recorded was a portion of Dali's autobiography. It took the phone company three weeks to track down the rogue machine. Reports were that a Nynex employee grabbed the ax from a nearby fireman's hand and callously murdered the innocent dialer.

Such simple yet satisfying misdeeds kept us busy while we hatched a more ambitious scheme. Neither did Burr and I neglect our landscaping business. Just because we were intent on introducing some fruitful chaos into society did not mean that people's grass stopped growing. Fiona, after being left home alone and bored for a few days, began to accompany us, pulling full weight with the landscaping chores. It was mighty pleasant to have her sweaty self working beside us.

At last we felt ready to embark on perhaps our most daring escapade yet.

"It's about time, too," said Burr forcefully. "I was starting to think we were going to go out with a whimper instead of a bang."

"You're saying this is our last prank?" Fiona asked.

"It's just an expression."

"Well, don't jinx us."

Once all the details were fixed, we set a date.

Late on the night before the big day someone knocked at my bedroom door. I was still awake.

"Come in."

Fiona closed the door softly behind her.

"Ever since Burr said that dumb thing, I've felt real freaky about this," she said.

It was important to keep breathing normally, as when a shy deer approaches, so I concentrated hard. "Nothing to worry about. All the bases are covered."

"Could I just—I mean, would you mind if I asked you a question?"

Not as long as I can kiss you afterward, I thought, but only said, "Course not."

"Sometimes I feel ugly. Do you think I'm ugly?"

My answer was the kiss.

We slept through the alarm. Burr had to knock on my door.

He jumped back an inch or two when Fiona came out and brushed past him on the way to the toilet.

But he didn't say anything.

More goddamn self-control than I would've shown, for sure.

Around the corner from Pleasant View Elementary School, I pulled the stolen Lincoln up to the curb. It was the mother of all understatements to say I felt like we could all benefit from a sincere heart-to-heart talk.

We sat three abreast, Fiona in the middle. When she had climbed in up front, Burr pushed in after her.

"Hey," I said weakly, "this isn't the way we planned it."

"Fuck you."

So I drove off.

Now I tried to think what to say to make things like they used to be.

It was hard to read Burr's frozen face behind his G-man shades. In that conservative suit, his hair slicked back, a suspicious bulge beneath one armpit, he looked too alien. Fiona too, in that stupid staid nurse's getup, winged hat, white stockings, and orthopedic shoes. I watched her chew noncommittally on a nonexistent hangnail.

I figured I looked equally weird to my friends, in my lab coat with its pocket full of nerd-tools, clipboard lying in my lap.

Suddenly I realized that the masks we had donned were now armor separating us, and I couldn't summon up any words to pierce them.

"Look," I temporized, "can we put aside icky personal stuff while we're trying to topple civilization as we know it? After—if there is an after—we can all roll around on the floor, gnashing our teeth and pulling our hair and similar emotional stuff. Okay?"

Fiona ceased chewing. "I'm up for it."

"Burr?"

Burr mumbled something.

"What? Speak up, for Christ's sake!"

"I said, 'Truce time.'"

A strange kind of achy sad nostalgia washed over me then. I remembered Burr and me playing war as kids, calling out "Truce time!" to each other.

I also remembered all the times the little shit had broken it.

I took the offer at face value, though. "Okey-doke. Can we assume dignified positions, please?"

Burr got out and let Fiona get in back. He resumed the front passenger seat, as far away from me as possible. I drove around the block.

Pleasant View Elementary faced a raised portion of the interstate that had bisected the neighborhood thirty years ago. That was why we had picked it.

As we had planned, no classes were in the schoolyard when we arrived. I parked in front of the main door. We all got out. Burr carried a crackling walkie-talkie, and Fiona a doctor's satchel. I held an army-surplus Geiger counter.

Inside, the fluorescent lights and crayon-disinfectant smells and even the color of the tiles intensified my earlier sense of déjà vu. I felt disoriented, and had to give myself a mental shake.

The principal's secretary was an old lady with violet-tinted hair and architectural eyeglasses.

"We need to see Principal Crumley immediately," I told her.

Plainly taken aback by our admittedly bizarre outfits, she hesitated. "Who . . . who shall I say is calling?"

Burr stepped forward and flashed his fake ID. "Government business, ma'am."

"Step this way."

Principal Crumley was a plump, middle-aged guy with a bad wig that I was sure the kids had a dozen derisive terms for. He rose awkwardly to greet us.

"What can I do for you?"

"Principal Crumley, my name is Doctor Andy Breton. My companions are Agent Naranja and Nurse Danvers. We're here because there's been a terrible accident."

Principal Crumley sat limply down. Sweat sprang from his brow. "Not Miss Angell's field trip—?"

"No, not that I know of. It's a trifle more complicated than that.

You see, a truck carrying radioactive wastes over our interstate highways system—in full compliance with all federal regulations, of course—just had a serious accident not long ago, about half a mile upwind of your school."

"Good Lord!"

"Don't panic, Principal Crumley. Panic is the last thing we need now. That's why there's been no broadcast of this disaster over the media. Emergency response teams like ours are circulating quietly through the affected area even as we speak, attempting to deal with the situation. May I?"

I gestured with the Geiger counter. Principal Crumley nodded When I clicked it on, the jammed circuits went wild with clicking. Principal Crumley turned the color of arithmetic paper.

"What . . . what are we going to do?"

"The very first thing is to tend to the children. With their smaller masses, they're much more vulnerable. Luckily, we've come prepared. Principal Crumley, do you have plenty of orange juice?"

"Orange juice?"

"We've got to administer potassium iodide right away. It's in pill form."

"Oh, I see. Yes, of course, we've got lots of juice."

"Very well, then. Can you assemble all the children in the gym?"

"Right away!"

Principal Crumley got on the speakers. Shortly after, we were heading toward the gym, just slightly in advance of the noisy, excited kids.

"I'll leave it to you to brief your staff, principal. Please stress the need for absolute compliance with our orders, and the need to maintain a closed environment here, at least until the blocking agents have been administered."

"Of course. They're good people. There won't be any trouble."

"We're holding you fully responsible," Burr said menacingly.

Soon we had a table set up at one end of the gym, quarts of OJ and Dixie cups on top. The kids had been formed into a single line that wound back and forth, youngest up front. Their initial excitement was giving way to mild unease, as they witnessed the somber expressions on the faces of their teachers, who formed a knot around a whispering Principal Crumley.

Fiona opened her satchel and reached inside. One by one, she took out several bottles of ominous-looking pills and set them on the table.

Over-the-counter multivitamins. A kid could never get enough vitamins.

From the knot of teachers we suddenly heard a raised shaky male voice. "But what about us!"

The three of us cast a withering glance at the teachers, and they shamefully shuffled their feet. There were no more outbursts.

With Burr setting up doses of juice and Fiona putting pills into individual foil hors d'oeuvres liners, we began to immunize the kids against trusting their government.

The line moved slowly along. Some of the kids had begun to sniffle and weep. I felt sad for them, but knew they'd appreciate this when they grew up.

Everything was going according to plan until Fiona spoke to Burr. "I need some more juice, Agent Naranja."

"Say please."

"Please."

Burr leered. "Pretty please."

Fiona was silent. She looked to me. Not over-hopeful, I nodded. She squeezed the words out. "Pretty please."

"Pretty please with sugar on top."

Fiona exploded. "Fuck you!"

"I wish you would," Burr said calmly.

Then he pulled the fire alarm on the wall behind him.

"Oh, mother . . ." I ventured over the shrill noise.

Principal Crumley and some of the teachers were advancing on us.

"We've got to split," I said softly.

"Not me," Burr said. "I'm staying right here." He collapsed to the floor and went limp.

Fiona tugged at my arm. "Let's go." I looked at Fiona. I looked at Burr. "No. It's all of us or no one. Help me with him."

"You sentimental jerk," said Fiona. But she went and grabbed Burr's wrists. I took his ankles, and we lifted most of him, though his ass dragged.

"What's the trouble?" said Principal Crumley, wringing his hands.

"The radiation's got to him. He took a bad dose at Chernobyl—"

A beefy phys-ed type blocked our way.

"I don't think you jokers are for real—"

Fiona kicked him in the ankle. He yelped, bent down to rub it, and she kneed him in the jaw.

While his comrades clustered around the stricken teacher and tried to calm the shrieking kids, we bumped a silent and complacent Burr down the corridor and out the door.

"Toss him in the back!" Fiona said, and we did.

It was only after we had ditched the Lincoln, transferred Burr to the back seat of the Toyota, loaded its trunk with a few possessions, and were on the interstate heading south out of town, that the cause of our rapid departure spoke.

"Why'd you do it?"

I thought about it. "Remember when we were six, and you got me real mad and I threw that rock at you and it hit you in the head and you fell down unconscious?"

"Yeah . . ."

"I owed you one."

"But now the score's even, right?" said Fiona.

"Right."

"Right."

And the three of us drove away.

One of my favorite Steely Dan songs is "Any World (That I'm Welcome To)," in which the narrator fantasizes about slipping through time and space and alternate dimensions to a more hospitable clime, some realm that consorts better with his temperament. This dream of fleeing to a personal utopia is a powerful one, rich enough for endless variations. Here's my take on the theme, with a reminder at the end that "in dreams begin responsibilities."

The Emperor of Gondwanaland

"Hey, Mutt! It's playtime, let's go!"

Mutt Spindler raised his gaze above the flat-screen monitor that dominated his desk. The screen displayed Pagemaker layouts for next month's issue of *PharmaNotes*, a trade publication for the drug industry. Mutt had the cankerous misfortune to be assistant editor of *PharmaNotes*, a job he had held for the last three quietly miserable years.

In the entrance to his cubicle stood Gifford, Cody, and Melba, three of Mutt's coworkers. Gifford sported a giant foam finger avowing his allegiance to whatever sports team was currently high in the standings of whatever season it chanced to be. Cody had a silver hip flask raised to her lips, imbibing a liquid that Mutt could be fairly certain did not issue from the Poland Springs cooler. Melba had already undone her formerly decorous shirt several buttons upward from the hem and knotted it, exposing a belly that reminded Mutt of a slab of Godiva chocolate.

Mutt pictured with facile vividness the events of the evening that would ensue, should he choose to accept Gifford's invitation. His projections were based on numerous past such experiences. Heavy alcohol consumption and possible ingestion of illicit stimulants, followed by slurred, senseless conversation conducted at eardrum-piercing volume to overcome whatever jagged ambient noise was passing itself off as music these days. Some hypnagogic, sensory-impaired dancing with one strange woman or another, leading in all likelihood to a meaningless hookup, the details of which would be impossible to recall in the morning, resulting in hypochondriacal worries and vacillating commitments to get one kind of STD test or another. And of course the leftover brain damage and fraying of neurological wiring would ensure that the demands of the office would be transformed from their usual simple hellishness to torture of an excruciating variety undreamed of by even, say, a team of Catholic school nuns and the unlamented Uday Hussein.

Gifford could sense his cautious friend wavering toward abstinence. "C'mon, Mutt! We're gonna hit Slamdunk's first, then Black Rainbow. And we'll finish up at Captains Curvaceous."

Mention of the last-named club, a strip joint where Mutt had once managed to drop over five hundred dollars of his tiny Christmas bonus while simultaneously acquiring a black eye and a chipped tooth, caused a shiver to surf his spine.

"Uh, thanks, guys, for thinking of me. But I just can't swing it. If I don't get this special ad section squared away by tonight, we'll miss the printer's deadlines."

Cody pocketed her flask and grabbed Gifford's arm. "Oh, leave the little drudge alone, Giff. It's obvious he's so in love with his job. Haven't you seen his lip-prints on the screen?"

Mutt was hurt and insulted. Was it his fault that he had been promoted to assistant editor over Cody? He wanted to say something in his defense, but couldn't think of a comeback that wouldn't sound whiny. And then the window closed on any possible repartee.

Gifford unself-consciously scratched his butt with his foam finger. "Okay, pal, maybe next time. Let's shake a tail, ladies."

Melba winked at Mutt as she walked away. "Gonna miss you, lover-boy."

Then the trio was gone.

Mutt hung his head in his hands. Why had he ever slept with Melba? Sleeping with coworkers was insane. Yet he had done it. The affair was over now, but the awkward repercussions lingered. Another black mark on his karma.

Refocusing on the screen, Mutt tried hard to proof the text floating before him. "Epigenetix-brand sequencers guarantee faster throughput . . ." The words and pictures blurred into a jittery multicolored fog like a mosh pit full of amoebas. Was he crying? For

Christ's sake, why the hell was he crying? Just because he had to hold down a suck-ass job he hated just to pay his grad-school loans, had no steady woman, hadn't been snow-boarding in two years, had put on five pounds since the summer, and experienced an undeniable yet shameful thrill when contemplating the purchase of a new *necktie*?

Mutt knuckled the moisture from his eyes and mentally kicked his own ass for being a big baby. This wasn't a bad life, and plenty of people had it worse. Time to pull up his socks and buckle down and all that other self-improvement shit.

But not right now. Right now, Mutt needed a break. He hadn't lied to Gifford and the others, he had to finish this job tonight. But he could take fifteen minutes to websurf his way to some amusing site that would lift his spirits.

And that was how Mutt discovered Gondwanaland.

In retrospect, after the passage of time had erased his computer's logs, the exact chain of links leading to Gondwanaland was hard to reconfigure. He had started looking for new recordings by his favorite group, Dead End Universe. That had led somehow to a history of pirate radio stations. And from there it was a short jump to micronations.

Fascinated, Mutt lost all track of time as he read about this concept that was totally new to him.

Micronations—also known as cybernations, fantasy countries, or ephemeral states—were odd blends of real-world rebellious politics, virtual artsy-fartsy projects, and elaborate spoofs. Essentially, a micronation was any assemblage of persons regarding themselves as a sovereign country, yet not recognized by international entities such as the United Nations. Sometimes micronations were associated with real physical territory. The Cocos Islands had once been ruled as a fiefdom by the Clunies-Ross family. Sarawak was once the province of the White Rajas, as the Brooke clan had styled themselves.

With the advent of the Internet, the number of micronations had exploded. There were now dozens of imaginary online countries predicated on different philosophies, exemplifying scores of different governmental systems, each of them more or less seriously arguing that they were totally within their rights to issue passports, currency, and stamps, and to designate ministers, nobility, and bureaucratic minions.

Mutt had always enjoyed fantasy sports in college. Imaginary leagues, imaginary rosters, imaginary games . . . Something about being totally in charge of a small universe had appealed to him, as an antidote to his lack of control over the important factors and forces that batted his own life around. He had spent a lot of time playing *The Sims,* too. The concept of cybernations seemed like a logical extension of those pursuits, an appealing refuge from the harsh realities of career and relationships.

The site Mutt had ended up on was a gateway to a whole host of online countries. The Aerican Empire, the Kingdom of Talossa, the Global State of Waveland, the Kingdom of Redonda, Lizbekistan—

And Gondwanaland.

Memories of an introductory geoscience course came back to Mutt. Gondwanaland was the supercontinent that had existed hundreds of millions of years ago, before splitting and drifting apart into the configuration of separate continental land forms familiar today.

Mutt clicked on the Gondwanaland button.

The page built itself rapidly on his screen. The animated image of a spinning globe dominated. Sure enough, the globe featured only a single huge continent, marked with interior divisions into states and featuring the weird names of cities.

Mutt was about to scan some of the text on the page when his eye fell on the blinking time readout in the corner of the screen.

Holy shit! Nine-thirty! He'd be here till midnight unless he busted his ass.

Reluctantly abandoning the Gondwanaland page and its impossible globe, Mutt returned to his work.

Which still sucked.

Maybe worse.

The next day Mutt was almost as tired as if he had gone out with Gifford and the gang. But at least his head wasn't throbbing and his mouth didn't taste as if he had French-kissed a hyena. Proofing the advertorial section had taken until eleven forty-five, and by the time he had ridden the subway home, eaten some leftover General Gao's chicken, watched Letterman's Top Ten and fallen asleep, it had been well into the small hours of the morning. When his alarm went off at seven-thirty, he thrashed about in confusion like a drowning man, dragged from some engrossing dream that instantly evaporated from memory.

Once in the office, Mutt booted up his machine. He had been doing something interesting last evening, hadn't he? Oh, yeah, that Gondwanaland thing—

Before his butt hit the chair, someone was IM-ing him. Oh, shit, Kicklighter wanted to see him in his office. Mutt got up to visit his boss.

He ran into Gifford in the hall. Unrepentant yet visibly hurting, Gifford managed a sickly grin. "Missed a swinging time last night, my friend. After her fifth Jell-O shot, Cody got up on stage at Captains. Took two bouncers to get her down, but not before she managed to earn over a hundred bucks."

Mutt winced. This was more information than he needed about the extracurricular activities of his jealous coworker. How would it be possible now to work on projects side-by-side with her, without conjuring up visions of her drunkenly shedding her clothing?

Suddenly this hip-young-urban-wastrel shtick, the whole life-is-fucked-so-let's-get-fucked-up play-acting that Mutt and his friends had been indulging in for so long looked incredibly boring and tedious and counterproductive, possibly even the greased chute delivering one's ass to eternal damnation. Mutt knew with absurd certainty that he could no longer indulge in such a wasteful lifestyle. Something inside him had shifted irrevocably, some emotional tipping point had been reached.

But what was he going to do with his life instead?

Making a halfhearted neutral comment to Gifford—no point in turning into some kind of zealous lecturing missionary asshole Gifford would tune out anyway—Mutt continued through the cube farm.

Dan Kicklighter, the middle-aged editor of *PharmaNotes*, resembled the captain of a lobster trawler, bearded, burly, and generally disheveled, as if continually battling some invisible perfect storm. He had worked at a dozen magazines in his career, everything from *Atlantic Monthly* to *Screw*. A gambling habit that oscillated from moderate—a dozen scratch-ticket purchases a day—to severe—

funding an Atlantic City spree with money the bank rightly regarded as a year's worth of mortgage payments—had determined the jagged progression of his résumé. Right now, after some serious rehab, he occupied one of the higher posts of his career.

"Matthew, come in. I just want you to know that I'm going to be away for the next four days. Big industry conference in Boston. With a little detour to Foxwoods Casino on either side. But that's just between you and me."

Kicklighter was up-front about his addiction, at least with his subordinates, and claimed that he was now cured to the point where he could indulge himself recreationally, like any casual bettor.

"I'm putting you in charge while I'm gone. I know it's a lot of responsibility, but I think you're up to it. This is a crucial week, and I'm counting on you to produce an issue we can all be proud of."

There were three assistant editors at *PharmaNotes*, so this advancement was not insignificant. But Mutt cringed at the temporary promotion. He just wanted to stay in his little miserable niche and not have anybody notice him. Yet what could he do? Deny the assignment? Wasn't such an honor the kind of thing he was supposed to be shooting for, next step up the ladder and all that shit? Cody would've killed for such a nomination.

"Uh, fine, Dan. Thank you. I'll do my best."

"That's what I'm counting on. Here, take this list of targets you need to hit before Monday. It's broken down into ten-minute activity blocks. Say, have you heard the odds on the Knicks game this weekend?"

Back in his cube, Mutt threw down the heavy sheaf of paper with disgust. He just knew he'd have to work through the weekend.

Before he had gotten through the tasks associated with the first ten-minute block, Cody appeared.

"So, all your ass-kissing finally paid off. Well, I want you to know that you haven't fooled everyone here. Not by a long shot."

Before Mutt could protest his lack of ambition, Cody was gone. Her angry strut conjured up images of pole-dancing in Mutt's traitorous imagination.

A short time later, Melba sauntered in and poised one haunch on the corner of Mutt's desk.

"Hey, big guy, got any plans for Friday night?"

"Yeah. Thanks to Kicklighter, I'll be ruining my eyesight right here at my desk."

Melba did not seem put off by Mutt's sour brusqueness. "Well, that's too bad. But I'm sure there'll be some other night we can, ah, hook up."

Once Melba left, Mutt tried to resume work. But he just couldn't focus.

So he brought up the Gondwanaland page.

Who was going to tell him he couldn't? Kicklighter was probably already out the office and halfway to the roulette wheels.

Below the spinning foreign globe was a block of text followed by some hot-button links: IMPERIAL LINEAGE, CUSTOMS, NATURAL HISTORY, POLITICAL HISTORY, ART, FORUMS, and so forth. Mutt began to read the main text.

> For the past ten thousand years of recorded history, Gondwanaland's imperial plurocracy has ensured the material well-being as well as the physical, spiritual, and intellectual freedom of its citizens. Since the immemorial era of Fergasse I, when the walled communities of the Only Land—prominently, Lyskander, Port Shallow, Vybergum, and Turnbuckle—emerged from the state of siege imposed by the roving packs of scalewargs and amphidonts, banding together into a network of trade and discourse, right up until the current reign of Golusty IV, the ascent of the united peoples of Gondwanaland has been unimpeded by war or dissent, despite a profusion of beliefs, creeds, philosophical paradigms, and social arrangements. A steady accumulation of scientific knowledge from the perspicacious and diligent researchers at our many technotoria, combined with the practical entrepreneurship of the ingeniator class, has led to a mastery of the forces of nature, resulting in such now-essential inventions as the strato-carriage, storm-dispeller, object-box, and meta-palp.
>
> The grateful citizens of Gondwanaland can assume—with a surety they feel when they contemplate the regular

rising of the Innermost Moon—that the future will only continue this happy progression.

Fascinated, Mutt continued to scan the introductory text on the main page, before beginning to bop around the site. What he discovered on these dependent pages were numerous intriguing photos of exotic scenes—cities, people, buildings, landscapes, artworks—and many more descriptive and explanatory passages that amounted to a self-consistent and utterly convincing portrait of an alien world.

"The Defeat of the Last 'Warg"; a recipe for bluebunny with groundnut sauce; *The Adventures of Calinok Cannikin*, by Ahleucha Mamarosa; Jibril III's tornado-struck coronation; the deadly glacier apes; the first landing on the Outermost Moon; the Immaculate Epidemic; the Street of Lanternmoths in Scordatura; the voices of children singing the songs of Mourners Day; the Teetering Needle in the Broken Desert; sunlight on the slate roofs of Saurelle; the latest fashion photographs of Yardley Legg—

Mutt's head was spinning and the clock icon on his screen read noon. Man, people thought Tolkien was an obsessive perfectionist dreamer! Whoever had put this site together was a goddamn fantasy genius! The backstory to Gondwanaland possessed the kind of organic cohesiveness that admitted of the random and contradictory. Why hadn't the citizens of Balamuth ever realized that they were sitting on a vein of pure allurium until a sheepherder named Thunn Pumpelly fell into that sinkhole? They just hadn't! A hundred other circumstantial incidents and anecdotes contributed to the warp and woof of Gondwanaland, until in Mutt's mind the whole invention assumed the heft and sheen of a length of richly embroidered silk.

Mutt wondered momentarily whether the whole elaborate hoax was the work of a single creator, or a group effort. Perhaps the name or names of the perps was hidden in some kind of Easter egg—

The one link Mutt hadn't yet explored led to the FORUMS. Now he went there.

He faced a choice of dozens of boards on different topics, all listing thousands of archived posts. He arbitrarily chose one—IMPERIAL NEWS—and read a few recent posts in chronological order.

Anybody heard any reports since Restday from the Liminal Palace on G4's health?

—IceApe113

The last update from the Remediator General said G4 was still in serious condition. Something about not responding to the infusion of nurse-hemomites.

—LenaFromBamford

Looks like we could be having an Imperial Search soon then. I hope the Cabal of Assessors has their equipment in good working order. When was the last IS? 9950, right?

—Gillyflower87

Aren't we all being a little premature? Golusty IV isn't dead yet!

—IlonaG

Mutt was baffled, even somehow a little pissed off, by the intensity of the role-playing on display here. These people—assuming the posts indeed originated from disparate individuals—were really into this micronation game, more like Renaissance Faire head-cases and Civil War reenactors than the art-student goofballs Mutt had envisioned as the people responsible for the Gondwanaland site. Still, their fervent loyalty to their fantasy world offered Mutt a wistful, appealing alternative to his own anomie.

Impulsively, Mutt launched his own post.

From everything I've seen, Golusty IV seems like a very fine emperor and a good person. I hope he gets better.

—MuttsterPrime

He quit his browser and brought up his word processor.

Then he resumed trying to fit his life into ten-minute boxes.

Kicklighter returned from the Boston trip looking as if he had spent the entire time wrestling rabid tigers. Evidently, his cure had not been totally effective. His vaunted invulnerability to the seductions of Native American–sponsored games of chance plainly featured chinks. An office pool was immediately begun centered on his probable date of firing by the publisher, Henry Huntsman. Ironically, Kicklighter himself placed a wager.

But all these waves of office scandal washed over Mutt without leaving any impression at all. Likewise, his dealings with his former friends and rivals had no impact on his abstracted equilibrium. Gifford's unceasing invitations to get wasted, Cody's sneers and jibes, Melba's purring attempts at seduction—none of these registered. Oh, Mutt continued to perform his job in a semicompetent, offhanded way. But most of the time his head was in Gondwanaland.

With his new best IM buddy, Ilona Grobes.

Ilona Grobes—IlonaG—had posted the well-mannered, respectful comment about not hastening Golusty IV into his grave. Upon reading Mutt's similarly themed post, she had contacted him directly.

> MuttsterPrime, that was a sensitive and compassionate sentiment. I'm glad you're not so thrilled by the prospect of an IS like most of these vark-heads that you forget the human dimension of this drama. I don't recognize your name from any of the boards. What clade do you belong to?
>
> —IlonaG

That question left Mutt scratching his head. He debated telling Ilona to cut the fantasy crap and just talk straight to him. But in the end he decided to go along with the play-acting.

> Ilona, is my clade really so important? I'd like to think that we can relate to each other on an interpersonal level without such official designations coming between us.
>
> —MuttsterPrime

When Ilona's reply came, Mutt was relieved to see that his strategy of conforming to her game-playing had paid off.

> How true! I never thought to hear from another Sloatist on this board! I only asked because I didn't want to give

> offense if you were an ultra-Yersinian. But it's so refreshing to dispense with such outdated formalities. Tell me some more about yourself.
>
> —IlonaG

> Not much to tell really. I'm an assistant editor at a magazine, and it sucks.
>
> —MuttsterPrime

> I'm afraid you've lost me there, Muttster. Why would a repository for excess grain need even one professional scurrilator, much less an assistant? And how can a condition or inanimate object "suck"? Where do you live? It must be someplace rather isolated, with its own dialect. Perhaps the Ludovici Flats?
>
> IlonaG

Mutt stood up a moment and looked toward the distant window in the far-off wall of the cube farm, seeing a slice of the towers of Manhattan and thereby confirming the reality of his surroundings. This woman was playing some serious games with his head. He sat back down.

> Oh, my home town is no place you've ever heard of. Just a dreary backwater. But enough about my boring life. Tell me about yours!
>
> —MuttsterPrime

Ilona was happy to comply. Over the next several weeks, she spilled her life story, along with a freight of fascinating details about life in Gondwanaland.

Ilona had been born on a farm in the Ragovoy Swales district. Her parents raised moas. She grew up loving the books of Idanell Swonk and the antic-tableaus (were these movies?) featuring Roseway Partridge. She broke her arm when she was eleven, competing in the annual running of the aurochs. After finishing her schooling, earning an advanced instrumentality in cognitive combinatorics, she had moved to the big city of Tlun, where she had gotten a job with the Cabal of Higher Heuristics. (Best as Mutt could figure, her job had something to do with writing the software for artificial mineral-harvesting deep-sea fish.) Every Breathday Ilona and a bunch of girlfriends—fellow geeks, Mutt conjectured—would participate in *zymurgy*, a kind of public chess match where the pieces were represented by living people and the action took place in a three-dimensional labyrinth. She liked to relax with a glass of cloudberry wine and the music of Clay Zelta. (She sent Mutt a sample when he said he wasn't familiar with that artist. It sounded like punk polkas with a dash of tango.)

The more Mutt learned about Ilona, the more he liked her. She might be crazy, living in this fantasy world of hers, but it was an attractive neurosis. The world she and her fellow hoaxers had built was so much saner and exotic than the one Mutt inhabited. Why wouldn't anyone want to pretend they lived in such a place?

As for the larger outlines of Gondwanalandian society and its finer details, Mutt learned much that appealed to him. For instance, the role of emperor or empress was not an inherited one, nor was it restricted to any particular class of citizen. Upon the death of the reigning monarch—whose powers were limited yet essential in the day-to-day functioning of the plurocracy—the Cabal of Assessors began a continentwide search for a psychic heir. At death, the holy spirit of the ruler—not exactly that individual's unique soul, but something like free-floating semidivine mojo—was believed to detach and descend on a destined individual, whose altered status could be confirmed by subtle detection apparatus. And then there was that eminently sensible business about every citizen receiving a lifetime stipend that rendered work not a necessity but a dedicated choice. Not to mention such attractions as the regular state-sanctioned orgies in such cities as Swannack, Harsh Deep, and Camp Collard that apparently made Mardi Gras look like the Macy's Thanksgiving Day Parade.

As for the crisis of Golusty IV's impending death, the boards remained full of speculation and chatter. The remediators were trying all sorts of new treatments, and the emperor's health chart resembled Earth's stock market's gyrations, one minute up and the next way down.

"Earth's stock market"? Mutt was shocked to find himself so convinced of Gondwanaland's reality that he needed to distinguish between the two worlds.

With some judicious self-censorship and the liberal use of generalities, Mutt was able to convey something of his life and character to Ilona as well, without baffling her further. He made up a lot of stuff, too, incidents and anecdotes that dovetailed with Gondwanalandian parameters. Her messages began to assume an intimate tone. As did Mutt's.

By the time Ilona sent him her picture, Mutt realized he was in love. The photograph clinched it. (It was too painful for Mutt even to dare to think the image might be a fake, the Photoshop ruse of some thirteen-year-old male dweeb.) Ilona Grobes was a dark-haired, dark-eyed beauty with a charming mole above quirked lips. If all cognitive combinatorics experts looked like this, Gondwanaland had proved itself superior in the geek department as well. With the photo was a message:

> Dear Mutt, don't you think it's time we met in the flesh? The emperor can't live much longer, and of course all nonessential work and other activities will be suspended during the moratorium of the Imperial Search, for however long that may take. We could use those leisurely days to really get to know each other better.
>
> —IlonaG

Finally, here was the moment when all charades would collapse, for good or ill. After some deliberation, Mutt attached his own photo and wrote back:

> Getting together would be really great, Ilona. Just tell me where you live, and I'll be right there!
>
> —MuttsterPrime

> You're such a joker, Mutt! You know perfectly well that I live at Number 39 Badgerway in the Funes district of Tlun! When can you get here? The aerial tramway service to Tlun

> is extensive, no matter where you live. Here's a pointer to the online schedules. Try not to keep me waiting too long! And I think your auroch-lick hairstyle is charming!
>
> —IlonaG

Mutt felt his spirits slump. He was in love with a clinically insane person, one so mired in her delusions that she could not break out even when offered genuine human contact. Should he cut things off right here and now? No, he couldn't bring himself to.

> Let me check those schedules and tidy up some loose ends here, Ilona. Then I'll get right back to you.
>
> —MuttsterPrime

Mutt was still sitting in a motionless, uninspired funk half an hour later when Kicklighter called him into his office.

All the editor's photos were off the walls and in cardboard boxes, along with his other personal possessions. The hairy, rumpled man looked relieved.

"I'm outta here as of this minute, kid. Security's coming to escort me to the front door. But I wanted to let you know that I put in a good word for you to take over my job. Huntsman might not like my extracurricular activities too much, but he's a good publisher and realizes I know my stuff when it comes to getting a magazine out. He trusts me on matters of personnel. So you've got a lock on the job, if you want it. And who wouldn't? But you've got to get your head out of your ass. I don't know where you've been the past few weeks, but it hasn't been here."

All Mutt could do was stare at Kicklighter without responding. Scurrilator, he thought. Why would I want to be head scurrilator?

After another awkward minute, Mutt managed to mumble some thanks and good-luck wishes, then left.

He dropped in to Gifford's cubicle. Maybe his friend could offer some advice.

Gifford looked like shit. His tie was askew, his face pale and bedewed with sweat. There was a white crust around his nostrils like the rim of Old Faithful. He smiled wanly when he saw Mutt.

"Hey, pal, I'd love to talk to you right now, but I don't feel so good. Little touch of stomach trouble. In fact, I gotta hit the john pronto."

Gifford bulled past Mutt. He smelled like spoiled yogurt.

Mutt wandered purposelessly through the cube farm. He found himself at Cody's box. She glared at him and said, "If you're here like the rest of them to gloat, you can just get in line."

"Gloat? About what?"

"Oh, come on, don't pretend you haven't heard about the layoffs."

"No—no, I haven't, really. I'm—I'm sorry, Cody."

Cody just snorted and turned away.

Melba wasn't in her cube. Mutt learned why from an official notice on the bulletin board near the coffee maker.

> If any employee is contacted by any member of the media regarding the sexual discrimination suit lodged by Ms. Melba Keefe, who is on extended leave until litigation is settled, he or she will refrain from commenting, upon penalty of dismissal.

Back in his cubicle, Mutt brought up the Gondwanaland web page. The coastline of Gondwanaland bore unmistakable resemblance to the geography Mutt knew, the way an assembled jigsaw puzzle recalled the individual lonely pieces. As far as he could make out, Tlun was located where Buenos Aires was on Earth.

> Ilona, I'm going to try to reach you somehow. I'm setting out today. Wish me luck.
>
> —MuttsterPrime

Mutt left his cheap hotel—roaches the size of bite-sized Snickers bars, obese hookers smoking unfiltered cigarettes and trolling the corridors 24/7—for the fifth time that day. He carried a twofold map. Before he had left the United States, he had printed off a detailed street map of Tlun. He had found a similar map for Buenos Aires and transferred it to a transparent sheet. Using certain unvarying physical features that appeared on both maps, such as rivers and the shape of the bay, he had aligned the two. This cartographic construction was what he was using to search for Number 39 Badgerway.

Of course, Buenos Aires featured no such street in its official atlas. And the neighborhood that Ilona supposedly lived in was of such a rough nature as to preclude much questioning of the shifty-eyed residents—even if Mutt's Spanish had been better than the "*Qué pasa, amigo?*" variety. Watched suspiciously by glue-huffing, gutter-crawling juveniles and their felonious elders hanging out at nameless bars, Mutt could only risk a cursory inspection of the Badgerway environs.

After checking out the most relevant district, Mutt was reduced to wandering the city's boulevards and alleys, parks and promenades, looking for any other traces of a hidden, subterranean, alternative city that plainly didn't exist anywhere outside the fevered imagination of a handful of online losers, as he prayed for a glimpse of an unforgotten female face graced by a small mole. Maybe Ilona was some Argentinian hacker girl who had been subliminally trying to overcome her own reluctance to divulge her real whereabouts by giving him all these clues.

But even if that were the case, Mutt met with no success.

He had now been in Argentina for ten days. All the trip's costs, from expensively impromptu airline tickets to meals and lodging, had been put on plastic. He had turned his last paycheck into local currency for small purchases, but Mutt's loan payments had left him no nest egg. And the upper limits on his lone credit card weren't infinite. Pretty soon he'd have to admit defeat, return the New York, and try to pick up the shambles of his life.

But for the next few days, anyhow, he would continue to look for Tlun and Ilona.

Returning today to the neighborhood labeled Funes on the Tlun map, Mutt entered a small café he had come to patronize only because it was marginally less filthy than any other. He ordered a coffee and a pastry. Spreading his map on the scarred countertop he scratched his stubble and pondered the arrangement of streets. Had he explored every possible niche—?

A finger tapped Mutt's shoulder. He turned to confront a weasly individual whose insincere yet broad smile revealed more gaps than teeth. The fellow wore a ratty Von Dutch T-shirt that proclaimed: I KISS BETTER THAN YOU.

"*Señor*, what is it you look for? Perhaps I can help. I know this district like the breast of my own mother."

Mutt realized that this guy must be some kind of con artist. But even so, he represented the best local informant Mutt had yet encountered, the only person who had deigned to speak with him.

Pointing to the map, Mutt said, "I'm looking for this street. Do you know it?"

"*Sí, seguro!* I will take you there without delay!"

Experiencing a spark of hope, Mutt followed the guide outside.

They came to a dank *calle* Mutt was half sure he had visited once before. The guide gestured to a shadowy cross-street that was more of a channel between buildings, only large enough for pedestrian traffic. A few yards along, the street transformed into a steep flight of greasy twilit stairs.

"Right down here, *señor*, you will find *exactamente* what you are looking for."

Mutt tried to banish all fear from his heart and head. He summoned up into his mind's eye Ilona's smiling face. He advanced tentatively into the claustrophobic cattle chute.

He heard the blow coming before he felt it. Determined not to lose his focus on Ilona, he still could not help flinching. The blow sent him reeling, blackness seeping over Ilona's face like spilled tar, until only her smile, Cheshire cat–like, remained, then faded.

Sunlight poured through lacy curtains, illuminating a small cheerful room. On the wall hung a painting which Mutt recognized as one of Sigalit's studies for his *Skydancer* series. Mutt saw a vase filled with strange flowers on a nearby small table. Next to the flowers sat a box labeled LIBERTO'S ECLECTIC PASTILLES and a book whose spine bore the legend "*Ancient Caprices*, Idanell Swonk."

Mutt lay in what was obviously a hospital bed, judging by the peripheral gadgetry around him, including an object-box and a pair of meta-palps. The blanket covering him diffused an odd yet not unpleasant odor, as if woven from the hairs of an unknown beast. He saw what looked like a call button and he buzzed it.

A nurse hurried into the room, all starched calm business in her traditional tricornered hat and life-saving medals.

Behind her strode Ilona Grobes.

Ilona hung back smiling only until the nurse assured herself that Mutt was doing fine and left. Then Ilona flung herself on Mutt. They hugged wordlessly for minutes before she stood up and found a seat for herself.

"Oh, Mutt, what *happened* to you? A Junior Effectuator found you unconscious a few feet from my door and brought you here. I was at work. The first thing I knew about your troubles was when I saw your picture on the evening propaedeutic. 'Unknown citizen hospitalized.' I rushed right here, but the remediators told me not to wake you. You slept for over thirty hours, right from Fishday to Satyrsday!"

Mutt grabbed Ilona's hand. "Let's just say I had kind of a hard time getting to Tlun."

Ilona giggled. "What a funny accent you have! That's one thing that doesn't come across online."

"And you—you're more beautiful than any photo. And you smell like—like vanilla ice cream."

Ilona looked shyly away, then back. "I'm sure that's a compliment, whatever vanilla ice cream may be. But look—I brought you some candy, and one of my favorite books."

"Thank you. Thank you very much for being here."

No ice cream, Mutt thought. He'd be a millionaire by this time next year.

They talked for several hours more, until the sounds of some kind of commotion out in the hall made them pause.

The door to Mutt's room opened and three men walked in. They were clad in elaborately stitched ceremonial robes and miters, and carried among them several pieces of equipment.

Seeing Mutt's puzzlement, Ilona explained. "It's just a team of Assessors. Golusty died yesterday, shortly after your arrival. The Imperial Search has begun."

One Assessor addressed Ilona. "Citizen Grobes, your testing will take place at your residence. But we need to assess this stranger now."

"Of course," Ilona said.

The Assessors approached Mutt's bedside. "With your permission, citizen—"

Mutt nodded, and they placed a cage of wires studded with glowing lights and delicate sensors on his head like a crown.

I offer the following story as a trial run for a book I wish to write that will focus on the science of the 1600s and 1700s: starring Bishop Berkeley, The Philosopher's Star *will indeed be an example of "horsepowerpunk"—if and when I ever find time to do the necessary research.*

But meanwhile we have the adventure below. It was not enough for me to conceive of using a young Cotton Mather as a narrator, although Howard Waldrop tells me that's a coup, since he can think of no other fiction that does so. No, I had to go and bring in a fictional hero from the canon of Robert E. Howard. Oh, well, the road to wisdom is through excess, and all that.

The chance to use local history—I live in Rhode Island—was another temptation. My thanks to Pamela Sargent, who commissioned this tale for her anthology Conqueror Fantastic.

Observable Things

Now that I have at long last, thro' simple Rolling Away of the weary Years, attained my threescore and a lustrum and acquired the status of Elderly Relick, honor'd and revered (yea, even feared), but likewise equally unlisten'd to, by Younger Generations busy with the affairs of a new Century, I am naturally disposed to cast my Eye backwards o'er the course of my life, questioning whether Events which once loom'd large as Mount Ararat in my Mental Apprehension did indeed hold all the Significance with which I once imbued 'em, and whether certain treasured Beliefs of mine, Polestars by which I erstwhile directed my Conduct and Career, were as trustworthy as I deemed, or whether these glittering Arrays of interlocking Axioms and Suppositions were not in fact Edifices built upon the Shifting Sands of Happenstance, Misunderstanding, and Deceit.

Chief among these Eidolons, perchance falsely dominant, I number my quondam Faith in the Existence and Prevalence of Witchcraft. Doubts as to the Mundane Workings of the Prince of Darkness thro' his mortal Slaves first began to trouble me shortly after the Trials at Salem, wherein I play'd no small Part. Convinced then that "an Army of Devils is broke in upon the place which is our very center," I staunchly maintained that Spectral Powers rampaged at will up and down our Earthly Stage, and that every Prayerful Man had a Duty to crusade against 'em.

Presently, however, in my Dotage (and I suspect in my weary Bones that I will not live much longer, certainly not managing to equal the vast Pile of Years once surmounted by my father, whose Christian Name Increase betokened his very longevity), I begin to doubt myself whether or not the Celestial Forces commonly make such Extraordinary use of Mortals as Actors in their Unknowable Dramas, imbuing 'em with Supernatural Powers for Good or Evil. I myself have, I now honestly aver, never *in my Maturity* witnessed any Occult Manifestations among the Pitiful Wretches accused in Salem or elsewhere and which would qualify without reservation as Extramundane. Certainly I would have no hesitation at this late date in abandoning all Credence in the Supernatural, were it not for one certain Man and the Events he brought in his train.

That Man was named Solomon Kane, and I met him when I was but thirteen years old, and all of Christian New England seemed doomed to Merciless Extinction at the hands of the Salvages and their Dreaded Conqueror, King Philip.

'Tis said, Reader, that the Spaniard De Leon quested after the Fountain of Youth in the Bermoothes and elsewhere, yet had he but considered the Power of Man's Memory to restore his Vanished Infancy as if not a Day had passed since he wore Bunting and Lisped his Cradle Songs, then would the Balked Romish Explorer have realized that said Prize dwelt nor further off than beneath our Pates. Thus when I in my Expiring Years cast my own Sensibilities backward down Time's Stream, I am instantly restored to the inquisitive and fleet-witted yet shallow-experienced and Headstrong Young Lad who once believed that he could understand any Observable Thing, and who found the World a Condign Marvel for his Seething Brain.

The Clime during that August of the Year of Our Lord 1676 had been a most unnatural one for the Colonies, Steamy, Enervating and Mephitic, as befitted the horrid Travails we Poor Souls in the English Israel had been undergoing for the past several Years.

Betimes it seemed that we upright New World Denizens were suffering the fate detailed in Deuteronomy: "wasted with Hunger, devoured with Burning Heat, the Teeth of Beasts against them." For two years now we had been battling for our Very Lives against the False Indians who had once befriended us, and with whom we had lived in tolerable Amity for some Decades. The Causes of their Bellicosity were numerous and hard to parse. An Enduring Catalogue of Innumerable Grievances had existed prior to actual Combat on both sides of the Affair, and the subsequent War had occasioned a Host of others. Slaughters and Outrages had been frequent during the course of the Struggle, and Blood both Pagan and Christian had flowed like Wine among the Nazarites.

At this Juncture, however, after much Tromping up and down the Countryside by Armed Militias, after many Grievous Setbacks and Retreats, Burnings of Homes and Stockados, Slaughter of Livestock, Despoiling of Grain and Fruit, Captivity of Innocent Maidens and Babes, the Tide seemed to have turned against the Tawny Tygers and in favor of the White Man. The Perfidious Canonchet, one of the Salvages' chief Sagamores, had been recently captured and executed, his Dying breath an Unrepentant Curse upon his Betters. Weetamoo, the Squaw Sachem, pursued across the Taunton River just days ago in her Canoo, had Drowned and Perished Utterly, her Head Alone paraded on a Pole thro' the Lanes of Taunton to Exultant Cheers. The Various Tribes Allied against us, the Bulk of the Nipmucs, the Narragansetts, the Wampanoags, and many lesser Clans, facing not only us English Lions but also our allies, the Mohegans and Mohawks, had been driven either Westward or Northward or into Guarded Encampments.

Yet one Redoubtable Foe remained uncaptured, and he the most Fearsome, Clever, and Undauntable Spectre of all. King Philip, Warrior Son of Massasoit, Sachem of all the Wampanoags, known before his English Christening as Metacomet. He it was who had Brew'd all the Storm amongst his Kith and Kin, he it was who had Wrought such clever Strategems against us, oft o'erwhelming our Superior Forces by Guile and Cunning. Now, 'tis true, Philip seemed helpless, a Portrait of the Chastized as we read of in *Amos:* "he who is stout of heart among the Mighty shall flee away naked in that day."

Yet just so long as Philip lived, so long would our Future Safety be uncertain. Prospects that the Renegade could Regroup his forces and return Some Far-off Day to Harangue and Belabor us again were all too Large, especially if he turned for help to our Rivals, the French and Dutch. (And may I interpolate here, Reader, Merest Mention of the well-known Irruption Twelve Years Later of just such Salvage Deviltry around Saco, Pemmaquid, Casco, and Elsewhere as proof of the Undying Enmity of these Redskins, as chronicled in my own humble tome, *Deccenium Luctuosum?*)

Moreover, there weighed in the Balance evidence of King Philip's Supernatural Allegiances. Many and many a time had reports come of Uncanny Forces at work on the side of the Salvages. Ill-faced Omens had oft abounded before Various Indian Attacks, *viz.*, Uncouth Storms, the clouding of the Moon and the Sun, St. Elmo's Fire, the Appearance of Unnatural Beasts, and the Disappearance of Common Game Animals. Such Tokens of the Dark Allies invoked by the Indians unnerved us, rightly so, and made Philip's Death all the more Imperative.

It was in this Spirit, and with this Aim, that a group of Statesmen, Militiamen, and Common Citizenry stood eagerly upon Hammett's Wharf that August Day in Newport, chief Establishment of the Plantations of Rhode Island, awaiting our Savior from across the Sea.

Standing atop a Tarry Piling and thus elevated above the Mass, with the Undimmed Eyes of Youth I was the first to spot the Ship we all anticipated, and gave a loud "Hulloo!"

"Here she comes! The *Black Gull* approaches!"

A general Stir went up among the Crowd congregated under the Unnaturally Blazing Sun. Even my own Father, ever a Figure of Stern Sobriety, evidenced a more agitated Mien 'neath his formal Wig, betokening a Ferment of Hope and Trepidation, than I had ever before seen him exhibit. He turned to Major Pynchon and said, "Let us pray that Kane has seen fit to answer our pleas. If this ship indeed bears that most fierce and noble of Puritans, we are saved, forsooth."

I clambered down from my Bituminous Perch, as the Stout Full-rigged Vessel drew e'en closer, and from the expectantly gathered Souls there began to arise a general unseemly Hubbub. Major Sanford and Captain Goulding, Major Gookin and Captain Church, took it upon themselves to quiet the Ladies and Husbandmen and their Babes, lest Solomon Kane receive a Wrongful Impression of our Character, deeming us less Stoic than the situation demanded.

Before much longer, Hawsers flew thro' the Air from the creeping Ship and the *Black Gull* was Warped into place alongside Hammett's Wharf. Navvies heaved a Gangplank up and over to bridge the Gap twixt Ship and Shore, and a Collective Suspension of Breath preceded the actual appearance of Solomon Kane.

When the Man Himself materialized like one of the Four Spirits of heaven mentioned in Zechariah, that Suspension turned to a Gasp.

Used as we all were to the Sober, Respectful, Crowfeather Garb of our Preachers and Leaders, we still received a Shock upon first sighting Solomon Kane. For he was Attired in a Manner that had not been General for at least a Hundred Years. His Unadorned, Close-fitting Garments harked back to the days of Good Queen Bess. From Slouch Hat to Unseasonable Mantle to Worn Boots, he presented a Stygian Form. Exceedingly tall, with long arms and broad shoulders, Kane exhibited features both Saturnine and Powerfully Focus'd. A kind of Dark Pallor lent him a Ghostly Visage, counterpointed but not relieved by the Thick Hedgerow of his Brows.

And his Accoutrements! Warlike and Vengeful in the extreme, raising in my Brain thoughts of the passage in Psalms: "two-edged swords in their hands, to wreak vengeance on the nations and chastizement on the peoples . . ." A Wicked Unscabbard'd Rapier depended from his wide leather belt, into which were thrust Twin Pistols. But the most Curious object carried by the Adventurer was a kind of short lance or Stave of Ebony Wood, its Pommel carved into the shape of a Cat's Head, its sharp tip stain'd with some Ocherous Substance.

At my elbow a Rude Fellow unknown to me whispered to his Companion, "'Tis said Kane was peer to Raleigh and Drake in their prime, during the century long gone."

"Aye. I have it on best authority that his Afric exploits earned him undying youth from Pagan sorcerers."

"If so, that fabled benison sits heavily on his shoulders."

I felt a righteous indignation in my Youthful Soul against the words of these Hayseed Poltroons. To my eyes, Solomon Kane was Justice Incarnate, the most Proper and Vengeful Christian my Gaze had yet to encounter. Moreover, he radiated an Aura of Romance, like a figure out of Spenser or Malory, a Dark Knight on a Perpetual Quest.

With Unreasoning Certitude, I knew then that I would follow this man wherever he led, and do whatever he bade, if he would but Consent for me to be his Page.

Kane broke the Awe-full Silence occasion'd by his entrance with a curt speech: "I have arrived as agent of thy solace, Brethren." Then he set foot on the Gangplank and began his descent.

Our Leaders were already moving solemnly toward the base of the Plank to usher Kane ashore, and the Visitor had nearly reached their warm Solicitude when the unexpected happened.

From the wat'ry gap twixt Wharf and Ship, a long scaled green Arm shot upward, and clamped its Mossy, Long-nailed fingers around the ankle of Kane's right Boot!

Before anyone else could summon up the Wits to react, Kane had whipped forth one of his Antique Pistols, and instantly primed and fired it straight into the Form of his Attacker!

The Unearthly Hand convulsed and withdrew, releasing Kane. Women screamed, and Men hastened to peer over the edge of the Wharf to descry the Nature of the Assailant. By virtue of my small size, I managed to push to the Vanguard.

The Humaniform Creature had been mortally wounded, staining the Harbor's Water's with its dark blood. Its Mortal Frenzy made Full Apprehension of its Lineaments impossible amidst the Froth, yet I thought to Glimpse a Barbed Tail and Webbed Hands. Upon its Expiration, the Chthonic Creature floated for a Short Moment, revealing its Naked, Reptilian Backside, before sinking like a Stone.

Kane had calmly replaced his matchlock. No expression of either Dismay or Triumph clouded his stony features. He uttered his assessment of the Attack with plainspoken Certitude. "A child of Dagon. Your suspicions of Indian complicity with ancient demiurges were not misplaced, my friends. Let us adjourn to some quarters affording more safety than the open air, and we can begin to plot our campaign against these abominations."

Major Pynchon was the first to regain his Composure. "By all means, Master Kane. We have adopted the house of one of our most esteemed husbandmen, Benedict Arnold, nigh to Spring Street, as our headquarters. Refreshment awaits us there."

En masse then, I staying close to my Father's side, so as not to be summarily dismissed from the Council of Greybeards, we set out up the Low Slope toward Spring Street, leaving at our back the waters of Newport Harbor, once so innocent and accommodating, yet now revealed to be the Lair of the Unspeakable.

All cram'd into the Narrow Quarters of the Keeping Room in Benedict Arnold's stout gambrel'd House hard by the Old Stone Mill (which some averred had been builded by Norsemen before e'er White Men arrived on these shores), we Settlers held Solomon Kane at our Worshipful Center as if he were the precious Beating Heart of our Body Politic. After his Masterful Display at the Wharf, he had commanded all our Respect. I was reminded of the passage in Luke, where the Christ is led into the council of priests and scribes and asked to furnish proof of his identity. Our Lord replied engimatically then: "If I tell you, you will not believe; and if I ask you, you will not answer." Yet still He carried the Day amongst the Disbelievers, and just so did Kane, despite his Stern Silence, evoke our Affections and Belief. And even the most Curious Statements he was later to make could not shake our Reliance on him.

Arnold's demure wife and dainty daughters served a modest Collation of Small Beer and Pasties, which were but sparingly consumed. Truth to tell, no man among us was particularly an-hungered, as the ennervating Heat of this most ungodly August robbed one of all Appetite, and the Closeness of the Room only accentuated the oppressiveness. I myself was able to down only three or four of the handy Meat Pies, whereas under other circumstances my Youthful Stomach—a Demanding Master whose Mature Edicts would lead to a later Corpulence of Frame—would not have been sated without Twice that Number.

Drinking only from a Tumbler of Well Water, his Stomach apparently set Sharp only for Fighting, Kane surveyed us silently, as if we were but Tools arrayed for his Handiwork, and he deeming how best to employ us.

The first order of Business was to make Suitable Introductions of all the Figures of Some Account in the Affairs of the Colonies to our Honored Visitor. We had here assembled men from Plimoth, Connecticut, Massachusetts, Rhode Island, and the Providence Plantations, each of the Polities that had suffered from the Depradations of the Salvages. Major Pynchon took this Affair into Hand, and Singularly Conducted each Colonist to shake the hand of the Brooding Puritan. Soon 'twas my Father's turn, and I trailed expectantly in his Wake.

"Mr. Kane, this stalwart man of the cloth is the Reverend Increase Mather, Pastor of Boston's North Church and President of Harvard College."

Father shook Kane's hand, and I awaited Acknowledgment of my Presence in turn. When such Token was not shortly forthcoming, I thrust forward and offered my own Hand, speaking boldly to the Corvine Adventurer from abroad.

"Cotton Mather, Sir, and most delighted to meet you."

To my surprize, Father discharged no Public Rebuke upon me, but smiled at my Presumption.

"You will forgive my son, I hope, Mr. Kane, for he is something of a prodigy. Already enrolled in the College at his tender age, he exhibits more wit than many an elder I could name."

Kane fixed upon me then a Stare of such Directness and Probing Intensity that I felt like moist, defenseless soil beneath the Farmer's Plough. I fancied he was reading a direct Impression off my very Soul, estimating the Cut of my Inner Qualities and Weighing 'em in some Obscure Balance.

Evidently I passed Muster, for Kane gripped my outthrust Hand with fervor and replied, "The blood of righteousness flows strongly in this one. Let him be a part of our councils."

Elated at this warm reception, half-dazed by Kane's Glory, I somehow retreated to the Periphery of the Crowd, where I watched and listened attentively to the following Discourse.

It fell to my Sire to give a Concise Summary of the Atrocities conducted by the Salvages, clothing the Stage of the Debate as it were with the Gory Curtains that would frame our Final Campaign. He spoke as Fervently as if he stood behind his wonted Pulpit, blasting Sinners.

"Many an innocent soul has lost his very scalp to these barbarians after being cruelly struck down from behind. Defenseless babes have had their brains dashed out upon tree trunks. Women have been trammeled and dragged at several removes across the harsh countryside as mere chattel of their redskinned captors. Why, recounting the tragedy at Nine Men's Misery alone would keep us here all day! And occasionally the cruel ingenuity of the tawny tygers has surpassed all boundaries of the imagination. There was one harmless fellow named Wright, whose strange conceit was that so long as he held his Bible, no harm would befall him. A praiseworthy belief, yet one that should have been supplemented by more practical measures. For when his salvage assailants understood the tenor of his defense, they but laughed coarsely, then slit open poor Wright from waistcoat to windpipe and inserted the Holy Book into his very guts."

The whole Room was Aghast at the repetition of this oft-told Tale, and one of Arnold's daughters swooned, dropping a Pewter Pitcher upon the stone floor with a loud Crash. But Kane evinced no comparable Reaction, instead admonishing us in a matter-of-fact yet grim Manner.

"Citizens, you may spare me your accounts of the simple grotesqueries that limited mortals may inflict on one another. I have stood beneath the Moon of Skulls and climbed the black stairs of an eldritch ziggurat to a sacrificial altar where an unnatural beast slavered over a naked princess. I have trod the streets of a city of vampires, the lone living man. I have wrestled with a murderous ghost who inhabited an English moor and was wont to rend his victims into small shreds. I have lived for months among a race of winged demons, fanged like wolves, who yet came to call me brother. Man is ever the sport and sustenance of titanic beings of night and horror. These primitive assaults by your rude tormentors are as piss in a tempest, compared to other bloody insults the cosmos holds in store for us. No, what matters most is not the atrocities performed upon you, but your manner of reply."

The Host of Militiamen and Counselors was taken aback by Kane's Implicit Diminishment of all the Wrongs they had so long Clasp'd close to their Breasts, and were silent awhile. Then Major Gookin spoke.

"Why, we have but answered 'em in kind. Upon capturing the lowest Indian soldier, we have performed upon 'em apposite punishments, such as the breaking of their fingers and other bones, and the pressing of their chests with heavy weights. Oft-times we employ our allies the Mohegan as our sanctioned executioners, for they know precisely what excruciations will justifiably extract the most pain from their stoic renegade compatriots. When possible, such as during our magnificent success last year in the Great Narragansett Swamp, when we attacked the winter encampment of the salvages, we have slaughtered their women and children and destroyed all their stores, the selfsame indignities they have inflicted on us. And of course, we regain some small measure of our lost economy by selling some captives as slaves in the Indies."

Kane smashed his pewter Tankard down hard upon the Board, causing all of us to jump as if Pitchforked. His face expressed naught but Disgust.

"This is not how you conduct a war, my brethren, but rather how infants wage a childish game of tit-for-tat. No wonder this petty conflict has persisted for so many years. Simple foot soldiers have no say in the duration or direction or intensity of the campaign. Abusing them earns you only the increased enmity of their race. But if ye make the leaders your target, you cut the problem off at the head. Champion against champion, that is how such a matter must be resolved, and how I myself intend to settle it."

Major Sanford took Offense at this Upbraiding. "Think you us utter nincompoops? We have chased Philip and his fellow sachems up and down the countryside, and we slew each pint-pot Caesar as directly as we could. Now only Philip is left, and our best intelligence has him hiding within a few leagues of our very seat here. But he is proving impossible to corner, thanks to his extraordinary assist from powers beyond our ken. That is why we have enlisted your aid, relying on your vaunted experience with matters arcane."

The Starkfaced Puritan accepted this Counterblow with a surprising

Temperance, cogitating upon Sanford's words for a full minute before finally saying, "Still and all, I maintain that 'tis your own unwise conduct that had prolonged this altercation."

Now stepped forward a man from the Ranks who had till this moment held Silence. People parted for him, opening a Path to Kane. Some gave way out of Deference, others out of Disdain, as if reluctant to let this man's touch Ataint 'em.

When the man had approached close to Kane, he extended his hand and offered his name.

"Roger Williams, Sir, and glad I am to hear you second the very sentiments I have been long pouring into the deaf ears of my peers. Their stubborn brutality has watered the thirsty root of this needless conflict with copious blood. And now my beloved Providence, that lively experiment at the head of the Salt River, is all burnt, save for three dwellings, because of the arrogant insensitivity of my comrades. I had parole from Philip himself for the safety of my settlement, but such treaties were expunged by a surfeit of betrayal, pain, and unnecessary cruelty."

Kane studied Williams for a moment before clasping his hand. "You are the fabled heretic, Sir, cast out of the Massachusetts colony for your deviant preaching."

Williams faltered not, neither in Glance nor in Grip. "Indeed, such an ignorant label has been applied to me, among others even less charitable. But what I preach is merely a brotherhood and equality of all the races, a sensible chariness toward all earthly authority, and a reliance on our inner voices in matters of conscience and action."

Releasing Williams's hand, Kane uttered a Judgment that ill consorted with the Prejudices of fully half the Audience. "Your ways are not mine, Sir, but I fully respect them. You are an authentic gentleman and visionary. I will not seek to enlist your help in this crusade, but I ask that you do nothing to hinder us from accomplishing the destruction of your erstwhile salvage *netop*."

With his use of this Aboriginal Word meaning friend, Kane gave some hint of the Depth of his Intimacy with New World Matters.

Williams sighed in a Dis-spirited Fashion. "I acknowledge your tact and good will, Sir, and altho' I could have wished you might be dissuaded from your bloody pursuit, yet will I give my bond not to stand in your way."

"In return," Kane replied, "you have my vow that when I am in striking distance of Philip, I will endeavor to withhold a mortal blow. Let us snaffle him and bring him to justice in a civilized manner, proving that our virtue is the greater. There will be no torture enacted upon Philip's person, so long as I can help it."

"My thanks, Goodman Kane. This is the most I could expect."

Williams departed the Arnold Lodgings then, and Kane made a request we found most curious.

"Is there one among you who has stood in Philip's actual presence? If there be more than one, let me speak to the one who has done so most recently."

A buzzing Consultation ensued, and finally a Verdict was reached. Major Pynchon said, "Sir, there is a goodwife now resident in this town named Mary Rowlandson. In February of last year she was taken captive by the Indians in a raid upon her garrison, and at one point was interviewed by Metacomet himself, all before attaining her present liberty. Shall we fetch her?"

"By all means."

A Messenger was Dispatched, and men took the occasion to venture outside, to stretch their Legs or enjoy a Bowl of Pipeweed, altho' little enough Relief from the Actual Heat was to be had, with the fully leafed Trees unstirring in the heavy stagnant Atmosphere. I myself remained inside, casting sly but constant Glances upon the Object of my Worship. Kane bided the interval like a patient predator, a Wolf or Catamount with an Eternal Perspective upon Events, or even like God Himself, Who, as we read in Peter's *Second Letter to the Romans*, regards a day as a thousand years and a thousand years as but a day.

Finally Kane chose to register my Ardent Eyebeams and motioned me to his Side. Tremulously I approached. Once within his Orbit, I made so bold as to ask a Boon, most especially now, whilst my Father was Absent. "Mr. Kane, I want to come with you when you strike out after the heathen prince."

Kane's Smile resembled a Hawk's Beakish Grin. "The little scholar desires to experience the warrior's lot? Not so wise a wish, young Cotton. Should your face be flecked but once with your foe's blood, you may well find yourself casting aside your primers in favor of the gun and the sword. And that is not a fate I would wish on anyone." Kane's eyes clouded over momentarily, as if he were watching a Parade of Phantasms from a Softer, more Luxurious Period in his own Career. "Had I heeded my own earliest inclinations, I might have become a simple schoolmaster, and never known the pains and tragedies I have endured. A wife, a fixed abode, children of my loins—all foreclosed to me now. But forsooth, absent also would have been the harsh glories of righteous conquest and retribution against sinners. And I surely would not be here speaking with you now, but long ago moldered to dust in my humble grave."

At this Juncture Kane negligently fondled the Cat-headed Stave at his waist, and my Eyes widened as I bethought to detect a Faint Glow emanating from the Fetiche.

There came a stir at the Door of the Room, and Kane summarily ended my short Interview. "I will not trammel thy spirit, Cotton. Every man must learn for himself which path he will tread. Let us see what eventuates. Stay alert, and take whate'er chance Dame Fortune presents."

Flanked by the returning Crowd, Mary Rowlandson entered the room. A short, pretty, chaste Woman of no great years, who yet evinced upon her Lineaments the Marks of her Travails as captive of the Indians, she came timorously into the presence of our Guest.

"Mary Rowlandson," said Kane decorously, "you received an audience from the Wampanoag sachem Metacomet during your captivity?"

"Yes, Sir, that I did. At first I was greatly afear'd of him, for he presented a fierce-some sight. He stood outside his rude wigwom, exceedingly tall, with mighty thews. He was girded with wampom, the Indian currency, and his stern face was bedizened with garish daubs of paint. But once he began to speak, in a calm and respectful manner, I someways lost my fright. He inquired as to my treatment, and I made complaint about the poor food afforded us, recounting how we slaves subsisted most days on naught but ground-nuts and hirtle-berries. Hearing this, Philip issued orders that we be given meat, bear or venison. Likewise, he ordered replacements for our tattered stokkins and shoos. When my audience was concluded, I retired with a fonder impression of him than I had expected to retain."

Kane seemed to come to some sudden decision. "Mary, you and I must now adjourn to a private chamber, where I intend to make use of your prior proximity to our enemy. For I have a method of ascertaining his current whereabouts thro' the spiritual bond established 'twixt you and the salvage. Mr. Arnold, where may we obtain the requisite privacy?"

Benedict Arnold hastened to say, "Pray employ the bedchamber my daughters use."

Kane stood, and escorted Mary Rowlandson to the designated Chamber.

Immediately I made for the Outer Door, but reckoned not with my Father's intervention.

"Cotton! Whither are you bound?"

"Ah, Sir, I—to the privy! 'Tis urgent!"

"Very well then. But stray not!"

Clutching my Privates as if to contain the Impulse to Micturate, I hastened outside.

Reader, I will confess to being no Plaster Saint in my Youth. As the Case was with Holy Augustine, the Tugs and Lures of the Flesh exerted their Devilish Sway over the immature Lad I once was. I oftssstimes sweated blood over my Sins of impurity, in the Wake of their Fulfillment, but could not find it in myself to firmly Excommunicate the Urges, so that I would, after some Days' piety, fall once again into the Slough of Onan. But at the Moment when I dash'd forth from the Arnold Household, I had cause to bless the Muddier Wellsprings of my Constitution, for it was these selfsame Peccant Ways which now afforded me a chance to spy upon Kane at his Conjurings.

I had removed from Boston to Newport many a Time before this day, accompanying Father on business matters concerning his Investments in the Carib Trade, *viz.*, Molasses, Rum, and Slaves. And we were often hosted by Benedict Arnold, one of Father's partners. In my aimless lonely Rambles about the Yard whilst boring Mercantile Affairs were conducted, I had discovered a small Chink or Slit in the outer wall of the House, a Gap which fortuitously gave upon the bedroom of the Arnold girls. Shielded by a dense stand of Pipeplants, whose lilac blooms would oft perfume my Vernal Peeping, this Spyhole had granted me many a Sweet Moment of Carnal Delight, as I witnessed the girls Making Water in their Chamberpots, or adjusting their Petty Coates and Stays.

Now I planted myself firmly before this Coign of vantage and was rewarded with the following Spectacle.

Mary Rowlandson sat on a sturdy straight-backed Chair, whilst Kane stood behind her. Their Speech, if any, I could not discern. But what Unfolded next made mere Words superfluous.

Kane laid his Left Hand upon Mary's collarbone, his Fingertips trailing tantalizing close to the Slope of her Bosom. I experienced a momentary Twinge of Suspicion. Was our Unassailable Puritan going to give way to his own Base Lusts and Molest his Subject? How could I follow him with Honor then? But no, Kane's Right Hand rose into view, clutching his Feline-Top't stave. That Instrument began to emit a Verdigrised Phosphorescence, a Lambent Glow that cloaked the actors in a veritable Corpselight. Kane uttered Something then, forcefully invoking Assistance or commanding Materialization.

Slowly, slowly, a third figure began to Cohere out of Thin Air. Surrounded by an Identifiable Landscape of Marshy Aspect, the Wraith gradually assumed its Wonted Lineaments, and I suddenly knew I was looking at none other than King Philip Himself.

Reader, you may rest assured that I felt at that Pivotal Moment like King David viewing Bathsheba nude at her Ablutions, all atingle with Mindless Exaltation. But as the Horrible Figure of Metacomet acquired more and more Solidity, my feelings transform'd to those which Actaeon must have felt, stumbling upon Artemis at her Sylvan Bath: a sense of Trespassing on the Cosmically Shrouded.

And when the Moment arrived that King Philip's puzzled, roving Eyes seemed to fasten on my Spyhole and engage my own Orbs in Spiteful Recognition, I nearly Fainted from fear.

Kane, howsomever, was nowise Discommoded by the Ghost. The Puritan's next actions were easy to interpret: he adjured the Ghost to speak. But this Astral Semblance of Metacomet, I soon saw, was no Obedient Smoak, but rather a Spectre of some Volition and

Malignance. Philip's only response to Kane's Adjuration was to Glower most Fearsomely and fasten his hands around Kane's throat!

Then ensued a brief but violent Tumult, as the two Warriors Contested against each other. Freed of Kane's steadying grip, Mary Rowlandson, drain'd of life, fell insensible to the Floorboards. My Heart was in my Gullet as Metacomet bent my Hero backwards, as if to crack his very Spine. But then Kane swung his Pagan Stave against the Skull of the Salvage King, and the Unnatural Apparition exploded in a Blaze of Light.

After spending just a moment longer at the Chink, to Ascertain that Kane yet Breathed and was making a Full Recovery, I hastily returned to the Gathering inside, making a Shew of buttoning my Trews.

Evidently, sounds of Kane's Struggle had penetrated to the Assembly, for much Consternation was abrew. Majors Pynchon and Gookin stood poised to burst in upon Kane. But just then the bedroom door opened, and a weary Kane emerged, half supporting his stun'd Female Accomplice.

Kane held up one hand in a Gesture of Reassurance. "All is well. I contended with the spirit of our enemy, and altho' he escaped me, I won the knowledge of his location, leaving him all unwitting of the theft, and, consequently, complacent of his own security. Philip is ensconced in the miry depths of a certain swamp at the foot of Mount Hope. We will set out under cover of darkness to bring the rogue down. But till then, let us all rest and prepare. I myself am sore fatigued."

Master Arnold conducted Kane to his own Bed. A General Exultancy reigned, albeit tinged with Sobriety at the Assault yet to come, as men slap'd each other upon their Backs and assured one another that at long last the Days of Terror were at an end.

Never prior to this Fateful Night had I ever considered myself to be one of the Sinners assailed by Paul in his *Second Letter to the Romans*. A Preacher's son, ever alert to maintaining Public Probity and a Cleanly Conscience, I had so long trodden the Path of Righteousness that by now such behavior was Second Nature to me, even as my Rectitude earned me Cuffings and Taunts from my Rowdy Errant Peers. Yet assuredly my actions of but a scant hour pass't had caused me to

Plummet into the ranks of those Sinners castigated by the Apostle, for Paul numbers among such Fiends as murderers, gossips, slanderers and inventors of evil, those who are "disobedient to their parents."

And so I had been.

But now, as I rode Unseeing thro' the Stifling August Night, bundled beneath the very Cloak of my Hero as the Mighty Steed lent to Kane carried us north to Tripp's Ferry, in Pursuit of the Greatest Villain and Conqueror these Arcadian Shores of the English Zion had yet known, I could not by any Dint of Conscience Regret my sins. For had I obeyed my Father's commands to remain behind in Newport, I would have missed all that Violent Glory that was to come, and thereafter Reviled my Overpunctiliousness for all Eternity.

At least such were my sanguine Feelings as I clutched the taut-muscled midriff of Solomon Kane whilst we gallop'd to our Destiny. Hang the Consequences till the Morrow! Tonight I was my own Man!

Kane had not Stirred from his Needful Sleep until well past eleven of the clock that eve, and the assembled Soldiers, Farmers, and Tradesmen had grown restless as Hens before a Storm, despite busying themselves with the preparations of their Weaponry and the Stoking of their Guts. But when the Grim Cavalier finally emerged with his Surly Magnificence Restored, and commanded, "Let us be off!" all Impatience and Incertitude vanish't, and a Lusty Huzzah spontaneously shook the very Rafters of the Arnold homestead.

As the men marshaled outside in the starlit Yard amidst the snorting Horses, Father approached me.

"Cotton, I have arranged for Faith and Charity to attend thee while we elders finish this dangerous and sordid matter. Thee need not go to bed at all on such a momentous night, for I know thy curiosity as to our success would certainly keep the awake. But I do trust that thee will make the most of thy time with the Arnold girls, perhaps by regaling 'em with some of thy lessons in natural history. Share with 'em the exciting news of the fossil record of God's abortive creations, those uncouth beasts which Noah spurned, and which perished afterwards in the Flood."

At any other time the Enticing Prospect of being alone with the Arnold Daughters would have commanded my whole attention. But tonight I was not to be Fobbed off so easily. Yet I made no Objection to my Father, but merely nodded mutely. Insofar as I kept Silent, so I chopped my logic, I could not be afterwards deemed a Liar.

As soon as Father exited, I made my same Privy-Desirous Excuse to the Arnolds, and was outside amidst the restlessly tromping Troop.

Spotting Kane, I acted unhesitantly. Racing to the side of his Horse, I thrust up my hand.

"Take me with you!" I whispered in a husky fashion.

Wordlessly Kane complied, hauling me off the ground with One-Handed ease. As I swung up into the saddle, he adjusted his long Mantle to Enshroud me, and the Deed was Done, with no one the Wiser.

Beneath my Woolly Concealment, bereft of any Actual Sense of the passing Terrain, I mentally rehearsed our Progress northward thro' Middle Town and Port's Mouth, along the sizable island whereof Newport occupied the Southern Portion. Our Terminus would be Tripp's Ferry, the Connexion to Mount Hope and Bristol on the Mainland. How I would avoid Father there, I could not say, and simply Entrusted my Survival as a member of the War Party to Luck and to Kane's Patronage.

After nearly an hour's hard Riding, we made the Slip wherefrom the Ferry wontedly departed. A messenger had been dispatched while Kane yet slumbered, and the Ferrymen awaited us, eager to do their part to end the Depradations of the Wampanoags and their kindred. The flickering light of Cressets and Torches filtered thro' the Weave of Kane's cloak, and I anticipated being Caught out upon perhaps some necessary Dismounting. But Kane simply trotted us onboard the rocking Ferry, taking up a Station at the Prow, and after another ten or so Horsemen followed, we poled off, leaving the rest of our party ashore until the craft returned.

I could hear the Oarlocks Engaged as we reached deeper Waters, and the Chaunts of the Laboring Scullers as they drew us across the half-mile of salty channel. The devilish August heat had hardly Abated with the fall of night, and the Closeness of my Little Tent made my eyes droop. But what Chanced next pulled me out of my drowse as surely as a Fisherman yanks a Cod from its Wat'ry Parlor.

"Mr. Kane," Major Pynchon said in a trembling voice, "what make you of those fast-moving clouds?"

When we had left Newport the begemmed nocturnal Skies had been clear as Ice. But obviously not so now.

"I like them not, major. They recall to me the boiling stormheads which I saw accrue when an Ethiope sorcerer of my acquaintance named N'Longa sought to dishearten his foes by magical means. Plainly these stormheads too are of supernatural origin."

A voice I did not recognize said, "I was with Captains Henchman and Prentice as we marched from Boston to Dedham last year to succor the garrison there, and we were overtaken by an eclipse of the moon. We all saw then strange portents on the moon's darkened face. A bloody scalp, an Indian bow. If the Tawnies can brand their evil upon Luna's very brow, what chance have we against 'em?"

"Nerve yourself to greater confidence, soldier!" Kane demanded. "Have ye forgotten you ride with God on your side?"

Some Instinct caused me to slip out of the Saddle then, to free Kane for easier Maneuvering. And 'twas well I did. For, as the Clouds clustering overhead began to Rumble and Spit, discharging crackling Lightnings as well, we were attacked!

"Watch yourselves!" yelled Kane, before Anyone else had taken Cognizance of the Assault upon us.

An enormous dripping Tendril as of some Unknown Leviathan of the Deeps, sucker'd over and round as a Hogshead Barrell, Hoary with Barnicles and Seawrack, burst from the water, arc'd thro' the air, and slapped down athwart the Deck, narrowly missing men and horses, who had scuttled away from its descent, thanks to Kane's warning. Horses scream'd, men curst, and a volley of Shots crack'd the night. But mere Musketballs seemed to have no effect upon the Creature, and the Awe-some Limb rose skyward again for another Plunge.

Kane was unhorsed now, and standing full beneath the shadow of the Kraken's Appendage. He flourished aloft his Cat-headed Stave, which Instrument commenced to Fulgurate in the manner I had earlier witnessed.

"Back to Hell with ye, demon! Back to the infernal depths!"

Pride in Kane's Staunch Demeanor and Apprehension that he would not Prevail against this Monster warred in my Juvenile Breast. Then all was decided, as a Lance of Cold Flame jabbed outward from

Stave to Tendril. A smell as of one of our traditional Clam Bakes multiplied an hundredfold filled the air, the Monst'rous Limb flailed about in obvious Pain before sliding away beneath the Turbid Waters, and silence descended upon the scene. At the same time the Unnatural Clouds began to Dis-sipate, and the Stars once more Smiled down on us.

Recovering with Admirable Alacrity, Major Pynchon soon had the Rowers back at work and order restored. In some further minutes the mainland beckoned us from no large distance. I came up to Kane, and was instantly heartened by his Praise.

"You did well to give me my liberty at the crucial moment, lad, and you did not quail before the hideous unknown. I do not believe anyone will raise any objections to your continued presence tonight."

"Thank you, Sir. I was inspired by your own noble bearing."

Kane returned me no Smile, but simply said, "If I exhibit no fear, young Cotton, it is only because all such emotions have been burnt from me by unfathomable hardships and privations. Anyone witnessing the horrors I have seen—assuming those hypothetical witnesses survived—would exhibit the same stoicism. I have no choice any longer in what I do, and this paucity of options represents a missing civilized luxury the lack of which I sometimes sorely regret. But such is my lot, and I am mainly content."

Leaving me to ponder this Chill Assessment of his Own Damaged Soul, Kane moved off to help with the docking. Soon we were on dry land.

Two Worthy and Vigorous men now separated themselves from the Mass of welcomers, introducing themselves as Captain Church of Plymouth and Captain Williams of Scituate. They delivered an Account of their forces, which included a Contingent of Praying Indians. These Friendly Salvages stood in a Cabal a ways off from us White Men, and I instantly mistrusted their Obsequious yet oddly Threatening Mien. In their adopted Civilized Garb, the Uppish barbarians seemed both Traitors to their own Race and Unreliant Allies, neither Fish nor Fowle, a Pack of Trained Apes or Dancing Bears.

"Mr. Kane," said Williams, "thanks to your veritable intelligence, we have been able to encircle the bog and ensure that Philip and any of his remaining myrmidons remain cloistered within. We await your subsequent direction."

Kane uttered then the chilling Words we had all been anticipating, but which nonetheless still Pricked our Courage. "There is naught for it but to enter the horse-repelling swamp afoot, in pairs. The separation of our forces will allow us to beat every bush most thoroughly. But the treacherous conditions underfoot, which the Indians know intimately, will confound and undo many of the teams. We can only pray that whoever of us meets Metacomet will be up to subduing him. Let us but agree to raise a commotion upon sighting our prize, and I will immediately hasten to aid whichever brave Ajax first grapples with the villain."

"Shall we wait until daybreak?" asked Captain Church.

"By no means. As soon as the rest of our party is ferried o'er, we strike."

Father arrived with the third Boatload of men, and I shall not recount the Bitter Upbraidings I thereupon received. I made humble yet cogent Response, employing all the finer Logic with which my mentors at Harvard had imbued me, citing the duty of every citizen, however Juvenile, to protect our Commonwealth. When mere Females could exhibit such Courage as to ward off their Vile Attackers with a scuttle of live Coals, could a strapping Youth such as myself do any less? Suffice it to say that not only did my words soothe and convince, but Kane's account of my Behavior under the Kraken's Buffets earned me Grudging Praise (once Father's Apoplexy abated), and also at last the Miraculous Privilege of Penetrating the Very Marsh itself, and in no other role than that of Patroclus to Kane's Achilles, to continue Kane's Grecian Simile.

In the end, Father seemed actually Prideful of my new Station in the Scheme of Things. He laid a hand on Kane's shoulder, signaling his assent to my new status, and earnestly bade the Puritan keep me safe by his Side, asserting that no other Warrior could offer his Cherished Son more Protection than Kane. Kane returned a simple, "That I will endeavor to do," and then we moved out.

The hour was now nearly Three in the Morning, and already hints of Aurora's debut were discernible. We welcomed even this negligible Lessening of darkness as an Aid to our Progress.

I carried no Weapon, but my Utility amidst the Thickets soon became apparent. Being Lighter and some'at more Nimble than my Protector, I served as Scout, probing ahead with a long stout Stick and testing the Hummocks and Tussocks that would serve us as Stepping Stones into the Depths of the Bog. This Service freed Kane to concentrate his Hunter's Senses on both repelling any Attack and Ferreting out any Hidden Salvages.

Not wishing to advertize our Presence too far in advance, we carried no Light, nor did any of the other Teams. Moving thro' the Sepulchral Gloom and Heat, with its Squelching Muck, Slithering Serpents, Apparitional Trees, and Hordes of Disturbed Insects, some of which made known their Appetite for Human Flesh, I felt like Dante Essaying some Lesser Circle of Hell, with Kane my Militant Virgil.

Now passed an Indeterminate Period of Time, an interval wherein my Sensible Universe narrowed to my own harsh Slogging, labored Breathing, and tensioned Nerves. However, I drew Courage and Stamina from Kane's unfaltering Harrowing of our Swampy Environs. Rapier in one hand and Pistol in t'other, he stalked behind me like an Avenging Angel in Judges or Zechariah, and I felt utterly safe within his Sphere of Protection.

Every now and then a distant Shot would resound, and I would pray that one less Salvage befouled the Earth, and also that our own men Fared Unharmed. But as time passed and no Hulloo summoned us to confront the Chief Object of our Search, I began to despair that our Fiendish Quarry would escape us once again.

In our unyielding Progress, Kane and I reached finally a largish expanse of solid ground, a little Islet sequester'd in the heart of the Swamp. Its O'ergrown Marge concealed its Interior from our eyes, and we penetrated cautiously.

But all our Deft Secrecy availed naught, for King Philip awaited us in full Cognizance of our advance, standing with Solemn Gravity upon a patch of clear Ground.

A grey Dawn now nearly nigh allowed me a good picture of the Formidable Warrior. Tall as Kane, the fearsome Metacomet wore his pursuit-tatter'd buckskins and robe as if they were Ermine or Sable. His painted face, all majestic angles, seemed hewn from our own New England granite or a block of lignum vitae. Strands of Wampom bedizened his brawny chest, across which he confidently cradled his

Musket, Indian fashion. A Rude Tom-a-Hawk, its Shaft carven with Pagan Glyphs, Feathers depending from its Butt, hung from his waist.

Ignoring me utterly, Philip spoke first, his Manly voice resonant with Suppressed Rage, Black Despair, and a most curious Forlorn Indifference to his own Fate. Of Fear I heard no syllable, but yet much of Intelligence and Refinement. Let me confess now that, by the end of his Speech, I had gained new Respect for our Opponent.

"What cheer, fellow Mage. After our spirit battle, we come face to face at last. Your reputation for independence and courage has reached me across the wide waters, yet I find you now entered into the service of these small men, who are all too timid and inept to confront me themselves. I see a proud lion yoked to a plough."

Kane responded soberly. "The choice of mission is my own, Metacomet. No man commands me. As ever, I respond to the sheer injustice of the situation."

King Philip spat upon the soggy soil. "Injustice! Where were you then when my people were enslaved and humiliated, when they were taken and imprisoned under false charges, when my brothers were executed and my sisters molested, when our lands were stolen from us? Is it only the sufferings of white men that can elicit your outrage?"

Kane seemed Stung by this Jab. "I have fought on behalf of all races and tribes, Metacomet, the sons of Ham as well as the sons of Shem. But by the time I learned of this war, your side was clearly in the wrong, having overstepped all bounds of civilized combat. Enlisting wicked allies, you turned your back on all courts and treaties—"

Philip's face contorted with anger. "Instruments of the conquerors, prejudiced against our kind from the start! And I piss on your ridiculous rules of war! Only victory matters."

Seemingly reconciled to the Futility of any further Argument, Kane assumed a more Agressive Footing. "Let us have at it then, King. Each cause will find embodiment in its champion, and victory will go to him who strikes hardest. And should it be within my powers to subdue you without dealing a mortal blow, I am pledged to do so, having given troth to your *netop,* Roger Williams."

"You must do what you deem honorable, as shall I. But I pray you, let us abandon our firearms, and allow our human muscles to hold sway."

King Philip nobly suited Deeds to Words then, and tossed aside his musket. Kane followed suit with his brace of Pistols and also his Rapier. Into his hand came the Cat-Headed Stave, its weird Radiance now matched by the cousin'd Glow from the Tom-a-Hawk.

Then Kane and Philip closed upon one another.

I watched Enrapt as the well-matched Fighters circled each other warily. But I was not prepared for what eventuated when their Weapons clashed.

An enormous Report like a barrage of Thunder issued from the smash of Fetiche against Hatchet. Jags of harsh Lightning shot skyward, illuminating the Scene as brightly as Noon. Neither man seemed disconcerted by the titanic Repercussions of their Contest, but, quite to the contrary, became e'en more fully Embroil'd in a Fantastic Dance of Death, darting around and about, each seeking a way thro' t'other's Defenses.

Once more my Heart was Socketed firmly in my Windpipe, as I observed my Worshipful Idol strive so Manfully, amidst the St. Elmo's Coruscations. From the Fringes, I watched this Eldritch Display with mute Fascination, unable to assign Dominance to either Combatant. But this much I knew: the Contest would not long go uninterrupted, for surely every Interested Participant within Leagues must be hastening to this very spot, drawn by the Tumult. If Kane would indeed settle Philip's Hash, it must be soon.

But then came Tragedy! Forced backwards, Kane stumbled upon a Root, and momentarily lost his Vigilance. Into that narrow crack of Inattention Metacomet plunged! A blow from his Tom-a-Hawk was only partially deflected before coming into Heavy Contact with Kane's Scull!

Now Kane measured his lanky Length upon the clammy Ground, Stunned and Bleeding. A Yawp of Sympathy and Alarm escaped my own Lips. My Beloved Conqueror had been felled, and All was Lost lest I could save him! I estimated how quickly I could reach one of Kane's discarded Pistols, but before I could move, Metacomet bestrode my prostrate Hero like the Colossus of Rhodes and raised his evil Axe.

"I took no such pledge of mercy as thee, Kane. Prepare to meet thy false God."

At that instant a Shot rang out, and King Philip plunged Rearward to the ground.

Into the clearing stepped one of the Praying Indians, named most inaptly, as I later learned, Alderman. He it was whose Cowardly Shot had ignobly finished the Great Sagamore, once the Bane of our Land, piercing the Body of the proud Leader precisely where "Joab thrust his darts into rebellious Absalom."

I rushed to Kane's side, seeking to Succor him. But his Wound was Gouting much blood, and he remained Insensate. There was little enough I could do, save cushion his Head and stroke his Gory Brow.

Within minutes, the Islet was crowded with exultant Soldiers. Somehow, between 'em all, both Kane and the corpse of Philip were Borne out of the Marsh.

Patient Reader, there is little enough more to indite in this Account anent the most Stirring Moments of my Young Life, now so far removed from my current Feeble Estate.

The fate of Philip's Mortal Remains is well known. Beheaded and quartered, the Punishment long reserved for Traitors, he was denied sanctified Burial according to either Christian or Pagan Customs. His mounted Head was displayed at Plimoth for twenty-five Years or more, and served as Grim Warning to his Dis-spirited and Dis-sheveled brethren.

This Brutal Decomposition of his Opponent, which Kane's Incapacitation made him unable to prevent, most assuredly occasioned Kane's Deepest Regrets, tho' he spoke not ever of it.

As for Kane himself, he recovered admirably, despite the Severity of his Wound, proving once agan that whereas one Man may die from cracking his Tooth upon a Plumb-stone, another may survive an Hatchet buried in his Scull. And I shall eschew False Humility enough to reveal that it was I who had the Inspired Notion to place his Stave upon his Bosom during the initial Stuporous stages of his Recovery. Indeed, the Magical Wand seemed to act as a Sovereign Incitement to his Speedy Healing. Before a fortnight had passed, the Old Puritan was ready to return to his Native Shores.

We made our Goodbyes at the same Newport Wharf where I had seen him step ashore, what seemed like a Small Eternity ago, so rich in Incident had the brief days been.

Kane clasped my hand firmly, regarding me from under his crumpled Slouch Hat with an iron Gaze.

"Think you still, young Cotton, to follow in the warrior's footsteps after all the gruesome things you have observed?"

I made ready Reply, having given much Consideration to this question while Kane recuperated. "No, Sir, I do not. I will most likely become a preacher, I think, like unto my father. The Reverend Cotton Mather has a nice sound to't. In that profession, I deem, a man's hands may remain virtuously unbloodied."

Kane neither disputed nor affirmed this Sentiment, but simply Saluted me, and stepped onto the vessel that bore him away.

This story exists only because the ingenious and far-sighted Lou Anders commissioned it for his original anthology, Live Without a Net. *Asked to imagine a scenario where the Internet had never been invented, or was no more, I was inspired by the work of Jack Vance, whose novella* The Dragon Masters *postulated a world where manipulation of animal and human breeding had accomplished all that physics ever could. And the classic motif of barbaric descendants of past glory clinging to things they half understood—a trope I had never worked with before—was also just too alluring to resist.*

Clouds and Cold Fires

Out of a clear sky on a fine summer morning, a buckshot rattle of hailstones across the living pangolin plates of Pertinax's rooftop announced the arrival of some mail.

Inside his cozy, low-ceilinged hutch, with its corner devoted to an easel and canvases and art supplies, its shelves full of burl sculptures, its workbench that hosted bubbling retorts and alembics and a universal proseity device, Pertinax paused in the feeding of his parrot tulips. Setting down the wooden tray of raw-meat chunks, he turned away from the colorfully enameled soil-filled pots arrayed on his bright windowsill. The parrot tulips squawked at this interruption of their lunch, bobbing their feathery heads angrily on their long succulent neck stalks. Pertinax chided them lovingly, stroking their crests while avoiding their sharp beaks. Then, hoisting the hem of his long striped robe to expose his broad naked paw-feet, he hurried outdoors.

Fallen to the earth after bouncing from the imbricated roof, the hailstones were already nearly melted away to invisibility beneath the temperate sunlight, damp spots on the undulant greensward upon which Pertinax's small but comfortable dwelling sat. Pertinax wetted a finger, raised it to gauge the wind's direction, then directed his vision upward and to the north, anticipating the direction from which his mail would arrive. Sure enough, within a minute a lofty cloud had begun to form, a flocculent painterly smudge on the monochrome canvas of the turquoise sky.

The cloud assumed coherence and substance, drawing into itself its necessary share of virgula and sublimula omnipresent within the upper atmosphere. After another minute or two, the cloud possessed a highly regular oval outline and had descended to within five meters of the ground. Large as one of the windows in Pertinax's hutch, the cloud halted its progress at this level, and its surface began to acquire a sheen. The sheen took on the qualities of an ancient piece of translucent plastic, such as the Overclockers might cherish. Then Pertinax's animated mail appeared across the cloud's surface, as the invisible components of the cloud churned in coordinated fashion.

Sylvanus's snouty whiskered face smiled, but the smile was grim, as was his voice resonating from the cloud's fine-grain speakers.

"Pertinax my friend, I regret this interruption of your studies and recreations, but I have some dramatic news requiring our attention. It appears that the Overclockers at their small settlement known as 'Chicago' are about to launch an assault on the tropospherical mind. Given their primitive methods, I doubt that they can inflict permanent damage. But their mean-spirited sabotage might very well cause local disruptions before the mind repairs itself. I know you have several projects running currently, and I would hate to see you lose any data during a period of limited chaos. I would certainly regret any setbacks to my ongoing modeling of accelerated hopper embryogenesis. Therefore, I propose that a group of those wardens most concerned form a delegation to visit the Overclockers and attempt to dissuade them from such malicious tampering. Mumbaugh has declined to participate—he's busy dealing with an infestation of hemlock mites attacking the forests of his region—but I have firm commitments from Cimabue, Tanselle, and Chellapilla. I realize that it is irksome to leave behind the comforts of your home to make such a trip. But I am hoping that I may count on your participation as well. Please reply quickly, as time is of the essence."

Its mail delivered, the cloud wisped away into its mesoscopic constituent parts. A light misty drizzle refreshed Pertinax's face. But otherwise he was left with only the uneasy feelings occasioned by the message.

Of course he would help Sylvanus. Interference with the tropospherical mind could not be tolerated. The nerve of those Overclockers!

Not for the first time, nor probably the last, Pertinax ruefully contemplated the dubious charity of the long-departed Upflowered.

When 99.9 percent of humanity had abandoned Earth for greener intergalactic pastures during the Upflowering, the leave takers had performed several final tasks. They had re-arcadized the whole globe, wiping away nearly every vestige of mankind's crude twenty-second-century proto-civilization, and restocked the seas and plains with many beasts. They had established Pertinax and his fellows—a small corps of ensouled, spliced, and redacted domestic animals—as caretakers of the restored Earth. They had charitably set up a few agrarian reservations for the small number of dissidents and malfunctioning humans who chose to remain behind, stubbornly unaltered in their basic capabilities from their archaic genetic baseline. And they had uploaded every vestige of existing machine intelligence and their knowledge bases to a new platform: an airborne network of minuscule, self-replenishing components, integrated with the planet's meteorological systems.

During the intervening centuries, the remaining archaic humans—dubbed the Overclockers for their uncanny devotion to both speed and the false quantization of holistic imponderables—had gradually dragged themselves back up to a certain level of technological achievement. Now, it seemed, they were on the point of making a nuisance of themselves. This could not be tolerated.

Hurrying back into his compact domicile, Pertinax readied his reply to Sylvanus. From a small door inset in one wall, which opened onto a coop fixed to the outside wall, Pertinax retrieved a mail pigeon. He placed the docile murmuring bird on a tabletop and fed it some special seed, scooped from one compartment of a feed bin. While he waited for the virgula and sublimula within the seed to take effect, Pertinax supplied his own lunch: a plate of carrots and celery, the latter smeared with delicious bean paste. By the time Pertinax had finished his repast, cleaning his fur with the side of one pawhand all the way from muzzle to tufted ear tips, the pigeon was locked into recording mode, staring ahead fixedly, as if hypnotized by a predator.

Pertinax positioned himself within the bird's field of vision. "Sylvanus my peer, I enlist wholeheartedly in your mission! Although my use of the tropospheric mind is negligible compared to your own employment of the system, I do have all my statistics and observations from a century of avian migrations stored there. Should the data and its backups be corrupted, the loss of such a record would be disastrous! I propose to set out immediately by hopper for 'Chicago.' Should you likewise leave upon receipt of this message, I believe our paths will intersect somewhere around these coordinates." Pertinax recited latitude and longitude figures. "Simply ping my hopper when you get close enough, and we'll meet to continue the rest of our journey together. Travel safely."

Pertinax recited the verbal tag that brought the pigeon out of its trance. The bird resumed its lively attitude, plainly ready to perform its share of the mail delivery. Pertinax cradled the bird against his oddly muscled chest and stepped outside. He lofted the pigeon upwards, and it began to stroke the sky bravely.

Once within the lowest layers of the tropospheric mind, the bird would have its brain states recorded by an ethereal cap of spontaneously congregating virgula and sublimula, and the bird would be free to return to its coop.

Pertinax's message would thus enter the meteorological medium and be propagated across the intervening leagues to Sylvanus. Like a wave in the ocean, the information was not dependent upon any unique set of entities to constitute its identity, and so could travel faster than simple forward motion of particles might suggest. To span the globe from Pertinax's home to the antipodes took approximately twelve hours, and Sylvanus lived much closer. Not as fast as the ancient quantum-entanglement methods extant in the days before the Upflowering. But then again, the pace of life among the stewards was much less frenzied than it had been among the ancestors of the Overclockers.

Having seen his mail on its way, Pertinax commenced the rest of his preparations for his trip. He finished feeding his parrot tulips, giving them a little extra to see them through his time away from home. If delayed overlong, Pertinax knew they would estivate safely till his return. Then from a cupboard he took a set of large saddlebags. Into these pouches he placed victuals for himself and several packets of multipurpose pigeon seed, as well as a few treats and vitamin pills to supplement the forage which his hopper would subsist on during the journey. He looked fondly at his neat, comfortable bed, whose familiar refuge he would miss. No taking that, of course! But the hopper would provide a decent alternative. Pertinax added a few other miscellaneous items to his pack, then deemed his provisions complete.

Stepping outside, Pertinax took one fond look back inside before shutting and latching his door. He went around shuttering all the windows as a precaution against the storms that sometimes accompanied the more demanding calculations of the tropospheric mind. From the pigeon coop he withdrew three birds and placed them in a loosely woven wicker carrier. Then he took a few dozen strides to the hopper corral, formed of high walls of living ironthorn bush.

Pertinax's hopper was named Flossy, a fine mare. The redacted Kodiak Kangemu stood three meters tall at its shoulders. Its pelt was a curious blend of chestnut fur and gray feathers, its fast-twitch-muscled legs banded with bright yellow scales along the lower third above its enormous feet. A thick strong tail jutted backward, almost half again as long as Flossy's body.

Pertinax tossed Flossy a treat, which she snapped from the air with her long jaws. In the stable attached to the corral, Pertinax secured a saddle. This seat resembled a papoose or backpack, with two shoulder straps. Outside again, Pertinax opened the corral gate—formed of conventional timbers—and beckoned to Flossy, who obediently came out and hunkered down. Holding the saddle up above his head, Pertinax aided Flossy in shrugging into the seat. He cinched the straps, then hung his saddlebags from one lower side of the seat and the wicker basket containing the pigeons from the other. Deftly Pertinax scrambled up, employing handholds of Flossy's fur, and ensconced himself comfortably, the seat leaving his arms free but cradling his back and neck. His head was now positioned above Flossy's, giving him a clear view of his path. He gripped Flossy's big upright ears firmly yet not harshly, and urged his mount around to face northeast.

"Gee up, Flossy," said Pertinax, and they were off.

Flossy's gait was the queerest mixture of hopping, vaulting, running, and lumbering, a mode of locomotion unknown to baseline creation. But Pertinax found it soothing, and his steed certainly ate up the kilometers.

For the first few hours, Pertinax enjoyed surveying his immediate territory, quite familiar and beloved, noting subtle changes in the fauna and flora of the prairie that distance brought. In early afternoon he stopped for a meal, allowing Flossy to forage. Taking out a pigeon and prepping the bird, Pertinax recited his morning's scientific observations to be uploaded to the tropospheric mind. Its data delivered, the bird homed back to Pertinax rather than the cottage. In less than an hour, the warden was under way again.

Pertinax fell asleep in the saddle and awoke at dusk. He halted Flossy and dismounted to make camp. With the saddle off, Flossy cropped wearily nearby. The first thing Pertinax attended to was the establishment of a security zone. A pheromonal broadcaster would disseminate the warden's exaggerated chemical signature for kilometers in every direction, a note that all of wild creation was primed by the Upflowered to respond to. Avoidance of the distinctive trace had been built into their ancestors' genes. (The bodily signature had to be masked for up-close work with animals.) Pertinax had no desire to be trampled in the night by a herd of bison, or attacked by any of the region's many predators. Sentient enemies were nonexistent, with the nearest Overclockers confined by their limited capacities nearly one thousand kilometers away in "Chicago."

After setting up the small scent-broadcast unit, Pertinax contemplated summoning forth some entertainment. But in the end he decided he was just too tired to enjoy any of the many offerings of the tropospheric mind, and that he would rather simply go to sleep.

The upright Flossy, balanced tripodally on her long tail, was already herself half adrowse, and she made only the softest of burblings when Pertinax clambered into her capacious marsupial pouch. Dry and lined with a soft down, the pouch smelled like the nest of some woodland creature, and Pertinax fell asleep feeling safe and cherished.

The morning dawned like the first day of the world, crisp and inviting. Emerging from his nocturnal pouch, Pertinax noted that night had brought a heavy dew that would have soaked him had he been dossing rough. But instead he had enjoyed a fine, dry, restful sleep.

Moving off a ways from the grumbling Flossy and casting about with a practiced eye, Pertinax managed to spot some untended prairie chicken nests amidst the grassy swales. He robbed them of an egg apiece without compunction (the population of the birds was robust), and soon a fragrant omelet, seasoned with herbs from home, sizzled over a small propane burner. (Pertinax obtained the flammable gas, like many of his needs, from his universal proseity device.)

After enjoying his meal, Pertinax dispatched a pigeon upward to obtain from the tropospheric mind his positional reading, derived from various inputs such as constellational and magnetic. The coordinates, cloud-blazoned temporarily on the sky in digits meters long, informed Pertinax that Flossy had carried him nearly one hundred and fifty kilometers during their previous half day of travel. At this rate, he'd join up with Sylvanus on the morrow, and with the others a day later. Then the five stewards would reach "Chicago" around noon of the fourth day.

Past that point, all certainty vanished. How the Overclockers would react to the arrival of the wardens, how the wardens would dissuade the humans from tampering with the planetary mind, what they would do if they met resistance—all this remained obscure.

Remounting Flossy, Pertinax easily put the uncertainty from his mind. Neither he nor his kind were prone to angst. So, once on his way, he reveled instead in the glorious day and the unfolding spectacle of nature reigning supreme over an untarnished globe.

Herds of bison thundered past at a safe distance during various intervals along Pertinax's journey. Around noon a nearly interminable flock of passenger pigeons darkened the skies. A colony of prairie dogs stretching across hectares mounted a noisy and stern defense of their town.

That night replicated the simple pleasures of the previous one. Before bedding down, Pertinax enjoyed a fine display of icy micrometeorites flashing into the atmosphere. The Upflowered had arranged a regular replenishment of Earth's water budget via this cosmic source before they left.

Around noon on the second full day of travel, with the landscape subtly changing as they departed one bioregion for another, Pertinax felt a sudden quivering alertness thrill through Flossy. She had plainly pinged the musk of Sylvanus's steed (a stallion named Bix) on the wind, and needed no help from her rider to zero in on her fellow Kodiak Kangemu. Minutes later, Pertinax himself espied Sylvanus and his mount, a tiny conjoined dot in the distance.

Before long, the two wardens were afoot and clasping each other warmly, while their hoppers boxed affectionately at each other.

"Pertinax, you're looking glossy as a foal! How I wish I were your age again!"

"Nonsense, Sylvanus, you look splendid yourself. After all, you're far from old. A hundred and twenty-nine last year, wasn't it?"

"Yes, yes, but the weary bones still creak more than they did when I was a young buck of a mere sixty-eight, like you. Some days I just want to drop my duties and retire. But I need to groom a successor first. If only you and Chellapilla—"

Pertinax interrupted his elder friend. "Perhaps Chellapilla and I have been selfish. I confess to feeling guilty about this matter from time to time. But the demands on our energies seemed always to preclude parentage. I'll discuss it with her tomorrow. And don't forget, there's always Cimabue and Tanselle."

Sylvanus clapped a hearty paw-hand on Pertinax's shoulder. "They're fine stewards, my boy, but I had always dreamed of your child stepping into my shoes."

Pertinax lowered his eyes. "I'm honored, Sylvanus. Let me speak of this with Chell."

"That's all I ask. Now I suppose we should be on our way again."

It took some sharp admonishments and a few coercive threats to convince Bix and Flossy to abandon their play for the moment and resume travel, but eventually the two wardens again raced northeast, toward their unannounced appointment with the Overclockers.

That night before turning in, Sylvanus suggested some entertainment.

"I have not viewed any historical videos for some time now. Would you care to see one?"

"Certainly. Do you have a suggestion?"

"What about *The Godfather*?"

"Part One?"

"Yes."

"An excellent choice. Perhaps it will help to refresh our understanding of Overclocker psychology. I'll send up a pigeon."

The sleepy bird responded sharply to the directorial seed and verbal instructions, then zoomed upward. While the wardens waited for the tropospheric mind to respond, they arranged their packs and saddles in a comfortable couch that allowed them to lie back and observe the night skies.

In minutes a small audio cloud had formed low down near them, to provide the soundtrack. Then the high skies lit with colored cold fires.

The new intelligent meteorology allowed for auroral displays at any latitude of the globe, as cosmic rays were channeled by virgula and sublimula, then bent and manipulated to excite atoms and ions. Shaped and permuted on a pixel level by the distributed airborne mind, the auroral canvas possessed the resolution of a twentieth-century drive-in screen, and employed a sophisticated palette.

Clear and bold as life, the antique movie began to unroll across the black empyrean. Snacking on dried salted crickets, the two stewards watched in rapt fascination until the conclusion of the film.

"Most enlightening," said Sylvanus. "We must be alert for such incomprehensible motives as well as deceptions and machinations among the Overclockers."

"Indeed, we would be foolish to anticipate any rationality at all from such a species. Their ancestors' choice to secede from the Upflowering tells us all we need to know about their unchanged mentality."

Midafternoon of the next day found Sylvanus and Pertinax hard-pressed to restrain their rambunctious hoppers from charging toward three other approaching Kodiak Kangemu. At the end of the mad gallop, five stewards were clustered in a congregation of hearty back-slapping and embraces, while the frolicking hoppers cavorted nearby.

After the general exchange of greetings and reassurances, Cimabue and Tanselle took Sylvanus to one side to consult with him, leaving Pertinax and Chellapilla some privacy.

Chellapilla smiled broadly, revealing a palisade of blunt healthy brown teeth. Her large hazel eyes sparkled with affection and her leathery nostrils flared wetly. The past year since their last encounter had seen her acquire a deep ragged notch in one ear. Pertinax reached up to touch the healed wound. Chellapilla only laughed, before grabbing his paw-hand and kissing it.

"Are you troubled by that little nick, Perty? Just a brush with a wounded wolverine when I was checking a trap line for specimens last winter. Well worth the information gained."

Pertinax found it hard to reconcile himself to Chellapilla's sangfroid. "I worry about you, Chell. It's a hard life we have sometimes, as isolated guardians of the biosphere. Don't you wish, just once in a while, that we could live together . . . ?"

"Ah, of course I do! But where would that end? Two stewards together would become four, then a village, then a town, then a city of wardens. With our long life spans, we'd soon overpopulate the world with our kind. And then Earth would be right back where it was in the twenty-second century."

"Surely not! Our species would not fall prey to the traps mankind stumbled into before the Upflowering."

Chellapilla smiled. "Oh, no, we'd be clever enough to invent new ones. No, it's best this way. We have our pastoral work to occupy our intelligence, with the tropospheric mind to keep us in daily contact and face-to-face visits at regular intervals. It's a good system."

"You're right, I suppose. But still, when I see you in the flesh, Chell, I long for you so."

"Then let's make the most of this assignment. We'll have sweet memories to savor when we part."

Pertinax nuzzled Chellapilla's long furred neck, and she shivered and clasped him close. Then he whispered his thoughts regarding Sylvanus's desired retirement and the needful successor child into her ear.

Chellapilla chuckled. "Are you sure you didn't put Sylvanus up to this? You know the one exemption from cohabitation is the period of parenting. This is all a scheme to get me to clean your hutch and cook your meals on a regular basis for a few years, isn't it?"

"Yes, I admit it. There's never been a universal proseity device made that was as nice to hold as you."

"Well, let me think about it for the rest of this trip, before I go off my pills. It's true that you and I are not getting any younger, and I am inclined toward becoming a mother, especially if our child will help ease Sylvanus's old age. But I want to make sure I'm not overlooking any complications."

"My ever-sensible Chell! I could have dictated your reply without ever leaving my hutch."

Chellapilla snorted. "One of us has to be the sober-sided one."

The two lovers rejoined their fellow stewards. Tanselle immediately took Chellapilla to one side, in an obvious attempt to pump her friend for any gossip. The feminine whispers and giggles and sidewise glances embarrassed Pertinax, and he made a show of engaging Cimabue in a complex discussion of the latter's researches. But Pertinax could lend only half his mind to Cimabue's talk of fisheries and turtle breeding, ocean currents and coral reefs. The other half was still contemplating his exciting future with Chellapilla.

Eventually Sylvanus roused them from their chatter with a suggestion that they resume their journey. Bix, Flossy, Amber, Peavine, and Peppergrass bore their riders north, deeper into the already encroaching forests of the Great Lakes region.

When they established camp that evening in a clearing beneath a broad canopy of lofty treetops, Sylvanus made a point of setting up a little hearth somewhat apart from his younger comrades. Plainly, he did not want to put a damper on any romantic moments among the youngsters.

The five shared supper together however. Sylvanus kept wrinkling his grizzled snout throughout the meal, until finally he declaimed, "There's a storm brewing. The tropospheric mind must be performing some large randomizations or recalibrations. I suspect entire registers will be dumped."

Baseline weather had been tempered by the creation of an intelligent atmosphere. Climates across the planet were more equitable and homogeneous, with fewer extreme instances of violent weather. But occasionally both the moderately large and even the titanic disturbances of yore would recur, as the separate entities that constituted the community of the skies deliberately encouraged random Darwinian forces to cull and mutate their members.

"I packed some tarps and ropes," said Cimabue, "for just such an occasion. If we cut some poles, we can erect a shelter quickly."

Working efficiently, the wardens built, first, a three-walled roofed enclosure for their hardy hoppers, stoutly braced between several trees, its open side to the leeward of the prevailing winds. Then they fashioned a small but sufficient tent for themselves and their packs, heavily staked to the earth. A few blankets strewn about the interior created a comfy nest, illuminated by several cold luminescent sticks. Confined body heat would counter any chill.

Just as they finished, a loud crack of thunder ushered in the storm. Safe and sound in their tent, the wardens listened to the rain hammering the intervening leaves above before filtering down to drip less heavily on their roof.

Sylvanus immediately bade his friends goodnight, then curled up in his robe in one corner, his back to them. Soon his snores—feigned or real—echoed off the sloping walls.

Swiftly disrobed, Cimabue and Tanselle began kissing and petting each other, and Pertinax and Chellapilla soon followed suit. By the time the foursome had begun exchanging cuds, their unashamed mating, fueled by long separation, was stoked to proceed well into the night.

The reintegrational storm blew itself out shortly after midnight, with what results among the mentalities of the air the wardens would discover only over the course of many communications. Perhaps useful new insights into the cosmos and Earth's place therein had been born this night.

In the morning the shepherds broke down their camp, breakfasted, and embarked on the final leg of their journey to "Chicago." Pertinax rode his hopper in high spirits, pacing Chellapilla's Peavine.

Not too long after their midday meal (Tanselle had bulked out their simple repast with some particularly tasty mushrooms she had carried from home), they came within sight of the expansive lake, almost oceanic in its extent, that provided the human settlement with water for both drinking and washing, as well as various dietary staples. Reckoning themselves a few dozen kilometers south of the humans, the five headed north, encountering large peaceful herds of elk and antelopes along the way.

They smelled "Chicago" before they saw it.

"They're not burning petroleum, are they?" asked Cimabue.

"No," said Sylvanus. "They have no access to any of the few remaining played-out deposits of that substance. It's all animal and vegetable oils, with a little coal from near-surface veins."

"It sure does stink," said Tanselle, wrinkling her nose.

"They still refuse our offer of limited universal proseity devices?" Pertinax inquired.

Sylvanus shook his head ruefully. "Indeed. They are stubborn, suspicious, and prideful, and disdain the devices of the Upflowered as something near demonic. They claim that such cornucopia would render their species idle and degenerate, and destroy their character. When the Upflowered stripped them of their twenty-second-century technology, the left-behind humans conceived a hatred of their ascended brethren. Now they are determined to reascend the same ladder of technological development they once negotiated, but completely on their own."

Cimabue snorted. "It's just as well they don't accept our gifts. The UPD's would allow them to spread their baneful way of life even further than they already have. We can only be grateful their reproductive rates have been redacted downward."

"Come now," said Chellapilla, "surely the humans deserve as much respect and right to self-determination as any other species. Would you cage up all the blue jays in the world simply because they're noisy?"

"You don't have any humans in your bioregion, Chell. See what you think after you've met them."

The pathless land soon featured the start of a crude gravel-bedded road. The terminus the travelers encountered was a dump site. The oil-stained ground, mounded with detritus both organic and manufactured, repelled Pertinax's sensibilities. He wondered how the humans could live with such squalor, even on the fringes of their settlement.

Moving swiftly down the pebbled roadway, the wardens soon heard a clanking, chugging, ratcheting riot of sound from some ways around the next bend of the tree-shaded road. They halted and awaited the arrival of whatever vehicle was producing the clamor.

The vehicle soon rounded the curve of road, revealing itself to be a heterogeneous assemblage of wood and metal. The main portion of the carrier was a large wooden buckboard with two rows of seats forward of a flatbed. In the rear, a large boiler formed of odd-shaped scavenged metal plates threatened to burst its seams with every puff of smoke. Transmission of power to the wheels was accomplished by whirling leather belts running from boiler to wood-spoked iron-rimmed wheels.

Four men sat on the rig, two abreast. Dressed in homespun and leathers, they sported big holstered side-arms. The guns were formed of ceramic barrels and chambers, and carved grips. Small gasketed pump handles protruded from the rear of each gun. Pertinax knew the weapons operated on compressed air and fired only nonexplosive projectiles. Still, sometimes the darts could be poison-tipped. A rack of rifles of similar construction lay within easy reach. The driver, busy with his tiller-style steering mechanism and several levers, was plainly a simple laborer. The other three occupants seemed to be dignitaries of some sort. Or so at least Pertinax deduced, judging from various colorful ribbons pinned to their chests and sashes draped over their shoulders.

Surprised by the solid rank of mounted wardens, looming high over the car like a living wall across the dump road, the Overclockers reacted with varying degrees of confusion. But soon the driver managed to bring his steam cart to a halt, and the three officials had regained a measure of diplomatic aplomb. The passenger in the front seat climbed down, and approached Pertinax and his companions. Leery of the stranger, the Kodiak Kangemus unsheathed their long thick claws a few inches. The awesome display brought the man to a halt a few meters away. He spoke, looking up and shielding his eyes against the sun.

"Hail, wardens! My name is Brost, and these comrades of mine are Kemp and Sitgrave, my assistants. As the mayor of Chicago, I welcome you to our fair city."

Pertinax studied Brost from above, seeing a poorly shaven, sallow baseline *Homo sapiens* with a shifty air about his hunched shoulders. Some kind of harsh perfume failed to mask completely a fug of fear and anxiety crossing the distance between Brost and Pertinax's sharp nostrils.

Sylvanus, as eldest, spoke for the wardens. "We accept your welcome, Mayor Brost. But I must warn you that we are not here for any simple cordial visit. We have good reason to believe that certain factions among your people are planning to tamper with the tropospheric mind. We have come to investigate, and to remove any such threats we may discern."

The mayor smiled uneasily, while his companions fought not to exchange nervous sidelong glances among themselves.

"Tamper with those lofty, serene intelligences, who concern themselves not at all with our poor little lives? What reason could we have for such a heinous assault? No, the charge is ridiculous, even insulting. I can categorically refute it here and now. Your mission has been for naught. You might as well save yourself any further wearisome journeying by camping here for the night before heading home. We will bring you all sorts of fine provisions—"

"That cannot be. We must make our own investigations. Will you allow us access to your village?"

Mayor Brost huddled with his assistants, then faced the wardens again. "As I said, the *city* of Chicago welcomes you, and its doors are open."

Pertinax repressed a grin at the mayor's emphasis on "city," but he knew the other wardens had caught this token of outraged human dignity as well.

With much back-and-forward-and-back maneuvering, the driver finally succeeded in turning around the steam cart. Matching the gait of their hoppers to the slower passage of the cart, the wardens followed the delegation back to "Chicago."

Beginning with outlying cabins where half-naked children played in the summer dust of their yards along with mongrels and livestock, and continuing all the way to the "city" center, where a few larger buildings hosted such establishments as blacksmiths, saloons, public kitchens, and a lone bathhouse, the small collection of residences and businesses that was "Chicago"—scattered along the lake's margins according to no discernible scheme—gradually assembled itself around the newcomers. Mayor Brost, evidently proud of his domain, pointed out sights of interest as they traversed the "urban" streets, down the middles of which flowed raw sewage in ditches.

"You see how organized our manufactories are," said Brost, indicating some long, low, windowless sheds flanked by piles of waste byproducts: wood shavings, coal clinkers, metal shavings. "And here's the entrance to our mines." Brost pointed to a shack that sheltered a pitlike opening descending into the earth at a slant.

"Oh," said Cimabue, "you're smelting and refining raw metals these days?"

Mayor Brost exhibited a sour chagrin. "Not yet. There's really no need. We feel it's most in harmony with, uh, our beloved mother earth to recycle the buried remnants of our ancestors' civilization. There's plenty of good metal and plastic down deep where the Upflowered sequestered the rubble they left after their redesign of the globe. Plenty for everyone."

"And what exactly is your population these days, mayor?" inquired Tanselle.

"Nearly five thousand."

Tanselle shook her head reflectively, as if to say, thought Pertinax, *Would that it were even fewer.*

After some additional civic boosterism, the party, considerably enlarged by various gawking hangers-on, arrived at a large, grassy town square, where goats and sheep grazed freely. Ranked across the lawn, tethered securely, were several small lighter-than-air balloons with attached gondolas of moderate size. The shiny lacquered patchwork fabric of the balloons lent them a circus air belied by the solemn unease which the mayor and his cohorts eyed the balloons.

Immediately, Pertinax's ears pricked forward at this unexpected sight and the humans' nervous regard for the objects. "What are these for?" he asked.

Mayor Brost replied almost too swiftly. "Oh, these little toys have half a dozen uses. We send up lightweight volunteers to spy out nearby bison herds so that our hunting parties will save some time and trouble. We make surveys from the air for our roadbuilding. And of course, the children enjoy a ride now and then. The balloons won't carry much more weight than a child."

"I'd like to examine them."

"Certainly."

Pertinax clambered down off Flossy. Standing among the humans, the top of his head just cleared their belt buckles. He was soon joined by his fellow wardens, who moved through the crowd like a band of determined furry dwarves.

The balloons featured no burners to inflate their straining shapes. Pertinax inquired as to their source of gas.

Highlighting the mechanisms, Mayor Brost recited proudly. "Each balloon hosts a colony of methanogenic bacteria and a food supply. Increasing the flow of nutrients makes more gas. Closing the petcocks shuts them down."

Pertinax stepped back warily from his close-up inspection of the balloons. "They're highly explosive, then."

"I suppose. But we maintain adequate safety measures around them."

The wardens regrouped off to one side and consulted quietly among themselves.

"Any explosion of this magnitude in the tropospheric mind would do no more damage than a conventional rain squall," said Cimabue.

"Agreed," said Chellapilla. "But what if the explosion was meant to disperse some kind of contaminant carried as cargo?"

"Such as?" asked Tanselle.

"No suitably dangerous substance occurs to me at the moment," Sylvanus said, stroking his chin whiskers.

"Nonetheless," cautioned Pertinax, "I have a feeling that here lies the danger facing the tropospheric mind. Let us continue our investigations for the missing part of the puzzle."

Pertinax returned to address the Mayor. "Our mounts need to forage, while we continue our inspection of your town. We propose to leave them here on the green. They will not bother people or livestock, but you should advise your citizens not to molest them. The Kangemu are trained to deal harshly with threats to themselves or their masters."

"There will of course be no such problems," said the mayor.

Sylvanus advised splitting their forces into two teams for swifter coverage of the human settlement, while he himself, in deference to his age and tiredness, remained behind with their mounts to coordinate the searching. Naturally, Pertinax chose to team up with Chellapilla.

The subsequent hours found Pertinax and his lover roaming unhindered through every part of the human village. Most of the citizens appeared friendly, although some exhibited irritation or a muted hostility at the queries of the wardens. Pertinax and Chellapilla paused only a few minutes to bolt down some cold food around midafternoon before continuing their so-far fruitless search.

Eventually they found themselves down by some primitive docks, watching the small fishing fleet of "Chicago" tie up for the evening. The fishermen, shouldering their day's bounty in woven baskets, moved warily past the weary wardens.

"Well, I'm stumped," confessed Pertinax. "If they're hiding something, they've concealed it well."

Chellapilla said, "Maybe we're going about this wrong. Let's ask what could harm the virgula and sublimula, instead of just expecting to recognize the agent when we see it."

"Well, really only other virgula and sublimula, which of course the humans have no way of fashioning."

"Ah, but what of rogue lobes?"

The natural precipitation cycles brought infinite numbers of virgula and sublimula down from their habitats in the clouds to ground level. When separated from the tropospheric mind in this way, the components of the mind were programmed for apoptosis. But occasionally a colony of virgula and sublimula would fail to self-destruct, instead clumping together into a rogue lobe. Isolated from the parent mind, the lobes frequently went insane before eventually succumbing to environmental stresses. Sometimes, though, a lobe could live a surprisingly long time if it found the right conditions.

"Do you think local factors in the lake here might encourage lobe formations?"

"There's one way to find out," answered Chellapilla.

It took only another half hour of prowling the lake shore, scrambling over slippery rocks and across pebbled strands, to discover a small lobe.

Thick intelligent slime latticed with various organic elements—pond weeds, zebra mussels, a disintegrating bird carcass—lay draped across a boulder, a mucosal sac with the processing power of a nonautonomous twenty-second-century AI. The slime was liquescently displaying its mad internal thoughts just as a mail cloud did: fractured images of the natural world, blazes of equations, shards of old human culture Ante-Upflowering, elaborate mathematical constructions. A steady whisper of jagged sounds, a schizophrenic monologue, accompanied the display.

Pertinax stared horrified. "Uploading this fragment of chaos to the tropospheric mind would engender destabilizing waves of disinformation across the skies. The humans don't even need to explode their balloons. Simply letting the mind automatically read the slime would be enough."

"We can't allow this to happen."

"Let's hurry back to the others."

"You damned toothy rat-dogs aren't going anywhere."

A squad of humans had come stealthily upon Pertinax and Chellapilla while their attentions were engaged by the lobe. With rifles leveled at their heads, the wardens had no recourse but to raise their hands in surrender.

Two men came to bind the wardens. The one dealing with Chellapilla twisted her arms cruelly behind her, causing her to squeal. Maddened by the sound, Pertinax broke free and hurled himself at one of the gun bearers. But a riflestock connected with his skull, and he knew only blackness.

When Pertinax awoke, night had fallen. He found himself with limbs bound, lying in a cage improvised from thick branches rammed deep into the soil and lashed together. He struggled to rise, and thus attracted the attentions of his fellow captives.

Similarly bound, Chellapilla squirmed across the grass to her mate. "Oh, Perty, I'm so glad you're awake! We were afraid you had a concussion."

"No, I'm fine. And you?"

"Just sore. Once you were knocked out, they didn't really hurt me further."

Sylvanus's sad voice reached Pertinax as well. "Welcome back, my lad. We're in a fine mess now, and it's all my fault for underestimating the harmful intentions of these savages."

Firelight flared up some meters away, accompanied by the roar of a human crowd. "Where are we?"

"We're on the town green," said Chellapilla. "The humans are celebrating their victory over us. They slaughtered our Kangemu and are roasting them for a feast."

"Barbarians!"

Tanselle spoke. "Cimabue and I are here as well, Pertinax, but he did not escape so easily as you. They clubbed him viciously when he fought back. Now his breathing is erratic, and he won't respond."

"We have to do something!"

"But what?" inquired Sylvanus.

"The least we can do," said Chellapilla, "is inform the tropospheric mind of our troubles and the threat from rogue lobe infection. Maybe the mind will know what to do."

Pertinax considered this proposal. "That's a sound idea, Chell. But I suspect our pigeons have already served as appetizers." He paused as an idea struck him. "But I know a way to reach the mind. First I need to be free. You three will have to chew my ropes off."

Shielded by darkness, without any guards to note their activities and interfere (how helpless the humans must have deemed them!), his three fellows quickly chewed through Pertinax's bonds with their sturdy teeth and powerful jaws. His first action after massaging his limbs back into a semblance of strength was to take off his robe and stuff it with dirt and grass into a rough recumbent dummy that would satisfy a cursory headcount. Then, employing his own untaxed jaw muscles, he beavered his way out of the cage.

"Be careful, Perty!" whispered Chellapilla, but Pertinax did not pause to reply.

Naked, dashing low across the yard from shadow to shadow, Pertinax reached one of the tethered balloons without being detected. Nearby stood a giant ceramic pot with a poorly fitting lid. Shards of light and sound escaped from the pot, betokening the presence of a malignant rogue lobe within. Plainly, infection of the tropospheric mind was imminent. This realization hastened Pertinax's actions.

First he kicked up the feed on one balloon's colony of methanogens. That vehicle began to tug even more heartily at its tethers. Moving among the other balloons, Pertinax disabled them by snapping their nutrient feed lines. At the very least, this would delay the assault on the mind.

Pertinax leaped onboard the lone functional balloon and cast off. He rose swiftly to the height of several meters before he was spotted. Shouts filled the night. Something whizzed by Pertinax's head, and he ducked. A barbed projectile from one of the compressed-air guns. Pertinax doubted the weapons possessed enough force to harm him or the balloon at this altitude, but he remained hunkered down for a few more minutes nonetheless.

Would the humans take revenge on their remaining captives? Pertinax couldn't spare the energy for worry. He had a mission to complete.

Within the space of fifteen minutes, Pertinax floated among the lowest clouds, the nearest gauzy interface to the tropospheric mind. Their dampness subtly enwrapped him, until he was soaked and shivering. His head seemed to attract a thicker constellation of fog. . . .

A small auroral screen opened up in the sky not four meters from Pertinax. He could smell the scorched molecules associated with the display.

Don Corleone appeared on the screen: one or more of the resident AIs taking a form deemed familiar from Pertinax's recent past viewing records.

"You have done well to bring us this information, steward. We will now enforce our justice on the humans."

Pertinax's teeth chattered. "Puh-please try to spare my companions."

The representative of the tropospheric mind did not deign to reply, and the screen winked out in a frazzle of sparks.

The night sky grew darker, if such was possible. Ominous rumbles sounded from the west. Winds began to rise.

The mind was marshaling a storm. A lightning storm. And Pertinax was riding a bomb.

Pertinax frantically shut off the feeder line to the methanogens. The balloon began to descend, but all too slowly for Pertinax's peace of mind.

The first lightning strike impacted the ground far below, after seeming to sizzle right past Pertinax's nose. He knew the bolt must have been farther off than that, but anywhere closer than the next bioregion was *too* close.

Now shafts of fire began to rain down at supernatural frequency. Turbulence rocked the gondola. Thunder deafened him. Pertinax's throat felt raw, and he realized he had been shouting for help from the balloon or the mind or anyone else who might be around to hear.

Now the cascade of lighting was nigh incessant, one deadly strike after another on the Overclockers' village. Pertinax knew he could stay no longer with the deadly balloon. But the ground was still some hundred meters away.

Pertinax jumped.

Behind him the balloon exploded.

Pertinax spread out his arms, transforming the big loose flaps of skin anchored from armpits to ankles into wings, wings derived from one of his ancestral strains, the sciuridae.

After spiraling downward with some control, despite the gusts, Pertinax landed lightly, on an open patch of ground near a wooden sign that announced the "City Limits" of "Chicago."

He had arrived just in time for the twister.

Illuminated intermittently by the slackening lightning, the stygian funnel shape tracked onto land from across the lake and stepped into the human settlement, moving in an intelligent and programmatic fashion among the buildings.

Even at this distance, the wind threatened to pull Pertinax off his feet. He scrambled for a nearby tree and held on to its trunk for dear life.

At last, though, the destruction wrought by the tropospheric mind ended, and the twister evaporated in a coordinated manner from bottom to top.

Pertinax ran back toward the town green.

The many fires caused by the lightning had been effectively doused by the wet cyclone, but still, buildings smoldered. Not one stone seemed atop another, nor plank joined to plank. The few Overclocker survivors were too dazed or busy to interfere with Pertinax.

Seared streaks marked the town green, and huge divots had been wrenched up by the twister. Windblown litter made running difficult.

But a circle of lawn around the cage holding the wardens was immaculate, having been excluded from electrical blasts and then cradled in a deliberate eye of the winds.

"Is everyone all right?"

"Perty! You did it! Yes, we're all fine. Even Cimabue is finally coming around."

Within a short time all were freed. Pertinax clutched Chellapilla to him. Sylvanus surveyed the devastation, clucking his tongue ruefully.

"Such a tragedy. Well, I expect that once we relocate the remnant population, we can wean them off our help and back up to some kind of agrarian self-sufficiency in just a few generations."

Pertinax felt now an even greater urgency to engender a heir or two with Chellapilla. The demands on the stewards of this beloved planet required new blood to sustain their mission down the years.

"Chell, have you decided about our child?"

"Absolutely, Perty. I'm ready. I've even thought of a name."

"Oh?"

"Boy or girl, it will have to be Storm!"

As with "Observable Things," this piece derives its existence from the solicitation of an excellent fiction writer who just happened to be playing editor for one project. Wil McCarthy's Once Upon a Galaxy *had as its premise the restaging of fairy tales in SF terms. I immediately jumped on the saga of Puss in Boots—ahem, long before a certain green cinematic ogre started palling around with Puss—and decided to incorporate as much homage as possible to SF I had loved. Hence the presence of Larry Niven's variable swords, Frank Herbert's sandworms, and so forth.*

Chosen to be reprinted in two best-of-the-year anthologies, this story seems to show the esteem in which displays of "galactic core values" are still held.

AILOURA

The small aircraft swiftly bisected the cloudless chartreuse sky. Invisible encrypted transmissions raced ahead of it. Clearance returned immediately from the distant, turreted manse—Stoessl House, looming in the otherwise empty riven landscape like some precipice-perching raptor. The ever-unsleeping family marchwarden obligingly shut down the manse's defenses, allowing an approach and landing. Within minutes, Geisen Stoessl had docked his small deltoid zipflyte on one of the tenth-floor platforms of Stoessl House, cantilevered over the flood-sculpted, candy-colored arroyos of the Subliminal Desert.

Geisen unseamed the canopy and leaped easily out onto the broad sintered terrace, unpeopled at this tragic, necessary, hopeful moment. Still clad in his dusty expeditionary clothes, goggles slung around his neck, Geisen resembled a living marble version of some young roughneck godling. Slim, wiry, and alert, with his laughter-creased, soil-powdered face now set in solemn lines absurdly counterpointed by a mask of clean skin around his recently shielded green eyes, Geisen paused a moment to brush from his protective suit the heaviest evidence of his recent wildcat digging in the Lustrous Wastes. Satisfied that he had made some small improvement in his appearance upon this weighty occasion, he advanced toward the portal leading inside. But before he could actuate the door, it opened from within.

Framed in the door stood a lanky, robe-draped bestient: Vicuna, his mother's most valued servant. Set squarely in Vicuna's wedge-shaped hirsute face, the haughty maid's broad velveteen nose wrinkled imperiously in disgust at Geisen's appearance, but the moreauvian refrained from voicing her disapproval of that matter in favor of other upbraidings.

"You arrive barely in time, Gep Stoessl. Your father approaches the limits of artificial maintenance, and is due to be reborn any minute. Your mother and brothers already anxiously occupy the Natal Chambers."

Following the inhumanly articulated servant into Stoessl House, Geisen answered, "I'm aware of all that, Vicuna. But traveling halfway around Chalk can't be accomplished in an instant."

"It was your choice to absent yourself during this crucial time."

"Why crucial? This will be Vomacht's third reincarnation. Presumably this one will go as smoothly as the first two."

"So one would hope."

Geisen tried to puzzle out the subtext of Vicuna's ambiguous comment, but could emerge with no clue regarding the current state of the generally complicated affairs within Stoessl House. He had obviously been away too long—too busy enjoying his own lonely but satisfying prospecting trips on behalf of the family enterprise—to be able to grasp the daily political machinations of his relatives.

Vicuna conducted Geisen to the nearest squeezer, and they promptly dropped down fifteen stories, far below the bedrock in which Stoessl House was rooted. On this secure level, the monitoring marchwarden hunkered down in its cozy low-Kelvin isolation, meaningful matrices of B-E condensates. Here also were the family's Natal Chambers. At these doors blazoned with sacred icons Vicuna left Geisen with a humid snort signifying that her distasteful attendance on the latecomer was terminated.

Taking a fortifying breath, Geisen entered the rooms.

Roseate illumination symbolic of new creation softened all within: the complicated apparatus of rebirth as well as the sharp features of his mother, Woda, and the doughy countenances of his two brothers, Gitten and Grafton. Nearly invisible in the background, various bestient bodyguards hulked, inconspicuous yet vigilant.

Woda spoke first. "Well, how very generous of the prodigal to honor us with his unfortunately mandated presence."

Gitten snickered, and Grafton chimed in, pompously ironical: "Exquisitely gracious behavior, and so very typical of our little sibling, I'm sure."

Tethered to various life-support devices, Vomacht Stoessl—unconscious, naked, and recumbent on a padded pallet alongside his mindless new body—said nothing. Both he and his clone had their heads wrapped in organic warty sheets of modified Stroonian brain parasite, an organism long ago co-opted for mankind's ambitious and ceaselessly searching program of life extension. Linked via a thick living interparasitical tendril to its younger doppelganger, the withered form of the current Vomacht, having reached the limits of rejuvenation, contrasted strongly with the virginal, soulless vessel.

During Vomacht Stoessl's first lifetime, from 239 to 357 Post Scattering, he had sired no children. His second span of existence (357 to 495 P.S.) saw the birth of Gitten and Grafton, separated by some sixty years and both sired on Woda. Toward the end of his third, current, lifetime (495 to 675 P.S.), a mere thirty years ago, he had fathered Geisen upon a mystery woman whom Geisen had never known. Vanished and unwedded, his mother—or some other oversolicitous guardian—had denied Geisen her name or image. Still, Vomacht had generously attended to all the legalities granting Geisen full parity with his half brothers. Needless to say, little cordiality existed between the older members of the family and the young interloper.

Geisen made the proper obeisances at several altars before responding to the taunts of his stepmother and stepbrothers. "I did not dictate the terms governing Gep Stoessl's latest reincarnation. They came directly from him. If any of you objected, you should have made your grievances known to him face to face. I myself am honored that he chose me to initiate the transference of his mind and soul. I regret only that I was not able to attend him during his final moments of awareness in this old body."

Gitten, the middle brother, tittered and said, "The hand that cradles the rocks will now rock the cradle."

Geisen looked down at his dirty hands, hopelessly engrained with the soils and stone dusts of Chalk. He resisted an impulse to hide them in his pockets. "There is nothing shameful about my fondness for fieldwork. Lolling about in luxury does not suit me. And I did not hear any of you complaining when the Eventyr Lode which I discovered came online and began to swell the family coffers."

Woda intervened with her traditional maternal acerbity. "Enough bickering. Let us acknowledge that no possible arrangement of this day's events would have pleased everyone. The quicker we perform this vital ritual, the quicker we can all return to our duties and pleasures, and the sooner Vomacht's firm hand will regrasp the controls of our business. Geisen, I believe you know what to do."

"I studied the proper Books of Phowa en route."

Grafton said, "Always the grind. Whenever do you enjoy yourself, little brother?"

Geisen advanced confidently to the mechanisms that reared at the head of the pallets. "In the proper time and place, Grafton. But I realize that to you, such words imply every minute of your life." The young man turned his attention to the controls before him, forestalling further tart banter.

The tethered and trained Stroonian life forms had been previously starved to near hibernation, in preparation for their sacred duty. A clear cylinder of pink nutrient fluid laced with instructive protein sequences hung from an ornate tripod. The fluid would flow through twin intravenous lines, once the parasites were hooked up, enlivening their quiescent metabolisms and directing their proper functioning.

Murmuring the requisite holy phrases, Geisen plugged an IV line into each head-enshrouding creature. He tapped the proper dosage rate into the separate flow pumps. Then, solemnly capturing the eyes of the onlookers, he activated the pumps.

Almost immediately the parasites began to flex and labor, humping and contorting as they drove an infinity of fractally minuscule autoanesthetizing tendrils into both full and vacant brains in preparation for the transfer of the vital engrams that comprised a human soul.

But within minutes, it was plain to the observers that something was very wrong. The original Vomacht Stoessl began to writhe in evident pain, ripping away his life supports.

The all-observant marchwarden triggered alarms. Human and bestient technicians burst into the room. Grafton and Gitten and

Woda rushed to the pumps to stop the process. But they were too late. In an instant, both membrane-wrapped skulls collapsed to degenerate chunky slush that plopped to the floor from beneath the suddenly destructive cauls.

The room fell silent. Grafton tilted one of the pumps at an angle so that all the witnesses could see the glowing red numerals.

"He quadrupled the proper volume of nutrient, driving the Stroonians hyperactive. This is murder!"

"Secure him from any escape!" Woda commanded.

Instantly Geisen's arms were pinioned by two burly bestient guards. He opened his mouth to protest, but the sight of his headless father choked off all words.

Gep Vomacht Stoessl's large private study was decorated with ancient relics of his birth world, Lucerno: the empty, age-brittle coral armature of a deceased personal exoskeleton; a row of printed books bound in sloth hide; a corroded auroch-flaying knife large as a canoe paddle. In the wake of their owner's death, the talismans seemed drained of mana.

Geisen sighed, and slumped down hopelessly in the comfortable chair positioned on the far side of the antique desk that had originated on the Crafters' planet, Hulbrouck V. On the far side of the nacreous expanse sat his complacently smirking half brother, Grafton. Just days ago, Geisen knew, his father had hauled himself out of his sickbed for one last appearance at this favorite desk, where he had dictated the terms of his third reincarnation to the recording marchwarden. Geisen had played the affecting scene several times en route from the Lustrous Wastes, noting how, despite his enervated condition, his father had spoken with his wonted authority, specifically requesting that Geisen administer the paternal rebirthing procedure.

And now that unique individual—distant and enigmatic as he had been to Geisen throughout the latter's relatively short life—the man who had founded Stoessl House and its fortunes, the man to whom they all owed their luxurious independent lifestyles, was irretrievably gone from this plane of existence.

The human soul could exist only in organic substrates. Intelligent as they might be, condensate-dwelling entities such as the marchwarden exhibited a lesser existential complexity. Impossible to make any kind of static "backup" copy of the human essence, even in the proverbial bottled brain, since Stroonian transcription was fatal to the original. No, if destructive failure occurred during a rebirth, that individual was no more forever.

Grafton interpreted Geisen's sigh as indicative of a need to unburden himself of some secret. "Speak freely, little brother. Ease your soul of guilt. We are completely alone. Not even the marchwarden is listening."

Geisen sat up alertly. "How have you accomplished such a thing? The marchwarden is deemed to be incorruptible, and its duties include constant surveillance of the interior of our home."

Somewhat flustered, Grafton tried to dissemble. "Oh, no, you're quite mistaken. It was always possible to disable the marchwarden selectively. A standard menu option—"

Geisen leaped to his feet, causing Grafton to rear back. "I see it all now! This whole murder, and my seeming complicity, was planned from the start! My father's last testament—faked! The flow codes to the pumps—overridden! My role—stooge and dupe!"

Recovering himself, Grafton managed with soothing motions and noises to induce a fuming Geisen to be seated again. The older man came around to perch on a corner of the desk. He leaned over closer to Geisen and, in a smooth voice, made his own shockingly unrepentant confession.

"Very astute. Too bad for you that you did not see the trap early enough to avoid it. Yes, Vomacht's permanent death and your hand in it were all neatly arranged—by mother, Gitten, and me. It had to be. You see, Vomacht had become irrationally surly and obnoxious toward us, his true and loving first family. He threatened to remove all our stipends and entitlements and authority, once he occupied his strong new body. But those demented codicils were edited from the version of his speech that you saw, as was his insane proclamation naming you sole factotum of the family business. All of Stoessl Strangelet Mining and its affiliates was to be made your fiefdom. Imagine! A young desert rat at the helm of our venerable corporation!"

Geisen strove to digest all this sudden information. Practical considerations warred with his emotions. Finally he could only ask, "What of Vomacht's desire for me to initiate his soul transfer?"

"Ah, that was authentic. And it served as the perfect bait to draw you back, as well as the peg on which we could hang a murder plot and charge."

Geisen drew himself up proudly. "You realize that these accusations of deliberate homicide against me will not stand up a minute in court. With what you've told me, I'll certainly be able to dig up plenty of evidence to the contrary."

Smiling like a carrion lizard from the Cerise Ergstrand, Grafton countered, "Oh, will you, now? From your jail cell, without any outside help? Accused murderers cannot profit from the results of their actions. You will have no access to family funds other than your small personal accounts while incarcerated, nor any real partisans, due to your stubbornly asocial existence of many years. The might of the family, including testimony from the grieving widow, will be ranked against you. How do you rate your chances for exculpation under those circumstances?"

Reduced to grim silence, Geisen bunched his muscles prior to launching himself in a futile attack on his brother. But Grafton quickly held up a warning hand.

"There is an agreeable alternative. We really do not care to bring this matter to court. There is, after all, still a chance of one percent or less that you might win the case. And legal matters are so tedious and time-consuming, interfering with more pleasurable pursuits. In fact, notice of Gep Stoessl's death has not yet been released to either the news media or to Chalk's authorities. And if we secure your cooperation, the aftermath of this tragic 'accident' will take a very different form than criminal charges. Upon getting your binding assent to a certain trivial document, you will be free to pursue your own life unencumbered by any obligations to Stoessl House or its residents."

Grafton handed his brother a hard copy of several pages. Geisen perused it swiftly and intently, then looked up at Grafton with high astonishment.

"This document strips me of all my share of the family fortunes, and binds me from any future role in the estate. Basically, I am utterly disenfranchised and disinherited, cast out penniless."

"A fair enough summation. Oh, we might give you a small grub-stake when you leave. Say—your zipflyte, a few hundred esscues, and a bestient servant or two. Just enough to pursue the kind of itinerant lifestyle you so evidently prefer."

Geisen pondered but a moment. "All attempts to brand me a patricide will be dropped?"

Grafton shrugged. "What would be the point of whipping a helpless, poverty-stricken nonentity?"

Geisen stood up. "Reactivate the marchwarden. I am ready to comply with your terms."

Gep Bloedwyn Vermeule, of Vermeule House, today wore her long blond braids arranged in a recomplicated nest, piled high atop her charming young head and sown with delicate fairylights that blinked in time with various of her body rhythms. Entering the formal reception hall of Stoessl House, she marched confidently down the tiles between ranks of silent bestient guards, the long train dependent from her form-fitting scarlet sandworm-fabric gown held an inch above the floor by tiny enwoven agravitic units. She came to a stop some meters away from the man who awaited her with a nervously expectant smile on his rugged face.

Geisen's voice quaked at first, despite his best resolve. "Bloedwyn, my sweetling, you look more alluring than an oasis to a parched man."

The pinlights in the girl's hair raced in chaotic patterns for a moment, then settled down to stable configurations that somehow radiated a frostiness belied by her neutral facial expression. Her voice, chorded suggestively low and husky by fashionable implants, quavered not at all.

"Gep Stoessl, I hardly know how to approach you. So much has changed since we last trysted."

Throwing decorum to the wind, Geisen closed the gap between them and swept his betrothed up in his arms. The sensation Geisen enjoyed was rather like that derived from hugging a wooden effigy. Nonetheless, he persisted in his attempts to restore their old relations.

"Only superficial matters have changed, my dear! True, as you have no doubt heard by now, I am no longer a scion of Stoessl House. But my heart, mind, and soul remain devoted to you! Can I not assume the same constancy applies to your inner being?"

Bloedwyn slipped out of Geisen's embrace. "How could you assume anything, since I myself do not know how I feel? All these developments have been so sudden and mysterious! Your father's cruelly permanent death, your own capricious and senseless abandonment of your share of his estate . . . How can I make sense of any of it? What of all our wonderful dreams?"

Geisen gripped Bloedwyn's supple hide-mailed upper arms with perhaps too much fervor, judging from her wince. He released her, then spoke. "All our bright plans for the future will come to pass! Just give me some time to regain my footing in the world. One day I will be at liberty to explain everything to you. But until then, I ask your trust and faith. Surely you must share my confidence in my character, in my undiminished capabilities?"

Bloedwyn averted her tranquil blue-eyed gaze from Geisen's imploring green eyes, and he slumped in despair, knowing himself lost. She stepped back a few paces and, with voice steeled, made a formal declaration she had evidently rehearsed prior to this moment.

"The Vermuele marchwarden has already communicated the abrogation of our pending matrimonial agreement to your house's governor. I think such an impartial yet decisive move is all for the best, Geisen. We are both young, with many lives before us. It would be senseless to found such a potentially interminable relationship on such shaky footing. Let us both go ahead—separately—into the days to come, with our extinct love a fond memory."

Again, as at the moment of his father's death, Geisen found himself rendered speechless at a crucial juncture, unable to plead his case any further. He watched in stunned disbelief as Bloedwyn turned gracefully around and walked out of his life, her fluttering scaly train visible some seconds after the rest of her had vanished.

The cluttered, steamy, noisy kitchens of Stoessl House exhibited an orderly chaos proportionate to the magnitude of the preparations under way. The planned rebirth dinner for the paterfamilias had been hastily converted to a memorial banquet, once the proper, little-used protocols had been found in a metaphorically dusty lobe of the marchwarden's memory. Now scores of miscegenous bestients under the supervision of the lone human chef, Stine Pursiful, scraped, sliced, chopped, diced, cored, deveined, scrubbed, layered, basted, glazed, microwaved, and pressure-treated various foodstuffs, assembling the imported luxury ingredients into the elaborate fare that would furnish the solemn buffet for family and friends and business connections of the deceased.

Geisen entered the aromatic atmosphere of the kitchens with a scowl on his face and a bitterness in his throat and heart. Pursiful spotted the young man and, with a fair share of courtesy and deference, considering the circumstances, stepped forward to inquire of his needs. But Geisen rudely brushed the slim punctilious chef aside, and stalked toward the shelves that held various MREs. With blunt motions, he began to shovel the nutri-packets into a dusty shoulder bag that had plainly seen many an expedition into Chalk's treasure-filled deserts.

A small timid bestient belonging to one of the muskrat-hyrax clades hopped over to the shelves where Geisen fiercely rummaged. Near-sighted, the be-aproned moreauvian strained on tiptoe to identify something on a higher shelf.

With one heavy boot, Geisen kicked the servant out of his way, sending the creature squeaking and sliding across the slops-strewn floor. But before the man could return to his rough provisioning, he was stopped by a voice as familiar as his skin.

"I raised you to show more respect to all the Implicate's creatures than you just exhibited, Gep Stoessl. Or if I did not, then I deserve immediately to visit the Unborn's Lowest Abattoir for my criminal negligence."

Geisen turned, the bile in his craw and soul melting to a habitual affection tinged with many memories of juvenile guilt.

Brindled arms folded across her queerly configured chest, Ailoura the bestient stood a head shorter than Geisen, compact and well muscled. Her heritage mingling a thousand feline and quasi-feline strains from a dozen planets, she resembled no single cat species morphed to human status, but rather all cats everywhere, blended and thus ennobled. Rounded ears perched high atop her densely pelted skull. Vertically slitted eyes and patch of wet leathery nose contrasted with a more-human-seeming mouth and chin. Now anger and disappointment molded her face into a mask almost frightening, her fierce expression magnified by a glint of sharp tooth peeking from beneath a curled lip.

Geisen noted instantly, with a small shock, the newest touches of gray in Ailoura's tortoise-shell fur. These tokens of aging softened his heart even further. He made the second most serious conciliatory bow from the Dakini Rituals toward his old nurse. Straightening, Geisen watched with relief as the anger flowed out of her face and stance, to be replaced by concern and solicitude.

"Now," Ailoura demanded, in the same tone with which she had often demanded that little Geisen brush his teeth or do his schoolwork, "what is all this nonsense I hear about your voluntary disinheritance and departure?"

Geisen motioned Ailoura into a secluded corner of the kitchens and revealed everything to her. His account prompted low growls from the bestient that escaped despite her angrily compressed lips. Geisen finished resignedly by saying, "And so, helpless to contest this injustice, I leave now to seek my fortune elsewhere, perhaps even on another world."

Ailoura pondered a moment. "You say that your brother offered you a servant from our house?"

"Yes. But I don't intend to take him up on that promise. Having another mouth to feed would just hinder me."

Placing one mitteny yet deft hand on his chest, Ailoura said, "Take me, Gep Stoessl."

Geisen experienced a moment of confusion. "But Ailoura—your job of raising me is long past. I am very grateful for the loving care you gave unstintingly to a motherless lad, the guidance and direction you imparted, the indulgent playtimes we enjoyed. Your teachings left me with a wise set of principles, an admirable will and optimism, and a firm moral center—despite the evidence of my thoughtless transgression a moment ago. But your guardian duties lie in the past. And besides, why would you want to leave the comforts and security of Stoessl House?"

"Look at me closely, Gep Stoessl. I wear now the tabard of the scullery crew. My luck in finding you here is due only to this very demotion. And from here the slide to utter inutility is swift and short—despite my remaining vigor and craft. Will you leave me here to face my sorry fate? Or will you allow me to cast my fate with that of the boy I raised from kittenhood?"

Geisen thought a moment. "Some companionship would indeed be welcome. And I don't suppose I could find a more intimate ally."

Ailoura grinned. "Or a slyer one."

"Very well. You may accompany me. But on one condition."

"Yes, Gep Stoessl?"

"Cease calling me 'Gep.' Such formalities were once unknown between us."

Ailoura smiled. "Agreed, little Gei-gei."

The man winced. "No need to retrogress quite that far. Now, let us return to raiding my family's larder."

"Be sure to take some of that fine fish, if you please, Geisen."

No one knew the origin of the tame strangelets that seeded Chalk's strata. But everyone knew of the immense wealth these cloistered anomalies conferred.

Normal matter was composed of quarks in only two flavors: up and down. But strange-flavor quarks also existed, and the exotic substances formed by these strange quarks in combination with the more domestic flavors were, unconfined, as deadly as the more familiar antimatter. Bringing normal matter into contact with a naked strangelet resulted in the conversion of the feedstock into energy. Owning a strangelet was akin to owning a pet black hole, and just as useful for various purposes, such as powering star cruisers.

Humanity could create strangelets, but only at immense cost per unit. And naked strangelets had to be confined in electromagnetic or gravitic bottles during active use. They could also be quarantined for semipermanent storage in stasis fields. Such was the case with the buried strangelets of Chalk.

Small spherical mirrored nodules—"marbles," in the jargon of Chalk's prospectors—could be found in various recent sedimentary layers of the planet's crust, distributed according to no rational plan. Discovery of the marbles had inaugurated the reign of the various houses on Chalk.

An early scientific expedition from Preceptimax University to the Shulamith Wadi stumbled upon the strangelets initially. Preceptor Fairservis, the curious discoverer of the first marble, had realized he was dealing with a stasis-bound object and had unluckily managed to open it. The quantum genie inside had promptly eaten the hapless fellow who freed it, along with nine tenths of the expedition, before beginning a sure but slow descent toward the core of Chalk. Luckily an emergency response team swiftly dispatched by the planetary authorities had managed to activate a new entrapping marble big as a small city, its lower hemisphere underground, thus confining the rogue.

After this incident, the formerly disdained deserts of Chalk had experienced a land rush previously unparalleled in the galaxy. Soon the entire planet was divided into domains—many consisting of noncontiguous properties—each owned by one house or another. Prospecting began in earnest then. But the practice remained more an art than a science, as the marbles remained stealthy to conventional detectors. Intuition, geological knowledge of strata, and sheer luck proved the determining factors in the individual fortunes of the houses.

How the strangelets—plainly artifactual—came to be buried beneath Chalk's soils and hardpan remained a mystery. No evidence of native intelligent inhabitants existed on the planet prior to the arrival of humanity. Had a cloud of strangelets been swept up out of space as Chalk made her eternal orbits? Perhaps. Or had alien visitors planted the strangelets for obscure reasons of their own? An equally plausible theory.

Whatever the obscure history of the strangelets, their current utility was beyond argument.

They made many people rich.

And some people murderous.

In the shadow of the Tasso Escarpments, adjacent to the Glabrous Drifts, Carrabas House sat desolate and melancholy, tenanted only by glass-tailed lizards and stilt-crabs, its poverty-overtaken heirs dispersed anonymously across the galaxy after a series of unwise investments, followed by the unpredictable yet inevitable exhaustion of their marble-bearing properties—a day against which Vomacht Stoessl had more providently hedged his own family's fortunes.

Geisen's zipflyte crunched to a landing on one of the manse's grit-blown terraces, beside a gaping portico. The craft's doors swung open and pilot and passenger emerged. Ailoura now wore a set of utilitarian roughneck's clothing, tailored for her bestient physique and matching the outfit worn by her former charge, right down to their boots. Strapped to her waist was an antique yet lovingly maintained variable sword, its terminal bead currently dull and inactive.

"No one will trouble us here," Geisen said with confidence. "And we'll have a roof of sorts over our head while we plot our next steps. As I recall from a visit some years ago, the west wing was the least damaged."

As Geisen began to haul supplies—a heater-cum-stove, sleeping bags and pads, water condensers—from their craft, Ailoura inhaled deeply the dry tangy air, her nose wrinkling expressively, then exhaled with zest. "Ah, freedom after so many years! It tastes brave, young Geisen!" Her claws slipped from their sheaths as she flexed her pads. She unclipped her sword and flicked it on, the seemingly untethered bead floating outward from the pommel a meter or so.

"You finish the monkey work. I'll clear the rats from our quarters," promised Ailoura, then bounded off before Geisen could stop her. Watching her unfettered tail disappear down a hall and around a corner, Geisen smiled, recalling childhood games of strength and skill where she had allowed him what he now realized were easy triumphs.

After no small time, Ailoura returned, licking her greasy lips.

"All ready for our habitation, Geisen-kitten."

"Very good. If the bold warrior will deign to lend a paw . . . ?"

Soon the pair had established housekeeping in a spacious, weatherproof ground-floor room (with several handy exits), where a single leering window frame was easily covered by a sheet of translucent plastic. After distributing their goods and sweeping the floor clean of loess drifts, Geisen and Ailoura took a meal as their reward, the first of many such rude campfire repasts to come.

As they relaxed afterward, Geisen making notes with his stylus in a small pocket diary and Ailoura dragging her left paw continually over one ear, a querulous voice sounded from thin air.

"Who disturbs my weary peace?"

Instantly on their feet, standing back to back, the newcomers looked warily about. Ailoura snarled until Geisen hushed her. Seeing no one, Geisen at last inquired, "Who speaks?"

"I am the Carrabas marchwarden."

The man and bestient relaxed a trifle. "Impossible," said Geisen. "How do you derive your energy after all these years of abandonment and desuetude?"

The marchwarden chuckled with a trace of pride. "Long ago, without any human consent or prompting, while Carrabas House still flourished, I sank a thermal tap downward hundreds of kilometers. The backup energy thus supplied is not much, compared with my old capacities, but has proved enough for sheer survival, albeit with much dormancy."

Ailoura hung her quiet sword back on her belt. "How have you kept sane since then, marchwarden?"

"Who says I have?"

Coming to terms with the semi-deranged Carrabas marchwarden required delicate negotiations. The protective majordomo simultaneously resented the trespassers—who did not share the honored Carrabas family lineage—yet on some different level welcomed their company and the satisfying chance to perform some of its programmed functions for them. Alternating ogre-ish threats with embarrassingly humble supplications, the marchwarden needed to hear just the right mix of defiance and thanks from the squatters to fully come over as their ally. Luckily, Ailoura, employing diplomatic wiles honed by decades of bestient subservience, perfectly supplemented Geisen's rather gruff and patronizing attitude. Eventually, the ghost of Carrabas House accepted them.

"I am afraid I can contribute little enough to your comfort, Gep Carrabas." During the negotiations, the marchwarden had somehow self-deludingly concluded that Geisen was indeed part of the lost lineage. "Some water, certainly, from my active conduits. But no other necessities such as heat or food, or any luxuries either. Alas, the days of my glory are long gone!"

"Are you still in touch with your peers?" asked Ailoura.

"Why, yes. The other Houses have not forgotten me. Many are sympathetic, though a few are haughty and indifferent."

Geisen shook his head in bemusement. "First I learn that the protective omniscience of the marchwardens may be circumvented. Next, that they keep up a private traffic and society. I begin to wonder who is the master and who is the servant in our global system?"

"Leave these conundrums to the preceptors, Geisen. This unexpected mode of contact might come in handy for us some day."

The marchwarden's voice sounded enervated. "Will you require any more of me? I have overtaxed my energies, and need to shut down for a time."

"Please restore yourself fully."

Left alone, Geisen and Ailoura simultaneously realized how late the hour was and how tired they were. They bedded down in warm body quilts, and Geisen swiftly drifted off to sleep to the old tune of Ailoura's drowsy purring.

In the chilly viridian morning, over fish and kava, cat and man held a war council.

Geisen led with a bold assertion that nonetheless concealed a note of despair and resignation.

"Given your evident hunting prowess, Ailoura, and my knowledge of the land, I estimate that we can take half a dozen sandworms from those unclaimed public territories proven empty of stranglets, during the course of as many months. We'll peddle the skins for enough to get us both off-planet. I understand that lush homesteads are going begging on Nibbriglung. All that the extensive water meadows there require is a thorough desnailing before they're producing golden rice by the bushel—"

Ailoura's green eyes, so like Geisen's own, flashed with cool fire. "Insipidity! Toothlessness!" she hissed. "Turn farmer? Grub among the waterweeds like some *platypus*? Run away from those who killed your sire and cheated you of your inheritance? I didn't raise such an unimaginative, unambitious coward, did I?"

Geisen sipped his drink to avoid making a hasty affronted rejoinder, then calmly said, "What do you recommend then? I gave my legally binding promise not to contest any of the unfair terms laid down by my family, in return for freedom from prosecution. What choices does such a renunciation leave me? Shall you and I go live in the shabby slums that slump at the feet of the Houses? Or turn thief and raider and prey upon lonely mining encampments? Or shall we become freelance prospectors? I'd be good at the latter job, true, but bargaining with the houses concerning hard-won information about their own properties is humiliating, and promises only slim returns. They hold all the high cards, and the supplicant offers only a mere savings of time."

"You're onto a true scent with this last idea. But not quite the paltry scheme you envision. What I propose is that we swindle those who swindled you. We won't gain back your whole patrimony, but you'll surely acquire greater sustaining riches than you would by flensing worms or flailing rice."

"Speak on."

"The first step involves a theft. But after that, only chicanery. To begin, we'll need a small lot of strangelets, enough to salt a claim everyone thought exhausted."

Geisen considered, buffing his raspy chin with his knuckles. "The morality is dubious. Still—I found a smallish deposit of marbles on Stoessl property during my aborted trip, and never managed to report it. They were in a floodplain hard by the Nakhoda Range, newly exposed and ripe for the plucking without any large-scale mining activity that would attract satellite surveillance."

"Perfect! We'll use their own goods to con the ratlings! But once we have this grubstake, we'll need a proxy to deal with the houses. Your own face and reputation must remain concealed until all deals are sealed airtight. Do you have knowledge of any such suitable foil?"

Geisen began to laugh. "Do I? Only the perfect rogue for the job!"

Ailoura came cleanly to her feet, although she could not repress a small grunt at an arthritic twinge provoked by a night on the hard floor. "Let us collect the strangelets first, and then enlist his help.

With luck, we'll be sleeping on feathers and dining off golden plates in a few short weeks."

The sad and spectral voice of the abandoned marchwarden sounded. "Good morning, Gep Carrabas. I regret keenly my own serious incapacities as a host. But I have managed to heat up several liters of water for a bath, if such a service appeals."

The eccentric caravan of Marco Bozzarias and his mistress, Pigafetta, had emerged from its minting pools as a top-of-the-line Baba Yar model of the year 650 P.S. Capacious and agile, larded with amenities, the moderately intelligent stilt-walking cabin had been designed to protect its inhabitants from climactic extremes in unswaying comfort while carrying them sure-footedly over the roughest terrain. But plainly, for one reason or another (most likely poverty), Bozzarias had neglected the caravan's maintenance over the twenty-five years of its working life.

Raised now for privacy above the sands where Geisen's zipflyte rested, the vehicle-cum-residence canted several degrees, imparting a funhouse quality to its interior. Swellings at its many knee joints indicated a lack of proper nutrients. Additionally, the cabin itself had been miscegenously patched with so many different materials—plastic, sandworm hide, canvas, chitin—that it more closely resembled a heap of debris than a deliberately designed domicile.

The caravan's owner, contrastingly, boasted an immaculate and stylish appearance. To judge by his handsome, mustachioed looks, the middle-aged Bozzarias was more stage-door idler than cactus hugger, displaying his trim figure proudly beneath crimson ripstop trews and utility vest over bare hirsute chest. Despite this urban promenader's facade, Bozzarias held a respectable record as a freelance prospector, having pinpointed for their owners several strangelet lodes of note, including the fabled Gosnold Pocket. For these services he had been recompensed by the tight-fisted landowners only a nearly invisible percentage of the eventual wealth claimed from the finds. Despite his current friendly grin, it would be impossible for Bozzarias not to harbor decades' worth of spite and jealousy.

Pigafetta, Bozzarias's bestient paramour, was a voluptuous

pink-skinned geisha clad in blue and green silks. Carrying perhaps a tad too much weight—hardly surprising, given her particular gattaca —Pigafetta radiated a slack and greasy carnality utterly at odds with Ailoura's crisp and dry efficiency. When the visitors had entered the cabin, before either of the humans could intervene, Geisen and Bozzarias had been treated to an instant but decisive bloodless catfight that had settled the pecking order between the moreauvians.

Now, while Pigafetta sulked winsomely in a canted corner amid her cushions, the furry female victor consulted with the two men around a small table across which lay spilled the stolen strangelets, corralled from rolling by a line of empty liquor bottles.

Bozzarias poked at one of the deceptive marbles with seeming disinterest, while his dark eyes glittered with avarice. "Let me recapitulate. We represent to various buyers that these quantum baubles are merely the camel's nose showing beneath the tent of unconsidered wealth. A newly discovered lode on the Carrabas properties, of which you, Gep Carrabas"—Bozzarias leered at Geisen—"are the rightful heir. We rook the fools for all we can get, then hie ourselves elsewhere, beyond their injured squawks and retributions. Am I correct in all particulars?"

Ailoura spoke first. "Yes, substantially."

"And what would my share of the take be? To depart forever my cherished Chalk would require a huge stake—"

"Don't try to make your life here sound glamorous or even tolerable, Marco," Geisen said. "Everyone knows you're in debt up to your nose, and haven't had a strike in over a year. It's about time for you to change venues anyway. The days of the freelancer on Chalk are nearly over."

Bozzarias sighed dramatically, picking up a reflective marble and admiring himself in it. "I suppose you speak the truth—as it is commonly perceived. But a man of my talents can carve himself a niche anywhere. And Pigafetta has been begging me of late to launch her on a virtual career—"

"In other words," Ailoura interrupted, "you intend to pimp her as a porn star. Well, you'll need to relocate to a mediapoietic world then for sure. May we assume you'll become part of our scheme?"

Bozzarias set the marble down and said, "My pay?"

"Two strangelets from this very stock."

With the speed of a glass-tailed lizard Bozzarias scooped up and pocketed two spheres before the generous offer could be rescinded. "Done! Now, if you two will excuse me, I'll need to rehearse my role before we begin this deception."

Ailoura smiled, a disconcerting sight to those unfamiliar with her tender side. "Not quite so fast, Gep Bozzarias. If you'll just submit a moment—"

Before Bozzarias could protest, Ailoura had sprayed him about the head and shoulders with the contents of a pressurized can conjured from her pack.

"What! Pixy dust! This is a gross insult!"

Geisen adjusted the controls of his pocket diary. On the small screen appeared a jumbled, jittering image of the caravan's interior. As the self-assembling pixy dust cohered around Bozzarias's eyes and ears, the image stabilized to reflect the prospector's visual point-of-view. Echoes of their speech emerged from the diary's speaker.

"As you well know," Ailoura advised, "the pixy dust is ineradicable and self-repairing. Only the ciphers we hold can deactivate it. Until then, all you see and hear will be shared with us. We intend to monitor you around the clock. And the diary's input is being shared with the Carrabas marchwarden, who has been told to watch for any traitorous actions on your part. That entity, by the way, is a little deranged, and might leap to conclusions about any actions that even verge on treachery. Oh, you'll also find that your left ear hosts a channel for our remote, ah, verbal advice. It would behoove you to follow our directions, since the dust is quite capable of liquefying your eyeballs upon command."

Seemingly inclined to protest further, Bozzarias suddenly thought better of dissenting. With a dispirited wave and nod, he signaled his acquiescence in their plans, becoming quietly businesslike.

"And to what houses shall I offer this putative wealth?"

Geisen smiled. "To every house at first—except Stoessl."

"I see. Quite clever."

After Bozzarias had caused his caravan to kneel to the earth, he bade his new partners a desultory goodbye. But at the last minute, as Ailoura was stepping into the zipflyte, Bozzarias snagged Geisen by the sleeve and whispered in his ear.

"I'd trade that rude servant in for a mindless pleasure model, my friend, were I you. She's much too tricky for comfort."

"But Marco—that's exactly why I cherish her."

Three weeks after first employing the wily Bozzarias in their scam, Geisen and Ailoura sat in their primitive quarters at Carrabas House, huddled nervously around Geisen's diary, awaiting transmission of the meeting they had long anticipated. The diary's screen revealed the familiar landscape around Stoessl House as seen from the windows of the speeding zipflyte carrying their agent to his appointment with Woda, Gitten, and Grafton.

During the past weeks, Ailoura's plot had matured, succeeding beyond their highest expectations.

Representing himself as the agent for a mysteriously returned heir of the long-abandoned Carrabas estate—a fellow who preferred anonymity for the moment—Bozzarias had visited all the biggest and most influential Houses—excluding the Stoessls—with his sample strangelets. A major new find had been described, with its coordinates freely given and inspections invited. The visiting teams of geologists, deceived by Geisen's expert saltings, reported what appeared to be a rich new lode. No single house dared attempt a midnight raid on the unprotected new strike, given the vigilance of all the others.

The cooperation and willing play-acting of the Carrabas marchwarden had been essential. First, once its existence was revealed, the discarded entity's very survival became a seven-day wonder, compelling a willing suspension of disbelief in all the lies that followed. Confirming the mystery man as a true Carrabas, the marchwarden also added its jiggered testimony to verify the discovery.

Bozzarias had informed the greedily gaping families that the returned Carrabas scion had no desire to play an active role in mining and selling his strangelets. The whole estate—with many more potential strangelet nodes—would be sold to the highest bidder.

Offers began to pour in, steadily escalating. These included feverish bids from the Stoessls, which were rejected without comment. Finally, after such high-handed treatment, the offended clan demanded to know why they were being excluded from the auction.

Bozzarias responded that he would convey that information only in a private meeting.

To this climactic interrogation the wily rogue now flew.

Geisen turned away from the monotonous video on his diary and asked Ailoura a question he had long contemplated but always forborne to voice.

"Ailoura, what can you tell me of my mother?"

The cat-woman assumed a reflective expression that cloaked more emotions than it revealed. Her whiskers twitched. "Why do you ask such an irrelevant question at this crucial juncture, Gei-gei?"

"I don't know. I've often pondered the matter. Maybe I'm fearful that if our plan explodes in our faces, this might be my final opportunity to learn anything."

Ailoura paused a long while before answering. "I was intimately familiar with the one who bore you. I think her intentions were honorable. I know she loved you dearly. She always wanted to make herself known to you, but circumstances beyond her control did not permit such an honest relationship."

Geisen contemplated this information. Something told him he would get no more from the close-mouthed bestient.

To disrupt the solemn mood, Ailoura reached over to ruffle Geisen's hair. "Enough of the useless past. Didn't anyone ever tell you that curiosity killed the cat? Now, pay attention! Our Judas goat has landed—"

Ursine yet doughy, unctuous yet fleering, Grafton clapped Bozzarias's shoulder heartily and ushered the foppish man to a seat in Vomacht's study. Behind the dead padrone's desk sat his widow, Woda, all motile maquillage and mimicked mourning. Her teeth sported a fashionable gilt. Gitten lounged on the arm of a sofa, plainly bored and resentful, toying with a hand-held hologame like some sullen adolescent.

After offering drinks—Bozzarias requested and received the finest vintage of sparkling wine available on Chalk—Grafton drove straight to the heart of the matter.

"Gep Bozzarias, I demand to know why Stoessl House has been denied a chance to bid on the Carrabas estate."

Bozzarias drained his glass and dabbed at his lips with his jabot before replying. "The reason is simple, Gep Stoessl, yet of such delicacy that you would not have cared to have me state it before your peers. Thus this private encounter."

"Go on."

"My employer, Timor Carrabas, you must learn, is a man of punctilio and politesse. Having abandoned Chalk many generations ago, Carrabas House still honors and maintains the old ways prevalent during that golden age. They have not fallen into the lax and immoral fashions of the present, and absolutely condemn such behavior."

Grafton stiffened. "To what do you refer? Stoessl House is guilty of no such infringements on custom."

"That is not how my employer perceives affairs. After all, what is the very first thing he hears upon returning to his ancestral homeworld? Disturbing rumors of patricide, fraternal infighting, and excommunication, all of which emanate from Stoessl House and Stoessl House alone. Leery of stepping beneath the shadow of such a cloud, he could not ethically undertake any dealings with your clan."

Fuming, Grafton started to rebut these charges, but Woda intervened. "Gep Bozzarias, all mandated investigations into the death of my beloved Vomacht resulted in one uncontested conclusion: pump failure produced a kind of alien hyperglycemia that drove the Stroonians insane. No human culpability or intent to harm was ever established."

Bozzarias held his glass up for a refill and obtained one. "Why, then, were all the bestient witnesses to the incident terminally disposed of? What motivated the abdication of your youngest scion? Giger, I believe he was named?"

Trying to be helpful, Gitten jumped into the conversation. "Oh, we use up bestients at a frightful rate! If they're not dying from floggings, they're collapsing from overuse in the mines and brothels. Such a flawed product line, these moreauvians. Why, if they were robots, they'd never pass consumer-lab testing. As for Geisen—that's the boy's name—well, he simply got fed up with our civilized lifestyle. He always did prefer the barbaric outback existence. No doubt he's enjoying himself right now, wallowing in some muddy oasis with a sandworm concubine."

Grafton cut off his brother's tittering with a savage glance. "Gep

Bozzarias, I'm certain that if your employer were to meet us, he'd find we are worthy of making an offer on his properties. In fact, he could avoid all the fuss and bother of a full-fledged auction, since I'm prepared right now to trump the highest bid he has yet received. Will you convey to him my invitation to enjoy the hospitality of Stoessl House?"

Bozzarias closed his eyes ruminatively, as if hearkening to some inner voice of conscience, then answered, "Yes, I can do that much. And with some small encouragement, I would exert all my powers of persuasiveness—"

Woda spoke. "Why, where did this small but heavy bag of Tancredi moonstones come from? It certainly doesn't belong to us. Gep Bozzarias—would you do me the immense favor of tracking down the rightful owner of these misplaced gems?"

Bozzarias stood and bowed, then accepted the bribe. "My pleasure, madame. I can practically guarantee that Stoessl House will soon receive its just reward."

"Sandworm concubine!" Geisen appeared ready to hurl his eavesdropping device to the hard floor, but restrained himself. "How I'd like to smash their lying mouths in!"

Ailoura grinned. "You must show more restraint than that, Geisen, especially when you come face to face with the scoundrels. Take consolation from the fact that mere physical retribution would hurt them far less than the loss of money and face we will inflict."

"Still, there's a certain satisfaction in feeling the impact of fist on flesh."

"My kind calls it 'the joy when teeth meet bone,' so I fully comprehend. Just not this time. Understood?"

Geisen impulsively hugged the old cat. "Still teaching me, Ailoura?"

"Until I die, I suppose."

"You are appallingly obese, Geisen. Your form recalls nothing of the slim blade who cut such wide swaths among the girls of the various Houses before his engagement."

"And your polecat coloration, fair Ailoura, along with those tinted lenses and tooth-caps, speak not of a bold mouser, but of a scavenger through garbage tips."

Regarding each other with satisfaction, Ailoura and Geisen thus approved of their disguises.

With the aid of Bozzarias, who had purchased for them various sophisticated semi-living prosthetics, dyes, and off-world clothing, the man and his servant—Timor Carrabas and Hepzibah—resembled no one ever seen before on Chalk. His pasty face rouged, Geisen wobbled as he waddled, breathing stertorously, while the limping Ailoura diffused a moderately repulsive scent calculated to keep the curious at a certain remove.

The Carrabas marchwarden now spoke, a touch of excitement in its artificial voice. "I have just notified my Stoessl House counterpart that you are departing within the hour. You will be expected in time for essences and banquet, with a half hour allotted to freshen up and settle into your guest rooms."

"Very good. Rehearse the rest of the plan to me."

"Once the funds are transferred from Stoessl House to me, I will in turn upload them to the Bourse on Feuilles Mortes under the name of Geisen Stoessl, where they will be immune from attachment. I will then retreat to my soul canister, readying it for removal by your agent, Bozzarias, who will bring it to the spacefield—specifically the terminal hosting Gravkosmos Interstellar. Beyond that point, I cannot be of service until I am haptically enabled once more."

"You have the scheme perfectly. Now we thank you, and leave with the promise that we shall talk again in the near future, in a more pleasant place."

"Goodbye, Gep Carrabas, and good luck."

Within a short time the hired zipflyte arrived. (It would hardly do for the eminent Timor Carrabas to appear in Geisen's battered craft, which had, in point of fact, already been sold to raise additional funds to aid their subterfuge.) After clambering clumsily onboard, the schemers settled themselves in the spacious rear seat while the chauffeur—a neat-plumaged and discreet raptor-derived bestient—lifted off and flew at a swift clip toward Stoessl House.

Ailoura's comment about Geisen's attractiveness to his female peers had set an unhealed sore spot within him aching. "Do you imagine, Hepzibah, that other local luminaries might attend this evening's dinner party? I had in mind a certain Gep Bloedwyn Vermeule."

"I suspect she will. The Stoessls and the Vermeules have bonds and alliances dating back centuries."

Geisen mused dreamily. "I wonder if she will be as beautiful and sensitive and angelic as I have heard tell she is."

Ailoura began to hack from deep in her throat. Recovering, she apologized, "Excuse me, Gep Carrabas. Something unpleasant in my throat. No doubt a simple hairball."

Geisen did not look amused. "You cannot deny reports of the lady's beauty, Hepzibah."

"Beauty is as beauty does, master."

The largest ballroom in Stoessl House had been extravagantly bedecked for the arrival of Timor Carrabas. Living luminescent lianas in dozens of neon tones festooned the heavy-beamed rafters. Decorator dust migrated invisibly about the chamber, cohering at random into wall screens showing various entertaining videos from the mediapoietic worlds. Responsive carpets the texture of moss crept warily along the tessellated floor, consuming any spilled food and drink wasted from the large collation spread out across a servitor-staffed table long as a playing field. (The house chef, Stine Pursiful, oversaw all with a meticulous eye, his upraised ladle serving as baton of command. After some argument among the family members and chef, a buffet had been chosen over a sit-down meal, as being more informal, relaxed, and conducive to easy dealings.) The floor space was thronged with over a hundred gaily caparisoned representatives of the houses most closely allied to the Stoessls, some dancing in stately pavanes to the music from the throats of the octet of avian bestients perched on their multibranched stand. But despite the many diversions of music, food, drink, and chatter, all eyes had strayed ineluctably to the form of the mysterious Timor Carrabas when he entered, and from time to time thereafter.

Beneath his prosthetics, Geisen now sweated copiously, both from nervousness and the heat. Luckily, his disguising adjuncts quite capably metabolized this betraying moisture before it ever reached his clothing.

The initial meeting with his brothers and stepmother had gone well. Hands were shaken all around without anyone suspecting that the flabby hand of Timor Carrabas concealed a slimmer one that ached to deliver vengeful blows.

Geisen could see immediately that since Vomacht's death, Grafton had easily assumed the role of head of household, with Woda patently the power behind the throne and Gitten content to act the wastrel princeling.

"So, Gep Carrabas," Grafton oleaginously purred, "now you finally perceive with your own eyes that we Stoessls are no monsters. It's never wise to give gossip any credence."

Gitten said, "But gossip is the only kind of talk that makes life worth liv—*oof!*"

Woda took a second step forward, relieving the painful pressure she had inflicted on her younger son's foot. "Excuse my clumsiness, Gep Carrabas, in my eagerness to enhance my proximity to a living reminder of the fine old ways of Chalk. I'm sure you can teach us much about how our forefathers lived. Despite personal longevity, we have lost the institutional rigor your clan has reputedly preserved."

In his device-modulated, rather fulsome voice, Geisen answered, "I am always happy to share my treasures with others, be they spiritual or material."

Grafton brightened. "This expansiveness bodes well for our later negotiations, Gep Carrabas. I must say that your attitude is not exactly as your servant Bozzarias conveyed."

Geisen made a dismissive wave. "Simply a local hireling who was not truly privy to my thoughts. But he has the virtue of following my bidding without the need to know any of my ulterior motivations." Geisen felt relieved to have planted that line to protect Bozzarias in the nasty wake of the successful conclusion of their thimble rigging. "Here is my real counselor. Hepzibah, step forward."

Ailoura moved within the circle of speakers, her unnaturally flared and pungent striped musteline tail waving perilously close to the humans. "At your service, Gep."

The Stoessls involuntarily cringed before the unpleasant odor wafting from Ailoura, then restrained their impolite reaction.

"Ah, quite an, ah, impressive moreauvian. Positively, um, redolent of the ribosartor's art. Perhaps your, erm, adviser would care to dine with others of her kind."

"Hepzibah, you are dismissed until I need you."

"As you wish."

Soon Geisen was swept up in a round of introductions to people he had known all his life. Eventually he reached the food, and fell to eating rather too greedily. After weeks spent subsisting on MREs alone, he could hardly restrain himself. And his glutton's disguise allowed all excess. Let the other guests gape at his immoderate behavior. They were constrained by their own greed for his putative fortune from saying a word.

After satisfying his hunger, Geisen finally looked up from his empty plate.

There stood Bloedwyn Vermeule.

Geisen's ex-fiancée had never shone more alluringly. Threaded with invisible flexing pseudo-myofibrils, her long unfettered hair waved in continual delicate movement, as if she were a mermaid underwater. She wore a gown tonight loomed from golden spider-silk. Her lips were verdigris, matched by her nails and eye shadow.

Geisen hastily dabbed at his own lips with his napkin, and was mortified to see the clean cloth come away with enough stains to represent a child's immoderate battle with an entire chocolate cake.

"Oh, Gep Carrabas, I hope I am not interrupting your gustatory pleasures."

"Nuh—no, young lady, not at all. I am fully sated. And you are?"

"Gep Bloedwyn Vermeule. You may call me by my first name, if you grant me the same privilege."

"But naturally."

"May I offer an alternative pleasure, Timor, in the form of a dance? Assuming your satiation does not extend to *all* recreations."

"Certainly. If you'll make allowances in advance for my clumsiness."

Bloedwyn allowed the tip of her tongue delicately to traverse her patina'd lips. "As the Dompatta says, 'An earnest rider compensates for a balky steed.'"

This bit of familiar gospel had never sounded so lascivious. Geisen was shocked at this unexpected temptress behavior from his ex-fiancée. But before he could react with real or mock indignation, Bloedwyn had whirled him out onto the floor.

They essayed several complicated dances before Geisen, pleading fatigue, could convince his partner to call a halt to the activity.

"Let us recover ourselves in solitude on the terrace," Bloedwyn said, and conducted Geisen by the arm through a pressure curtain and onto an unlit open-air patio. Alone in the shadows, they took up positions braced against a balustrade. The view of the moon-drenched arroyos below occupied them in silence for a time. Then Bloedwyn spoke huskily.

"You exude a foreign, experienced sensuality, Timor, to which I find myself vulnerable. Perhaps you would indulge my weakness with an assignation tonight, in a private chamber of Stoessl House known to me? After any important business dealings are successfully concluded, of course."

Geisen seethed inwardly, but managed to control his voice. "I am flattered that you find a seasoned fellow of my girth so attractive, Bloedwyn. But I do not wish to cause any intermural incidents. Surely you are affianced to someone, a young lad both bold and wiry, jealous and strong."

"Pah! I do not care for young men, they are all chowderheads! Pawing, puling, insensitive, shallow and vain, to a man! I was betrothed to one such, but luckily he revealed his true colors and I was able to cast him aside like the churl he proved to be."

Now Geisen felt only miserable self-pity. He could summon no words, and Bloedwyn took his silence for assent. She planted a kiss on his cheek, then whispered directly into his ear. "Here's a map to the boudoir where I'll be waiting. Simply take the east squeezer down three levels, then follow the hot dust." She pressed a slip of paper into his hand, supplementing her message with extra pressure in his palm, then sashayed away like a tainted sylph.

Geisen spent half an hour with his mind roiling before he regained the confidence to return to the party.

Before too long, Grafton corralled him.

"Are you enjoying yourself, Timor? The food agrees? The essences elevate? The ladies are pliant? Haw! But perhaps we should turn our mind to business now, before we both grow too muzzy-headed. After conducting our dull commerce, we can cut loose."

"I am ready. Let me summon my aide."

"That skun— That is, if you absolutely insist. But surely our marchwarden can offer any support services you need. Notarization, citation of past deeds, and so forth."

"No. I rely on Hepzibah implicitly."

Grafton partially suppressed a frown. "Very well, then."

Once Ailoura arrived from the servants' table, the trio headed toward Vomacht's old study. Geisen had to remind himself not to turn down any "unknown" corridor before Grafton himself did.

Seated in the very room where he had been fleeced of his patrimony and threatened with false charges of murder, Geisen listened with half an ear while Grafton outlined the terms of the prospective sale: all the Carrabas properties and whatever wealth of strangelets they contained, in exchange for a sum greater than the Gross Planetary Product of many smaller worlds.

Ailoura attended more carefully to the contract, even pointing out to Geisen a buried clause that would have made payment contingent on the first month's production from the new fields. After some arguing, the conspirators succeeded in having the objectionable codicil removed. The transfer of funds would be complete and instantaneous.

When Grafton had finally finished explaining the conditions, Geisen roused himself. He found it easy to sound bored with the whole deal, since his elaborate scam, at its moment of triumph, afforded him surprisingly little vengeful pleasure.

"All the details seem perfectly managed, Gep Stoessl, with that one small change of ours included. I have but one question. How do I know that the black sheep of your House, Geisen, will not contest our agreement? He seems a contrary sort, from what I've heard, and I would hate to be involved in judicial proceedings, should he get a whim in his head."

Grafton settled back in his chair with a broad smile. "Fear not, Timor! That wild hair will get up no one's arse! Geisen has been effectively rendered powerless. As was only proper and correct, I assure you, for he was not a true Stoessl at all."

Geisen's heart skipped a cycle. "Oh? How so?"

"The lad was a chimera! A product of the ribosartors! Old Vomacht was unsatisfied with the vagaries of honest mating that had produced

Gitten and myself from the noble stock of our mother. Traditional methods of reproduction had not delivered him a suitable toady. So he resolved to craft a better heir. He used most of his own germ plasm as foundation, but supplemented his nucleotides with dozens of other snippets. Why, that hybrid boy even carried bestient genes. Rat and weasel, I'm willing to bet! Haw! No, Geisen had no place in our family."

"And his mother?"

"Once the egg was crafted and fertilized, Vomacht implanted it in a host bitch. One of our own bestients. I misapprehend her name now, after all these years. Amorica, Orella, something of that nature. I never really paid attention to her fate after she delivered her human whelp. I have more important properties to look after. No doubt she ended up on the offal heap, like all the rest of her kind."

A red curtain drifting across Geisen's vision failed to occlude the shape of the massive auroch-flaying blade hanging on the wall. One swift leap and it would be in his hands. Then Grafton would know sweet murderous pain, and Geisen's bitter heart would applaud—

Standing beside Geisen, Ailoura let slip the quietest cough.

Geisen looked into her face.

A lone tear crept from the corner of one feline eye.

Geisen gathered himself and stood up, unspeaking.

Grafton grew a trifle alarmed. "Is there anything the matter, Gep Carrabas?"

"No, Gep Stoessl, not at all. Merely that old hurts pain me, and I would fain relieve them. Let us close our deal. I am content."

The starliner carrying Geisen, Ailoura, and the stasis-bound Carrabas marchwarden to a new life sped through the interstices of the cosmos, powered perhaps by a strangelet mined from Stoessl lands. In one of the lounges, the man and his cat nursed drinks and snacks, admiring the exotic variety of their fellow passengers and reveling in their hard-won liberty and security.

"Where from here—son?" asked Ailoura with a hint of unwonted shyness.

Geisen smiled. "Why, wherever we wish, mother dear."

"*Rowr!* A world with plenty of fish then, for me!"

III
Two Plus Two Equals Infinity

Something about the nature of science fiction makes collaborating both fun and natural. As a literature of ideas, SF definitely benefits from the "two heads are better than one" philosophy. Plus, most SF writers, I've found, really care about the state of the genre as a whole. Literary achievements are not seen solely as unsharable personal triumphs, but rather as part of a contribution to the great flowing stream of science fiction. We're not all isolated Stephen Daedaluses, but rather a cooperative of individual voices joined in a chorus.

I've collaborated so far in my career with Bruce Sterling, Rudy Rucker, Marc Laidlaw, Don Webb, Barry Malzberg, Pete Crowther, and Michael Bishop, and expect to add more names to that list.

Now, let's see: There're over one thousand members of the Science Fiction Writers of America. At the rate of a story per week, without any time off . . . I should be set for partners until about the year 2025!

Simply put, Don Webb, with whom I collaborated on the next story, is one of the finest fantasists working these days. I've always enjoyed his fiction, and we leaped at a chance to write together, even before we had met in the flesh. Our shared love of Steely Dan—from whom we've borrowed our title—provided a springboard for this tale, a fusion of Lem's Solaris *and Blish's "Common Time." When I finally did get a chance to meet Don in his hometown of Austin, at a Turkey City writer's workshop, he did me an immense favor by reminding me that fluency of narrative did not always equal the passionate conviction that the best stories exhibited.*

And I say all this without compulsion, even though Don is also a master of the occult arts on a par with Doctor Strange, and threatened to turn me into a frog if I didn't write a glowing introduction.

Ribbit!

YOUR GOLD TEETH, PT. 2

[written with Don Webb]

The *Nepthys* was leaking brains.

Just prior to the catastrophic Reality Transvaluation that had overwhelmed the Singularity Complex for Assessment of Metanoia, the *Nepthys*'s onboard AOI had begun to undergo an undetected metastasis. Colonies of rogue neurons had come free and traveled through the SCAM's various pipings, vacuum chutes, and paralymphatic system, establishing uncoordinated ganglia throughout the small orbiting city. Seizing control of various functions, both critical and nugatory, these independent, even mutually combative, pieces of the AOI had revealed their existence through severe yet comprehensible mechanical derangements of the environment.

But just as the crew was about to take remedial measures to reestablish control, the Transvaluation had washed over the *Nepthys*, plunging its citizens into a nightmare of giggling death and screaming metamorphosis.

In the midst of this chaos, Howard Exaker alone remained untouched.

Or so he dared hope, with a guilty twinge at how his new comrades—ill-known and emotionally distant as they had been from him—had perished or still bizarrely suffered.

Regarding the spill of faintly pulsing gray matter—so similar to baseline human brains, yet oddly *other*—that tumbled from the split seams of a Gradient Seven corridor, Howard thought for the hundredth time, *If only there were someone left to talk to . . .*

When the mock sisal–textured wall of the corridor began to change before his eyes, as if in response to his silent wish, Howard prayed he would not have cause to regret his unspoken supplication.

What he saw now in place of the familiar corridor was a (brain-free) freshly plastered wall of an Egyptian tomb. The paint smelled wet, and the hieroglyphs had begun to speak. The voice of one, a golden two-headed lion, lifted above the chatter: "If you know my name, Howard, you know my nature."

Only a week ago, when life had still retained its familiar parameters, Howard had been old-fashionedly absorbing a book on Egyptology. Had the Transvaluator—who, Howard still faintly suspected, might be the damaged AOI, but was probably not—plucked the reading from his mind and used it to couch its latest appearance?

Howard tentatively replied. "You are Routi, the twin lions Shu and Tefnut, and your name is Yesterday-Tomorrow."

Apparently satisfied with his response, the agent behind the Transvaluation—if sentient agent there even were—returned this portion of Gradient Seven to what passed for normality these days. Howard was free to continue his aimless ambling, stepping over the bodies of his recently fallen acquaintances. Those who had worked most closely with him had been the last to die or change. He wondered if the Transvaluator had a special fate in mind for him, toward which it built and ascended along a spiral of bodies?

From time to time in his peregrinations through the SCAM, the deranged AOI would attempt to touch his mind as of old. But nothing coherent could be gleaned from these brushes.

It was strange not to be able to form a question and have a ready-made answer appear. Humans had lived so long with AOI morphic fields. In many ways, Howard was the first human being to be alone in five hundred years.

But the last puzzling thing the AOI had told him before it went mad was "You are not alone. There is another at Gradient Zero. She is . . ."

She is. What? Dying? Safe? Responsible for the Transvaluation? A multilifer? A registered berdache? She is.

Add to that the fact that the SCAM's layout boasted no Gradient Zero, and the AOI's final contact had proved less than enlightening.

Howard stepped over the contorted, barely recognizable body of Cheng Anderson, who had been brought down by a carapace of fungal plaques. Like all the others, he had died with that look of shock. What was the damn final revelation, the answer that killed?

If conventionally dead the victims even were.

Again, guilt at his lack of deep remorse coursed through Howard. Two months he had been aboard the *Nepthys*, hardly long enough to form any solid bonds. And most of the SCAM's inhabitants had hated him instantly, placed him at the focus of their unease and suspicions.

But then to occupy that focus was his job.

His previous assignment had been a nasty little totalitarian world called Fagen III. (Neofascism and primitive agriculture unfortunately worked very well together.) There he had had to manipulate the fourfold plectic symbol of the organic *nation* into the fivefold symbol of a multicultural *state*. With luck the changed symbol would permeate the psyches of the population, effecting certain civil justice feelings.

Happily, the riots and cultural unrest had erupted on the day of his departure. The government thanked him profusely, and paid a bonus. There would be a culmination of the glorious creative unrest when the time to move beyond an agricultural economy arrived.

In fact he had done so well that he could pick his next assignment, so he went for that very mysterious, newly available plum that had the whole Sophontic Commensality atwitter.

Nepthys.

He had written in his Diary then: "I will voyage to the edge of the unknown to find both my undiscovered self and something the universe has never before seen." (He had not then formulated the thought that these two things might be one and the same.)

The Diary's oracle function had written back: "Who are these children who scream and run wild?" He had thought it a marvelous oracle, referring perhaps to some Inner Child, an old archetype recently resurfacing

Now, of course, after the Transvaluation he tended to interpret the oracle more disturbingly . . .

Leaving Anderson's body behind, refraining from casting a backward glance for fear the corpse might choose to change, Howard took slow, deliberate steps. It wasn't wise to run. Beatrice Somerville, the first victim, had discovered that. A glaucous mist had chased her from the gravitic engine room. She had run, and the mist laughed as she turned inside out before vanishing. Briefly displaying on its shimmering self scenes from Beatrice's childhood, the mist soon faded away, leaving everyone with a headache and the smell of her perfume, which stood out even above the raw sewage unleashed by the rogue ganglia.

Everyone soon learned the best way to react, for what such knowledge was worth.

If you let the Transvaluator touch you at will, play with you, you lived longer.

Howard focused his attention away from his memories and onto his next few steps. If the Gradients hadn't been reconfigured too terribly, there would be a dining hall twenty meters ahead to the left. He would only have to pass two doorways. Doorways were the worst. The Transvaluator, perhaps reflecting its own liminal nature, had some fascination with doorways.

There were no apparent changes as he passed by the first entrance.

No, that wasn't right.

Something had changed.

Subjective time sped up, making the world around him, including his own body, seem super-slow.

Howard moved like a superannuated sloth, kicking a dropped scanner and watching it rise underwater-slow. He wondered how many mental hours it would take him to reach the next portal a mere eight meters away. Maybe this slowing had produced the shocked faces on his fallen companions. They had enjoyed what most humans never had—time to think it all out.

And judging by their faces, the answer to all of life's questions wasn't a nice one.

The director of the station, Sharon Dewdney, had been one of those who had hated him on sight.

"We don't need a socio-plectic engineer! The dynamics of our interpersonal situation are firmly established, maximally optimized."

"You're probably right," Howard agreed, "insofar as you go. There are enough humans here to produce a critical mass of affinities and discharges. If this were a boring, routine assignment, of course, you'd still need an engineer for conventional reasons."

"No one will have the time to be bored, or play out the little rituals you devise in the name of psychic health, Com'sal Exaker. And since you admit as much, I fail to see your utility."

"Allow me to share some data with you, commander." Howard routed the dump from his personal nodes through the AOI and into Dewdney. He was gratified to note Dewdney's eyes widen. "As you see, intense research groups such as yours generally avoid psychosis. But you risk blind spots and self-sustaining inversions that can lead to mission failure. And that would mean that the Kamakirians would get the concession, and take over your precious SCAM."

Well, that was a definable fear, and enough of a fear to quash any further opposition from the commander.

For over a hundred years, both Kamakirians and humans had been aware of the black hole around which the SCAM now orbited. The singularity had been merely a navigational hazard of some fifty standard solar masses, with nothing to mark it as any more interesting than any other piece of dark matter that held the universe together.

Then a disabled Kamakirian ship had been caught by the greedy dead star. Before being completely sucked into the singularity, its crew had launched a message packet. Picked up decades later, it stunned the Commensality.

As they fell into the star pit, the Kamakirian crew reported experiencing strange mental adjustments bordering on the transcendental, adjustments that came to be subsumed under the catchall term "metanoia." And deep within the singularity's domain, where nothing should be able to exist, they could discern something. Something big in a stable orbit, which wasn't being sucked into that awful gravity well.

The Kamakirians announced that they would study the anomaly exclusively, since one of their ships had discovered it (and died doing so). The Commensality ruled for them, but it was an academic decision, since neither Kamakirians nor humans could get anywhere near the hole, and long-range studies proved inconclusive.

Then a human named Octavia Xibalba-Fitzsimmons developed the gravitic engine, a device that utilized the long-sought Fifth Force and permitted maneuvering in ultrahigh gravity fields. The gravitic engine created an island of stability—like a bubble caught in a vortex; it was able to remain stable by its complex movement and interaction with the forces around it.

Plainly, this was the means whereby the mysterious Object maintained itself against the black hole's perpetual desire, deep inside the event horizon.

The humans declared their right now to study the whole enigma alone, since they had developed the technology to make it possible. The SCAM—existing at this point as only a CAD-gleam in an AOI's neurons—would be fitted with a gravitic engine, allowing it to swirl round and about the hole, occasionally "surfacing" to take on supplies and download information.

Diplomacy, negotiations, eventual mediation by the Free Machines, resulted in the birth of the *Nepthys.*

Four standard years ago when Howard had first heard of the project, he had written in his Diary: "Nepthys, the Lady of the Temple, goddess of the future of the unknown." And the oracle function had responded: "What are the secrets they trace in the sky?"

The unique *Nepthys,* also denominated SCAM, assembled itself at a nearby red dwarf, and when it was ready, its AOI grown, it called for its citizen crew, all volunteers. Impelled within the hole's reach, station and crew began a crazy spin orbit, a glyph so plectically ramified that the minicity would never repeat its position twice in the whole of Time. When the "bubble" of low gravity was farthest from the hole, crew and supplies could be taken on, data sent out.

The first standard year of its assignment passed before the *Nepthys* shot far enough away from the hole to relay its first databurst.

It told news of the Object.

And of the death of its original socio-plectic engineer, the need for a replacement.

The humans had twice passed between the Object and the hole. At those times *Nepthys*'s sensors had been able to intercept the infalling radiation of all energies emanating from the Object and to draw a limited picture of it.

It didn't look like any ship or station ever seen in the Commensality. It looked like a castle designed by a mescal-crazed Escher. In its angular windows lights glowed, something vast and dark moved.

The Transvaluator? Howard had since had cause to wonder. Or simply, it would soon be plausible, another mortal victim of that unknown agency?

As for Howard's predecessor, supposedly, by training, the most stable of minds, he had inexplicably committed suicide in a novel way, making an EVA outside the protective field of their gravitic engines.

Was it his ghost, perpetually caught in some wormhole, that was raising havoc onboard?

Howard had no feeling one way or the other. All theories seemed equally valid.

Time was discongealing around him now.

Howard's foot, suspended infinitely in midstride, now fell normally toward the floor.

The second doorway drew near.

It was very, very hard to be certain, but Howard felt he had three standard days to make it to the escape pod. At the end of that period, *Nepthys* would be at one of its infrequent apogees. He could launch the pod and have some hope of not being sucked into the hole.

During that time, he would search the Gradients for any survivors —at least those who could move under their own power and sustain themselves. It would be no favor to bring the irrecoverably ultrawarped out into the glare of a disgustedly fascinated populace.

In some ways, he felt the decision to leave was the supreme act of cowardice. What human being before him had had the chance to explore Pandemonium? If he could only grasp the mechanics of the Transvaluation, its necessary (?) laws and rules, he would be the first cartographer of hell. Unless Hieronymous Bosch had had similar visions. Did theory not offer the possibility of travel backwards in time? Perhaps the metanoia resonated pastwards, awakening others to the strangeness. Perhaps, he thought, I am the mother of all weirdness.

His thoughts had gotten more and more unruly. Was this what had overtaken his predecessor? Was his cadre hypersensitive by training to the Transvaluation? Could he turn that training now to his survival? He should be able to channel his thoughts and feelings, however odd. Make a game of them. Even the drug-induced visions of ancient shamans had gained order from the ability of the mystics to think ascriptively.

Could he summon a spirit guide? A Virgil, an Isis?

But what if there were no ordered system behind the chaos? A hell of concentric rings rang true for the Renaissance, but the hell for an ungraphable orbit—? Perhaps there is no poetry in chaos . . .

He stepped through the second doorway—

Untouched? Seemingly.

A large dining hall stretched out before him, pleasingly empty of bodies, though not of looping vines and fleshy flowers. He could smell food. He crossed toward the swinging doors that led to the kitchen. There, he hesitated. Entered.

One of the rogue ganglia had subverted the servocooks, which now poured out liters of spaghetti and meatballs. The floor was awash in them.

Howard attempted to assert control, speaking aloud.

"I am hungry and about to eat. I am hungry and think about five hours of objective time have passed since my last meal. Therefore, I will now eat." For good measure he added, "I am Howard Exaker."

All of this brave facade melted away as pink rose petals began to rain from the ceiling. A woman's voice trilled out "The Caverns of Altamira," a hit from the twenty-third century. "They heard the call, and they wrote it on the wall . . ."

Howard recognized the voice wistfully as belonging not to a professional singer, but to a musicologist he'd met many years ago on Fezzon. She had been his first real lover. It made him sad and angry that such a sweet memory should manifest itself amidst such alienage. Even the dearest, most familiar parts of his life were being estranged from him.

He fell to his knees amid the edible slop.

As he ate and cried and choked, some of the rose-petal rain began to turn blue. By the time he was sated, the blue petals covered every surface. He had eaten several, despite his best efforts.

Apparently, that had been a bad mistake.

As he stood, Howard felt a change overtaking him.

His arms fused to his side, his legs melded. Rotundity shaped him. Simultaneously, he felt himself stretching upward toward the ceiling, rooting downward.

In less time than it would take to tell a nonexistent companion, the transformation was complete.

The reflective surface of a storage unit across the kitchen revealed his new appearance to his eyes.

He was a fluted column with living kohl-outlined eyes embedded in it. Colorful animated hieroglyphics—including the twin lions Shu and Tefnut—cavorted across his surface.

Suddenly the kitchen vanished, to be replaced by—

By a space that could never have existed aboard the SCAM. A space of such alien geometries that even the Transvaluation could not have rendered it with the *Nepthys* as a starting point.

Howard knew without a doubt that he was now aboard the Object.

Futilely, he writhed nonexistent muscles, struggling to break free. Then, enervated by the effort, he tried to study his new ambiance, in preparation for the approach of the castle's ogre-owner, the barely glimpsed shadow thrower.

This exercise was nearly as pointless. Howard couldn't decide which blocks of improbable color in his vision were the walls and which the space. Acute angles swapped identities with obtuse ones. Dimensions exfoliated and curled around him.

The strain made his kohl-rimmed eyes drip tears. He could feel them run down his marmoreal column-body. The hieroglyphs there had ceased to cavort, apparently as frightened as he. A buzzing pink light inside his tubular ?body? filled him with a taste of hot pewter. Two other groups of sensations presented themselves to him, but like a blind man confronted suddenly with sight, he had no words or orderings to represent them.

He floated ?without moving? for twenty-five years or a second or two.

Then the Object's resident approached.

The sensors aboard the *Nepthys* had seen a "shadow," and deemed it necessarily a shadow of something.

But the shadow *was* the something.

A convoluted black sheet composed of innumerable scintillating particles, particles that seemed to wink in and out of existence, down ways as complex as the orbit of the *Nepthys.* Plainly, each mote was independent, yet the whole was cohesive, moving by space-time warpage. Its size was impossible to discern in this alien environment.

The sheet wrapped itself around the column that was Howard, blanking his vision. An impression of intelligence similar to that of an AOI filtered through to Howard.

A construct. A matrix of information and processing. This thing was not one of the Object's builders, but simply one of their tools. The originators of the Object were gone, Howard instantly knew, gone for millennia, Transvaluated.

Confirmation of a sort seeped through to him. Desperately, without a mouth, he tried mentally hurling questions at the shadow. But the questions just spawned and proliferated horribly in his own ?mind?. All and everything became an incandescent blur as his own thoughts echoed and re-echoed in his ?mind?. Stream of consciousness be came white noise. Without sensory input, a deadly solipsism was threatening to swallow him like—

Like a black hole.

Someone, Howard managed to conceptualize, someone to talk to.

At that instant, the matrix-shadow was gone.

Everything was quiet in his !mind!.

Howard stood in a comprehensible yet impossible (because so far removed) environment.

The sky was blue-green, the sun too large for Earth.

But just fine for Fagen III, a familiar scene, his last triumph, obviously plucked from his psyche.

Around Howard stood a few of Fagen III's famous kilometer-high pinelike trees. Between the pines, binding them to each other—and binding Howard to the trees!—were countless sticky threads woven by—or at least tenanted and traversed by—hundreds of tiny slate-gray caterpillars.

But none of these features surprised Howard as much as the body he wore.

That of Beatrice Somerville, the Transvaluator's first human victim.

He had once seen Beatrice naked, in the null-gee natatorium. He found her exquisitely beautiful, and an ache to possess her blossomed in his loins. But any pursuit would have screwed up the 'plectics he was trying to generate. So he, celibate priest of social engineering, had acted cold, and she, once appreciative, then quite stung, had dived up into the water bubble and swum away from him.

First Osiris, now Arachne, thought the bound Howard wryly. The Transvaluator is obviously not a small mind, for it is unbothered by any foolish inconsistencies.

Several of the caterpillars were making their way across the webbing, heading for Howard's oddly nonmale pubis. Feeling a disinclination to be crawled upon, Howard—or Beatrice—wrenched violently, breaking his—or her—body free from the elastic webbing. It coiled away from her in all directions.

Stepping back from the web, she realized that despite the high big sun, it was chilly.

No garments around, and the idea of covering herself in the webbing was distasteful, almost as if the substance would form a—poison shirt?

Herself a female Heracles, now? There was a thought. What baker's dozen of Labors awaited? What could be expected of her?

Howard knew this was not really Fagen III. Plainly, she was still in the grip of the Transvaluator. She suddenly had the feeling that its goal was simply to communicate with her or another human, had been all along. All the horrid carnage aboard the *Nepthys* was merely fumbling attempts at speech in a medium it did not fully comprehend.

If that were the case, then there should be further objective correlatives here to the Transvaluator's intentions.

She carefully scanned her immediate environment.

Yes, there, high in the web.

Twin flashes of green and gold. The objects seemed to swell in her vision, as if the eyes in this (imaginary? artificial?) body had telescopic properties.

Green earrings, jade wrapped with golden threads.

Those rings of rare design . . .

Half-memories swamped her. She had owned those earrings, perhaps across innumerable lifetimes! They were hers by right. If only she could lay her hands on them, she would remember everything!

Tentatively, she advanced to the web. The caterpillars ignored her, save for forming complex icons with their bodies. She began pulling the webbing with both hands. This produced the opposite effect of what she had intended. Releasing the tension in some of the strands had caused the earrings—formerly in dynamic balance—to shoot upwards.

Frustration, intense! She was not Howard or Beatrice in mind now, but only the emotion of Wanting. There seemed to be no rocks or branches to throw at the earrings, only a soft green moss covering the ground, and the webbing certainly wouldn't support her weight.

Studying the matrix (was it composed of black motes that glimmered?), she began to discern in it elements of the puzzling geometry exhibited by the interior of the Object. That angle there corresponded to the direction from which the computer-shadow had approached, for instance . . .

Slowly, using her modified intuition, she began to see how the webbing held together. If she could oscillate these several strands in just the right pattern, the earrings would fall—if not to the ground, then at least to a reachable support strand.

After minutes of running mental simulations, she knew just how to do it.

In a short time the green earrings, which had begun about six meters over her head (and at one point in the process soared to at least twelve), were within grasping distance.

Her eager hands closed around them.

A chorus of piping voices immediately sounded.

"Isolate and oscillate, meditate and palpitate! Make a hole in the system, make the system your whole!"

Clutching the earrings, Howard turned.

Hovering in the air were nine winged cherubs. Babyish chubby-cheeked heads without bodies, they sprouted their wings in some improbable fashion from where necks should have been.

The Nine fluttered hummingbird-like, dipping and chittering.

"Integrate the potentate, exacerbate the precipitate! Take your soul into the storm, take the storm into your soul!"

After this last Oracle, the cherubs seemed to be gathering themselves to leave. "Wait!" shouted Howard. "Tell me! What happened to those who built the Object?"

"We ate them," giggled the cherubim. "They tasted fine, and we learned a lot. But we made a mistake! A bad mistake!"

Now the cherubs fell to chastising each other, each one yelling simultaneous accusation and defense.

"It was your fault! No it wasn't!"

"We broke the Object's gravitic-engine controls. We had to go and play with them, didn't we! It was stuck inside us. We couldn't make it carry us outside the event horizon. Trapped! Always and forever, trapped!"

Plainly disturbed, the flock of cherubim began to depart. As they arrowed off, Howard heard them utter a last, disturbing phrase.

"Until you came! Until you!"

With the departure of the cherubim, Howard realized that she was clutching the earrings so tightly that they were digging painfully into her palms.

Reaching up, she applied them to her earlobes.

The earrings gripped flesh.

Burrowed—or melted, or fused—inward, with a sensation of frozen hydrogen sublimating.

One of the pines was now a column. A column with eyes.

Was it himself? Was he still aboard the Object?

Howard walked toward it.

Into it.

And out.

Howard found himself in his own body again, sitting at a small table with a clothed Beatrice Somerville. They seemed to be in the private room of a restaurant. Or was it the dining chamber aboard the *Nepthys,* where this whole madness had begun?

Howard found words unbidden rising to his tongue. "So, you were the template . . ."

Beatrice smiled alluringly. "The human template only. Don't forget, the hole had already swallowed and integrated a shipful of Kamakirians and the builders of the Object. Who, by the way, called themselves something approximating "Wudocs."

"Are you still alive?"

Beatrice fluttered the question away with a butterfly-like hand gesture. "Not relevant. It's like that unresolvable philosophical game you can play. Am I someone else's dream? Well, I've actually lived that game, and it doesn't interest me very much anymore."

Howard looked around the room, expecting a sommelier to appear at any moment. "Where are we?"

"My guess would be somewhere aboard the *Nepthys.* But I wouldn't make any bets."

"And our next move?"

"Is not ours to make. It's his."

"The Transvaluator? Are you just using conventional pronouns? Or do you feel a maleness about him'?"

Beatrice looked embarrassed. "Oh, a definite maleness. At least in his relations to me, as he dreams my existence."

Obviously seeking to change the subject, she said, "He was born through the concatenation of forces we have no understanding of, during the collapse of the progenitor star that formed the hole and he's lived here ever since, subsisting on infalling matter and energies, trying to puzzle out what lies beyond the inescapable event horizon.

"Inescapable, that is, until the gravitic engine."

A deep fear gripped Howard. "The Transvaluator wants out? To wreak his mad changes on the universe at large? We can't possibly help him do that!"

"You don't understand. He's neither wholly good nor wholly evil, any more than one of us is. He's just a being who's trapped and alone! Besides, there seems some question as to how much power he will retain, once he leaves the special conditions here and enters the broken symmetry of the universe at large. It will probably take most of his strength and attention just to maintain his identity."

Howard lowered his head into the cradle of his hands. "What a mess . . ."

Beatrice clasped one of his wrists. "Cheer up. It's out of our hands anyway. Listen, let's order a meal."

A red velvet menu appeared before each of them. Reluctantly, Howard picked up his, opened it.

Every single item was labeled "My Story."

Howard snorted ruefully. "I guess," he said, "I'II try this," tapping one line at random.

The menu became a piece of yellow paper with nine numbered statements. Beatrice had vanished. Howard recalled Dante's remark that his Beatrice was a Nine. Not symbolized by Nine, but was a nine.

Howard read:

I. In the beginning was the Collapse, which begat the Mind, and He could detect no others.

II. Then He had his first Thought, and Mind and Thought lived in endless play, as She traced out all things with and within Him.

III. They came to know there was a Universe beyond Them, which fed and sustained Them with a rain of food.

IV. They longed to achieve Oneness with Their glowing source of Life.

V. They turned Their source of Life upon itself so that They could have a play Universe of Their own, limitless mock Creation.

VI. In the fullness of time, the Mind and the Thought exhausted Their play, and died away into a quiescence of boredom.

VII. Then the First New Thing fell into Their dark tomb and by its disturbing symmetry awakened the Mind. At first He imagined it was a bad dream, and so erased it. Then the Second New Thing arrived, and

He chose to study it. But in his ignorance and eagerness, He broke it.

VIII. When the Third New Thing appeared, he knew he must learn to talk with it.

IX. And this was the way: not to greedily subsume all into Himself, but to create a mediator, a space between Himself and the universe.

Howard placed the paper carefully on the table.

Beatrice reappeared. Howard noticed she was now wearing the green earrings.

"You're not real, are you?" asked Howard.

"Not quite as real as you. But then again, what's ten—or infinity—times zero?"

Beatrice cocked her head, as if listening to something, then informed him, "The *Nepthys* is thirty seconds away from apogee. We reenter normal space then."

"And at that point the Transvaluator is free?"

"Yes."

"And us?"

"Wait and watch."

The restaurant vanished. Howard was whelmed in prismatic blackness, devastating and crushing, blanking his thoughts.

After a period of no time, he became aware through highly sophisticated sensors of normal starfields all around him. The volume of space around the black hole was filled with Commensality ships, all eagerly awaiting the fate of the SCAM.

A shout of glee blared across all bands, broadcast by the freed Transvaluator. Howard felt the immaterial Mind shoot across the universe, eager to play.

And himself?

Where was he?

What was he?

Slowly, he realized what the Transvaluator had done.

The *Nepthys* had been amalgamated with the Object, a fusion of Wudoc and human technology and forms. And Howard's self, his body long ago destroyed, was running on the platform of the AOI.

He searched the mutated interior of the SCAM for companions.

Alone. The Mind had left him intolerably alone!

Then, up from out of Planckian inscrutability, the Wudoc shadow-matrix arose. In it, Beatrice was embodied.

Don't despair, she counseled gently. *We have a job.*

Then he realized. There were innumerable black holes left to visit.

And Minds to set free.

My career began with Barry Malzberg.

While still a college student, I sold my first story: a pastiche of Mister Malzberg's work, great jeroboams of which I had deliriously imbibed. During the mid-seventies, Barry Malzberg was a dominant figure in the genre, his engaged, sardonic, prolific voice everywhere, hectoring the field of science fiction to new heights. Thirty years later he remains a master, his accomplishments gratefully acknowledged by the cognoscenti.

The SF field being the tightly knit circle it is, as I became more and more a part of it, I found myself making the personal acquaintance of the man I had once so crudely imitated for a lark. Barry proved himself a big enough soul to forgive my youthful transgressions, and we soon came to call ourselves friends.

The results of our friendship, on display below, seem to me somehow emblematic of a certain stage in my career. After three decades, I might just be done with my apprenticeship.

Beyond Mao

[written with Barry Malzberg]

Halfway to Mars, Wu Yuèhai calls out to He Keung. He Keung is startled. More than startled, alarmed and shaken. Even terrified.

In the close quarters of the *Radiant Crane*, a *Shenzhou-11* module only three times the size of the compact *Shenzhou-5* that lofted Yang Liwei into his historic orbit twenty years ago, there is no room for stowaways. He Keung and his two fellow taikonauts are jammed into quarters that even Mao on his fabled Long March would have found primitive and uncomfortable. The cockpit of the *Radiant Crane* is studded with instrumentation and storage lockers holding the ample supplies of freeze-dried shredded pork with garlic sauce on which the taikonauts mainly subsist. The three form-fitting chairs which double as bunks are separated by only centimeters.

He Keung, occupying the middle of the couches, turns first to his left, to confront Huang Shen. A thin, ascetic figure, Huang Shen reminds He Keung of one of those dedicated cadre members you could see on old digitized newsreels of the Cultural Revolution, who would turn in his own parents for ideological trespasses. How such an archaic man—notable prior to this expedition mainly as the chief tax enforcer for Shanghai—came to arise in the twenty-first-century market-socialist China, which has been in existence since before any of the taikonauts were born, is a puzzle to He Keung. Perhaps such creatures are eternal, springing up despite external circumstances.

Whatever the mystical explanation for Huang Shen's origins, it is plain that the sober-sided, calculating man would not be the one to play a cruel practical joke involving the taping and disseminating through the ship's cabin speakers of Wu Yuèhai's voice.

That leaves Wang Yu, on He Keung's right. Now, Wang Yu is a likely suspect. Burly and overfull of energy, the piggy-faced taikonaut has been renowned for his jests and japes since the days when he was a famous fighter pilot in the short war with Taiwan. Wang Yu has chafed on this long mission, finding little to occupy his enormous energies as the *Radiant Crane* hurtles under precise cybernetic control toward Mars. Yes, Wang Yu possesses the kind of coarse nature that would conceive of such a mean-spirited burlesque.

Yet, He Keung recalls, Wang Yu was once romantically linked with Wu Yuèhai. He Keung himself saw the authentic flow of his comrade's tears when Wu Yuèhai broke up with Wang Yu. There was no bitterness or desire for revenge then on Wang Yu's part, only black despair. Surely he would not disgrace her memory in such a manner.

The ventilation unit blows clammy air redolent of that uncontrollable HVAC mold-spore infestation over He Keung's face, adding to his unease. Odd pinging noises from the skin of the *Radiant Crane*, evoked under the almost unimaginable stresses of interplanetary space, sound like the temple bells of some unearthly monastery.

Discarding his only two suspects as agents of the jest, He Keung is left with a pair of equally repellent alternatives.

Either He Keung is going insane.

Or Wu Yuèhai is truly addressing him.

From beyond the grave.

For Wu Yuèhai is dead.

The first female taikonaut perished in orbit during an unpredicted solar storm seven years ago. Her body riddled with radiation, her craft disabled by electromagnetic surges along its circuitry, Wu Yuèhai lasted for a week after the storm hit, broadcasting her final experiences to a world that hung on her every steadily weakening word. She became the very emblem of Chinese strength and courage, the shining symbol of both the triumphs and the necessarily harsh costs of the Chinese conquest of space.

Like everyone in his generation of the taikonaut corps, He Keung idolizes Wu Yuèhai. He has had frequent dreams in which she figures, both erotically and heroically. True, she surfaces randomly in his thoughts every day, a beacon inspiring him onward toward Mars when his spirit flags.

But this instance is different. He Keung can swear he actually heard her voice.

And then, even as he seeks to replay the incident in his mind, Wu Yuèhai appears in the cabin of the *Radiant Crane.*

The female taikonaut's form is translucent, shimmering like a bad holo. Yet there is some indisputable element of vitality about the apparition, a sense of living interactivity and presence that would belie any mere recording.

"I am come for you," Wu Yuèhai says. She seems to be addressing He Keung directly. At least the others, drowsing almost narcoleptically, as they all three often do to pass the interminable hours, pay this apparition no regard. "You have been waiting for me, yes? All of your life?"

Her face is radiant; her features now fully formed, well defined in the haze of the enclosure; if he did not know that she was dead, if he had not listened to her death agonies transmitted by private circuit long after the inspirational sections of her address had run out, he would have thought that she was alive. She beckons toward him. "Come with me," she says.

The situation is absurd. On his left in the module Huang Shen, dreaming of double-entry bookkeeping, arms folded across his chest, the little drafts of his breath stirring embers in the space surrounding; on his right in the *Radiant Crane* the formerly merry Wang Yu similarly gripped in slumber. The woman with whom he was rumored to have had liaisons—all in the name of China's greater glory in space—drifts within two feet of him but he pays her no heed, no mind. Only He Keung seems to be alert to her presence, and yet her imminence, rather than stirring him as it had through all of the years he idolized her, seems rather to stun; he finds himself shifting toward lower levels of inhabitancy.

"I have long been dreaming of you," Wu Yuèhai says. "In all the stuffy and infinite volume of space, an empire vaster than any ruled by the Yellow Emperor. But only of you. You and you alone."

Her tone startles; it is the same lustrous, slurred enunciation with which she had called from the broken craft, the *Lacquered Barge*, announcing her travail, from the first jolt of the storm to the slow and unintelligible jargon with which some time later she announced the end of consciousness. Her voice in his ear had been like her voice all over the globe: personal, intimate, focused, as if she were drawing him not to her death but to her bed. It is this Wu Yuèhai whom he sees before him, and He Keung turns left and right again, sees his drugged or sleeping companions as they fail to remark upon this at all, and finally, feeling foolish—as well he might—he speaks.

"Why are you still alive?" He Keung says. "Why are you here? You died far from the *Radiant Crane*, locked in darkness. You were mourned. The Honorable Companion described the heavens as your shrine. There was mourning for three days. Now you are here. Is this you or have you only found the spirit of your ancestors to blame?"

I am babbling, he thinks, I am not being scientific. I am not being precise. I am overwhelmed. I should be brave and decisive, like Lin Xiangru when he faced the fearsome King of Zhao. So much is depending on this flight, which will have repercussions that radiate throughout the Chinese economy and culture. Why, already action figures of the three taikonauts are available in the department stores of Beijing. Commemorative wristwatches bearing the likeness of the *Radiant Crane* are being sported by proud teenagers in the Tibetan province. A beer bearing He Keung's visage on its label is being quaffed this very moment in Macao.

"Watch this now," Wu Yuèhai says. "Attend to the spirit of the Suns." She bridges the distance between them and embraces him; even through the intelligent metal and sophisticated fabrics that swaddle him he can feel the force of that embrace. She is garbed in the simplest way, not in the equipment of space but almost as a courtesan. He Keung knows that he cannot be aroused, thanks to the antipriapic treatments enforced upon the taikonauts prior to the flight, but he finds himself mockingly considering what Wu Yuèhai's embrace would feel like if he *were* aroused. There is no love in space, only engineering; that had been the link of their training. But this spectral clasp has been an utterly startling experience.

"The Suns are revolving," she says. "They are rotating within your spirit. I am infusing you with my portion of the Tao."

At any moment, He Keung knows, the two others will come to awareness and the situation will become uncontrollable. The accountant soul of Huang Shen will demand to know what his teammate is babbling about, what sensory derangements the youngest of the three taikonauts is experiencing. If He Keung reveals the truth of his encounter with the ghost of Wu Yuèhai, the others will surely clamp him into one of the American-made neural-restraint devices that the *Radiant Crane* carries as a precaution against just such a lunatic spree. (Nowadays the Americans excel at nothing so much as the "deaccessioning of transgressive personal liberties." The Waldrop-McAuley Shock Carapace is one of their finest and most in-demand export products, rated with a 1.5 Hulk-disabling factor.) Nor can He Keung count on the jovial nature of Wang Yu to help him slough off any charges that Huang Shen might level. Wang Yu is only two years away from the iron rice bowl of retirement. He need only complete this mission, then adjourn to his state-owned mansion on the banks of the virgin lake formed by the Three Gorges Dam. Wang Yu will not jeopardize such a sweet deal to cater to the erotic, cosmic delusions of a youngster.

No, he will have to lie to his teammates, tell them that he was merely reciting aloud the text of some fondly recalled Japanese manga, for his own amusement. (The music MP3s and compressed video files and engineering PDFs supplied by the National Space Administration have already palled for all of them, and they are only a quarter of the way in what will hopefully be a round trip.) But will his comrades believe such a shabby pretext? And if they do believe it, will they not still forevermore look askance at He Keung, as one who betrays the necessary vigilance and concentration demanded by this historic mission? (And yet dual supercooled cross-checking computers, no bigger than one of the many gold Olympic medals China will surely reap this year, are the real pilots of the vessel, at least at this uneventful stage.)

Even as He Keung parses his options regarding his fellow taikonauts, Wu Yuèhai, squirming in his lap, renders both truthfulness and deceit moot by her next words.

"He Keung, I can sense that your soul is fully invigorated by the immortal solar fluids which I have shared with you, a portion of the aetheric stellar radiation which did not end my life, but caused me to be reborn, along with the ministrations of the Tian Shi Yu. And now that your *qi* is flowing richly, I need you to terminate your fellows. They are a poisoned cargo you must jettison."

He Keung feels his heart stop beating, suspending itself for a seeming eternity, then hurl itself against his ribs like one of the oxen on his grandfather's farm in Honan province, maddened by flies, running full tilt into a barn wall. To kill his comrades, the men with whom he trained so long and hard! He Keung recalls the weeks they lived in simulated Mars quarters in Antarctica, relying on each other for sheer survival. The time the two older men took him on a bawdy drinking binge in Hong Kong. What has either man done to deserve such a cruel end?

As if half cognizant that their fates are being debated, both Huang Shen and Wang Yu stir fitfully on their couches, their respectively cadaverous and infantile cheeks bedewed with sweat. Their hair, though close-cropped, stirs under the ministrations of the personal blowers which prevent the carbon dioxide of their own exhalations from hanging around their faces in zero gravity and smothering them as they sleep. (How easy, simply to shut those fans off. What a reputedly comfortable death.)

Seeking to delay the mortal answer he must make to Wu Yuèhai, recalling the proverb that advises, "When you want to test the depths of a stream, don't use both feet," He Keung seeks initially to unravel the mystery of her continued existence. "You claim the solar flux did not kill you, but instead brought new life. How can this be? And who are the Tian Shi Yu?"

Wu Yuèhai rears back from her close proximity to He Keung's face (is that her breath he feels, or only his own anti-CO_2 fan?) and assumes a serious yet still somehow flirtatious mien. "The radiation triggered ancient programming buried in my cells, in the human genome. When I fell silent, it was because I was encysted in a cocoon. My nascent transformation sent FTL impulses along the Tao, and summoned my new mentors, the Tian Shi Yu, the Jade Angels. They were waiting to receive me into their loving arms when I hatched into my superior form, and to teach me the true meaning of the cosmos. They brought me to Mars, where I found a community of endless bliss and perfection. A community I wish to share with you. But only if you reach me alone."

He Keung would like to believe this fairy tale. Wu Yuèhai alive, and desirous of him. And Mars, a world thought to be forbidding and sterile, instead hosting some kind of pan-galactic utopian outpost. It resonates with his fondest hopes and dreams. But the sticking point is Wu Yuèhai's insistence that he murder his fellow taikonauts.

"Why cannot Huang Shen and Wang Yu also enter into this lotus land? Are they not as human as you or I, just as susceptible to the beneficial influences of your Jade Angels?"

"No, they are not. Human, I mean. Earth has always hosted two species, true humans and a parasitic mimic race. It is the mimics who are responsible for the endless litany of human suffering down the ages. You are human, holding within you the potential to become as I am. Your false mates are not. In fact, they and their ilk know of the existence of the Jade Angels and the Martian redoubt. They are ancient enemies. And their intention is to destroy it utterly. Have you never wondered why the habitable space of the *Radiant Crane* is so small, why it represents such a slight improvement upon the ancient *Shenzhou-5*?"

Sensing the answer will not please him, He Keung asks, "Why?"

"It is because the bulk of this vessel is given over to weapons of mass destruction, bombs of surpassing ferocity which your fellows intend to rain down from orbit upon the heads of all we Martians."

We Martians. This is a startling statement, and He Keung feels his sensibility tilt at its outrageousness, but before he can contemplate further (Wu Yuèhai a Martian? but was that before or after her soliloquy of mourning and farewell?), Wu Yuèhai speaks in a dramatic new tone, a voice of imperiousness and certitude.

"The amplitude and oscillations of your *qi* indicate you are loath to rid the ship of these two parasites, even though they are like camels standing amidst a flock of sheep. But how can you expect to put out a cartload of wood on fire with only a single cup of water? Yet even this contingency has been foreseen. In different circumstances, you will find the strength perhaps to do what needs to be done. Remember, He Keung: Great souls have wills; feeble ones have only wishes."

The ship, subjectively stationary until then, seems to tilt, lurching and bucking improbably like a fragile life raft in the wake of a robot supertanker. At the same time, the yawning, gleaming haze which has surrounded the apparitional Wu Yuèhai seems to bloom and exfoliate, filling the small cabin. An odor of dusty poppies infiltrates He Keung's space-dulled nostrils.

Their restraints suddenly rotting like the Yellow Emperor's ancient silk robes, the three taikonauts are propelled into that gaping, devouring haze with enormous force, and before He Keung can access the stabilizers, which might possibly arrest the situation, he is instead pressed with enormous force against the bulkhead. He tries to struggle against the alien gravities pinning him in place but cannot, and from the others come strange, bleating cries as they emerge from their drugged state into some kind of transitive half-life in which they neither achieve consciousness nor lose it.

The *Radiant Crane* is shaking now; shaking in the vacuum of space as was never supposed to be possible, and, caught in some approximation of fetality, He Keung is shaking too, in sympathetic and terrible vibration. If the other two are in a half-state of ascension toward consciousness, He Keung is now otherwise—he seems to be descending toward some dark star which will envelop him. Wu Yuèhai, invisible in the dominant cold nebulosities contained in the cabin, is giggling; the embrace that locks him is not hers but some aspect of descent and yet he has never felt as close to her as he has at this moment.

"Be not afraid of growing slowly, be afraid only of standing still," Wu Yuèhai's voice whispers close to him. He cannot touch her but she is there. "You are embarked fully now upon your journey. We greet you, we raise the flag of liberation. Soon you will join us on the surface of the Red Planet and we shall together celebrate the will of the people. And remember: Even a single ant may well destroy a dike." He feels invisible lips against his ear, hears another harsh giggle, and then space itself in its full and irreversible emptiness seems to swaddle him, not the illusory haze which the *Radiant Crane* has furnished its three voyagers but the vast and abandoned tableland of the heavens themselves. Breathing seems an outmoded luxury. His companions appear to be flickering before him. He wants to speak but cannot. He wishes to confer or, failing that, at least make their new condition known to Grand Mao Station back in Earth orbit, but he is beyond speech.

"Thus ends the first part of your journey," Wu Yuèhai whispers. "Now the true testing can begin."

Mars hangs in the sky like the mass of Jupiter's Great Red Spot scooped from the mother planet and given independent existence, or like the promise of a placid uterine existence, all artery-filtered light and dear protective enclosure. He Keung feels resilient solidity beneath his back. His limbs are free of the encumbering space suit for the first time in months, protected from whatever environment surrounds him only by the skintight green undersuit he donned before departure from Grand Mao Station.

Shakily, He Keung rises to his feet and gazes about.

He is evidently standing on a smallish world, for the very curvature of the globe is half perceivable, the horizon oddly close. The ground beneath his booted feet is irregular in a natural manner, but covered with a kind of uncanny springy mouse-gray turf composed of long interlocking cilia finer than the downy hairs of a woman's back. The sky above his head is a cloudless violet, with the brighter stars of the Milky Way shining through, where the Mars light permits. The air he breathes is redolent of novel proteins and pheromones.

Incredible as it may seem, He Keung can draw but one conclusion. He is standing on one of the satellites of Mars, either Phobos or Deimos. He takes a tentative step, and the bounciness of his stride supplies another confirming datum. But how came the airless, barren moon known to science for centuries to host an entire ecology and atmosphere, however primitive? Is the change so recent that terrestrial telescopes have not yet detected it? Or if they have done so, why were He Keung and his comrades not informed of this miracle? Can it be that their masters do not want them to know of such a crucial change in their destination? Would the taikonauts hesitate to deliver their putative cargo of WMDs if they knew in advance they were bombing a living world?

He Keung can only assume that this enlivening of the formerly dead satellite is a result of cosmic machinations by Wu Yuèhai and her unseen peers in the Martian community, and possibly by their mentors, the Tian Shi Yu, the Jade Angels. This satellite must have been set up as an anteroom to the glories of the Red Planet, a kind of quarantine chamber for imperfect visitors. Realizing this, he regards the hovering bulk of Mars with altered sensibilities. Now the planet looks like a monitoring eyeball or the working end of a telescope, sucking in data to be processed by the no-longer-human minds that dwell there.

Have He Keung's cabin mates also been deposited here? If so, why were they not all three dumped side by side? Is it intended that He Keung rest alone for a moment to muster his energies and willpower for some upcoming competition? These must be the "different circumstances" into which Wu Yuèhai promised to transplant him, the arena in which he must decide whether to slaughter Huang Shen and Wang Yu, according to her instructions, to earn celestial merit and her undying love.

Or his place in hell.

He Keung realizes that he can advance no further in his destiny until he reunites with his two comrades, whether they be fellow humans or an antagonistic species. Since every direction appears identical, He Keung sets off on an arbitrary vector.

It is his own Long March, his trudge toward some kind of goal shrouded now but only by his ignorance. All he can hope is that his ignorance will dissipate as he trudges and so He Keung stumbles across the slick panels of the Moon (Deimos or Phobos? he cannot know; very well, he will call it Mao and claim it in the name of the People's Army) feeling all of the elements of his life to this moment impelling him, dragging him through this strange, expressionless landscape.

The repetitive muted squelch of his boots upon the living carpet of Mao falls into a metronomic rhythm, lulling He Keung slightly, despite the toxic, the absolute, strangeness of it all. At one moment in the capsule his companions on either side of him, at the next the strange and intimate discourse with Wu Yuèhai, the breath of her confession, her shocking revelation, as shocking as the landscape of Formosa must have been for the evil and exiled Chiang Kai-shek in those early, frantic, wonderful days of the Revolution, and then to the asteroid itself, no transition: truly the *Little Red Book* was filled with alerts of a world gone suddenly incomprehensible and threatening . . . but still the experience is overwhelming.

And then also there is He Keung's sense of shame and failure, his betrayal of his glorious mission. He feels like Su Qin, the "criss-cross philosopher" of the Warring States Era, returning in defeat to his native Luoyang, going back home in despair and rags, having spent all his resources fruitlessly. Is it possible he can ever atone for his moment of doubt and indecision in the *Radiant Crane*, can somehow salvage his mission?

The lonely man pushes forward across the unvaryingly desolate landscape for hours. His mind begins to drift back to his childhood, his early manhood, the time spent on his grandfather's farm, when everything seemed so certain and straightforward. Half dreaming, He Keung continues to lift and plant one foot after another, until he is brought to an abrupt halt by a voice at once anticipated and dreaded.

"He Keung," Wu Yuèhai says out of the empyrean. Her voice is intimate, confidential, as if she were resting her chin on his shoulder, and yet there is that iciness as well; that glaze of distance that has always surrounded her, even in life. "You are not doing well. You are set upon a course of betrayal, betrayal of the true cause of all humanity. You must cease your impetuousness, you must think."

"Think?" he says, speaking the word into the violet atmosphere, and, in sudden, lurching panic, "What is there to think? I am here because of what you have done to me. I was in the *Radiant Crane* dreaming, then you spoke to me, then I was dislodged. What do you want?"

Wu Yuèhai says something so shocking that He Keung feels his frail senses waver, the small lamp of his sensibility, of his struggling intellect, which once seemed able to cast some light on this wretched moon, seeming to gutter and die.

"I want nothing," she says. "I failed in my mission, don't you understand? Now I am reduced to searching here, searching there, looking for you to bring this to an end. The Martians, my Martians, cannot help me. They say that I have been corrupted, that I have chosen the path of an exile, allowing my memories of mere flesh and blood existence to contaminate my proper relationship with you. What I should have done, by their ethical standards, was to assume control of your neural structures in the *Radiant Crane* and forced you to carry out my wishes. But I could not bring myself to damage in such a fashion one whom I . . . respected.

"And so I unbalanced the Tao, they claim, and their words have disarmed me. I cannot help myself because I have lost all belief. It is there for you then to change or it cannot be at all."

Wu Yuèhai as desolate as He Keung? Herself bereft of her comrades' trust? All her seemingly godlike powers rendered impotent by some breaching of the finer parameters of her arcane assignment, by mission creep that came to include sympathy and empathy and—and affection?—for a young taikonaut who once worshipped her? He Keung would like to believe this, but cannot rid his mind of the suspicion that this confession is merely another strategem to ensure his cooperation. So his response to Wu Yuèhai is rather formal and chilly, tepid as the noodle soup young He Keung would eat upon his midnight return home from his university cram courses.

"And what kind of end do you want?"

"It does not matter to me; what matters is that I be at last permitted to sleep. They promised me sleep; they said that if I made my appeal, if I stayed to mark the truth no matter how painful, I would be permitted to move on to another plane, where life is effortless and uncontested. But they were lying. I have no sleep, I have no peace."

As if excited by her intensity the satellite Mao begins to shake, the fibrous panels underfoot surge and heave with the volatility of liquid. He Keung finds himself in perilous balance. Space madness! It must be that ultimate discomfiture of which they had been warned throughout all of the arduous training. The madness which cuts like a knife through all the truisms and teachings of the Great Revolution itself!

"Wu Yuèhai, help me!" calls out the young man alone in the seeming face of imminent destruction, just as, centuries past, the brave warrior Han Xi made his desperate plea prior to the descent of the headsman's ax. And just like Han Xi, who was pardoned at the last moment by a prince eager for brave soldiers, He Keung is saved.

After a complicated fashion.

The surface of Mao blisters upward just a few meters in front of him, the gray tapestry formed by the cilia stretching to cover the new extrusion. It is as if the planet's elastic skin sprouts an immense boil or sarcoma that swells in speeded-up malignancy. This is an objective phenomenon; He Keung is certain of that. In the face of this enormity, all his self-pity and epistemological uncertainty implode. No delusion or hallucination, hence not space madness, but rather the alien workings of a globe rendered intelligently totipotent by the Jade Angels and their unfathomable technology.

The blister ceases its exponential growth when it is as large as a peasant's cottage. Then a portion of the curved surface facing He Keung melts away, revealing a cavern, a wetly crimson interior that is a mockingly obscene echo of the dry russet planet hanging above as mute witness.

And inside the hollow blister stand Huang Shen and Wang Yu, his fellow taikonauts. They stand, but not unsupported, instead hanging like puppets. They are wired into the substance of the blister by numerous living tendrils and conduits, neural bundles piercing them like the claws of a sky dragon. Surely this is their unmerited punishment, imposed by Wu Yuèhai for daring to approach Mars, the sanctuary of the Jade Angels.

"Wu Yuèhai!" shouts He Keung. "What have you done? Release my friends!"

The voice of the martyred female taikonaut whispers despondently in He Keung's ear. "This is not my doing. Rather, it is the end of all hope."

As if to confirm the woman's speech, Huang Shen now speaks, his pinched bookkeeper's face bearing a malicious leer incommensurate with any real suffering.

"Your ghostly bitch is correct, He Keung. Wang Yu and I have assumed control of this construct, the moon you once called Deimos. We found the supervisory ganglia exactly where the Jade Angels always install them. They are such trusting creatures, so intent on making it easy for their subordinate races to adopt and work their puny gifts. But this time their mania for standardization has betrayed them. We have made a long and diligent study of these so-called Angels and their technologies, across a thousand thousand solar systems, until we know them better than they know themselves. For any race that limits itself to only half the spectrum of existence—that which is conventionally called goodness—cannot, by definition, understand as much as another race, one that spans the whole continuum of motivation and desire, from light to dark."

He Keung is nearly dumbstruck. At last he babbles out, "But, but—what are you? What have you done with my comrades?"

Wang Yu speaks like a jolly demon. "We are still your same comrades in truth, He Keung, but we were always more than you knew. Our kind is called the Shih Chieh Hsien."

The Bodiless Immortals. Only an ancient myth—or so He Keung has always believed.

"The birth-souls of your fellows," continues Wang Yu, "were driven out years ago by the force of our superior *qi,* to perish howling in the aether. We used their bodies as we have used many in the past, as meat machines to accomplish our goals. In this case, we always intended to crush the beachhead established by the Jade Angels in this solar system. We have enjoyed unimpeded rule of your primitive sphere too long to relinquish it now. Therefore, Mars must be destroyed."

"What do you intend?"

Huang Shen makes an answer, quite forthrightly and unconcernedly, as if He Keung were a child being told the reason why grass is green. "This modified satellite possesses powerful engines. We will drive the whole globe now out of orbit and into the Red Planet, creating a world-shattering cataclysm such as that which, eons ago, wiped ninety-nine percent of life off Earth itself. The colony of the hybrid Martians will be extinguished; all individuals no matter where or how concealed will be destroyed. Including your precious Wu Yuèhai. These mortal containers temporarily housing our essences will of course be evaporated as well, along with yourself. But our essential selves will simply be released back into the Tao."

The Tao! The Jade Angels! The Bodiless Immortals! Celestial layers upon layers! It is of such enormity to He Keung that he feels the cosmos or at least this small part of it to which he has been sentenced lurch. Meat machines! All of the curses of the Ancients seem to have descended upon him through this sudden and shocking confidence, and He Keung, his legs like his soul seemingly encased in cement, finds himself unable to move. He stands helpless before Huang Shen's valediction waiting for some awful judgment to descend upon him, to tell him what must come next, but nothing at all happens in this glazed and sudden circumstance.

He Keung realizes he has reached the nadir of his quest. All roads leading either to fulfillment of his original mission or to wholehearted adoption of Wu Yuèhai's imperatives seem barricaded. Within He Keung's heart, mind and soul, all the tugging, tensioned polarities that have kept him ajitter and incapable of decision making resolve into one gaping nullity, a black hole compounded of the impossibility of wisdom in a delimited framework of knowledge and the utterly dire necessity of action.

At this moment of He Keung's inverted satori, Huang Shen and the silent Wang Yu suddenly implode, collapse, as if those hanging puppets had been deflated and with no transition whatsoever they have become are ragged blotches staining the red cavern of the blister with a soup of foul yellow matter.

His nemeses are naught but small, indistinct puddles upon which he glances, and then his perspective shifts, rises toward the ruddy and damaged surface of Mars hanging above, and Wu Yuèhai, returned inexplicably from the exile of her abysmal and despairing silence as He Keung never expected she would or could resurface, says: "Amazing! It is the most ancient, the greatest of powers you have shown! An unflagging warrior's spirit, like that of Su Wu when sent to face the Huns. You have vanquished them!"

The wavering, exultant exclamation of her voice is so unlike that quiet, insidious tone with which she had so movingly tracked her own orbital expiration that He Keung's own spirits are comparably lifted.

"Come with me," she says, "Come with me now before these two perfidious Immortals are reconstituted in some other vessels. On Mars, we shall devise counterschemes that will yet secure this solar system as a bastion of the Jade Angels."

Reconstituted? He Keung, deep in service to the Great Revolution, deep in his fathoming and dedication to the cultural enlightenment which the space program has brought to his country and his life, has never felt as confused as he does at this moment; it is as if he were not a taikonaut but an innocent, somehow stripped of memory and desire, hanging (hanging like a puppet?) within some deep well excavated in the name of the Ancients. He cannot move; movement is beyond him, and yet he can feel some force, perhaps generated by Wu Yuèhai, which flutters at the rim of sensibility and begins to guide him, stumbling, away from the decaying blister and its slimy contents.

"You must hurry!" she is saying, "you must not let this triumph pass; you must be opportune and take the moment," and the shuffling He Keung, lashed by a kind of insistence that he cannot comprehend, stumbles forward, stumbles under the guidance of the more-than-human Wu Yuèhai toward some dim conception of the light.

Is he going to Mars? Has he been granted entrance to the community of transfigured souls whose existence Wu Yuèhai has hinted at, a comity of blissful demigods who, under the tutelage of the Jade Angels, all work toward evolving the plenum to some form of transcendental perfection? Will he make his ascent toward the mythic planet that has for so long fascinated mankind? Or he is instead doomed to shuffle like some broken automaton across the gray plains of Deimos? Can this be some monstrous illusion, some hallucination on the Journey of a Thousand Knives patched into his dying sensorium only to torment him?

He does not know. He cannot know.

How he loved Wu Yuèhai in those hours of dictation of her loss; how he loved the Great Leader in all of the years before that; how, dreaming, he loved the skies and stars when even the issue of the Revolution fell away and it was only he and possibility close and alone in the night.

He takes a step. He takes another step. Something systematic, something greater than he, seems to be guiding. Wu Yuèhai laughs in his ear and it is a laugh both gentle and ferocious, laughter of absolute insistence and yet yielding. Mars, the great Red Planet of dreams, hangs ever lower in the distance. If he could but expand his arm by just a little, if he could just reach a little farther, he would be able to touch that great snare, hanging low like fruit in the heavens. All that he must do is stretch a little farther . . .

Behind the ripe beckoning pomegranate of Mars, misty figures larger than the prominences of the solar flare that killed or metamorphosed Wu Yuèhai now appear, viridian specters whose outlines fluctuate like flames in accordance with some half-sensed cosmic tempo. Are these the Jade Angels, come to assist He Keung in his transition, or only artifacts of his derangement?

Wu Yuèhai says, "And soon, believe me, He Keung, as it did for me as I lay dying all alone, the Earth so near, yet so far, in this darkness everything will appear," and he reaches adamant to embrace her.

Soon.

Soon all will be revealed.

Soon he will be a Martian, too.

IV

Children of André Breton

Surrealism and its offshoots are surely some of the most significant literary inventions of the twentieth century. And science fiction has adapted these narrative strategies to its own goals. Just consider, as one example, how seminal the surreal works of Philip K. Dick or J. G. Ballard are to the development of the genre. But as with any technique, it's easy to overdose on such a dramatically in-your-melting-watchface style. That's why the best such work is generally short.

I hope the following stories hew to that standard of amusing brevity.

As someone raised on the songs of Bob Dylan, I always wanted to title a story "[Yadda Yadda Yadda] 1 & 2." Or maybe it was the Isley Brothers' influence. Who is that lady?!? In any case, the title came first in this instance. Then I had to imagine two blasphemous anecdotes to accompany it. Religious blasphemy is easy, but politically incorrect blasphemy was more fun.

Time-Travel Blasphemies I and II

I

Joe Carpenter had undergone a strict Catholic upbringing: weekly confession; Sunday School till age thirteen; nuns as teachers right through twelfth grade; and then straight to Notre Dame.

It was only natural then that his favorite sexual fantasy should be to imagine himself fucking the Virgin Mary.

Ever since his first wet dream, the original Madonna had been the focus of his sexual longings. As the nuns of Joe's youth frequently referred to themselves as "the brides of Christ," it was an easy step for him to imagine himself "the husband of Mary."

Seeing the *Pietà*, Joe would imagine himself in Christ's place and get a hard-on. Russian icons substituted in the bottom of his underwear drawer for the more traditional copies of *Penthouse*. He made a shameless pastiche of the "Hail Mary," which he would recite mentally whenever he was called on to perform the prayer. It began, "Hail, Mary, full of cum," and went downhill from there.

Quite predictably, Joe's sex life was rather unsatisfactory. Mere mortal women held no delight for him.

Luckily, Joe was a genius. And a driven genius at that. More often than not, being a driven genius allows you to achieve all you *think* you want, with generally bad results. (Just consider, for instance, Thomas Wolfe the Elder and Robert Oppenheimer.)

Joe therefore bent all his talents and intelligence toward building the world's first time machine. With a firm mastery of quantum physics, he soon perfected a tachyonic field modulator small enough to fit into a belt.

Now the belt device was around his waist, under a sackcloth robe. Sandals on bare feet, a pouch of antique coins in his pocket, and Joe was ready.

In less than no time, Joe stood in pre-Christian Judea.

He tracked down Mary's family and found her still a teenager.

From a distance, laying eyes on her for the first time, he had an involuntary spontaneous orgasm and collapsed in a faint.

The next day—speaking the Latin drilled into him at school—he introduced himself to Mary's mother as a prosperous merchant and trader from Rome.

Within a month, he was married to Mary.

For the next few weeks, Joe lived out all his sexual fantasies. Mary was a hot if inexperienced lay. It was heaven.

But then one morning Mary announced: "Josephus—I think I am with child."

Understandably somewhat alarmed, Joe decided then and there to abandon Mary and return to the twenty-first century. He had a hunch that he could relive these weeks whenever he wanted. Here's how Joe saw it: he would arrive so as to intercept his earlier self, kill that self, and then take his place. Over and over, innumerable times, he could murder his earlier doppelganger so that the (n + 1)th Joe could enjoy Mary afresh.

It occurred to Joe—as it probably has to you—that the fact that he himself hadn't been murdered yet by any of these later Joes was a bad sign that his plan had some hidden flaw. But he easily made up some quantum explanation about branching timelines to satisfy himself that his plan was plausible.

"Goodbye, Mary," said Joe, and vanished.

Back in his time of origin, a few twenty-first-century seconds after he had first set out, Joe could be found in his bathroom, enjoying the delights of a modern shower.

As he was toweling himself dry, the doorbell rang.

Joe opened the front door.

It was the Jewish babe he had skipped out on.

And she had her kid with her.

II

Sandra Birkenstock hated men.

Her father had been an abusive bully. Her brother had raped her. Her first husband had been an alcoholic. The president was a warmongering, anti-abortion fanatic.

These seemed good and sufficient reasons to Sandra for her to engineer the extermination of the entire male gender.

So she did.

In her capacity as a biohacker for Merck Pharmaceuticals, Sandra fashioned a lethal virus that attacked only humans with Y chromosomes. It was gruesomely fatal within days of being contracted, and so cunningly wrought that all men would be dead before its mysteries could be unraveled.

Rather selfishly, Sandra had no desire to live through the short-term chaos that was sure to follow her purge. On the other hand, she wanted to see the sane and healthy all-womyn society that was sure to follow the Interregnum.

Her work provided a solution.

After unleashing the indestructible airborne anti-male virus, Sandra injected herself with stasis-inducing nanodevices. These tiny machines would put her into suspended animation for a century, at the end of which period little bioclocks would shut the machines down and she would awake.

The injection was made while Sandra was shivering in a cave high in the Swiss Alps. Here her body would be safe from the social chaos to come. She had taken the precaution of leaving a sealed envelope with the National Organization of Women. The envelope contained the story of what she had done, and how to find her body.

As Sandra's cells shut down, snow drifted over her . . .

Sandra awoke to tropical heat.

Several womyn were bending over her.

They were all sun-bronzed, their features a mix of different races, and they wore only sarongs. They were smiling down at her.

"Welcome, Savioress," said one of the womyn in barely understandable, time-shifted English.

Sandra struggled creakily to her feet. A frond roof was above her head. Glassless windows revealed lush vegetation washed in bright sun. Sea breezes wafted in.

"Where am I?" asked Sandra.

"You are on the Isle of the Blue Conch, and I am Queen Frangipani."

"How did I get here?"

"Your body was recovered by one of the last expeditions to venture north, just before the ice sheets came down."

"Ice sheets? What happened to global warming?"

"The fever which Mother Gaia had, induced by the evil workings of male technoculture? Once industry was abandoned and the atmosphere was cleansed, the ice age that was geologically overdue quickly settled in. All of womynkind now lives in a small belt around the equator. I believe you once called this part of the world 'Polynesia.'"

Sandra could hardly believe what she was hearing. This was not something she had counted on. However, she quickly adjusted to the news. The diminished womyn territory and population was a small price to pay for ridding Gaia of males.

"If you feel well enough," Queen Frangipani said, "we have arranged a feast in your honor."

"Of course," said Sandra. "I am eager to sample your brave new world."

Sandra and her host stepped outside, followed by the other womyn. They were greeted by cheers from the entire population of Blue Conch Isle. Sandra's heart was lifted by the sight of the exuberant womyn.

Down on the sandy beach, a pit full of coals held roasting vegetables. Over another fire, a roasting pig—male, noted Sandra gleefully—turned on a spit.

Some kind of alcoholic beverage began to circulate. Songs and dancing started. Soon, Sandra felt right at home.

After the drink had loosened her inhibitions, Sandra felt free enough to inquire about reproduction.

"Is it by parthenogenesis? Or cloning?"

Queen Frangipani laughed. "Neither, I'm afraid, would be much fun, or very practical to sustain in our low-tech culture. No, you see, before the last laboratories ceased functioning, womyn scientists succeeded in permanently modifying the genome of dolphins to the point where we could mate with them. Of course, all male babies from such unions die immediately, since we are all still latent carriers of your splendid virus."

Sandra gagged on her pork. "You mate with dolphins?"

"Of course. Everyone here had a dolphin father. What troubles you about that? Are they not our equals in Gaia's eyes? Look! I will introduce you to them and you will see."

The Queen signaled for a conch to be sounded. Soon, the water around the beach was thronged with lustful dolphins. The drunken Blue Conchers waded into the shallows and embraced the dolphins. The water began to surge with fucking.

Sandra passed out.

In the morning, she awoke with a wicked hangover. During a breakfast of fruit, she tried to convince herself that the interspecies orgy of the prior night had been a bad dream.

As Sandra was finishing her third banana, the sound of a conch drifted in from far out at sea.

"It's the Pink Conch womyn!" shouted Queen Frangipani. "Queen Jacaranda promised she would try to take the Savioress away from us, but I thought she was only boasting. Quickly! To the canoes!"

Seemingly from nowhere, the tribeswomyn brought out plaited armor, spears, and war clubs. These latter were caked with dried blood, gristle, and tufts of hair.

Queen Frangipani gripped Sandra's arms. "You must come with us. Your mana will ensure victory."

Numbly, Sandra let herself be led away.

Soon the Blue Conch fleet was afloat. The womyn paddled vigorously, chanting imprecations and blood-curdling death threats.

Within minutes, the fleet of the Pink Conchers was sighted.

Queen Frangipani stood up in the prow of the lead canoe, where Sandra sat, too.

"I swear by the Savioress that I will eat your heart, Jacaranda!"

It was then that Sandra noticed for the first time that the Queen's teeth were filed to sharp points.

Leaning over the gunwale, Sandra puked her breakfast.

Screams suddenly sounded. Surely the fleets hadn't engaged yet—

Sandra looked portside.

The ocean floor was rising up through the surface.

No. It was only a whale.

"Orca!" screamed Frangipani. "They have Orca on their side!"

The building-sized mammal opened its immense jaws. It was like looking into a train tunnel.

As Sandra's canoe shot into the whale's gullet, she could only think—

I hope it's a female.

At an SF convention known as Readercon some years ago, the rabble-rouser and avant-popist Larry McCaffrey was hot on a new project. "Paul, I'm going to create an anthology of fiction devoted solely to the O.J. Simpson case. Would you contribute something?" How could I refuse such an outrageous invitation? I wrote the story you're about to read, but the project died stillborn, alas. Nonetheless, Larry was kind enough to include my piece in the Italian edition of one of his books, its first appearance in print, where it doubtlessly mystified and alienated a vast foreign readership.

If you can cast your thoughts back to the day when we were all fixated on this scandal, and recall the various personalities involved, and then summon up memories of some icons from Pop. Lit. 101, you might still enjoy this little jape.

PULP ALIBIS

Pop. 7 Million

Sheriff Fuhrman swung his massive hairy fist into the gut of the unsuspecting tramp—some bottle-blond nancy-boy he had picked up for vagrancy—and felt it connect with the man's backbone. Stepping back with a neat practiced motion to avoid the spew of vomit from the unshaven hobo, Fuhrman began to laugh.

"Told ya that cheap wine wouldn't agree with ya, Kato old son!"

Leaving the crippled bum to wallow in his own filth, Fuhrman swung shut the cell door, twisted the key in the lock, and moved across the tiny jailhouse to his desk. Seated with his booted feet up, a pint of whiskey opened for chugging, he ran through some pleasant options for how to spend the rest of his day.

After he visited the Cowlings ranch and delivered the foreclosure papers, he might take a spin up to ol' Marcia's house. The purty lady lawyer should be home today—warn't nothing scheduled down at the county courthouse, and maybe—hell, no maybes about it!—for sure he'd feed her a little raw turkey neck. Most days she didn't need no convincing anyhow, being randier than an Okie roustabout fresh from a three-week stint in the oil fields with his pocket full of pay. After that little interlude, he could head out to Dogtown, see what action he could stir up among the niggers, Mexes, and white trash who lived there. It had been too long since the last lynching, and there was danger them half-breeds and coons might be getting uppity. No sense letting things get to the point where he'd have to call the Klan up. Most of the boys were getting too old to ride anyhow, and they mostly took queen-size sheets for their robes.

Dropping his feet to the floor with a satisfying thud, adjusting his holster, Sheriff Fuhrman once more thanked his lucky stars for making him the only law in this two-bit town.

Lord knows, it was a dang sight better being on this side of the nightstick than t'other!

O.J. of Melnibone

From behind the golf clubs in the closet, Stormbringer called insistently to him.

"Blood," whined the cursed devil sword in its eerie voice only Prince O.J. of Melnibone could hear. "I need blood!"

Huddled on the couch, hands cupped to his ears, Prince O.J. strove with every ounce of his royal strength to resist the call. Why had he not destroyed the evil instrument of chaos when he had last had a chance, back at the End of Time? Was it his destiny always to lose those he loved to the insatiable maw of the black sword? For days now it had been demanding souls to drink. Preferably the souls of those most beloved by its owner. How much longer could even one of such deep superhuman strengths as he possessed resist the foul urgings of the sentient nigrescent blade?

Concentrate, he must concentrate!

As the last heir to the glory that once was the far-off exotic kingdom of Melnibone writhed on the couch, the phone rang, shattering his single-pointed psychic resistance like a battering ram against a castle's gates.

"Argh!" yelled Prince O.J. "Curse you, Arioch!"

Fumbling the phone off its cradle, Prince O.J. bellowed, "What the fuck is it!"

"Uh, sorry to bother you, sir. This is the limo service. We just wanted to confirm your appointment—"

"Yes, damn you! Eleven tonight!"

Prince O.J. slammed the receiver back down. Then he moved to the closet, opened the door, roughly pushed aside the golf bag.

There lay his sweet doom.

"Ah," whispered Stormbringer in its oily voice, "my old friend. Do we feast tonight?"

Prince O.J. grabbed the sheathed instrument of carnage and strapped it on. Instantly a thrill as of his veins filling with pure essence of poppy surged through him. Once more he knew why he could never part with Stormbringer. Filtered through its presence, the world assumed a clarity of purpose and vision.

"We will feast," agreed Prince O.J. "I have someone in mind—someone quite *special.*"

"Perhaps there will even be another with her," the sword said greedily.

"Naw, I got that bitch so scared she don't *dare* date."

She

At the ornately carved, vine-cloaked entrance to the abandoned temple, O. J. Simpson paused. Pushing back the pith helmet that had protected him from the African sun for the seemingly endless months of his trek into the unexplored interior of the Dark Continent, he stopped to contemplate what he had achieved. No civilized explorer had ever penetrated this far during recorded history! O.J. Simpson was about to become a legend. His name would stand in the history books as a shining example of the heights a man could reach if he followed his dream.

Ending his reverie, pushing aside some vines, O.J. stepped through the ancient portal—

And was snared!

Natives of a peculiar degenerate type (myths O.J. had never countenanced till now referred to them as "mediamen," an apparent reference to their status midway between beasts and humans) quickly bound him up, lifted him off his feet, and carried him through torch-lit tunnels deep underground.

In what appeared to be a throne room of sorts, he was deposited still bound in a stone chair. Weird drums and flutes began to play. And from the shadows stepped—a woman!

But what a woman! Clad only in diaphanous silks and ropes of pearls, she was femininity distilled into its purest essence, regal, imperious, seductive. Moreover, she was a white woman, although bronzed by the sun.

Most strange to find one such here in Africa's heart of darkness.

"So," said the queenly figure in a not unkindly tone, "you have returned to me at last."

"Returned? What do you mean?"

"Ah, my dearest one, don't you recall how, in another life long ago, you were Prince O-ren-thal, and I was your lover, Princess Faye-res-nik. How we pledged eternal troth, even unto death—and beyond! And now here we are, reincarnated and drawn together by the stars."

"Lady, I don't know what you've been smoking, but I don't buy all that New Age hooey."

The woman reared back violently. "Sacrilege! You dare to defy me? Don't you know the name the natives use for me? 'She Who Must Be Obeyed'!

"I shall possess you, body and soul, even if I must reduce you to my slave! Hmmm, let me see. I shall set you a task, one even repugnant to your noble nature, in order to prove the folly of resisting me. What shall it be, what shall it be— Ah, I have it! A murder!"

O.J. fought his bonds without success. He could feel an occult narcotic haze wrapping his normally lucid thought processes, drawing him deeper and deeper into a whirlpool of damnation—

One from which he would be incredibly lucky—even with the assistance of the most highly paid lawyers—ever to emerge.

The Hornet's Sting

One lovely June night, Britt "O.J." Reid, crusading editor and publisher of *The Daily Sentinel*, summoned his faithful manservant, Kato, to his side. Reid sat in the parlor of his mansion (paid for by the honest sweat of his brow and his paper's lucrative advertising income) drinking a healthful glass of that fine California fruit juice, an "addiction" to which had earned him his jocular nickname.

"Kato, have you finished polishing the Black Beauty yet?"

"Yes sir! She's fueled and ready to go!"

"Let's don our costumes and hit the road then! I have news of a malignant sore upon the body of this fair city that needs some of our special kind of surgery!"

"You got it, Boss!"

Soon the Green Hornet—none other than Reid himself; and how his buddies would have been surprised by his transformation! —accompanied by his martial-arts-trained sidekick, Kato, were seated in their astonishing crime-fighting vehicle, a customized ebony Ford Bronco dubbed "Black Beauty."

"So as not to attract undue attention, and also obey the relevant traffic laws, what say I drive us to our destination at approximately ten miles per hour, Boss!"

"Good thinking, Kato! I'll direct you!"

After approximately an hour of easygoing travel, the pair found themselves parked inconspicuously outside a familiar locale.

"But Boss—can this be right? Isn't this your ex-wife's place?"

Emerging from the car and checking his various weapons—gas gun, "stinger"—the Green Hornet replied, "Indeed, Kato. It is with sincere regret that I must spring a perhaps shocking surprise on you. My former wife has seen fit to tread the path of the world's oldest profession. Out of sheer greed, not content with my generous stipends, she has started soliciting weak-willed males for sex. I have no doubt, in fact, that we shall find one such here tonight. In the words of the street-wise, she's now nuthin' but a goddamn ho! And we're going to bring her to justice, much as it might hurt us personally. Unfortunately, lawless times require that we masked avengers take justice into our own hands! Now, here's my plan. I want you to render my wife and any of her 'johns' we discover to be with her unconscious with your dazzlingly swift karate moves. Then leave the rest to me!"

Kato's expression—never that of a brilliant man—now reflected a puzzled acquiescence. "Sure, Boss. Whatever you say."

"Okay! Let's move!"

Within seconds, Nicole Simpson and an unidentified male lay quiet on the stone walkway.

"Very good, Kato! Now, you just go back to the car and polish the head lamps a bit, okay? And oh—make ready the Hornet Handiwipes! I have a feeling I'll be needing them!"

The Dream Life of Ronald Mitty

Driving through the evening after his boring, dreary job was over, Ronald Mitty began to indulge himself in his favorite pastime. The mental cinema of which he was scriptwriter, director, projectionist, and sole audience member started to play.

I'll walk up her front path, suave and cool, pretending I'm not impressed at all by such a fancy place. She'll probably think I live in such swell digs myself! I'll ring the bell, straighten out my uniform—Oh, heck, this uniform! But I had to come straight from work or miss my big chance! Well, the heck with it, all the girls say my butt looks cute in my waiter pants. Where was I? Oh, yeah, right. The door opens, I smile, she says hi, I say hi, then I hold up the sunglasses, maybe twirling them a little on my finger, and say, "Do these look familiar, Mrs. Simpson?" No, wait, that's wrong! How dumb can you get! Miss Brown, that's what I'll call her. Or should it be Ms. Brown-Simpson? Oh, rats! I'll just go with Nicole. "Do these look familiar, Nicole?" "Why, yes, they do! However did you find them? You must be an extremely smart and observant fellow! I'd be absolutely lost without them! Glare of publicity and all, don't you know! Now, how can I possibly reward you?" So I say, "Well, a ginger ale would go down nice about now," and she invites me in, and then we—

The images in Ronald Mitty's brain acquired that peculiar vaporish insubstantiality imposed by the Hays Code at the most interesting moments in the narrative. Forcing himself to concentrate on his driving, Ronald Mitty began to whistle a sprightly tune from the current Hit Parade, congratulating himself all the while on his most excellent good fortune.

Condo of the Damned

The children—if *children* they still were—had been tucked into bed for the night.

But that didn't mean they were *safe*.

Or that anyone was safe from *them*.

Armed with a glass of Perrier to soothe her nerves and wet her nervously parched throat, Nicole Brown Simpson, mother of Sydney and Justin, curled up on the couch in her condo at 875 South Bundy, and prayed that she would survive the night.

Once more, for the umpteenth time, she racked her brains for anything she could have done differently since that fateful morning in Cancun, when her world had come undone. But as always, she could come up with no alternative paths to the ones she had taken.

How *could* she have known on that day—when the children (then still blessedly normal) had come running to her where she lay sunning her lissome form on the beach, happily babbling of their mysterious find—that her life and theirs were about to undergo a precipitous change for the worse?

Sydney and Justin had been so thrilled with their sandy find—a small gold casket, encrusted with barnacles and draped with seaweed—that Nicole had never imagined that anything *dangerous* could be lurking inside it. Then, when her two beautiful youngsters—the beloved products of the wonderful marriage between Nicole and her worshipful, adoring O.J.—had finally cracked the casket open and that horrid cloud of green noxious gas had enveloped them, causing them to fall unconscious for a full twenty-four hours—only then had she shrieked and pulled her darlings away.

But too late. Much too late.

Nicole didn't *care* what the doctors said. The children were *different* now. And not in a pleasant way. Thank God that she had managed to isolate O.J. from the worst of their bizarre new behavior, thanks to the ruse of pretending she wanted to maintain a separate household.

Of late, Sydney's and Justin's unchildlike demands and veiled threats had become nearly overwhelming—

"Mother, we need to talk."

Nicole screamed and launched her nonalcoholic drink in an arc across the room.

Beside her, having crept up quietly as dust, stood the children.

Their eyes glowed in the dimly lit room. Liquid pools of golden fire, the orbs seemed to spin hypnotically in the eye sockets of their once-pleasant mulatto faces.

"Wha—what do we need to talk about?" stammered Nicole.

"Opening the way," said Sydney, age nine, in a voice resonant as a tomb.

"So that more of us may come through," explained Justin, age six.

"It requires blood, you see," Sydney continued. "The blood of a relative and the blood of a stranger."

Before Nicole could deny this horrifying request, the doorbell rang.

"And there's the stranger," said little Justin. "Just in time."

Nicole made to leap up and flee, but was stopped by the paralyzing touch of her possessed daughter.

"Now," said Sydney, "you'll walk outside and pretend nothing's wrong. Keep him talking. We'll be right with you—as soon as we visit the kitchen for the tools we need."

Helpless, silently screaming inside, Nicole did as she was programmed.

Beyond the door stood Ronald Goldman. "Hey, Nicole—do these look familiar?"

Run! Nicole tried to yell. *Save yourself!* But instead of the warning, all that emerged was foolish talk of the dinner she had just enjoyed and her unfelt gratitude for the return of her meaningless property. Moving her visitor outside with talk of not wanting to wake the children (!), Nicole admitted to herself at last that she was a dead woman.

But oh, she selflessly thought a few seconds later as the knives wielded by the small but capable hands of her own children struck and struck again, *how will my poor darling O.J. ever manage all alone?*

Elementary, My Dear Cowlings

"Allow me to recapitulate," said Sherlock Simpson in his familiar ratiocinative, brandy-mellowed, erudite tones. "Then perhaps you shall finally begin to grasp what is so patently obvious, Cowlings."

Seated beside his mentor and friend in a slow-moving horseless carriage now cruising down the turnpikes of southern California, Dr. Cowlings replied in his hearty, bluff, and game manner, "Why,

I'm always absolutely thrilled to listen to you, Simpson. You know that, of course, as you know everything! I've been carefully recording all your deductions and adventures for years now. Why, perhaps there'll even be a book composed of them someday!"

"All beside the point, Cowlings, although I do appreciate your houndlike loyalty. The matter before us now is to ascertain the motives and probable destination of a certain party, based on the contents of his 'getaway' vehicle. We can see, first off, that he has made certain to obtain approximately ten thousand dollars in U.S. currency. A rather large sum, wouldn't you say, for a simple 'visit to the cemetery'? In addition, he carries a weapon, his passport, a map of Mexico, a fake beard, and a year's supply of antivenereal sheaths. Left at home is a maudlin 'suicide' note plainly intended to send the authorities—so tiresomely blinkered, as always—on a wild goose chase. Very well—given all this, what conclusions can you draw, Cowlings?"

Cowlings crinkled his brow in deep cogitation before finally blustering out with a guess. "Why, by Jove, I should say the bounder and cad was fleeing directly for the border and planning never to return, all to avoid prosecution and sentencing for a foul deed he most surely committed!"

"Oh, bravo, Cowlings! Well done! Now, step on it!"

O.J. Stover at Yale

It was the twenty-sixth reunion of the class of '68, held as always in the month of May, so that the "alums" could witness another perennial graduation: in this case the sterling class of '94. From far and near the old school chums had assembled behind the gates of their beloved alma mater, there gleefully to reminisce and gaily disport themselves. It was a sparkling assemblage, for the class of '68 had done well by themselves, fulfilling their youthful promise. Present were lawyers and doctors, judges and politicians, graying executives and their young wives. Yet even amidst such a stellar crowd, one couple stood out.

That former Big Man on Campus, the star Negro football player who had led Yale to its finest four seasons and innumerable trophies, repository of so many hopes and fond memories: Orenthal

James Simpson, accompanied by his beautiful second wife, the Caucasian Nicole Brown Simpson.

These days "O.J." and his wife lived in exotic California, far from the sites of his old East Coast triumphs. Seen constantly on "television" and in the moving picture palaces, his face featured on the covers of national magazines, "O.J." had never been far from the minds and hearts of his old chums. Clustered around this handsome couple now stood a crowd of adoring compatriots offering what amounted almost to worship.

"Can I get you another drink, Nicole?" one gentleman now considerately asked Mrs. Simpson.

"Sure, sweetie," replied "O.J.'s" spouse in a charmingly slurred voice perhaps in vogue on the West Coast.

"No, she's had enough," interpolated "O.J." "Haven't you, dear?"

"Fuck, no!" countered Mrs. Simpson. "In fact, I'm ready to do a few lines! Who's holding here? C'mon, don't be selfish!"

"Hey, 'O.J.'," queried one rapscallion, "where'd you get this slut?"

"Any more like her at home?" chimed in another banterer.

"Slut?" echoed the furious "O.J." "Who're you calling a slut?" The burly ex-pigskinner now thrust his hand between Mrs. Simpson's legs so as to cup her loins. "See this! This belongs to me! This is where my children come from!"

In a similar joshing manner, Mrs. Simpson now tossed the contents of her glass in her husband's face. "Pig! Bastard!"

Displaying the same gridiron panache with which he had broken through many a defensive line, "O.J." silenced his wife with a deft backhand, knocking her to the floor. Bending down as if to raise her, he ejaculated sotto voce, "You shamed me, you whore! Just wait till we get home! You're gonna pay big time!"

Mrs. Simpson only whimpered.

U.F.O.J.

Blissfully asleep in his home, O.J. was snared by the tractor beam of the mother ship. Drawn through his bedroom window and upward through the night sky, his pajama-clad form rigid as a board, he would have presented an incredible sight to any witnesses—save that the Men in Black make sure there are *never* any witnesses to such abductions.

Through the opened iris of the saucer-shaped ship ringed with multicolored lights he was guided, finally to rest upon an examination slab, the focus of scores of mysterious instruments. Attenuated, nakedly gray-skinned, big-eyed forms emerged from the depths of the ship to cluster excitedly around their captive.

Now the various probes were inserted and samples taken. The E.T.'s huddled together, examining holographic displays and twittering musically. Returning to their patient, they proceeded to make the Changes.

After a time, when O.J. had been sealed up again, he was levitated off the slab, out the port, and back to his bed, all while it was still dark.

In the morning he awoke normally and stretched vigorously. "Damn, that was a solid night's sleep! But those dreams! Crop circles, man! Never dreamed of any crop circles before! Hell, I even think there was something in there about cattle mutilation!"

The Limo Driver Always Rings Twice

Paula Barbieri, widowed owner of a little juke joint halfway between LA and Vegas known as the Playboy Lounge, sauntered into the kitchen where her hired hand, a young, naïve lad known as O.J. Simpson, was busy sweeping the floor. It was June, the desert was brutally hot, and Barbieri's thin cotton dress was pasted to the wicked curves of her sweaty body like the shirt on a drowned man's chest. She fanned herself with a sheaf of fifty-dollar bills, licked her lips, and purred, "What's a girl to do with herself when there's no customers in sight for miles, it's so damn hot all you can do is lie naked in bed, and the only person with her is a handsome stud?"

O.J. stopped lashing the floor with the corn bristles and regarded his employer grimly. "Miss Barbieri, I wish you'd tone down your language and lewd ways a trifle. I can't be responsible for my actions much longer, if you keep on torturing me this way."

Flinging the wad of cash aside, Barbieri hurled herself at the boy.

With her arms draped around his neck, grinding her nubile form against him, she raved like a madwoman. "*Don't* be responsible! Take me! What do I have to do to break down your honest and moral nature? Oh, damn the day I ever fell in love with an ethical man!"

O.J. unpeeled the temptress from him. "Ma'am, you know I didn't have no ulterior motive in taking this job. It was the only one I could find, times being so tough and all. And I need it! I'm trying to support an ex-wife back home—"

Barbieri jumped away from her prey like a tiger in reverse, vehemently spitting out, "So! That's it! You're still in love with her! Admit it!"

O.J. glanced shyly at the floor, blushed, and dug the tip of one shoe into the boards. "Well, maybe a little . . ."

"But if she were out of the picture," Barbieri continued, musing out loud, "then I'd have you for myself!"

O.J. came alert. "Nothing better happen to that sweet little girl, or I swear—"

"Do you know, honey," cooed the viperish Barbieri, "the penalty for rape in this state? All I have to do is lodge a complaint, and your ass is grass!"

O.J. fell to his knees, wailing, "Oh, Lord, what have I gotten myself into?"

Barbieri grabbed her hapless victim's head by his hair and pulled his face against her throbbing loins. "There, there, baby, let Mama handle everything—"

The Puppetmasters

Wandering in its aimless canine way, sniffing the familiar pavements, the Akita named Kato strayed under the low-hanging branches of a tree, little realizing what deadly creature lurked patiently above.

In those branches hung a deadly parasite not of this world. A protoplasmic tendriled mass the size of a football, it was equipped with a cunning intelligence dedicated to the conquest of this new globe.

Now it dropped down with a squishy plop onto the furry back of the dog. Kato yelped and bolted, but it was too late. Tendrils burrowed into its spinal cord, and thence to its brain.

Now the dog was under complete alien control!

Tapping the animal's memories, the Puppetmaster guided it home.

Standing in the secluded walkway were two figures.

Not good, thought the Puppetmaster. The humans would never let their dog access the television, computer, or phone! And the young Puppetmaster was not yet mature enough to handle a human host.

No, there was only one solution.

"Hey, Nicole, shouldn't your dog be inside?" said one of the humans.

"Why, how did he ever get loose? Here, Kato! Come to Mama!"

Kato began to trot. When he was within range, letting loose a savage growl, he leaped!

At their throats!

The Wiles of Lance Manchu

Tied to a chair in the dim, dank basement of a sushi factory in the heart of Los Angeles's mysterious and impenetrable-to-Occidentals Japtown, the valiant O. J. Simpson could only squirm helplessly. Beside him in a precisely identical fix—save for the added fillip of having been beaten unconscious—slumped his sidekick, Nayland Kaelin.

"Drat!" exclaimed O.J. "If only those thugs hadn't taken my pocket jackknife away, there might be some hope. But as things stand—"

From behind O.J. came a voice rich in Oriental menace to complete his thoughts.

"But as things stand, Honorably Despised O.J.-san, you and your precious friend have reached the end of the line!"

From the crepuscular shadows now stepped that most dreaded archvillain, bane of the world's law-enforcement systems, perpetrator of innumerable arcane crimes and plots, a figure to strike terror into the hearts of the superstitious—Lance Manchu!

"Lance Manchu!" ejaculated O.J. "I knew it had to be you behind this kidnapping! No one else could have been so devilishly clever! Imagine luring the two of us to that hamburger joint with the anonymous tip that offered the promise of breaking up a drug-smuggling ring! What fiendish scheme have you in mind now?"

Rubbing together his long-nailed yellow hands, Lance Manchu

smiled like a cream-fed feline, contorting his pitiful facial hair along repugnant leer-lines.

"Oh, not much, my good sir. Simply the end of your career as a thorn in my side. After I'm done with you, you'll perhaps wish I had killed you outright!"

"You demon! What unnatural doings are afoot?"

"Oh, nothing too complicated or bizarre, my old enemy! I have simply sent some highly reliable assassins to visit your wife. And with them they carry your jackknife! With your fingerprints upon it! Some of her blood will find its way back to your vehicle and domicile. A certain detective on the force is also in my pay. With all these factors, I think you'll be lucky to avoid the electric chair and merely spend the rest of your life behind bars!"

O.J. rocked furiously back and forth in his chair, his enormous muscles straining to no avail against his bonds. Curiously, his first words were not a plea of mercy for his beloved Nicole. "Gosh darn you, Lance Manchu! You won't succeed! No jury would believe such a circumstantial case in the face of my reputation and character!"

Lance Manchu seemed unfazed by O.J.'s assertion. "Perhaps not. But you'll certainly spend months and millions defending yourself. At the end, you'll be a broken shadow of your old self. And I—I shall be unstoppable!"

The insidious slant-eyed underworld mastermind turned to leave. "By the time you and Kaelin succeed in freeing yourselves, you'll be a wanted man!"

With a flourish of his black robes and a peal of chilling laughter, Lance Manchu disappeared through a secret door that closed behind him.

Subsequent to the departure of the evil archcriminal O.J. seemed to relax, as if dropping a pose. "We'll see who laughs last, Lance baby!" the redoubtable O.J. exclaimed to the stone wall. "Oh, and thanks for saving me the trouble of wasting the old ball-and-chain!" Then, with a smile, our hero settled back to await his freedom.

For years, the gifted SF writer Carter Scholz was rumored to be working on a novel to be titled, simply, Science Fiction. *I envisioned this unborn masterpiece as a kind of* Miss Lonelyhearts *of the genre, akin to some of Barry Malzberg's riffs on the sad and lonely life of the SF writer. When Carter finally told me that the project was dead, I knew the title, in all its stark allusiveness, was too good to let die. When asked by Claude Lalumière and Marty Halpern for a contribution to* Witpunk, *their anthology of black-humored, satirical SF, I realized I had found the perfect home for my diminutive take on Carter's abandoned masterpiece. How I decided to attach the style and tone of one of my favorite mainstream writers, J. P. Donleavy, to this tale is less clear in memory. But I think the combination of subject matter and angle of attack work well.*

SCIENCE FICTION

Pissing warily but with immense somatic relief in one of the ill-maintained and rather frightening rest rooms at Penn Station. And Corso Fairfield blissfully directs his golden urine into the commodious porcelain basin. Distilled from several cups of tedious Amtrak coffee. While trying not to eyeball the spectacle around him. Motivated not by anti-homosexual anxiety. Certainly not a prejudice found in Corso's liberal soul. But rather a discretionary maneuver directed at the homeless men. Who throng the room, with its scatter of smudged, wet paper towels across the tiled floor. Washing their feet in the sink. And other even less savory parts.

Corso finishes his own noisy voiding. And replackets his penis. Certainly nothing special, and in no wise superior to the members of the surrounding indigents. But indisputably all his own. Yet regrettably not likely to be shared with any female. Since his wife, Jenny, left him. Eloping with his exceptional car mechanic. Jack Spanner. A double loss. And hard to quantify the ratio of injury between bedroom and garage.

But his lonely penis is now safe. Behind the sturdy zipper of his best pants. Donned this morning back home, several hundred miles northward. With a white shirt and camphor-smelling wool jacket suitable for meeting editors. And agents. And his bosom pal

Malachi Stiltjack. That rich bastard. And also an ensemble entitling one to enter fine restaurants. For expense-account meals. Moreover and finally, pride-enhancing when encountering with unfeigned glee any of one's public. Adoring public. Who should chance to recognize one from dustjacket photos. However unlikely. Granted his small and undemonstrative readership. Which, one must forever believe, is always just on the verge of growing exponentially.

The problem of washing one's hands. When bums barricade the sinks. Corso hesitates, shifting his soft modern satchel from hand to socially unsanctioned postmicturating hand. When one of the mendicants departs. Leaving the taps running. So that one does not even have to touch them. Saving one from contact with numerous New York–mutated germs too vile to mention.

At the sink. Satchel secured between pincering knees. Pumping some opalescent soap the shade of cheap rosé wine into a palm. Lathering up. While one's elflock-bearded, multishirted neighbor to the right is balanced on one bare foot. The other unshod appendage embasined. Caked absolutely black with street grime. Causing Corso to flinch inwardly. But his initial reaction is mild. Compared to the emotions that flood him as the foot comes clean. For the foot is not human. By any stretch of even Corso's trained imagination.

Putrid water runnels down the trap. Depriving the scrubbed foot, like a fish stick denuded of crust, of its concealing coating. Revealing something that looks like an ostrich's appendage. Hard yellow-ringed bony digits. Terminating in claws. That could disembowel one with a kick. And a spur above the ankle. Also potentially lethal.

Falling back from the sink. Dripping soapy water on one's best pants. Knock-knee'd as one strives valiantly to prevent the satchel from dropping to the contaminated floor. And now the bum with the avian foot taking umbrage. At such evident revulsion. So ungentlemanly expressed.

"Hey, dude, what's your problem?"

Corso seeking suitable words for a polite response. But unable to link any placatory syllables together in his confusion. So as finally to mutter bluntly only, "Your foot."

The bum regarding his elevated foot, sunk still below Corso's new line of sight in the fount. So recently laved of its dirt disguise.

To reveal the underlying otherness. "Okay, so it ain't pretty. But Jesus, you'd think I was some kinda alien, way you jumped."

Which of course is the exact dilemma. Only it is no longer. A dilemma.

For the homeless stranger has removed his foot from its bath. And now the instrument of Corso's disconcertment is revealed to be fully anthropomorphic. Scabbed, cracked, and horny-nailed, yes. But otherwise unremarkable.

Corso recovers. As well as possible. "I am exceedingly sorry. Please accept this donation toward the future care and refreshment of your foot."

Corso tenders a five-dollar bill. Retrieved from pants pocket. The retrieval having somewhat dried at least one hand. In a manner most unbecoming to his best pants. Which now exhibit a damp stain. Much too close to the groin.

"Gee thanks pal."

"Think nothing of it."

Paper towels from the dispenser complete Corso's ablutions. Although some slight stickiness of soap remains. Not wholly rinsed in the confusion. He turns to depart. Cannot resist one last backward glance. And sees the bum re-donning a tattered sock. Which piece of clothing features a hole strategically placed. To allow a spur to protrude.

Corso shakes his head. He should have expected some visitation of this nature. For this is not the first time reality has played the deceitful trull with him.

> And when he's asked again
> what his problem is
> he will lay all blame
> squarely yet perhaps unfairly
> on his profession
> of science fiction.

Twenty years now. Two decades of writing science fiction. And before that, naturally. Two prior decades. Of reading it. Subsisting in youth on an exclusive diet. Of pulp adventures. Sophisticated extrapolations. Space operas, dystopias, and technological fantasies. Millions of words that shaped his worldview. Ineluctably. Like so many hands molding raw clay into an awkward shape. And baked him. In a kiln fueled with paraliterature. So that ever afterwards no other kind of fiction would make any real impress. On the pottery of his mind.

Then came the adolescent dream. Forgotten circumstances of its birth. Lost in the mists of his SF-besotted youth. But quickly becoming an omnipresent urge. To write what he loved. Despite no one's inviting him to do so. In fact, barring the gates. With shotguns cradled across the chests of the genre guardians. The hard years of apprenticeship. Hundreds of thousands of words. Laboriously composed. Read and rejected. By hardhearted editors. Who emitted the mustard gas of their dreadful intelligence. To paraphrase Ginsberg. And proving Corso Fairfield could quote. From someone other than Asimov, Bradbury, or Clarke. The ABC's of the genre. Superseded by newer names, surely. Yet still talismanic to ignorant outsiders.

Improvement by micro-degrees. Understanding himself better. And what made a story. Tools honed. Finally his first sale. Ecstasy soon replaced by despair. At the realization of how hard this path was going to be. Yet not relenting. Further sales. To better markets. Then a book contract. For a novel titled *Cosmocopia*. Which allowed him to leave the day job. Managing an independent bookstore-cum–Bavarian beer garden. Named with dire whimsy. Chapter and Wurst.

And Jenny so supportive throughout. Married straight out of college. Ever faithful. Rejoicing in his eventual success. Even attending various conventions. Unlike most SF spouses. Who would all rather undergo tracheotomies with spoons. Than meet the odd-shaped and weirdly intelligent readers whose necessary and even lovable support underpinned the books. Not to mention encountering disgruntled and jaded peers. Deep in their cups. Looking up from below the liquor with the hapless expressions of drowning victims.

And a future that seemed to stretch ahead fairly brightly, albeit labor-intensively. Until Corso's recent blockage. Due to massive failure of suspension of authorial disbelief. In one's own conceptions. And vision. And even chosen medium. And the advance for the overdue project already long spent. On septic-tank replacement, a trip to Bermuda, and a new transmission. Putting some of Corso's unearned future royalties for *The Black-Hole Gun* directly into the pockets of the treacherous Jack Spanner. Who had been eagerly present to rescue Jenny when she jumped the Federation Starship *Corso Fairfield*. When it was beset by the mind-parasites of Dementia VII.

The first hallucination occurred at the supermarket. A watermelon developed a face. A jolly face, but nonetheless unnerving. And began talking to Corso. Who failed to heed the import of the melon's speech. So fixated was he on the way that parallel rows of black seeds formed the teeth in the pulpy mouth. Doubtless the melon had had much to say. Words that might have given Corso some guidance. During future outbreaks.

Needless to say, Corso did not share this vision with Jenny. But subsequent manifestations proved less easy to conceal. Since Jenny was present. Staring in shock. As Corso attempted to open a door that wasn't there. In the sidewalk. In front of the local multiplex theater. On a busy Saturday night. And other peculiar delusions at other times as well. Until she reached her breaking point. And fled.

Corso felt curiously unfearful of these eruptions. Of surrealism. And dire whimsy. Granted, they were momentarily shocking at times. When he was taken by surprise. His mind elsewhere. As with the bird-foot man. But once engaged with each new derangement, for however long it persisted, Corso felt a decided sense of liberation. From duties and expectation. From his own persona. From consensus reality.

> And what more
> after all
> did any reader
> of science fiction
> demand.

The offices of *Ruslan*'s *Science Fiction Magazine*. Low-rent quarters on lower Broadway, parsimoniously leased by the parent corporation. Klackto Press. And shared with the publishing chain's stablemates. *Fishbreeder's Monthly*, *Acrostic Fiend's Friend*, *Tatting Journal*. One receptionist for all the wildly incompatible magazines.

A bored young woman with a scatter of freckles. Across acres of exposed cleavage. A vista that stirs Corso's penis in its hermitage. But like any solitary's spasm, the moment inevitably passes without relief.

"Um, Corso Fairfield for Sharon Walpole. She's expecting me."

"Hold on a minute please. I'm right in the middle of printing."

Corso sits perforce. Resting his satchel across his damp lap. In case of renewed lust attack. As the woman dances her enameled fingertips noisily across her keyboard. Generating finally some activity in the printer beside her. Corso painfully reminded of his own vain attempts recently to coerce output magically from his own printer. The buffers of which hold not the unborn chapters of *The Black-Hole Gun*. But only pain.

Picking up the phone. Reaching Sharon Walpole. Humiliatingly, from the receptionist: "What did you say your name was." Name conveyed to receptionist again and thence to Walpole. Grudging admittance secured.

Through a busy bullpen of interns and editorial assistants and graphic designers. Photos of loved ones on the desks. Free donuts by the coffee urn. Happy chatter. All workers earning a regular paycheck. With regular health-coverage deductions, unthinkingly groused over. Yet so willingly would they be assumed by Corso. In exchange for some stability.

The view from Walpole's cluttered corner office. A wooden rooftop water tank. A ghost sign for Nehi soda. A sliver of one stalwart tower of the Brooklyn Bridge. Walpole behind her desk. Hugo Awards on a shelf behind her. Trim and blonde. Dressed in a mustard-colored pantsuit. Chunky gold necklace and earrings and bracelets. Fixing Corso with a beam of bright-eyed welcome. Behind which is the message. DON'T WASTE MY TIME.

"Corso, it's always a pleasure." Air kisses. Floral-vanilla scent of perfume. "What brings you into the city."

"Oh, mainly meeting with my editor at Butte Books."

"That would be Roger Wankel."

"Yes, Wankel." Inwardly, Corso winces. At the memory. Of the recent reaming out endured over the phone. As Wankel screamed about missed deadlines. And penalties incurred at the printing plant. Which would accrue to Corso's accounts. If not literally, then karmically.

"And of course I need to touch base with my agent."

"Clive Multrum."

"Still, yes. And it's very likely I'll have dinner with Malachi."

No need for a last name. Since everyone in science fiction knew Malachi Stiltjack. Fixture on the best-seller lists. And at many conventions. And on a number of committees. Of the Science Fiction Writers of America. And PEN. Not to mention adjudging many awards. Or making media appearances. As SF's unofficial ambassador to the mundane world. To discuss cloning. Or the Internet. Or virtual sex. And by God, where did he find the time to write.

Walpole positively frisking at the mention of Stiltjack. Disconcertingly girlish timbre to her voice now. "Oh please give Malachi my best. Ask him when he'll have something new for us. We haven't seen anything from him since he had the cover story two whole months ago."

"Ah, certainly, Sharon. Two whole months. Imagine." Corso's last appearance in *Ruslan's* so long ago the millennium has since rolled over. "Happy to act as go-between, ha-ha. Which actually brings me to the reason for my visit. I was hoping you might take something from me."

Walpole begins fidgeting with a bracelet on her left wrist. "Well, of course we're always happy to look at any story of yours, Corso. After all, our readers are still talking about 'The Cambrian Exodus.' But I didn't think you were currently working at shorter lengths. Do you have the manuscript with you."

"Ah, but that's the rub. I don't. Damnable oversight. Dashing from the house to catch my train. In fact, the story's only just begun. It's a winner, though. I'm certain of it." Corso's fugitive mind has blanked on the impressive title he earlier prepared to woo Walpole. Now he has to fashion one out of thin air. He looks desperately out the window. "'The Towers— The Towers of Nehilyn.'"

Walpole spins one bracelet on her left wrist. Evident excess of impatience. Corso finds it hard to focus. On her unsympathetic face. The golden motion around her wrist is seductive. The bracelet a blur of uncanny energy. He feels the beginning of a fugue. Onset of one of his science-fictional hallucinations. But the prospect of visiting an unreal world is seductive. More enticing than this humiliating begging ritual.

Walpole speaking schoolmarmishly. "Well, you know we hardly ever commission anything, or buy from an outline. You do have an outline to show me at least, don't you."

"An outline. Not with me, alas. How foolish. Forgotten likewise at home. But if you could signal your faith with, um, a contract, or even a check perhaps, I'd email the whole project folder on Monday. Very extensive notes. World-building, in fact. Equal to Anderson or Clement."

Sharon Walpole stands up now. And is plainly unscrewing her hand. Corso fully embracing the revelation. Of Walpole's cyborg nature. The bracelet revealed as not jewelry, but as the rim of some prosthetic fixture. And now the threaded extension is disclosed. Shiny metal. Reminding one of such familiar terms as "plastalloy" and "durasteel." And the corresponding threaded hole into her forearm. And Corso is fixated by the dismantling. Overly intimate dismantling. His lower jaw drops further. For now the hand is detached. And the editor lays it upon the desk. Like a fleshy paperweight. And reaches into a drawer. To come up with a substitute hand. A giant lobster claw. Bright red. Which she starts to attach.

And all the while talking. "Corso, I'm afraid I can't help you. Your lateness with your novel for Butte is already a scandal. And such a track record does not inspire confidence. There's no way I can advance the good money of Klackto Press on such a tenuous project."

The lobster claw is firmly seated now. And waving. At the incongruous end of a feminine arm. A hybrid. Of sternness and guile. Which Corso should acknowledge. Except how can he honor in others the commonsensical standards which he never upheld in his own life.

Walpole's voice. Descending into a droning alien monotone. Now Corso's calm begins to dissipate. The fantasy no longer an alluring alternative to his problems. But rather menacing, in fact.

"Send me the story. Send me the story. Then we'll see. Then we'll see." And the claw looming larger and larger. Audibly clattering. Directly in Corso's wide-eyed blood-drained face.

And then he's scuttling backward
out of the office,

> the building,
> into the streets,
> thinking only
> of the giant pot one would need
> to boil a crustacean that big.

Lines of office workers at hot-dog and falafel and gyro carts. With nothing on their mundane minds. Save mortgage payments, love affairs, television shows, shopping sprees, and ferrying hordes of overindulged children from event to event. No obsessions with intergalactic ambassadors. Nor fifth-dimensional invaders. Nor the paradoxes of time travel. Only solid, sensible quotidian activities concern them. The eternal verities. Home and family. Sex and status. Untainted with abnormal speculations derived from technological angst. Of sense of wonder. They know naught. They flip the wall switch for the overhead light. And never think. About the infrastructure behind the scene. And why should they really. That's what engineers are for.

Corso's stomach rumbling. Yet he turns reluctantly from the line of vendors. Why purchase a cheap lunch. If Clive Multrum will stand him to a meal. And doesn't his agent owe him that much. For the monies earned by *Cosmocopia*. Which was a Featured Selection. Of the Science Fiction Book Club. And optioned by a Hollywood studio. Named Fizz Boys Productions. Which proved to be two ex–parking lot attendants from LA. Temporarily flush with profits from an exceedingly large Ecstasy deal. And with no more realistic chance of actually making a film. Than two orangutans fresh from the jungles of Kalimantan. And by the time their option expired. Interest in *Cosmocopia* was dead. And another flavor of the week was all the rage. Probably something by Stiltjack.

Multrum's building on Park Avenue South. Classier by far than the *Ruslan's* quarters. Concierge in a Ruritanian uniform. Your name, sir. May we inspect your briefcase, sir. Multrum and his peers here obviously a prime target. For enraged terrorists. Eager perhaps to avenge injustices against disenfranchised writers. Of whom Corso is certainly one. But he manages to disguise his true affiliations from the vigilant guardian. A fat sixtyish man with a dandruff-flecked comb-over. Who directs Corso to the elevators.

Eleventh floor. Corridor with doors to numerous suites. Into number 1103, anticipatorially unlocked upon notification by the admiral downstairs. Impeccable furnishings. Rugs from Araby and Persia. Paintings by artists as yet unknown outside New York. Yet inevitably destined for fame and fortune. Such is Multrum's unerring taste. Leather couch. Wet bar. Bookshelves holding hundreds of titles by Multrum's clients. Looking like some Hollywood set designer coordinated them. *Cosmocopia* on the lowermost shelf, partly shadowed.

Multrum's personal assistant emerging from the back. Well known by Corso. And likewise. An imperturbable Korean woman. Soberly dressed in black linen. Flat face and hair so jet-dark it should be sprinkled with stars. Named most improbably Kichi Koo. And Corso has always longed to ask her. Did you assume this cognomen deliberately. In some kind of madcap Greenwich Village fit of bohemianism. Or were your parents so blithely cruel. But he never has nor will he. Since Koo has never once so much as cracked a smile in his presence.

"Mr. Fairfield, hello. Mr. Multrum is on the phone presently. But he will see you soon."

"Thank you, ah, Ms. Koo. I believe I will help myself to a drink then. To ease the wait."

Koo's wall-like face assumes an even sterner mien. "As you wish."

Corso pours himself some of Multrum's finest single-malt. Often dreamed of, seldom tasted. By writers. Of Corso's stratum. Sipping it with pleasure. Letting his eyes rove over the shelves. Where they encounter a long row of books by Malachi Stiltjack. Stiltjack being Corso's entry point into Multrum's aegis. Not the only debt Corso owes the man. And the rightmost title not familiar. *Gods of the Event Horizon*. Taking it down. Published last month. And probably already in a second printing. Reading spottily in the text. Yes, yes, transparent style, stirring action, big ideas. That's the winning formula. To be applied to *The Black-Hole Gun*. As soon as one returns home. With a face-saving check in pocket. To stave off the bill collectors. And stock the fridge. With beer and jugged herring.

"Corso you bastard, are you drinking up my entire bar."

Multrum slapping Corso jovially on the back. Causing expensive liquor to slosh. Onto Corso's shirt.

"Ah but no, of course not, Clive. Just a small tot. To enliven the humors. And prime the digestive track. For lunch."

Multrum has Corso by the elbow. A large fragrant cigar projects from Multrum's face. His agent steering him away from the bar. A silver-haired man of middling height. Clean-shaven and smelling not only of Cuban tobacco but also of expensive aftershave. Available only to literary agents above a certain income level. No doubt. His face engraved with lines that oddly map both a habit of smiling and one of sneering. Not plump but layered with a generous amount of self-satisfied tissue. As if to say, *I am insulated by my success.*

"So you haven't eaten yet. Surprise, surprise. Well, me neither. Let's go to Papoon Skloot's. I have something important to discuss with you."

"And is this, um, Skloot's a pricey establishment."

Another slap rattles Corso's bones. Hail fellow well met. We're all adults here. Don't give your shameful poverty a thought. Old bean.

"Don't sweat it, my friend, it's all on me."

"So very kind of you, Clive."

"Can the shit and let's move."

A taxi ferries them to Papoon Skloot's. During the ride Corso can ponder only Multrum's mysterious words. Something important to discuss. One senses the ax about to fall. Ass meeting sidewalk. Creditors gnawing on one's bones. Unjust fate for a simple soul. Who never asked for much. And since youth dreamed only of traveling the star lanes in prose. And who deserves some slack. Now that he is temporarily stymied. By a lack of belief in his own fictions. While at the same time beset. By those very science-fictional conceits made real.

Corso nearly gives way to self-pitying tears by the end of the ride. But manfully stifles them. Instead adopting an eager air of gaiety. Commensurate with the atmosphere inside the posh restaurant. Where various literati and glitterati clink flutes of champagne. Amidst expensive fabrics, elaborate chandeliers, and servile attendants. And consume tiny portions of elaborately mangled foodstuffs. From plates big as the shields of warriors. In a bad fantasy trilogy.

Buck up. In the face of elitist pretensions. One must go out in style. This is Corso's vow. Despite liquor-sticky shirt, soapy trousers, and satchel containing only a return Amtrak ticket, a toothbrush, and a recent issue of *Fantascience Journal*. With a picture of Hugo Gernsback on the cover.

"What'll you have, Corso. Can't decide, huh. Used to ordering through the drive-up window, hey. Okay, let me get us started." Multrum rattles off a litany of dishes. The server brings their drinks. Corso allowed one sip. Before Multrum launches into business.

"Now listen to me, Corso. You and I both know you're in deep shit with Wankel and Butte Books. But I've negotiated you one final extension. However, the grace period hinges on you going over there in person and kissing some ass."

"Exactly my own strategy, Clive. Of course, kowtow and touch cap. Not too proud to beg. Yes, certainly. I already have an appointment later this afternoon with Roger."

"Excellent! Then back home to dig into *Neutron Cannon*."

"Ah, *The Black-Hole Gun*."

"Sure, whatever. But before then, you're going to do both of us a big favor. You're going to knock out a tie-in novel. Vestine Opdycke from Shuman and Shyster called me, desperate for a last-minute replacement for Jerome Arizona. Arizona bailed on this project, and they need it yesterday."

His second drink of the day is inflating Corso's brain. Leery of visionary states. But no untoward incidents so far. No smerps or thoats rampaging through the restaurant. As they once did in the Wal-Mart. Where the beasts received no cheerful hello. From the oblivious store greeter.

Allowing a drift of mellowness to overtake his anxiety-plagued day. "But Arizona is usually so reliable. Never misses a deadline."

"True. But that was before he was caught by the local cops in bed with two sixteen-year-olds."

"Oh."

"So, are you on board."

"But what's the nature of the project."

"A novelization of the *Starmaker* movie."

Corso misbelieves his ears. "The Stapledon classic."

"I think that's the guy's name."

"But there's already a book. Hundreds of pages of impeccable speculative text. They must have used that as a source of the script. Can't they just reissue the original."

"The movie doesn't exactly follow the original anymore. Just the new love interests and space battles alone demand a different version. C'mon, it's easy money. No royalties though. Strictly work for hire."

Corso is bewildered. Lowering his glance to his immaculate napkin in his lap. How to answer. Traducing one's youthful idol. But quick cash. And a foot in the door at Shuman and Shyster. Maybe a good way to dissolve one's block. Crib from a master. What choice does one have.

Corso raises his eyes to Multrum's face.

The agent's brow is mutating to a jutting ledge. Features thickening. Facial pelt growing. Stained horsy teeth protruding. Multrum has devolved. To Neanderthal status. And so have the other diners. And staff. Walking awkwardly with curved backs and bowed legs. Their neckties cinching their enlarged necks. Like barbed wire overgrown by a tree.

Multrum grows impatient. His voice remains unchanged. Thankfully. No primordial grunts to misinterpret. "Well, Corso, what's your answer."

Even as Corso rummages for his own voice, Multrum continues to devolve. Scales. Fangs. Horns. Spiked tail. Multrum now an anthropomorphic saurian. A dinosaur in Hugo Boss. And the rest of the patrons. Similarly antediluvian. One female dinosaur. Categorized by her dress. Picks up her steak with disproportionately small forelimbs. And pops it entire into her slavering, razor-toothed mouth.

Sweat soaks Corso's shirt. Reptilian stench emanates from his table companion. Must phrase one's acceptance of the odious assignment in the most genial terms. Lest agent take offense. And disembowel one with a casual kick.

For Corso sincerely doubts
Multrum would stop
after only fifteen percent
of his client
was eaten.

One's third female gatekeeper of the day. The receptionist at Butte Books. Cheeks still hamstery with adolescent avoirdupois. Purple nail polish. Gingery hair secured in two outjutting tails on either side. Of a face both too wise and utterly naïve. A recent graduate, no doubt. Of a prestigious school. That should be ashamed of itself. For culturing and feeding innumerable such starry-eyed hapless romantics. Into publishing's voracious low-wage maw.

"Ah, Mr. Fairfield to see Mr. Wankel."

"Go right in, please."

Corso expected to wait. The easy access discommodes him. For he needs to utilize a "jakes."

"Is there, um, a restroom I could avail myself of first."

"Certainly. Here's the key. Left down that corridor."

Carrying the sacred key. Almost as if he works here. At the firm which ignored all his suggestions. For the cover of *Cosmocopia*. And instead of Whelan or Eggleton. He got the defiantly pastel work of Murrell Peurifoy. Whose oeuvre consists almost entirely of covers for humorous fantasy novels. And the image Peurifoy supplied for the eponymous device of Corso's book. Looked like a hybrid of a juicer, the postmodern VW Bug, and a penile-extension pump.

Through the limited-access door. Into the uttermost stall. Hanging satchel from a coat hook. Gratefully dropping one's trousers and boxers. Taking a seat. Peristaltic relief. Still blessedly easy to obtain. Unlike the mental variety.

Additional patrons entering noisily. A familiar voice and an unknown one. Wankel himself the former. Jovial banter above hardy plashing of piss.

"So you're meeting with Corso Fairly Fried. What's his story these days."

"Pathetic case. Fair amount of talent. But he's gotten too deep into this whole mythos of the genre thing. Thinks SF is some kind of mystical calling. Instead of just another job. Imagines he's writing for a fraternity of supermen. Instead of a bunch of dorky, overintelligent fifteen-year-olds."

Laughter from the unidentified interlocutor. "Jesus! Can't he see it's all interchangeable. Mysteries, techno-thrillers, westerns. Just a load of identical crap. Well, I know one thing. I won't make *that* mistake. I'm not getting trapped in this dead-end field. Another year or two and I'm outta here. I've already got some feelers out at *Maxim.*"

Zippers laddering upward. "*Maxim*, huh. Must meet a lot of beautiful women there."

"You bet."

Sounds of hand washing. Departure. And a sob betokening black desolation in the farthermost stall.

Corso Fairly Fried. His public image. Known to everyone but oneself. Passion and dedication to one's chosen field. Derided and cast aside. One's motivation laughable. If not predicated strictly on commercialism. Not to mention exclusion of any artistic striving. To build upon the work of past heroes. Giants of the medium. Who no doubt received similar treatment. From their own traitorous editors.

And how will he face Wankel now. Without spitting in his eye. Or punching same. But he of course cannot. For Multrum would rend his impetuous and violent client into bite-sized pieces. To be shared with the other velociraptors. Corso's only choice. To swallow his shame. And carry on.

Back to the receptionist. Return the key. Into Wankel's sanctum.

Roger Wankel standing by a table near the window. View of steel and glass canyons. Assaultive in their uncaring facades. Birds in flight. Boyish shock of tawny hair angling across the editor's wide brow. Close-set eyes. Nose and lips chosen from a child's catalogue of facial features then misplaced in an adult facial template. Sorting through a stack of cover proofs. Perhaps Peurifoy already engaged to limn *The Black-Hole Gun*. If so, one has only a dual question. Is that window shatterproof. And how far to the ground.

"Corso! A real pleasure to see you! How's Ginny doing."

"You must mean Jenny. She's fine." Unspoken of course. That she is fine with someone else.

"Great, great. Now I assume you're here to talk about the extension. Never thought it would get approved. But Multrum's one tough negotiator. You're lucky to have him on your team."

"Yes. He has a thick hide."

"True, true. Now what can you share with me to convince me you've got a handle on this project."

Restraining oneself from "sharing" venomous accusations. Of

venality and double-dealing. Instead babbling in a stream-of-consciousness fashion. About likely plot developments. Which might occur. To Corso's protagonist. Russ Radikans. Owner of the Black-Hole Gun. Ancient artifact of a vanished race. The Acheropyte. And Russ's lover. Zulma Nautch. Starship pilot. Of the *Growler.* Zulma's evil clone sister. Zinza, deadly assassin. And so forth. With Wankel taking it all in. And nodding sagely. The hypocritical bastard.

A knock at the office door. Which Wankel ignores. But a workman enters regardless. Mustache, dirty brown coveralls, hammer hanging from a loop, work gloves tucked in a back pocket. And without a word. The man begins to dismantle one of the office walls. Using a putty knife. To peel sheets of thin substance away. Not plaster or particleboard, but a resinous veneer. To reveal not girders and joists. But rather the raw blue air several dozen stories up. A breeze strokes Corso's cheek.

Corso flummoxed into silence. Wankel confused. But only by his author's hesitation. "Go on, I'm listening." So that Corso realizes. This is another hallucination. And he tries to continue. Tries to embrace the unpredictable unreality of his senses.

Now several more workman arrive. All twins to the first. A busy horde of disassemblers. They fall to aiding the original in deconstructing the walls. Until soon Corso and Wankel sit at the top of a lofty naked pillar. A few square feet of carpeted floor. Exposed on all sides. To Manhattan's brutal scrutiny. Since the rest of the office has inexplicably vanished. A stage set struck. By the Hidden Puppet Masters. Who intend to decimate. Corso's solipsistic self.

Breezes riffle Corso's hair. He cannot go on. Because of the actions of one workman. Who has stepped confidently off the pillar. And now climbs the sky itself. As if the air were a gentle blue slope. He heads for the sun. And as he approaches the orb he does not shrink. But rather puts the "sun" into its true scale. A disk as big as a hubcap. And donning his gloves. The workman begins to unscrew the sun.

At the same time other workman have shut down Wankel. Employing a switch at the back of his neck. Corso's enduring suspicions of the existence of some such switch now validated. And they pick up the editor's chair with him in it. And tip it upside down. But Wankel remains attached. Grinning moronically.

And then as the sun is finally completely unthreaded from its socket descends the ultimate darkness.

> As if Russ Radikans
> just employed his
> Black-Hole Gun
> on his very Creator.

"Corso, my boy. Wake up!"

That plummy voice. Steeped in all the luxuries of a cozy life. So familiar. From a credit card commercial. And one for Saturn automobiles. And many a convention panel. Not to mention the occasional phone conversation. In the nighted hours. When despair crept up. On the protégé. And he dialed the mentor's home phone. A number millions of fans would have killed for. One such being the vanished younger Corso himself. And even now when one is accorded one's own small professional stature. Still half disbelieving. One has been granted such a high privilege.

Corso unshutters his eyes. He is recumbent. Half naked. Atop a wheeled stretcher. Shielded by dirty curtains on rings. From the pitiful and pitying gazes of fellow sufferers. Evidently in a hospital emergency room. And by his side sits Malachi Stiltjack.

Stiltjack wears an expensive charcoal suit. Many yards of Italian fabric girdling his extensive acreage. Of a finer cut even than Multrum's. Vest. Watch chain. Other dandyish accoutrements. Silver hair razor-cut and styled to perfection. His middle-aged shiny pontifical face beaming. Presumably at Corso's reattainment of consciousness.

"What—what happened to me."

"You passed out in your editor's office. Bad show, my boy. Many of us have longed for such an escape, but it's pure cowardice to make such a melodramatic exit. Reflects poorly on your endurance and stamina. How could you handle a multicity book tour if one little bout of tedium causes you to crumple like an empty potato-chip packet. So they'll ask. In any case, an ambulance rushed you here. I tracked you down when you failed to meet me."

"Oh, Christ, Wankel will put me at the top of his shit list now for sure."

Wry expression on Stiltjack's face. "And you weren't there already."

Corso chagrined. "You know then about me missing my deadlines."

"But who doesn't. *Locus* even did a sidebar on your predicament in the December issue. Didn't you see it then."

"I let my subscription lapse. Money was tight. And reading *Locus* just makes me nervous. All those big-money deals, all those brilliant, joyous, glad-handing *professionals.* How does it all relate to the actual dreaming—"

"Come now, Corso, you should know better than to believe all that printed hyperbole. None of us is ever really secure. Most writers just put up a good front."

An ungenerous feeling of anger and envy at his friend. "Easy enough for you to say, Malachi, with your castle and contracts and—and concubines!"

The padrone unoffended by the peon's eruption. Magnanimous and solicitous from on high. "Now, now, Corso, such resentment ill becomes you. But I understand completely that it's your creative blockage talking. That's the crux of your trouble. Not your material circumstances. Or your wife's desertion."

A wail of despair. "My God, has *Locus* run a sidebar on that, too!"

"Not at all. But the grapevine—"

"Do my goddamn peers ever stop gossiping long enough to collect their awards."

"Let's put aside the all-too-human deficiencies of our comrades for the moment, Corso, and consider my diagnosis. Think a minute. If *I* were the one suffering the blockage, would all my money and possessions make me feel one whit happier. Of course not. Same thing with one's physical health. Psychological or somatic, an easy and natural functioning is the one essential to your peace of mind. Clear up your creative logjam, and you'll be back on top of the world."

"An easy prescription. But hard to administer to oneself."

"Let's work on it together a little longer. It's not that late in the evening. We can still have dinner. But first we need to get you discharged."

Doctor summoned. Corso reluctantly given a clean bill of health. Possibly a small case of food poisoning adduced. From Papoon

Skloot's. Spoiled coelacanth in the prehistoric kitchen. Which would serve all the egregiously wealthy diners right. Bidden by a surly yet attractive red-haired nurse to dress oneself. Nurse not lingering to peek at Corso's neglected manhood. As half fantasized. By a lonely and too-little-of-late-fondled professional daydreamer. And soon out on the twilit streets.

Stiltjack swinging a cane with a golden grip. Casting a radiant appreciative gaze at the whole wide world. Scurrying business drones. Sweaty delivery persons. Idling teenagers. A cherry for his picking. Or kicking. Should any viciously magisterial whim overtake him. *Droit du seigneur.* My mundane subjects. Corso striding silently alongside. Certain that if any pigeon shits. The excrement will hit the one who presents the most abject target.

"Now then, tell me about your problems, lad."

Corso complies. Recounts his disenchantment with the work. Displacement of tropes into real life. And the fugue states. And even as he describes his disease. He nervously awaits another strike. But nothing. Yet Corso's sigh of relief is undone. By Stiltjack's next words.

"So you've got the dicky fits. I thought they wouldn't have hit you for another few years yet. But they do occur in direct proportion to one's talents. So I shouldn't be surprised."

Corso simultaneously flattered and alarmed. "The dicky fits."

"Named after you-know-who, of course. Our patron saint."

"But you mean to say—"

"That I've had them, too. But of course! Every cold stone writer of science fiction goes through them at one point or another. Most come out the other side. But of course a few don't. With luck you won't be numbered among the latter."

"It's an occupational disease then."

"Oh it's not a disease. It's a privileged glimpse of reality."

Corso stops. "What are you saying, Malachi."

"Aren't you listening to me. You've been vouchsafed a vision. Of the plastic, unstable nature of reality. The illusory character of the entire cosmos. It's the god's-eye perspective. Conceptual breakthrough time."

Corso's tone sneering. "And I suppose then that you've benefited immensely from these visions. Maybe even learned how to become a deity yourself. Maybe I'm just a character in one of your fictions."

"Well, yes, I have become rather a demigod. As to who created whom, or whether we're both figments of some larger entity—well, the jury is still out."

"I would appreciate some disproof of your insanity."

"Naturally. How's this."

The surging pedestrian crowd freezes in place. And the traffic, too. On the sidewalk appear Sharon Walpole, Clive Multrum, and Roger Wankel. In their standard configurations. But then each morphs to his or her abnormal state. Walpole's prosthetic lobster claw. Multrum's reptilian guise. Wankel's android fixity. Corso approaches the marmoreal figures. Pokes them. Turns to Stiltjack.

"Satisfied now. Or shall I trot out Jenny and her new beau. I believe they're attending a car show in Duluth at the moment. I could bring onstage that derelict from Penn Station as well. His name, by the way, is Arthur Pearty. A fascinating fellow once you really get to know him."

"No. Not necessary. Just send these—these specters away."

The editors and agent vanish. Life resumes. Stiltjack moves blithely onward. Corso numbly following. The world's deceptive insubstantiality now confirmed. A thin shambles. A picture painted on rice paper. Corso sick to his stomach.

"It's best not to cause such large-scale disruptions. The universe, whatever it is, is not our toy. We did not create it. We do not run the hourly shadow-show. We are unaware of the ultimate rationale for its existence. But a small tweak here and there. Aimed at personal betterment. Such little perquisites are permitted those of us who have come out the other side of the dicky fits."

"But, but—but even if you decide to go on living, how can you continue to write science fiction! In the face of such knowledge."

Malachi pausing. To signal importance of his words. "Well, as to motivation, now, Corso, it's all a question of whose imagination is superior, isn't it. Weird as the universe is when you finally comprehend it, a trained mind such as yours or mine demands that our own imagination be even more potent in its conceptions. If you're a real science fiction writer, that is. Now why don't we go enjoy a fine meal. I can guarantee that we won't be interrupted."

And Corso laughs
loud enough to cause strangers
to gape
for his appetite
is suddenly prodigious
and not just for food.

For Horselover Fat, Jonathan Herovit, and, of course, the Ginger Man.

Thom Metzger is quietly, diabolically insane. Oh, you'd never know it just by meeting him. He presents a demure, affable face to the world. But I ask you this: What kind of fellow could write transgressive tomes on such topics as the history of opium and the history of the electric chair, as well as the landmark posthorror novel, Big Gurl, *and then go on to write authentically affecting young-adult novels, under a pen name meant to spare wandering teens from discovering his Mr. Hyde half? Only someone with a massive alien brain whose neurons do not fire in conventional sequences.*

When I tell you that Thom also invented the figure of the Hypmogoogoopizin' Man, the protagonist of the story that follows, you'll have no choice but to acknowledge that Mr. Metzger does not inhabit the same continuum as the rest of us.

The Curious Inventions of Mr. H

1. 7000 B.C.

Setting out from their village one bright dawn for the day's hunt, the barefoot tribesmen were half asleep. They scratched under their gamy furs, farted, belched, poked each other with the butt-ends of their spears. One loosed a practice arrow at a rabbit, missed, and was pummeled by the leader, a hulking male with arms the size of elk haunches. Hooting and laughing, the hunters trouped with maximum disorganization into the woods.

In a familiar clearing not far from their settlement, they came to an unplanned halt. Clustering closer together, they gaped with astonishment at a disconcerting sight.

Across the patch of open grassy ground stood a stranger. Big as their leader, the newcomer was oddly attired. Instead of a single drape of clumsily sutured hide, he wore multiple pieces of clothing: a fur-trimmed top that covered his arms and back and shoulders but left his chest bare, tapered leggings, and tasseled square-toed foot coverings. Atop his head perched a wide, peaked, shade-making device of some sort. The stranger's skin was dark, the color of sooty fire-scorched hearthstone, something never seen before. But the man's weirdest, most disagreeable feature was his left eye, an enormously protruding, arterially crimsoned orb of commanding magnificence and eerie mana.

Now the stranger called brashly out, in the villagers' own tongue, "Gen-tuhl-*men*! Heads up! This is your *big* day!"

He moved across the clearing, simultaneously reaching behind his back. Miraculously, he produced from behind himself an object much bigger than he could have hidden with his body.

Whispering among themselves as the black man approached, the tribesmen nervously divided their attention between the man and his out-held offering. The object, its like never before seen, was plainly artificial. Constructed of wood, it had no edges, as if it were some sort of miraculously flattened egg. In its center was a hole.

The newcomer was quickly upon them. Up close, he brandished the wooden thing proudly, as if it were a new child or freshly killed game. In a loud voice, he said, "Friends, will you kindly lookee here! What we got here is, we got a *wheel.* Can you say that?"

Several of the hunters obediently repeated the strange word. Their chief, however, only grunted his growing disapproval.

"Now I know you're all asking yourself, what's a wheel *do*? What's it *good* for? How's it gonna put a slab of cave bear on *my* table? Well, there's hardly anything a wheel *can't* do! But I don't expect you to take my word for it. I'll be happy to *demonstrate* this little charmer for y'all. Completely free, no charge of any kind, except whatever your generous hearts might be inclined to offer by way of minor recompense for my valuable time. So let's forget all your half-ass chasing and jabbing plans for today. We'll run your posse back to your crib, and I'll put this baby through its paces. Believe me, you won't regret one minute of this lucky day."

The stranger took a step down the path that led back to the village, and the majority of the transfixed tribesmen fell in obediently behind him. All, in fact, except the chief. The village leader stood fuming for a moment, his bearded face flushing clay-red, before bellowing out, "No! No go!"

Everyone stopped. The headman bulled through his compatriots, coming right up to the stranger, brandishing his spear and thrusting his face nearly against the black hyperocular visage.

"Who *you* to say? Who *you*? I boss here! Only me! I say time to hunt!"

The stranger was unintimidated by the blustering man. "Well, friend, I'm glad you asked for my handle. Allow me to introduce myself. I'm the one and only Hypmogoogoopizin' Man."

With these words, the stranger's throbbing bad eye seemed to swell a little and even to swirl. The weaker of the villagers held their heads and tottered. To his credit, the chief was mostly unswayed.

"I say you no good! I say you *die*!"

Preparing to thrust, the chief was stymied by the Hypmogoogoopizin' Man's raising the wheel like a shield. Into the wheel *thunked* the flint point, and the stranger's eye flared like the sun on the sea, freezing the chief where he stood.

"Chief, I think you need a little demonstration of this here wheel's cosmic *potency*!"

After easily dislodging the spear, with both hands the Hypmogoogoopizin' Man raised the wheel above the stunned chief so that it hung like a flat stone above the frozen leader. Then the stranger began to bring it down. When the wheel touched the chief's head, a very strange thing happened. The man began to disappear, as if being consumed by the center hole.

Within moments, the wheel lay flat on the ground. The remaining villagers stood hushed and stunned. As they watched, a tiny figure pulled itself out of the center hole. It was the chief, big as a mouse. The miniature leader capered and squeaked, waving a doll-proportioned bow. The mannikin shot a splinter-sized arrow at the Hypmogoogoopizin' Man, causing him to laugh heartily.

Recovering his wheel, the Hypmogoogoopizin' Man turned away from the minuscule man. "Okay, friends, back home!"

Bending slightly, the Hypmogoogoopizin' Man tossed his magic wheel before him. Seemingly of its own volition, like a live thing it rolled all the way back to the encampment, negotiating every twist and turn of the path.

The women were startled to see the hunters returning so soon, without their chief and led by a stranger. Soon, however, every mother, wife, and sister, as well as all the children, were shyly clustered around the magnificent newcomer, who seemed to have earned the approval of their men.

"Okay, *ladies*! Break out the food and drink. We are gonna have us a par-*tay*!"

Within a short time, the entire village was on a festival footing. Meat crackled over fires, skin pouches of fermented fruit drink were circulating, and children were running and screaming delightedly in games of tag. After everyone had gorged themselves—the Hypmogoogoopizin' Man taking first honors—the promised lecture and demonstration began. Moving from the simplest applications of the marvelous new wheel to others that would not be realized for millennia, the Hypmogoogoopizin' Man decanted through the force of his speech and his mean ol' pulsating eye all the pure knowledge of the innate masterful powers of human mind over brute matter that the villagers could handle. After many hours, his audience lay stupefied, their brains plainly stuffed with fecundly breeding ideas.

At this point the Hypmogoogoopizin' Man held up the wheel and stuck a finger illustratively through its hole, waggling and poking it to make his meaning clear. His eel-like eye began to protrude and waggle also. The effect on the villagers was instant invigoration and concupiscence.

"Time for a little *sen*-shoe-uhl fun, folks!"

Dropping the wheel, scooping up seven of the prettiest women, four in one arm and three in the other, leaving the rest of the clan to shed their clothes and begin to rut in the dirt, the Hypmogoogoopizin' Man made a beeline toward the headman's hut.

"Damn! I am gonna *hate* to leave this place! But—duty calls!"

2. 2000 B.C.

The madam of the most exclusive whorehouse in Thebes came to the door of her establishment, summoned thence by an incoherent message passed down a chain of babbling servants who had made no sense at all.

"The giant Ethiop—his eye—flames—the glare—a wheel that knows time—"

Absolute blather, all of it. Probably some deformed beggar or soothsayer, even a harmless tradesman, dull of intellect, who had mistaken the customer's entrance for the delivery door. What good were slaves if they couldn't exercise a little intelligence? Perhaps she would have them all whipped.

In her slippered feet, skirted and bare-breasted, braceleted and kohl-eyed, the madam padded past the erotic wall paintings and into the front antechamber, harsh words ready to spring from her lips.

Framed in the doorway in an insouciant attitude was an alarming man who robbed the speech from her. Some kind of huge black barbarian, he wore an *outré* costume that escaped attention thanks only to the wrenching weirdness of his great goggling left eye, so vibrant it seemed an entity in its own right.

"*Shake* that moneymaker, girl," the Hypmogoogoopizin' Man called out upon spotting the madam. "Time is money, and money is time, and I've got plenty of both to share with you. If you're interested, of course."

The madam understood a business proposition, however unconventionally phrased. "What could one of your uncouth mien and savage cast have to offer a citizen of mighty Thebes, fount of all wisdom and material goods?"

"Just this little gizmo, sister." From beneath his upper garment, the Hypmogoogoopizin' Man whipped out a queer device. A flat disc with numerals running around its edge, and in its middle a slanted flange of bronze.

The madam snorted. "I prefer my sculpture to be representational. The least you could have done, considering my profession, is shape that pointer into a phallus."

Stepping inside, the Hypmogoogoopizin' Man seemed unabashed. "You don't know what you're looking at, girl. This handy gadget is gonna double and triple your profits. And my fee is nothing but chicken feed—nothing you haven't given out before."

Here the Hypmogoogoopizin' Man winked, closing his normal eye. The effect of his lone monstrous orb shining fulsomely without counterbalance sent the madame staggering. Moving quickly, the Hypmogoogoopizin' Man steadied her, with big hands on waist and elbow.

"Let's go into the courtyard, honey, and I'll show you the elephant. Oh, and let's have us some drinks. This is one *dusty* burg."

Dazedly, the madam signaled to the servants to bring beer. Half leading, half led, she accompanied the stranger to the atrium. Sunlight poured in, falling onto a stone bench. There they sat, and the Hypmogoogoopizin' Man laid the odd device between them.

"How long your customers take with the gals, honey? No hard data, just a guess about the average fuck duration. You can't say? Of *course* you can't say! You got no good way of marking the hours! You know that if you tried to enforce a limit without solid proof, you'd get into endless hassles with the johns. 'Shit, I only been here half an hour, whose ass you trying to burn!' Am I right, or am I right?"

The madam could only sip at her beer and mutely nod. The enormous eye had her in its thrall.

"Well, that's no way to maximize your merchandise, honey. Your fillies could probably pull twice as many tricks as they do. They're slackin' and your purse is hurtin'. But you can thank your natal stars, I'm here to introduce some pure *efficiency* into this operation."

The beer lubricated the madam's tongue somewhat. "Huh—how?"

"With this here *sundial.* Just watch this magic baby for a few minutes."

The madam gazed upon the instrument. The projection caused a slim shadow to fall upon the face where the numbers were. As the sun moved across the sky, so did the shadow, tracing out the hours.

Fascinated, the madam said, "Very intriguing. But what of my busy nighted hours?"

Winking briefly, the Hypmogoogoopizin' Man said, "Can't put one over on *you.*" He pulled another device from his clothes: a thing of bowls and floats and a measured bar. "I call this one a *clepsydra.* You're gonna love it."

Calculations roiled in the madam's had. If what this odd fellow promised was true, then she would soon be the richest woman in Thebes. "And your price?"

"Can't even rightly call it a fee," said the Hypmogoogoopizin' Man.

The madam suddenly noticed that somehow her skirt had disappeared. Overhead, the always present yet generally unseen maculations on the sun seemed to float and coalesce in the solar center, turning the celestial orb into a giant eye. The Hypmogoogoopizin' Man was pressed up against her now, his breath hot in her ear.

"You see, honey chile, I'm just interested in a little widespread *dissemination.*"

3. A.D. 1150

The captain of the Spanish caravel stood on the bridge, which was shrouded in fog as thick as wool on a sheep's back. He knew the Canaries were out there somewhere. But navigation had become impossible in this witch's broth.

Looking hopefully over the rail for signs of floating vegetal wrack that might hint at the nearness of land, the captain was startled to see a pale swath of luminescence far below the sea's surface. As he watched, transfixed, the glowing area grew larger and better defined. Soon its nature was plain: a cyclopean eye the size of a kitchen garden. Bulking around and beyond the eye was the creature it belonged to, some kind of kraken or enormous grampus.

The captain began to pray, aloud and with fervency. He was certain his ship was about to be swamped, that he and his crew were downward bound, their new home the hoary nighted seabed that had claimed so many in the past.

But to the captain's immense surprise and tentative relief, the underwater monster stopped while still some distance beneath the surface. Movement below seemed to indicate the presence and action of a gigantic tentacle. Then the actual limb broke the surface, swept through the air, and deposited something wetly on the deck. Within seconds the kraken was gone.

Hesitantly, the captain advanced toward the object left on his ship. It appeared to be the clothed corpse of a blackamoor. With trepidation, the captain poked the sodden corpse with a finger.

"Boo!"

The captain shrieked as if the gates of hell had opened in his face, and he fell back. When his mind resumed functioning, he saw that the blackamoor, now standing, was alive and laughing. His only hurt—echoing the monster which had delivered him—seemed to be that his vein-threaded, fluid-packed left eye bulged like a hanged man's.

When his guffaws ceased, the stranger said, "Sorry, man, I just couldn't resist!"

The captain's cry and the blackamoor's laughter had brought sailors armed with belaying pins and swords. Now the captain's fear turned abruptly to rage. "Seize this caitiff jester! We'll see if he laughs so heartily after being clapped in irons and given a sound drubbing!"

The sailors began cautiously to move forward. The stranger appeared untroubled, merely raising a hand of caution.

"Now hold on, boys, you don't want to come across the wrong side of the Hypmogoogoopizin' Man, do you?"

The men halted. The name stirred vague ancestral memories, evoked fireside whispers and the obscure tales told by gimlet-eyed grannies.

"Besides, I'm here to offer you and Cappy the neatest piece of maritime science since the invention of the astrolabe. We call it the *compass.*"

From nowhere the Hypmogoogoopizin' Man whipped out a shallow bowl with markings around the lip. Held out for their inspection, the bowl proved to contain only water and a cork with a needle laid in a groove. One end of the needle was painted red.

The Hypmogoogoopizin' Man strode briskly up to the captain. "Which way you figure is north, Sinbad?"

The captain paused thoughtfully, then pointed in a certain direction. The Hypmogoogoopizin' Man made an offensive buzzing noise, then exclaimed, "Wrong! Look how we align the magic north-loving needle, like so—" The Hypmogoogoopizin' Man rotated the bowl so that the floating needle lined up with the marking on the bowl's rim representing north. The Captain regarded the bowl thoughtfully before speaking.

"This is always accurate?"

"Always. Lessen you go near certain geomantic bad spots—but they're rarer than feet on a snake. Plus, this gadget's so easy to make. The magic's contagious to regular iron, by the way—all's you need is a source of lodestone for the needles. And it just so happens I got this here handy map of lodestone deposits."

Narrowing his eyes, the captain said, "What do you ask for this miraculous device and information?"

"Not one red cent, cuz. Only that you use my little gift to haul your Euro-asses around the whole globe. Go forth and multiply. *Sub*-ju-gate and *dom*-in-nate, that's all I'm asking. Just what your nature is set up for anyhow. You see, for what I got in mind, I gotta build me up a critical mass of tech-no-*logical* civ-i-lie-*zay*-shun!"

The captain stuck out his hand. "Done!"

Instead of shaking in the normal fashion, the Hypmogoogoopizin' Man slapped palms. "Now you're *talking*! This calls for a little celebration!"

Putting fingers between his lips, the Hypmogoogoopizin' Man emitted a piercing whistle. Instantly, the sounds of many medium-sized creatures breaking the water were heard. Everyone rushed to the ship's rails. In the sea floated dozens of beauteous mermaids, their naked bosoms exposed as they rode high on their tails.

"Get your nets, boys!" called the Hypmogoogoopizin' Man. "It ain't every day you make a catch like this'un!"

4. A.D. 1878

Illuminated by a crazily flickering, sharp-nippled prototype of his as-yet unperfected "electric light," Thomas Alva Edison lay on his workbench, napping. It was midnight on Easter Sunday, and his lab was empty of coworkers. Only the dedicated Great Man remained behind, ever diligent, ready after this short restorative to resume his inspired creation. All was quiet and peaceful, until the door to the lab was violently hurled open.

In strode the Hypmogoogoopizin' Man, all dancing flash and prancing sass.

"Wake up, T.A.! Time's a-wastin'! We're almost there! End of the millennium's right around the corner, but there's still a *shitload* of work to be done! Chop-chop!"

Edison came awake quickly. He swung his legs around to dangle off the bench and sat up. "Who are you? What do you want?"

"The Hypmogoogoopizin' Man don't *want* nothing, Eddie. He *causes to be*! Now, rumor has it you're looking to perfect a device for the recording of sound. 'Zat true?"

"Yes, that is one of the many projects I am working on. What is it to you?"

"I really need you to finish this one quick, Eddie. Move it up to the top of the queue. Lotta important voices and music we gotta get down on wax. It's all crucial to the plan. Now, I got a few mechanical suggestions involving cylinders and disks and such—"

Edison levered himself off the counter. "Forget it. I don't take advice or outside help—mercenary pressure least of all. Being steered removes all my intellectual pleasure. If you're any kind of inventor yourself, you should understand that."

The Hypmogoogoopizin' Man cupped his chin with one hand and his elbow with the other. His outsized eye throbbed as if in anticipation of being put to work, then subsided. "Hmmm, you got a point, T.A. I could coerce you, of course—bathe you in the slosh of my optojism—but that might skew the results of your undisturbed creativity somehow, throw all my schemes off. Let me see now—is there any bribe I could offer you to accelerate the phonograph work?"

Edison waved a hand dismissively. "I am confident that my patents will soon bring me all the wealth and power I could use. What else is there?"

"Well, Eddie, I'm talking about your Faustian dee-*lights*, stuff no amount of regular worldly influence could ever get you. Interviews with ghosts, assignations with famous women—"

Now it was Edison's turn to ruminate. "Women, you say?"

"You name the babe, and she's yours."

"Now that my mind moves in that direction, well, I—"

"Spit it out, son. Don't be shy. We're all bull moose here."

Edison took the plunge. "I have always wished to witness Madame Blavatsky engaged in a catfight with Jenny Lind, culminating in Sapphic sex."

"Is *that* all? I thought you were gonna give me a *challenge*." The Hypmogoogoopizin' Man snapped his thick fingers, and the two denominated women appeared, blinking and confused. "In this corner, wearing red knickers and a whalebone corset, the Swedish Nightingale. And her opponent, the lama-robed author of *Isis Unveiled*. Okay, girls, show us what you got."

Instantly the women dashed at each other and began tussling. Clothes were rent, and hair pulled. The women tumbled to the floor and rolled back and forth in violent struggle. A stool went down with a crash, followed by a rack of test-tubes jostled off a bench.

Fascinated, Edison resumed his seat. The Hypmogoogoopizin' Man joined him. Reaching beneath his jacket, the monocularly magnanimous mojo man took out a large paper tub.

"Popcorn, Eddie?"

"Don't mind if I do."

5. The Present

You sit behind the wheel of your speeding car, which is encapsulated as if in a featureless golden cloud.

The hands on the analogue watch on your wrist offer the hour as 13:99.

The needle of a compass suction-cupped to the dashboard is spinning wildly.

You pop a CD into the onboard player; out of the speakers emerge alien wailings in an unknown language.

From the rearview mirror hangs a small stuffed effigy of a black man, pimpishly dressed with one protuberant eye.

The effigy comes alive, winks, and demands: "Now tell me, son: where the *hell* you think you're *going*?"

V

Counterfactual Curiosities

Lately, the "alternate history" story has become both popular and reviled. SF purists claim that mucking about with historical trivia is not intellectually equal to fabricating vast cosmological speculations or blue-skying biological riffs. Yet many SF readers seem to appreciate stories that use history as a laboratory, showing us how mere accidents of place and person and circumstance can divert the course of the world. At their best, these "uchronias" do indeed serve as rigorous examples of historical speculation. At their worst, they become nothing more than excuses to parade the lives of celebrities across the page, lending the stories a cheap glamour that the author would otherwise have failed to invent by employing an original character.

I've probably perpetrated some of each type. Here are three of my counterfactual curiosities so that you may decide for yourself.

The theme of America in decline first appeared at least as long ago as 1889, with John Mitchell's The Last American, *in which a triumphant Persia gloats over the ruin of the United States. Since then, America's possible downfall has become a perennial topic, one that provokes joy in the country's enemies and despair in her friends. But it's a useful lesson for both parties to contemplate a world where the United States no longer bestrides the global stage in quite so majestic a manner.*

And you just can't beat the mandatory image of the Statue of Liberty's torch sticking up out of the sand or ice or water that these stories allow. It's iconic.

I almost included this story in my Lost Pages *collection, until I realized that while a famous writer was central to the tale, he wasn't precisely the protagonist—a prerequisite for inclusion in that volume. Now at last the piece finds a new home, long after the gracious Gordon Linzer first published it.*

Shake It to the West

Shake it to the east, my darling,
Shake it to the west, my darling,
Shake it to the very one that you love the best.

—Street rhyme cited by Aaron Siskind in "Harlem Document"

Professor Rufus Sexwale found it vexingly hard to concentrate. It was seven in the morning, the time he normally began to write (starting so early usually gave him several uninterrupted hours before having to teach his first class at Lusaka University, a freshman introduction to the Unification years). It was a daily ritual Rufus cherished and anticipated.

The problem was that Rufus was not in his normal environment, the quiet and prosperous middle-class suburb of Lusaka known as Sugar Hill. There, most mornings, he would have had no distracting noises louder than tropical bird calls or the rumble of one of Lusaka's shiny new "Memphis"-model garbage trucks. In his book-lined study, the new tubeless "Nile"-brand radio was tuned softly to the classical strains of Radio Pan-Africa's early jazz program. Rufus could marshal his research, ponder his facts, become lost in the vastness of time, and compose his popular-history books, which commanded a sizable audience from Tangier to Durban.

But here, right now, in his first-class cabin aboard that newest, biggest, and most glamorously appointed ship of the Black Star Line—the *Chicago Bluesman*—Rufus had to contend with the party still going on outside on deck.

Not just any old party, either. This was the party of the century. The hundredth anniversary of the first president's birth.

The party had begun a week ago, when the *Chicago Bluesman* was in the middle of its passage from Monrovia to New York. The festive atmosphere of being at sea had encouraged the early start—not that the passengers needed much excuse. Last night had been the climax, though: the actual eve of the first president's birth (the date popped obediently into Rufus's trained mind: August 17, 1887). And the celebration's finale had been boisterous and anarchic out of all proportion to anything Rufus had ever seen.

Rufus had attended the opening hours of last night's celebration, had a few drinks—White Zombies—danced a slow dance or two with a charming Zulu girl six inches taller than he, then decided to leave. Such events quickly lost their luster for him. Truth to tell, he felt more at home at a faculty wine and cheese reception. Retiring to his cabin, he'd drifted off to an uneasy, booze-tinged sleep.

Around 3 A.M. he was jolted out of his slumber by an enormous round of fireworks. Poking his head out of his cabin, he witnessed a scene that could have come straight out of the climax of Ibrahim Reed's fantasy masterpiece, *A Night in the Bush.*

The electric lights mounted on the liner's superstructure had been extinguished, and the deck was lit by flaring torches. Everyone Rufus could see was buck-naked. Their bodies—some already elaborately scarified and tattooed—had been decorated in various modes: paint, mud, glued feathers, colored ink (markers from the children's lounge, he supposed).

The bodies were in elaborate syncopated motion, propelled by the sweaty band laboring atop a raised stage.

The band was not the suave jazz one that had earlier played at the slow tempos Rufus favored, nor even a somewhat more racy ragtime assemblage. It was one of these new "jit-jive" groups, a bunch of wild-haired teenagers who had taken traditional African rhythms, bred them with certain neglected Western forms such as Appalachian fiddle music, and mutated the bastard into something incredibly brazen, suggestive, and hypnotic.

The band found a primeval beat and wouldn't let go. Circular pulses of sound washed over a stunned Rufus like the waves on the Capetown beach where he and Mudiwa and the children had spent their last vacation. To Professor Sexwale's muzzy brain, it appeared the liner had passed through some kind of time warp out of the British mode of "experimentifiction" favored by his son Pete and had emerged in some primitive past before the civilizing effects of the Great Return and the subsequent Unification.

At this point, the snakes appeared.

Suddenly, many dancers were partnered not with fellow humans, but with an assortment of large, sinuous reptiles. The dancing became positively indecent. A shuffling circle of foot-stomping, howling celebrants spontaneously formed. Into it leaped a single man and a single woman, both barely clothed in leopard skins.

They began circling each other in mock predation.

Suspecting what would come next, Rufus retreated to his bunk, clamping a pillow to his head.

For once he regretted the largesse of Lusaka University, which had booked him first-class passage. In steerage, at least, he could have slept.

Now, for the tenth time, as the inexhaustible jit-jivers, laboring on past dawn, launched into a song even Rufus recognized (ironically, a furious version of "The Lion Sleeps Tonight"), the professor tried to focus on the single-spaced sheet of paper in the gently humming Ovambo electric typewriter before him, the beginning of chapter 5 of the tentatively titled *Our Destined Start.*

> *The year 1921 witnessed the convergence and alliance of two groups that could not on the surface have appeared more dissimilar and antipathetic. I refer, of course, to First President Marcus Moziah Garvey's United Negro Improvement Association and the Ku Klux Klan. Although unequal in size and resources, both groups were led by powerful, crafty,*

charismatic figures who managed to put aside their mutual distaste and hatred to form an uneasy détente in order to achieve a mutual goal.

In this crucial year, the UNIA tallied its membership in the middling six figures and derived its not insignificant treasury from the donated pennies and quarters of maids and barbers, porters and dancers. Contrariwise, the KKK boasted six million followers and the backing of rich businessmen and politicians, industrialists, and farmers. Led by their Grand Cyclops (William Simmons, formerly a Georgia minister), the KKK stretched its tentacles into nearly every boardroom and ward-heeler–stuffed voting booth in the United States.

The point of agreement upon which these two seemingly irreconcilable groups could meet was plainly stated.

Both organizations desired to empty the United States of its Negro population.

First President Garvey, in his early role as the "black Moses" of our childhood textbooks, wished to lead his people back to their ancestral homelands, which would at the same time contribute to the liberation and uplift of the African continent—in this not-so-remote period completely dominated by European colonial regimes, save for the two free countries of Liberia and Ethiopia.

Grand Cyclops Simmons and his numerous followers, on the other hand, wished to restore America to a mythical sixteenth-century white pristinity (perhaps—nay, certainly—mythical, when one acknowledges the presence of the indigenous red men), a homogeneous Anglo-Saxon, High Germanic, and Nordic culture, where little Virginia Dare would have no longer to fear the always lurking insults and assaults of Sambo.

Despite the root difference in their philosophies, both the UNIA and the KKK convinced even their most moderate and reluctant followers to cooperate in the mass repatriation we now call the Great Return.

They caused their shared program to be made the law of the land.

We now know, thanks to recent daring research efforts by a group of courageous and sympathetic Britons who smuggled certain key documents out of the Library of Congress, that the KKK had President Harding in the pockets of its robes, so to speak. The Harding administration (1920–1932) was as large an assortment of crooks and grafters, con men and swindlers, as has ever held the American White House. The simple threat to divulge the scandalous doings of the Hardingites to the press—controlled in large part by KKK sympathizers anyway—was enough to elicit President Harding's complete cooperation (speculation has emerged that, had Harding been a man of stronger will and defied the Klan, the KKK planned to assassinate him in 1923 and run their own candidate).

First President Garvey, in a move of dubious ethical validity yet understandable practicality, given his position of inferior strength, was a full participant in this blackmail, piggybacking his schemes atop the enemy's.

The passage and signing of the Negro Exclusionary Act in May of that fateful year set in motion the Great Return, the largest planned exodus in the history of humanity.

Over the course of a mere seven years, using the ships of the UNIA's Black Star Line and numerous supplemental vessels (including some of the U.S. Navy fleet), more than one million Amero-Africans of all ages were funneled into the "Dark Continent" through the port of Monrovia, which quickly became the largest city in sub-Saharan Africa.

The importance of the rider to the Exclusionary Act barring all immigration into the United States from a long list of countries (basically, only England, Germany, the Netherlands, and the countries of Scandinavia were exempted) went unnoticed amid the general uproar occasioned by the uprooting of the native-born Negroes—

A drum solo from the jit-jivers broke Professor Sexwale's concentration for the eleventh time. Sighing, he toggled off the typewriter.

Perhaps it was just as well he abandon his manuscript at this point for a short time. Early this afternoon, they were scheduled to dock in New York. The official celebrations attendant on this historic return of the first Black Star Line ship to America in over sixty-five years would doubtless occupy several days in which it would be impossible to work. After that, his researches would in all likelihood uncover so much new material—New York had been Jamaican-born Garvey's headquarters—he might have to revise the first four chapters anyway.

Rufus stood up from the zebra hide–covered seat at his desk.

Time for breakfast and, more important, coffee. How he missed lovely Mudiwa and her considerate attentions. Had he been home, a steaming pot of Kampalan brew would have been waiting before he even began. It was a shame she and the children couldn't come, but Mudiwa had her job as manager of the Lusakan Fabric Works to consider.

Straightening the lapels of his full-cut kente-cloth suit jacket (Mudiwa had his clothes made exclusively from conservative LFW prints), Rufus stepped outside.

Almost immediately, he encountered an entirely displeasing figure.

Forced to maneuver over and around unconscious bodies littering the deck, Rufus found his convoluted path bringing him directly toward the man in the leopard skin whose vulgarity had precipitated Rufus's hasty retreat to his cabin. Slouched over the rail, the man appeared comatose. Just as Rufus was edging past, the party victim straightened, confronting the professor face to face.

That man, only shadowily apprehended last night, turned out in the bright light of day to be none other than the egregious Banga Johnson.

Banga was one of Rufus's fellow Lusakans on board. Incredibly rich, slim and self-assured, the dapper owner of the Springbok Motor Company had a reputation as a playboy and bon vivant. Rufus had encountered him socially once or twice and been unimpressed. Granted, the man had a certain amount of guile and street smarts—he could hardly have brought his company so far if he had been a complete idiot—but his brusque speech and coarse manners were utterly disagreeable.

Banga gripped Rufus by the elbow, an imposition Rufus detested.

Banga's eyes in his somewhat narrow head were bloodshot, and his thin mustache was flecked with dried beer froth (or worse). Yet he appeared relatively in control of himself.

"Professor Sexwale! Just the man I want to see! I've been meaning to speak with you the whole trip, but you know how these things can slide. We must talk before the ship docks. There's not much time. Now would be perfect."

Rufus tried to temporize. "I was just on my way to dine. Couldn't it wait . . . ?"

"No. I've made an appointment with a charming Ashanti girl for ten, and we'll probably be quite busy up till noon." Banga leered in the manner of the lecherous Mister Bushpig in Alake Walker's *Shades of Violet.* "I could go for something to eat myself. We'll breakfast together."

Rufus regarded Banga, appalled. "Would you care to change—?"

"No time. Besides, every woman on board has already seen this leopard's tail—fore and aft! Let's go!"

Captured by his own good manners and by Banga's bad, Rufus let himself be led to the liner's vast and elegant chandelier-lit dining room, which turned out to be only sparsely occupied at this early hour. Nevertheless, a full buffet was laid out, everything from groundnut stew to grits.

Helped by liveried attendants, the two men soon carried heaped plates and cups of steaming coffee on their trays to an empty table. Bessie Smith and Ma Rainey played softly over the room's speakers.

Banga dug into his food like a starving man. Rufus tried to recall the last time he had seen anyone deal so savagely with a meal. Real hunger was rare nowadays—at least on the Dark Continent. More delicately, Rufus cut up his monkey livers, waiting for the other man to broach his reasons for wanting to converse.

After demolishing a good portion of his meal, Banga slurped noisily from his cup, half draining it. Abruptly he fixed Rufus with a piercing look and demanded, "Why are the Americans letting us in now, after six decades of isolationism and a self-imposed virtual quarantine?"

Taken aback, Rufus could only parrot the standard editorial

stance of *The Lusakan Daily Gleaner* and other conservative papers of its ilk.

"Why, they've finally repented of their harsh and inhuman treatment of our ancestors—"

Banga's sardonic laughter filled the room, causing the few other diners to swivel and look.

"I don't see what's so funny—" began Rufus, who hated being the center of a public display.

Still guffawing, Banga held up his Egyptian cotton napkin like a surrender flag, as if to say, "No more witticisms, I give up!" Finally, he ran out of energy. Wiping his eyes, the automobile magnate said, "Oh, please forgive me, Professor Sexwale. It's just that you and others of your class are so predictable. Having read your books, I had hoped the glint of independent thinking I discerned might manifest itself in your conversation. I was laughing more at the inevitable disappointment of my own foolishness than at your prosaic blindness."

Pleased that Banga had actually read his books and insulted at being called blind, Rufus could only equivocate in his own defense. "I don't feel that attributing the actions of a person—even a white person—to an underlying sense of repentance or exculpation should be arbitrarily— That is, I realize international affairs seldom proceed from a basis of charity or altruism—"

"Seldom! Try never!" Banga picked up his fork and pointed it at Rufus. "Did the British leave South Africa and Rhodesia and the Sudan out of altruism? Did the Portuguese leave Angola and Mozambique out of compassion? Did the French leave West Africa out of charity? Did the Belgians leave the Congo out of the goodness of their hearts? Did the Italians leave Libya after some divine revelation of their wickedness? Of course not! They left because we kicked their butts out! And because they faced a very distracting war at home."

"What of the role of Gandhi and his nonviolent methods? Surely that amounts to awakening the oppressor's conscience and letting his better self take over—"

"That little South African lawyer was as nonviolent as a crocodile! When I think of how he dealt with intertribal rivalries—! No, he wielded supernatural power, that's all that differentiated him from Garvey. Did you ever meet the man? No? Well, I did. I was only five. It was 1950, and Garvey had sent his vice president to negotiate an end to the steelworkers' strike in Bulawayo. My father was the union leader. He had a closed-door meeting with Gandhi and came out gray as a ghost. I remember Gandhi making a speech to the press afterward, about how the fabric of society required both warp and weft, and how the cutting of any thread could unravel the whole piece. When he made a snipping motion with his fingers, my father fainted dead away. Now, there was power for you!"

Rufus had no rejoinder. Banga continued.

"No, if the Americans are suddenly opening up their country to us—even in a limited way—you can rest assured self-interest lies at the heart of it."

"Oh, come now. What could a powerful country like the United States want from us?"

Banga regarded Rufus incredulously. "Professor, you truly are living in the past. You hark back to the era of the Great Return, when the United States sat at the top of the heap and Africa was an undeveloped morass of poverty and sickness. I must inform you now the tables are turned. The Americans are desperate for our help."

"Ridiculous! I could see if they had been devastated by the Hitlerian war as Europe and Russia were. There, Pan-Africa was indeed able to extend a helping hand to clean up the aftermath and rebuild. Even Lenin, proud as he was, took our aid in the end, though he had to execute argumentative comrades like Stalin first. But America never suffered such depredations. Even the loss of their own colonies, Hawaii and the Philippines, during the Japanese Expansion, was not enough to lure them out of their secure shell. No, our old homeland has gone from strength to strength, I'm sure."

"Now you're talking through your hat. How can you know anything about the current state of America, given the Old Glory Curtain?"

"How can *you*?"

Banga narrowed his eyes. "I have my sources. A trickle of information slips out. Industrial spies, who also report on cultural matters. My government contacts back home also pass on certain information."

Rufus dismissed the assertion. "I can't give credence to such a wild tale."

"What an Uncle Sam you are, professor!"

Rufus stood, radiating dignity. "I know you intend that epithet as an insult, but I take it as a compliment. I shall always honor the country of our diaspora, however shabbily they once treated us."

Banga stood also. "Are you an African, professor, or not?"

Airily waving the question aside, Rufus responded, "Who among us is a true African these days, Mr. Johnson? Extensive interbreeding over three generations—which you should know all about—has diluted all the pure bloodlines of antiquity. As for attitude and culture, look around you. We're all as much American as African these days."

Banga nodded wisely. "You have me there, professor. I can only add that perhaps we are more American than the Americans, if that word still means what it used to."

With this cryptic remark, Banga bowed and made his exit, leopard tail dragging on the parquet floor.

Rufus sat and finished his meal, trying to convince himself he had triumphed.

But, leaving the dining room, he found himself still pondering Banga's closing sally.

Was Pan-Africa the true heir to the ideals and freedoms of old, pre-Exclusionary America?

Born in a revolution nearly identical to that of 1776, the Dark Continent's constitution and government were modeled exclusively on the that of the U.S. system. Her borders were open to immigrants and refugees of all stripes: Europeans who fled the Hitlerian conflagration of 1939–1948; Chinese and Indochinese and Malaysians on the run from Japanese; even some nervous Australians (true, the complexion of the vast land was 90 percent black, but so had early America been overwhelmingly white, and the blacks were just as heterogeneous as had been America's assorted ethnic whites). Pan-Africa's booming economy was relentlessly capitalistic and individualistic, and English had emerged as the lingua franca. Religious freedom embraced animists, Muslims, and Christians alike.

Professor Sexwale had always viewed Pan-Africa as America's

little brother, a child constantly striving to emulate its elder. Suddenly to imagine the relationship reversed was highly disorienting.

With a deliberate shrug, Rufus dismissed the notion and returned to his cabin to pack.

After his bags and typewriter were dealt with, Rufus succumbed to a short nap to make up for his uneasy night. He wanted to be fresh and alert for the historic moment of their arrival.

Dreams of Banga Johnson fornicating with a lively, willing, and suitably proportioned Statue of Liberty troubled the professor's sleep until the moment they were mercifully shattered by a mighty blast of the *Chicago Bluesman*'s whistle.

Hastily donning his jacket and dress sandals and leaving his bags for the liner's stewards to attend to, Rufus hurried outside.

The vessel was well into the Narrows of Upper New York Bay, almost at the northern point of Staten Island. Buildings reared on the Jersey and Brooklyn shores (surprisingly, they were rather unassuming, decrepit, and ugly buildings; Rufus supposed most post-Exclusionary construction had been concentrated on Manhattan). Excited passengers continued to rush toward the prow like a river of ink, as if to gain an extra foot or two in their inevitable progress to the soil of their ancestors, and they blocked Rufus's forward view.

"Professor! Up here!"

Turning toward the source of the hail, Rufus saw Captain Owole de Klerk.

Owole was a three quarters Hottentot. In his elaborate formal uniform (First President Garvey had been inordinately fond of ornate regalia for himself and his lieutenants), he stood approximately four foot seven. Despite his short stature, he was a vibrant man who inspired confidence and admiration.

Accepting the captain's invitation, Rufus ascended a steel staircase and soon found himself on the bridge, enjoying its excellent view.

Below, Rufus was grateful to note, his fellow passengers had abandoned their barbaric finery of the night before in favor of civilized garments.

There were four classes of passengers, each with a distinct style. Businessmen and traders such as Banga wore mainly various colorful skirts and soft hand-tooled leather vests, and carried the ceremonial fly-whisks currently in fashion. Rufus's academic fellows were clothed in conservative trousers and jackets, mostly in various combinations of red, green, and yellow. The diplomats wore their incredibly elaborate Garvey-inspired uniforms, including plume-crested hats. Finally, the simple tourists—generally speaking, well-off middle-class families with an interest in discovering their Amero-African roots—wore whatever was fashionable in either Paris, London, Luanda, or Cairo.

All in all, an eclectic assemblage betokening a healthily diverse nation.

A sudden concerted gasp from the crowd caused Rufus to raise his eyes.

The Statue of Liberty had come into view.

Headless, spattered with faded paint, and garlanded with a noose made from a ship's hawser, the Statue seemed to crouch in shame beneath the blue August skies. Her up-raised arm, jaggedly truncated and blackened by an apparent explosion, gaped like her neck, open to the elements. Her hand and torch, flame downward, lay below, embedded in the soil beyond the base's perimeter.

As the condition of the monument sank into the souls of the crowd—Rufus had a momentary flash of horror picturing a similar fate somehow befalling the half-sized Negro-featured replica that stood offshore from Monrovia—an angry murmur began to rise.

"I had better give my little lecture now," said Captain Owole calmly, picking up a microphone and depressing its button. His voice boomed out across the ship.

"Attention, people. This is your captain speaking. I want to offer some information and advice before we dock, and remind you of some salient facts.

"I fully comprehend the depth of your feelings at the sacrilege and devastation you currently witness.

"Although I myself have seen hitherto-classified photos of Miss Liberty, I too was unprepared for the actual sight. Please remember the destruction you are viewing is over fifty years old. The current United States government disavows the actions of its predecessors and has promised to repair the damage once their resources allow.

"This brings me to what we can expect from the current leaders and citizens of the United States. It is not generally known—and the details of what is known are hazy—but for many years the popularity and influence of the Klan has been fading.

"Without internal enemies, they gradually became vitiated and relatively powerless. A recent purge—somewhat bloody, I'm afraid—has removed them from federal positions, although parts of the country remain firmly in their grip. Needless to say, we shall not be visiting these regions.

"In fact, our itinerary will be somewhat rigidly controlled by our hosts. Until relations are normalized and the sight of a Negro is once again no longer an oddity on these shores, we must be protected from unwanted attentions—harmful or benign.

"Finally, I wish to remind you that each and every one of us will be on constant display as we go about our business and pleasures. And each one of us will be regarded—fairly or unfairly—as a representative of our whole race and nation. It is up to each of us to do nothing that could discredit or dishonor our Negritude. We must show the Americans our best natures, and convince them we have put our differences behind us and are extending a hand of friendship.

"Please bear all this in mind, and thank you for listening."

Replacing the mike, Captain de Klerk turned to Rufus.

"Well, what do you think, professor?"

Rufus's head spun. He had just received more new information about his chosen field of study than in the past ten years. "'Think'? About what?"

"You're the expert on America. Will they reciprocate our friendly overtures? Or are they planning to take us for all we're worth, then discard us, as they did our ancestors?"

"Right now, captain, I haven't the slightest idea. For all I know, we could be heading straight into a cannibal's pot."

Laughing, Captain Owole clapped Rufus on the back as high as the short man could reach. "I hardly think a mythical metaphor casting our hosts as anthropophagists would be welcome, professor. Best to keep such flights of fancy to yourself. If you'll excuse me, I've got to bring us in."

Leaving the bridge, Rufus joined the crowd on deck.

A pair of old tugboats, their smokestacks rusty, put out from the

Battery. Slowly, slowly, the massive Black Star liner decreased her speed, allowing the tugs to match vectors and nudge her. Crewmen tossed lines down from the Pan-African ship. At the appearance down below of the first American white faces yet seen, a friendly roar of acclamation rose spontaneously from the assembled Africans. The white sailors appeared uneasy and embarrassed and, after securing the ropes, quickly disappeared back inside their cabins.

Now the *Chicago Bluesman* was entirely under the guidance of the tugs, which drew her gradually toward the appointed dock.

Excitement filled Rufus's breast as he contemplated the legendary towers of Manhattan. Oddly, the skyline looked much as it had in pre-Exclusionary photos. Where were all the new skyscrapers, the effusions of America's famous vitality—?

"Gee, Mom," said an adolescent standing near Rufus, "I've seen bigger buildings in Accra."

"Hush, dear. Remember your manners."

From the ship's position of approximately a hundred yards out, the crowd on shore began to assume rough details. Standing on tiptoe, Rufus scanned the largest mass of white faces he had ever seen, outside of the time he and Mudiwa and the children had attended the quaint Boer Trek Festival held by that rapidly dwindling reservation-sheltered minority.

What struck Rufus first was the uniform grayness of the crowd's dress. There was not a spot or scrap of colored adornment amidst the acres of dingy, fustian fabric except for the small Pan-African flags being waved desultorily, as if by command.

As the ship drew nearer its allotted berth at one of the Midtown docks (she could have chosen from any number of empty slots, since no other vessel of her magnitude was present), individual faces among the front ranks came into focus, causing Rufus to gasp.

These were not the keen-eyed, tanned, semi-Caucasian visages he was used to seeing here and there on the streets of Lusaka, belonging to highly regarded Pan-African "citizens of no color." Nor did the American faces exhibit the paler but still handsome features of visiting European faculty members or, say, League of Nations officials.

The pasty faces collected to welcome the Africans were frighteningly and uniformly slack-jawed and chinless, dull-eyed, sparse-haired, and clogged-pored. It looked to Rufus like a sea of drooling imbeciles and half-wits.

From behind Rufus came the familiar droll voice of Banga Johnson.

"Three generations of inbreeding as contrasted to Africa's three of exogamy, professor. What do you think?"

Rufus turned to confront the beskirted, bare-chested auto magnate. "Surely three generations is too short a time to produce the wrecks we see here."

"It depends on the stock you begin with. In the Northeast, I understand Jukes and Kallikaks are preferred. Granted, these are undoubtedly extra tractable specimens massed with an eye toward good behavior and crowd control. And most assuredly there are many wild Americans who resemble your revered pioneers of yore. But I assure you, Professor Sexwale, the mass of urban Americans today are precisely as you see them now."

"But how?"

"Have you never heard of the American Eugenics Society, Professor Sexwale, and its notorious founder, Davenport? At the turn of the century, its ostensible program was to 'improve' and 'perfect' Caucasian bloodlines. After the Exclusion, it became an arm of the government, with quite a different covert program including mass sterilizations of all remaining Asians, Mediterraneans, Catholics, Jews, homosexuals, and other minorities. As for the startling degenerative effects you now witness—well, the only science in which the United States outstrips us is a kind of narrow-minded, twisted biology. Mutagenic agents, both chemical and radionic, along with manipulation of the embryo with hormones, enzymes, and other subtle factors— Well, as a layman myself, I don't pretend to understand all the details, but my government contacts were quite explicit. I still have nightmares about some of the photos I saw."

At this long-dreamed-of moment, the most exciting opportunity of his professional career, when he had expected to feel only a sense of exultance and intellectual challenge, tinged perhaps with ancestral nostalgia, Rufus experienced quite a different set of feelings: primarily heartsickness and disgust. Quite a bit of this latter was directed at Banga Johnson, who Rufus now realized had been highly disingenuous in their earlier conversation.

"If you and others knew this," challenged the professor, "why was this trip even sanctioned?"

Banga stroked his mustache with a forefinger. "I told you, my dear Rufus, that self-interest makes the world go round. America is still a rich land, if only in terms of her natural resources. Oil, timber, minerals, what have you—they've hardly been touched in the past sixty years of delusion and decay. You know the population of the United States in the year of the Exclusion, I assume?"

"One hundred five million, seven hundred ten thousand, six hundred and twenty," replied Rufus with a stunned pedantic automatism.

"It's half that now. The Americans are having a hard time even maintaining their current infrastructure. That's why they've let us in. With a little luck, Pan-Africa will own this continent in a few years."

"Why haven't they turned to Europe or the Canadians for help?"

"Pride. Paradoxically, it's harder for them to beg from their fellow white folks. With us, they can delude themselves that they are still the masters and we, the slaves."

During their disturbing talk, the ship had come to rest. A broad canopied gangway was let down. In a few moments, the first of the passengers disembarked.

Meekly, in a daze, Rufus let himself be swept up in the flow.

The feebly cheering crowd, held back behind temporary barriers by mounted police, gawked and gaped as the Africans marched proudly along, following the Pan-African diplomatic delegation, which had been first off the ship. Arrayed at the foot of Broadway were dozens of horse-drawn wooden buckboards.

Into these piled the visitors for a ceremonial procession up the Great White Way.

Rufus thought initially that the antique mode of transportation was an anachronistic flourish. Then doubt assailed him.

"No autos?" inquired the professor of Banga.

"Reserved for the privileged. And most of them are vintage models held together with baling wire. Hardly comparable, say, to the Gazelle ISO that you drive."

The first wagons set off. Down the shallow canyon they trundled at barely more than a walking pace. From those windows not boarded up leaned more Americans, emitting weak, unconvincing huzzahs and tossing shredded-newspaper confetti.

Rufus removed some of the debris from atop his head. The print was big and smeary, the few words he could discern only one syllable long. The ink stained his fingers a darker black.

After an interminable journey, they reached City Hall. In front of the building stood a stage covered with red, white, and blue bunting.

The wagons stopped to discharge the passengers, and Rufus found himself standing in the front row of the Africans at the foot of the stage.

Atop the platform was a row of folding chairs and a lectern without any visible electronics. A collection of fairly intelligent-looking dignitaries sat in the chairs. Naturally, they were all white; more remarkably, they were all males of a certain age (Rufus thought briefly of how young their current vice president, Ayobunmi Carter, would look, were she magically placed alongside these politicians). Each of the men had longish white hair and drooping planter-style mustachios. Dressed in sparkling whites, they looked to Rufus as if they'd only recently doffed their conical face-concealing hoods.

Repressing such a baseless reaction as bigoted, Rufus sought to calm himself, to appreciate the moment at hand and the days to come. Although his initial shock at the conditions here had been highly disconcerting, he was determined to make the most of this visit to this glorious country his great-grandparents had been forced to abandon.

One of the Americans approached the podium, and the murmuring Africans fell quiet.

The man spoke in the legendary New York accent (still recalled by elderly survivors of the Great Return), but larded with Southernisms. His countenance displayed unease barely masked by professional civility. Sweat dotted his brow.

"Ahem, I—that is, all of us here extend a big welcome to our visitin' nig—free negroes. As mayor of Noo Yawk, the greatest city in the world, I'm downright proud to play host to this delegation from the upstandin' country of Pan-Africa, which has come so far from such humble beginnins. I'm sure y'all gonna have a helluva time here. We've got some great activities lined up for y'all—"

"Harlem!" yelled a black voice. "We want to see Harlem!"

A chant went up among the Africans. "Harlem! Harlem! Harlem!"

The mayor's air of nervousness visibly increased. He held up his hands for silence and was eventually rewarded, whereupon he resumed his set speech without acknowledging the interruption.

"But before then, I just wanna innerduce a little ol' down-home boy who has a few words to say. Ladies and gentlemen and Negroes, the leader of these here United States, President Coughlin!"

The Africans applauded politely as the eldest figure on stage creakily stood and shuffled to the lectern, clutching a handful of papers. When he spoke, his age-stricken voice hinted at what must have once been a remarkably resonant instrument.

"Thank you, Mayor Duke. Good afternoon, my fellow Amero-Africans, if I may be so bold as to claim kinship with such a splendid collection of bucks and hoochie-coochie girls as I see here before me. Considering the centuries when we lived side by side, there's probably a tiny touch of the tar brush in all of us here on this stage."

The president paused, obviously expecting his own chuckle to be echoed. Receiving only stony silence, he squinted with a touch of irritation, at the same time shuffling his speech as if to skip over a large part.

"Well, I realize that after the rigors of your long journey you're all eager to rest up a tad, so I won't protract this occasion, however pleasant it might be. Let me just conclude by saying I hope America and Pan-Africa can put the past behind us and resume a fruitful relationship of long standing after an unfortunate interregnum. And now, with your permission, I'll ask Reverend Billy to lead us in a short prayer."

Another indistinguishable old man changed places with the president and was greeted with polite applause.

"Thank you. Let us please bow our heads. Holy Father, grant us victory over our enemies, Papist, furrin, heathen, or otherwise, and let us see them crushed into the dust and relegated to the outermost blackness of your ass-smitin' disdain."

Rufus withdrew a fetish of Unkulunkulu hanging from a leather cord beneath his shirt. Gazing at his compatriots, he saw many of them doing likewise, with their own particular deities.

Praying along in his own way with Reverend Billy, Rufus felt he and his countrymen could use all the celestial help they could get.

After Ambassador Jimiyu Hendricks received a golden key to the city from Mayor Duke, the Africans were reloaded onto the buckboards and transported crosstown to their lodgings at the Waldorf-Astoria.

Soon, Rufus found himself alone in what he had to admit was a luxurious and spacious room. If it had had running water, it would have been perfect.

Gazing out his window at Park Avenue, where sheep grazed on the median, Rufus fell into a reverie that was interrupted by a knock on his door.

"Come in," said the professor, half expecting Banga Johnson.

But the visitor was an American.

The sight of him, framed in the open doorway, riveted Rufus to the spot.

Barefoot, shirtless, wearing a straw hat with attached artificial cornrow braids, dressed in patched bib overalls with one suspender strap dangling, a red bandanna hanging from a back pocket, the young man was smeared with burnt cork or some similar substance all over his exposed skin.

"Dey calls me Virgil," said the apparition. "Virgil Cane. I'se gwine ter be yer guide."

Rufus found his outraged voice somewhere deep down in his socks.

"What in the name of all that's sacred are you rigged out like that for?"

Virgil looked down at himself wonderingly. "Why, Lawdy, we done figgered dis way ob dressin' would put y'all at ease, make y'all feel at home."

"Well, it doesn't. Anyone in Lusaka dressed like you would be hauled off for a mental exam."

"Lawdy, how was we'all to know—"

"And quit speaking that abhorrent patois!"

Virgil scrunched up his features. "You mean I can talk normal?"

"That's precisely what I mean. Now, why don't you use that pitcher and basin over there and wash that insulting makeup off?"

Fear took up residence on Virgil's face. "Oh, no, I couldn't do that. I was ordered to— I mean, if I ever dared—"

Rufus sighed. "You may as well just go. I don't need a guide anyway."

Virgil's terror jumped an order of magnitude. "No, please, you have to use me. They won't let you out on the streets alone, and if I fail, then—"

The boy—he was hardly more than that—began to sob, and Rufus walked over to comfort him.

As he endeavored to assure the lad he could remain as guide, Banga Johnson emerged from the room across the hall. With him was a woman. Also in blackface, she wore a gingham outfit and headrag. Voluminous padding endowed her with an enormous rear end.

"Ah, professor, I see you've met your guide. Mine was identical, but I pulled a few strings and exchanged him for his female equivalent. May I introduce you to the beautiful Pearl—"

The woman tittered. "Lawdy, you gwine ter make a gal go all ober shibbers."

Banga smirked. "Charming, is she not?"

Emboldened by Banga's amiability, Virgil stopped sniffling and spoke up. "If y'all be ready, dere's fried chicken and chitlins and watermelon waitin' downstairs."

Somehow, Rufus got through the dinner and the "entertainment" that followed.

But it was neither easy nor pleasant, nor anything like what he had once envisioned back in faraway Lusaka.

The buffet was as Virgil had promised. As Rufus tried to enjoy the foreign food, he was approached by a middle-aged white man, balding and bespectacled. The man wore a small gold pin in the shape of a noose on his lapel.

"Professor Sexwale?"

Rufus extended a hand. "Yes, sir. And you are—?"

The man took Rufus's hand gingerly, as if it were a rotten fish. "Professor Jefferson Davis Hurt. Columbia History Department. We're looking forward to establishing contacts with your school."

"At last, a fellow scholar! I can't tell you, Professor Hurt, how glad I am to find higher learning represented amidst all these political and mercantile types. I trust Columbia fares well these days? The campus is still flourishing?"

Hurt looked nervous. "Ah, well, our circumstances are somewhat reduced. We had to abandon the Harlem campus because of the—for various reasons. Nowadays, we occupy the tenth floor of a very nice midtown building."

Rufus thought of the shady, sprawling grounds of Lusaka University, of the spanking new Kamau Clay History Building and his office therein. "I see. Your department has the tenth floor—"

Hurt looked at the carpet. "No, that's the whole school."

"I beg your pardon?"

"Columbia University rents the tenth floor. It's quite reasonable, really."

After this embarrassing incident, Rufus kept to the company of his fellow Africans for the rest of the meal.

Soon, a general exodus from the Waldorf-Astoria was organized. The Africans piled into the buckboards—which were already becoming as familiar and tedious as the splinters they inflicted—and headed toward Sixth Avenue. At the doors of a large wooden barn-like structure whose sputtering multibulb sign spelled out RADIO CITY MUSIC HALL they disembarked and went inside.

Rufus found himself seated—not accidentally, he reckoned—next to his guide, Virgil. The boy took pleasure in pointing out the various dignitaries assembled.

"Dat's Mistuh Clark, he's a membuh ob de Order ob de White Rose. Next ter him is Colonel Groopman. He's a Grand Titan in de Men ob Justice. Up in the balcony dere, you can see Mistuh Lee. He owns half of Charlotte, Nort' Caroliner—"

"The inhabitants?"

Virgil was shocked. "Mistuh Sexwale, I'se 'prised at you! You know dere ain't no sech thing as slayberry here no more."

At that moment the house lights went down. Virgil whispered

excitedly, "We'se gwine ter see a bunch of willrogers, den some jennylinds, den a moobin' pickture. Finally, dey'se gwine ter be a play!"

"I can hardly wait," said Rufus wearily.

First on stage was a succession of cowboys, all of whom told tiresome cracker-barrel jokes while ineptly spinning lariats. Following them came one female singer after another, their faces caked with white makeup so that Rufus imagined he was watching a Kabuki performance. The ladies all warbled sentimental and lugubrious ditties with names such as "Down by the Old Mill Stream" and "Father, Whither Goest Thou?" Rufus longed for the jit-jivers.

After the departure of the last coloratura, a movie screen was lowered manually in fits and starts. A projector sprang to life, and the screen filled with grainy, scratchy black-and-white images. There was no sound.

"I'se seen dis pickture a hunnerd times!" whispered Virgil. "It's great!" THE BIRTH OF A NATION, read Rufus resignedly.

A black man in the row ahead turned around. Rufus was unsurprised to see his nemesis, Banga Johnson. Banga had his arm well around Pearl's neck, his hand down her collar.

"I wager it's the only film they own, professor. Take me up on it?"

"No thank you."

Banga returned to fondling Pearl, and Rufus settled resignedly in.

When the film was finally over, the screen was lifted. Behind it, the stage had been set for the play.

A placard on an easel stood stage-left.

"AN AMERICAN COUSIN"

AS ENACTED IN FORD'S THEATRE

ON THE NIGHT OF APRIL 14, 1865

Rufus buried his head in his hands.

A short time later, despite his muffled ears, he heard the pistol shot, followed by a sea of uproarious applause and an island of black silence.

That night, his dreams were not pleasant.

The next few days were spent in what soon became a boring routine. Accompanied by Virgil, Rufus was allowed to meander both solo and with groups of his fellows and their guides anywhere he wished on the isle of Manhattan, so long as he stayed south of

Central Park. Beyond this point, the authorities refused them permission to go.

Naturally, being forbidden to enter Harlem—the ancestral territory one and all had traveled so far expressly to see—caused great irritability and many complaints. But the American government was adamant. Harlem was not fit to be visited yet. It needed cleaning. It was unsafe.

And many other similar excuses.

Nothing the Africans said, no promises not to hold the United States liable for any accidents, could shake the determination of the implacable officials.

Barred from doing hoped-for on-site research, Rufus turned to the main city library on Fifth Avenue.

The stone lions—African animals, after all—were smashed and headless.

Rufus and Virgil ascended the broad steps. All doors save one were well barred with planks.

At the lone entrance, an old caretaker greeted them. He appeared well advanced into senility, yet touchingly attentive.

"Yes, yes, the stacks are not all they once were, I fear. And the pigeons—nasty birds!—have made a mess of the Reading Room. But I'll try to find what you request. If only the card catalogue hadn't gone for fuel during the winter of 'fifty-nine! But where there's a will, there's—something or other. I forget precisely what—"

Needless to say, results were less than stupendous.

One morning thereafter, Rufus stood at the Waldorf-Astoria's lobby souvenir stand, eyeing for the fiftieth time the replicas of Lady Liberty for sale, complete with paint spatters and hemp necklace, and shaking his head ruefully.

A hand on his shoulder caused him to turn.

It was Banga.

Eagerly, Rufus turned and clasped the auto magnate's hand.

"I never thought I'd be glad to see you, Mr. Johnson. I confess this city is getting me down. I trust your negotiations have been more successful than my researches."

"Hardly, professor. In fact, they're damn well stalled. These Americans possess an inflated notion of their worth and stature. They're holding out for ridiculous concessions. I understand the ambassador is having no greater luck with his treaties. In fact, I'm thinking of taking today off. Would you like to accompany me on a little expedition?"

"Where to?"

"Ah, to tell would spoil the surprise. Are you game?"

"At this point, I'd follow the devil into hell and call it a vacation."

Banga smiled in his sardonic manner. "Remember those words, professor. Let's go."

"What of our guides?"

"I've arranged a little concert for all the Pearls and Virgils. The jit-jivers are playing in the ballroom right now. The whites love it, but I fear their attempts to dance along are truly pathetic."

Banga conducted Rufus out to the hotel's stables, where they secured a pair of horses. Banga slung a mysterious saddlebag over his horse's rump. Mounted, they rode first west as far as Fifth Avenue, then north.

Before long, they reached Central Park South, where guards armed with Great War–era rifles accosted them.

Banga flashed a pass. They were permitted to continue.

Although burning with questions, Rufus kept silent. He fixed his thoughts on Harlem, assuredly their destination.

Harlem the beautiful. Harlem, the throbbing heart of pre-Exclusionary Negro culture. There, legendary artists had painted, sung, and written. There, churches, taverns, and theaters had flourished. There, First President Garvey, from his offices on 135th Street between Lenox and Fifth, had dreamed of his liberation of Africa, mustered his forces, avoided jail and assassination and duplicity, and eventually won through to victory.

Rufus could hardly wait. This would make up for all the earlier indignities.

They entered a buffer zone of rubble-strewn untenanted acres. Rufus smelled Harlem at the same time he saw the wall around it. A ripe stench as of gangrenous flesh, open sewers, and unburied garbage, carried on breezes to which the high brick wall stretching east and west as far as the eye could see was no impediment.

A wooden gate in the wall blocked Fifth Avenue's uptown progress.

Here, too, stood a pair of feeble-minded guards. Impressing them with his pass, Banga secured entrance.

As the gates closed behind them and they trotted on, Rufus felt his stomach drop.

The buildings on the far side of the wall were no more than crumbling, fire-blackened shells. The damage was old, a product of the same period as Liberty's beheading.

Rufus pictured the hordes of victorious, vengeance-seeking whites who must have rampaged here, making sure no Negroes lingered after the last boat left.

Stopping a few dozen yards inside the walled ghetto, Rufus saw that the physical heritage of Harlem was totally destroyed.

But the district was still populated.

From the ruins they crawled and leaped and hopped and dragged themselves, an army of defectives and cripples. Half-men, animal-women, brutish children, naked with every missing limb or flipper or extra organ on display. Snakes and frogs and apes they resembled, and other, less savory, things. Their calls and cries rang abominably.

Banga smiled, less convincingly than usual.

"The culls, professor. The failed experiments. Not put down out of hand, as a merciful people might ordain, but stored here as a measure of perverse thrift, fed with the city's slops."

Rufus choked out his words. "What—what do you intend?"

"Liberation, professor. Plain and simple. With a tidy profit down the line."

Banga turned to address the crowd of mutants, which, still swelling, easily numbered in the thousands. They did not seem unduly surprised by the appearance of two black men, almost as if they had been prepared by forerunners.

"Friends, it is as prophesied! I am here to lead you to reclaim what's yours! You have only to follow me!"

The noise of the mob grew until it resembled feeding time at the Lusaka zoo.

Without further delay or speech making, Banga swung his horse around. Digging into his saddlebag, he brought out two grenades.

Having pulled the pins, he chucked both at the gate.

Twin explosions rocked the ground.

Then Banga shouted, "Ride! Ride for your life, professor!"

Rufus chose to obey.

He did not look back until they were well down Fifth.

Behind, the monstrous horde spilled out unchecked. Sirens went off all over the city.

Their horses were in a lather by the time they reached the Waldorf-Astoria.

Assembled on the street were what seemed to be all the Pan-African guests.

"To the ship!" yelled Banga, and turned to lead.

On Broadway, the retreating Africans came face to face with a white militia. Led by a saber-waving, medal-bedecked general on horseback, the nervous troops blocked the way with bayonets leveled. Only a few dozen yards separated the two groups.

"Will you let us pass?" demanded Banga.

"Never! Your nigger treachery is known, and you must pay!"

Banga seemed to be stalling for time. "An incident like this spells war."

"So be it! The white man is not afraid to spill either his blood or your sickly juices!"

At that moment a clattering noise was heard. As it grew louder, one and all looked up.

A Tutsi-class helicopter gunship, previously a tarp-shrouded mystery on the decks of the *Chicago Bluesman*, bore down on them.

The whites scattered as the gunship's Gatling guns rattled. Then an expertly aimed air-to-surface missile exploded in their midst.

Rufus was deafened. His horse reared violently, and it was all he could do to hang on. Shrapnel and chips of cement zipped through the air. Several blacks went down with minor flesh wounds. The militia, however, took the brunt of the blast and was utterly devastated and demoralized.

Carrying their wounded, the Africans surged past the dead and dying soldiers and their general buried beneath his gutted horse.

With the omnipotent helicopter shadowing them, they met no further resistance.

Before he realized it, Rufus was back on board the Black Star liner.

Rufus saw Captain Owole calmly supervising affairs from the bridge. A crewman called up, "All accounted for, sir!"

"Engine room, quarter-power reverse!"

The *Bluesman* pulled away from the dock, the airborne gunship covering any possible attacks from land.

Rufus watched the receding shore with queer feelings he had never known before. Already it seemed like a horrid dream.

The first of the mutants spilled out onto the docks. Heedless of the demarcation between land and water, they plunged into the Hudson and swam after the liner, with unclear motives. The gunship picked them off easily.

Now the *Bluesman* was opposite the Statue of Liberty, and well under way.

Banga came to stand beside Rufus.

The factory owner who had proved so adept at intrigue said nothing. Finally, Rufus spoke.

"All planned, wasn't it?"

Banga shrugged. "Of course. I had some freedom from the president to alter my strategy, if the Americans seemed tractable, but there was never much doubt, once I arrived, about what policy would best serve Pan-Africa."

"So now our country has the pretext she needs to invade."

"Precisely, professor. And can you doubt the war will be a short and easy one, given what we've seen of the Americans' military prowess?"

Rufus shook his head sadly. "It seems we never learn—"

Banga's smile was restored to its usual luster. "To the contrary, professor. Need I cite the well-attended lessons of the Spanish-American War, the Mexican-American War, the Guatemalan incursion—"

Rufus was forced to chuckle wryly.

"You're saying the Americans taught us everything we know."

"Your words, professor. Not mine. But then, you'll write the book."

Rufus wondered, though, if he would.

Does anyone read Camus these days the way they once did, several decades ago? He hardly seems the cultural touchstone he once was. Yet I took a chance that enough readers would still identify with him to give him the starring role in the following story. The main point of this alternate history, of course, was to put a certain hegemonic shoe on another national foot. I hardly think the United States is perfect, especially considering some of its more problematic actions in the international arena, but I wanted to pose the question of which country could do a better job, given a similar role.

And the French are just such easy targets!

Sisyphus and the Stranger

Albert Camus was tired. Tired of his job. Tired of his life. Tired of the vast empire he daily helped, in however small a manner, to sustain.

Yet he had no choice but to continue, he felt, like Sisyphus forever rolling his stone up the mountain. His future was determined, all options of flight or rebirth foreclosed.

Sitting in his office in the Imperial Palace in Algiers, Camus held his weary head in his hands. He had been awake now for thirty-six hours straight, striving to manage all the preparations for the dual anniversary celebrations about to commence. This year, 1954, marked fifty years since the glorious discovery of N-rays, and forty years since the birth of the French Empire out of the insufficient husk of the Third Republic. All around the empire, from the palmy isles of the Caribbean to the verdant coasts of South America, from the steaming jungles of Indochina to the tranquil lagoons of Polynesia, across the tawny veldts and plains of Africa and into the lonely islands of the Indian Ocean, wherever the proud French flag flew, in scores of colonies and protectorates, similar preparations were under way.

Poster-sized images of the stern-faced emperor and of the genius inventor René Blondlot, bald and Vandyked, had to be mounted everywhere under yards of tricolor bunting. The facades of public buildings had to be cleansed with a mild application of N-rays. Ballrooms had to be decorated, caterers consulted, parade routes mapped, permits for vendors stamped, invitations issued. Indigent street Arabs had to be rounded up and shipped to the provinces. The narrow, stepped streets of the Casbah had to be locked down to prevent any awkward demonstrations, however small and meek, against the French and their festivities. (Listening to the complaints of merchants whose trade was peremptorily hurt in advance of any unlawful gatherings was infinitely preferable to answering the questions of cynical reporters concerning the corpses of demonstrators charred to cinders by the N-ray cannons of the police.) And perhaps most important, security measures for the visit of the emperor had to be checked and double-checked.

And of course, Camus's superior, Governor-General Merseault, was absolutely no help. The fat, pompous toad was excellent at delivering speeches once they were written for him, and at glad-handing businessmen and pocketing their bribes. But for achieving any practical task the unschooled Merseault (an appointee with relatives in high places back in France) relied entirely on his underling, Camus, trained in the demanding foreign-service curriculum of the prestigious École Nationale d'Administration.

Camus lifted his head from the cradle of his hands and smiled grimly, his craggily handsome face beneath a thick shock of oiled black hair seamed with the lines of stress. *Ah, Mother and Father*, he thought, *if only you could see your little boy today, for whom you scraped and saved so that he might get the best education in the ancestral homeland. At a mere forty-one years of age, he has become the power behind a certain small throne, yet finds himself utterly miserable.*

But of course Camus's parents could not witness today his abject state. They had both perished in Algiers in the anti–*pieds noirs* riots of 1935, roughly twenty years into the existence of the empire, when Camus himself had been safely abroad in Paris. So many had died in that holocaust, both Europeans and Arabs, before the soldiers of the empire with their fearsome N-ray weapons and N-ray–powered armored vehicles had managed to restore order. Since that harsh exercise of power, however, peace and harmony had reigned in Algeria and across the empire's many other possessions, several of which had received similar instructional slaughters.

Camus's sardonic smile faded as he contemplated the bloody

foundations of the current era of global peace and prosperity emanating from Paris. He reached for a pack of cigarettes lying next to an overstuffed ashtray, secured one, and lit up. An abominable, necessary habit, smoking, but one that was slightly excusable in these days when lung cancer could be cured by medically fractionated N-rays, as easily as the rays had cured Camus's childhood tuberculosis —at least if the patient was among the elite, of course. Puffing his cigarette, leaning back in his caster-equipped chair, Camus permitted himself a few minutes of blissful inactivity. Two flies buzzed near the high ceiling of his small, unadorned, spartan office. The blinding summer sunlight of Algiers, charged with supernal luminance by reflection off Camus's beloved ancient Mediterranean, slanted in molten bars through the wooden Venetian blinds, rendering the office a cage of radiance and shadow. Yet the space remained cool, as N-ray-powered air conditioners hummed away.

Camus's mind had drifted into a wordless place when the screen of the interoffice televisor on his desk pinged, then lit up with the N-ray-sketched face of his assistant, Simone Hié, an austere woman of Camus's own years.

"M'sieur Camus, the American ambassador is here to see you."

Camus straightened up and stubbed out his cigarette. "Send him in, please."

As the door opened, Camus was already on his feet and moving around his desk to greet the diplomat.

"Ah, Ambassador Rhinebeck," said Camus in his roughly accented English as he shook the American's hand, "a pleasure to see you. I assume your office has received all the necessary ducats for the various celebrations. There will be no admission to events without proper invitations, you understand. Security demands—"

The silver-haired, jut-jawed Rhinebeck waved away the question in a gruff manner. Not for the first time, Camus was simultaneously impressed and appalled by the American's typical bluntness.

"Yes, yes," the ambassador replied, "all that paperwork is being handled by my assistants. I'm here on a more important matter. I need to see the governor-general immediately, to register a formal protest."

One of Camus's many duties was, if at all possible, blocking just such annoying demands on Merseault's limited capacities. "A formal protest? On what matter? Surely such a grave step is not required between two nations with the amiable relations that characterize the bonds between the United States and the empire. I'm certain I could be of help in resolving any trivial matter that has arisen."

Rhinebeck's blue eyes assumed a steely glint against his sun-darkened skin. Despite the air conditioning, Camus began to sweat. The two flies that had been hovering far above had now descended and were darting about Camus's head, making an irritating buzz. Camus wanted to swat at them, but refrained, fearing to look foolish.

"This is not a trivial matter," said Rhinebeck. "Your imperial soldiers have detained a party of innocent American tourists on the southern border with Niger. They are refusing to release them until they have been interrogated by your secret service. There's even talk of transferring them to Paris. These actions are in violation of all treaties, protocols, and international standards. I must see Merseault immediately to demand their release."

Camus considered this news. There was a large military installation on the border with Niger, where N-ray research deemed too hazardous to be permitted in the homeland took place. Was it possible that these "innocent American tourists" were spies, seeking to steal the latest developments in the technology that had granted France uncontested global supremacy? Quite possibly. And if so, then Merseault, in his amateurish, naïve, blundering way, might very well cave in to Rhinebeck's demands and grant the American concessions that would prove damaging to the best interests of the empire. This possibility Camus could not permit. Best to let the military and the omnipresent Direction Générale de la Securité Extérieure handle this affair.

Camus was tired of the empire, yes. But when all was said and done, he knew nothing else. His course became clear, and any hesitancy vanished.

Time to push the rock uphill once again.

"Ambassador Rhinebeck, I regret that I cannot forward your request for an audience to the governor-general. However, you may rest assured that I will personally monitor the situation and keep you informed as to the fate of your countrymen."

Rhinebeck's resolve and bluster seemed to evaporate in a moment, in the face of Camus's brusqueness. He suddenly looked older than his years. "So, more stonewalling. I had hoped for better from you, Albert, since I thought we were friends. But ultimately I should have expected such a response from someone in your superior position of strength. You realize that America is toothless against the empire. There's nothing we have to offer in exchange, nothing we can do, no threat we can make, to sway the empire toward our point of view."

"Oh, come now, Henry, don't take that tack. Surely you exaggerate—"

"Do I? Maybe you know something about my country's international stature that I don't. We face French outposts on all sides of our nation, limiting our actions, forbidding our natural expansion. Quebec, Cuba, Mexico, the Sandwich Islands, all of them under French control and bristling with N-ray armaments. Our trade deficit with France and its possessions grows more burdensome every year. Our allies are equally weak. Spain, Germany, even the formerly majestic United Kingdom, have all proved powerless in the face of French conquests. Your empire has become something totally unprecedented in human history. Let's call it a superpower. No, no—a *hyper*power. There is no nation left to offer a counterweight to your actions. You do exactly as you please, in any situation, and tell the rest of the world to be damned. Yet frustrating as the political situation is, we could contend with fair competition in international matters. But it's your cultural dominion back home that's really killing us. Our young people are aping French fashions, watching French cinema, reading French books. Our own domestic arts are dying. We're being colonized mentally by your empire. And that's the most insidious threat of all."

Camus was about to attempt to refute Rhinebeck's unblinkingly realpolitik analysis of global affairs, when he realized that everything the ambassador had said was absolutely true. Disdaining hypocrisy, Camus merely said, "I am sorry, Henry, that the world is as it is. But we must both make the best of the reality presented to us."

"Easy enough to say from where you sit, in the catbird seat," said Rhinebeck. The ambassador turned away sharply then and exited.

The encounter left Camus unsettled. He had to get away from his desk. Consulting his watch, Camus saw that it was past one P.M. He would go have lunch at Céleste's restaurant.

Camus activated the televisor. "I will be out of the office for the next hour."

"Yes, m'sieur."

Outside, the heat of the July day and the sheer volume of the sunlight smote Camus brutally, yet with a certain welcome familiarity. Born and raised here, Camus had integrated the North African climate into his soul. He recalled his time in Paris as years of feeling alien and apart, distressed by the city's foreign seasons almost as much as by the natives' hauteur when confronted by a colonial upstart. At graduation he had been most relieved, upon securing his first posting, to discover that he had been assigned to the land of his birth. He had never left in all the years since. The love he felt for Algiers, a place open to the sky like a mouth or a wound, was a secret thing in his life, but also the engine that sustained him through all his angst and anomie.

Walking easily down the broad boulevard of the Rue d'Isly, with its majestic European-style buildings nearly a century old, Camus felt his spirit begin to expand. If only he had time for a swim, his favorite pastime, life would begin to taste sweet again. But he could not permit himself such indulgences, not, at least, until after the emperor's visit. Flanked by sycamores, the Rue d'Isly boasted parallel sets of trolley tracks running down its middle. At one point the tracks bellied outward to accommodate a pedestaled statue of Professor Blondlot, holding aloft the first crude N-ray generator.

Camus enjoyed watching the cool-legged women pass, the sight of the sea at the end of every cross-street. From an Arab vendor (license prominently displayed) he purchased a glass of iced lemonade flavored with orange-flowers. Sipping the cool beverage, Camus was attracted to a public-works site where other onlookers congregated. From behind the site's fence spilled the edges of a crackling glare. Camus knew the source of the radiance. N-ray construction machinery was busy slicing through the earth to fashion Algiers's first metro line, running from Aïn Allah through downtown and on to Aïn Naadja. Camus looked through a smoked-glass port at the busy scene for a moment, then continued on his way. He hoped the new metro would not mean the extinction of the nostalgia-provoking trolley cars, and made a mental note to arrange some subsidies for the older system.

A few blocks farther on, Camus arrived at his destination.

In the doorway of the restaurant, his usual place, stood Céleste, with his apron bulging on his paunch, his white mustache well to the fore. Camus was ushered into the establishment with much to-do and seated at his traditional table. He ordered a simple meal of fish and couscous and sat back to await it with a glass of cold white wine. When his lunch came, Camus consumed it with absent-minded bodily pleasure. His thoughts were an unfocused kaleidoscope of recent problems, right up to and including Rhinebeck's visit. But eventually, under the influence of a second glass of wine, Camus found his thoughts turning to his dead parents. He recalled specifically his father's frequent anecdotes surrounding the elder man's personal witnessing of the birth of the empire.

The year was 1914, and the Great War was newly raging in Europe. Camus's father was a soldier defending France. Far from his tropical home, Lucien Camus and his comrades were arrayed along the river Marne, preparing for a titanic battle against the Germans, and fully expecting to die, when the miracle happened that saved all their lives. From the rear lines trundled on their modified horse-drawn carriages some curious weapons, guns without open bores, strange assemblages of batteries and prisms and focal reflectors. Arrayed in an arc against the enemy, the uncanny weapons, upon command from Marshal Joffre himself, unleashed deadly purple rays of immense destructive power, sizzling bolts that evaporated all matter in their path. The German forces were utterly annihilated, without any loss of life on the French side.

After this initial trial of the new guns, the Great War—or, as most people later ironically called it, "the Abortive Great War"—continued for only another few months. Impressive numbers of the futuristic weapons were deployed on all fronts, cindering all forces who dared oppose the French. The Treaty of Versailles was signed before the year was over, and the troops of the Triple Entente occupied Germany, with the French contingent predominant, despite objections from its allies England and Russia. (Just four years ago, Camus had watched with interest the results of the very first postwar elections allowed the

Germans. Perhaps now the French civil overseers in the defeated land could be begin to be reassigned to other vital parts of the empire.) The transition from Third Republic to empire was formalized shortly thereafter, with the ascension of the emperor, the dimwitted, pliable young scion of an ancient lineage.

Of course, the question on all tongues at the time, including Lucien's and his comrades', concerned the origin of the mystery weapons. Soon, the public was treated to the whole glorious story.

Ten years prior to the Battle of the Marne, Professor René Blondlot had been a simple teacher of physics at the University of Nancy when he became intrigued by the newly discovered phenomenon known as X-rays. Seeking to polarize these invisible rays, Blondlot assembled various apparatuses that seemed to produce a subtle new kind of beam, promptly labeled N-rays, in honor of the professor's hometown of Nancy. At the heart of the N-ray generator was an essential nest of prisms and lenses.

In America, a physicist named Robert Wood had tried to duplicate Blondlot's experiments and failed to replicate the French results. He journeyed to Nancy and soon concluded, quite erroneously, that Blondlot was a fraud. Seeking, in the light of his false judgment, to "expose" the Frenchmen, Wood had made a sleight-of-hand substitution during a key demonstration, inserting a ruby-quartz prism of his own construction in place of Blondlot's original. When, as Wood expected, Blondlot continued to affirm results no one else could see, the American planned to step forward and reveal that a crucial portion of the apparatus was not even consistent with the original essential design.

Ironically and quite condignly, the ravening burst of disruptive violet energy that emerged from the modified projector when it was activated incinerated Wood entirely, along with half of Blondlot's lab.

Accepting this fortuitous modification, the scorched but unharmed Blondlot was able to swiftly expand upon his initial discovery. Over the next several years, he discovered dozens of distinct forms of N-rays, all with different applications, from destructive to beneficent. Eventually his work came to the attention of the French government. When hostilities commenced in June of 1914, the French military had already secretly been embarked on a program of construction of N-ray weapons for some time. Under the stimulus of war, the first guns were hastily finished and rushed to the Marne by September.

Now, forty years later, N-rays technology, much expanded and embedded in France's vast navies, armies, and aerial forces, remained a French monopoly, the foundation on which the ever-expanding empire rested, and the envy of all other nations, which waged constant espionage to steal the empire's secrets, spying so far completely frustrated by the DGSE. Not the Russian czarina nor the British Marxist cadres nor the Chinese emperor nor the Ottoman pashas nor the American president had been able to successfully extract the core technology for their own use. And as France's dominion grew, so all these aforenamed nations shrank.

So much did every schoolchild of the empire learn. Although not many of them could claim, as Camus could, that their fathers had been present at the very first unveiling of the world-changing devices.

Camus's ruminations were interrupted by the arrival of Céleste at his table. The plump proprietor coughed politely, then tendered a slip of paper to his patron.

"A gentleman left this earlier for you, m'sieur. Please pardon me for nearly forgetting to deliver it."

Camus took the folded sheet of note paper and opened it. Inside was a simple message.

> Dear Sisyphus,
> Meet me tonight at the dance hall at Padovani Beach. I have a proposition that will change your life, and possibly the world.

Camus was dumbstruck. How did some stranger come to address him by his unrevealed sardonic nickname for himself? What unimaginable proposition could possibly involve Camus in world-altering events?

Camus summoned Céleste back to the table.

"What did this fellow look like?"

The restaurant owner stroked his mustache. "He was an odd duck. Completely bald, very thin, with odd smoked lenses concealing his eyes. But most startling was his mode of dress. If he's wearing the same clothes when you see him, you won't be able to mistake him. A queer suit like an acrobat's leotard, made of some shiny material and covering even his feet, poked out of the holes of a shabby Arab robe that seemed like some castoff of the souks. At first I thought him part of the circus. But upon reflection, I believe that no circus is in town."

Camus pondered this description. This stranger was no one he knew.

Camus thanked Céleste, folded the note into his pocket, paid his bill, and returned to the office.

The rest of the afternoon passed in a stuporous fog. Camus consumed numerous cups of coffee while attending in mechanical fashion to the never-ending stream of paperwork that flowed across his desk. All the caffeine, however, failed to alleviate the dullness of his thoughts, the dark befuddlement that had arrived with the stranger's note. Merseault called on the televisor once. The governor-general wanted to ensure that his counterpart from the French Congo was bringing all the native women he had promised to bring during the upcoming festivities. Merseault had a weakness for Nubians. Camus promised to check.

At eight o'clock Camus bade his equally hard-working secretary goodnight, and left the palace. Two streetcar rides later, he arrived at Padovani Beach.

The famous dance hall situated in this location was an enormous wooden structure set amidst a grove of tamarisk trees. Jutting with awnings, the building's entire seaward side was open to the maritime breezes. With the descent of darkness, the place came alive with the violet-tinged N-ray illumination from large glass globes. (Suitably modulated, N-rays could be conducted along copper wires just like electricity.) Couples and single men and women of all classes streamed in, happy and carefree. Notes of music drifted out, gypsy strains recently popular in France. Camus wondered briefly why the intriguing "jazz" he had heard at a reception at the American embassy had never caught on outside America, but then realized that Rhinebeck's tirade about the unidirectional flow of culture from France outward explained everything.

Inside, Camus went to the bar and ordered a pastis and a dish of olives and chickpeas. Halfheartedly consuming his selections, Camus wondered how he was to meet the writer of the note. If the stranger remained dressed as earlier described, he would be immensely out of place and immediately attract notice. But Camus suspected that the meeting would not occur so publicly.

For an hour, Camus was content simply to admire the dancers. Their profiles whirled obstinately around, like cut-out silhouettes attached to a phonograph's turntable. Every woman, however plain, swaying in the arms of her man, evoked a stab in Camus's heart. No such romantic gamine occupied his life. His needs were met by the anonymous prostitutes of the marine district, and by the occasional short-term dalliance with fellow civil servants.

Finally Camus's patience began to wear thin. He drained his third pastis and sauntered out to a deck overlooking the double shell of the sea and sky.

The stranger was waiting for him there, sitting on a bench in a twilit corner nominally reserved for lovers, just as Céleste had depicted him.

The stranger's voice was languorous and yet electric. His shrouded eyes disclosed no hints of his emotional state, yet the wrinkles around his lips seemed to hint at a wry amusement. "Ah, Albert, my friend, I was wondering how long it would take you to grow bored with the trite display inside and visit me."

Camus came close to the stranger, but did not sit beside him. "You know me. How?"

"Oh, your reputation is immense where I come from, Albert. You are an international figure of some repute."

"Do not toy with me, m'sieur. I am a simple civil servant, not an actor or football hero."

"Ah, but did I specify those occupations? I think not. No, you are known for talents other than those."

Camus chose to drop this useless line of inquiry. "Where exactly do you come from?"

"A place both very near, yet very far."

Growing impatient, Camus said, "If you don't wish to answer me sanely, please at least keep your absurd paradoxes to yourself. You summoned me here with the promise of some life-altering program. I will confess that I stand in need of such a remedy for the moribund quandary I find myself in. Therefore state your proposition, and I will consider it."

"So direct! I can see that your reputation for cutting to the heart of the matter was not exaggerated. Very well, my friend, here it is. If you descend to the beach below and walk half a kilometer north, you will encounter a man sleeping in the dunes. He looks like a mere street Arab, but in reality he is a trained Spanish assassin who has made his laborious covert way here from Algeciras and on through Morocco. He intends to kill the emperor during your ruler's visit here. And he stands a good chance of succeeding, for he is very talented in his trade, and has sympathizers in high places within your empire."

Camus felt as if a long thin blade were transfixing his forehead. "Assuming this is true, what do you expect me to do about this? Do you want me to inform the authorities? Why don't you just go to them yourself?"

The stranger waved a slim hand in elegant disdain. "Oh, that course of action would be so unentertaining. Too pedestrian by half. You see, I am a connoisseur of choice and chance and character. I believe in allowing certain of my fellow men whom I deem worthy the opportunity to remake their own world by their existential behavior. You are such a man, at such a crucial time and place. You should consider yourself privileged."

Camus tried to think calmly and rationally. But the next words out of his mouth were absolute madness. "You are from the future then."

The stranger laughed heartily. "A good guess! But not the case. Let us just say that I live in the same *arrondissement* of the multiverse as you."

Camus pondered this response for a time, striving to reorder his very conception of the cosmos. At last he asked a broken question. "This multiverse is ruled—?"

"By no one. It is benignly indifferent to us all. Which makes our own actions all the more weighty and delicious, wouldn't you say?"

Camus nodded. "This is something I only now realize I have always felt."

"Of course."

"Can you give me a hint of the alternate outcomes of my actions? Will one decision on my part improve my world, while its opposite devastates it?"

The stranger chuckled. "Do I look like a prophet to you, Albert? All I can say is that change is inescapable in either case."

Camus contemplated this unsatisfying response for a time before asking, "Do you have anything to aid me if I choose to accept this challenge?"

"Naturally."

The stranger reached beneath his robe and removed a curious gun unlike any Camus had ever seen.

"Its operation is extremely simple. Just press this stud here."

Accepting the gun, Camus said, "I need to be alone now."

"Quite understandable. An act like this is prepared within the silence of the heart, like a work of art."

The stranger arose and made as if to leave. But at the last moment he stopped, turned, and produced a book from somewhere.

"You might as well have this also. Good luck."

Camus accepted the book. The faint violet light reaching him from the dance hall allowed him to make out the large font of its title, *The Myth of Sisyphus.*

The author's name he somehow already knew.

After the stranger had gone, Camus sat for some time. Then he descended to the sands and began walking north, carrying both the book and the pistol.

Just where the stranger had specified, Camus found the sleeping man. His hands were pillowing his head as he lay on his side. The waves crashed a maddening lullaby. In the shadows, the sleeper's Iberian profile reminded Camus of his mother, Catherine, who boasted Spanish ancestry herself, a blood passed down to her son.

It occurred to Camus that all he had to do was turn, walk away, and think no more about this entire insane night. His old life would resume its wonted course, and whatever happened in the world at large would happen without Camus's intervention. Yet wasn't that nonaction a choice in itself? It crossed his mind that to fire or not to fire might amount to the same thing.

The assassin stirred, yet did not awake. Camus's grip on the pistol tightened. Every nerve in his body was a steel spring.

A second went by. Then another. Then another. And there was no way at all to stop them.

I think of this story as a cousin to my novella about Whitman and Dickinson, Walt and Emily, *to be found in* The Steampunk Trilogy. *Poets—at least the majestic icons of the past—offer such perfect ready-made protagonists, full of weltschmerz and other high emotions. Grab a poet as your leading man or woman, and you've instantly got a wealth of human feeling, and likely also some ditzy, unconventional lifestyles to play with.*

Even when you plunge them into a milieu of penny-a-word pulp fiction.

A Monument to After-Thought Unveiled

"Life is an after-thought . . ."

—Robert Frost, "A Monument to After-Thought Unveiled" (written when he was eighteen)

Up the steep ascent of College Hill in Providence, Rhode Island, in March of 1924, at a wintry, shadow-thronged hour long past midnight, labored the attenuated, castoff-swaddled form of the horror writer.

He had been tramping about through both city and countryside since 10 A.M. of the previous day, seeking to quiet his tumultuous brain, where thoughts raced like chips in a millstream. That selfsame morning had seen the dawn of his natal day, marking his fiftieth year of existence on this cursed globe. The intense self-reflection occasioned by this portentous milestone had immediately overwhelmed all the makeshift defenses of sanity he had erected over the past twelve years, since that tragic day in 1912 when his life went so radically off course. In anticipation of this sad anniversary, unable to pen either new fiction or correspondence, his wonted reading materials bleached of interest, the horror writer had hastily donned several layers of moth-eaten sweaters atop his omnipresent union suit, wool trousers, and broadcloth shirt. Against the exterior cold (hardly any worse than that in his cheap rented rooms; would spring never arrive?), he completed his outfit with the long tatty cloth coat kindly passed down to him by two of his few local friends, the similarly impoverished poetess Muriel Eddy and her husband, a fellow *Weird Tales* contributor, Clifford Eddy. Thus accoutered, with less than thirty cents in change to supply his nourishment for the day's exertions, he plunged out of his grim widower's flat.

In the ensuing hours he covered much ground. Heading north out of the city, he made for Quinsnicket Park, one of his favorite sylvan locales, where, during temperate seasons, he oft composed his work al fresco. But for once, sight of the massive boulders like Cyclopean monuments, and large, dark, mysterious Olney Lake had failed to raise his spirits. The leafless trees seemed to mock all human ambition, betokening a terminus to life upon the planet, a day when no living thing would stir from icy pole to pole.

From there he sought solace in several of his favorite small villages bordering the park, such as Saylesville and Fairlawn. But the hustle and bustle of factory workers and tradesmen and schoolchildren held no distraction for him today.

Despairing of his old haunts, he struck out for pastures less well trodden, crossing into Valley Falls and thence into neighboring Massachusetts. But even the suggestive, moss-covered, anciently disused rural cemeteries he chanced upon, with their weathered stones listing like drunken sailors, failed to lift his thoughts out of their weary self-pitying maelstrom.

From here, he had little memory of the paths and byroads he took. A vague sensation of having eaten at a lunch wagon—some noxious meat pie swilled down with coffee—remained with him. All he knew was that when dusk fell he was some score miles away from home, in the town of Bristol, on the East Bay. Weary and dispirited, he spent his last five cents on a trolley ride, but got off impulsively some few miles outside Providence. The rest of the hours until his footsore ascent of College Hill were spent at a nighted overlook of the bay, as he revolved the idea of self-destruction in his fatigued brain. The nigrescent tidal waters seemed to whisper alluring invitations to his soul.

But at last he not so much positively decided against such a cowardly way out of his troubles, as he merely acknowledged that today he lacked the initiative to consummate such a frequently considered relief. And so, without having either surmounted or been beaten by his nightmares, but rather merely exhausted them while they exhausted him, he once more turned his feet toward home.

Now, climbing from the sidewalk up the steps to his shabby Waterman Street residence, he fumbled for the key to a place he could hardly distinguish with the term "home," a place equally meaningless to him as every other place on earth.

Beyond the front door, in the common hall, the smell of early-morning greasy breakfasts cooking on illicit gas burners came to him. Before he could attain the relative sanctuary of his own rooms, a door opened and a burly, shirtless laborer emerged, making for the communal lavatory. Through the open apartment door, the horror writer caught a glimpse of a teeming family scene—slatternly wife and mother, a pack of grimy children—and the mockery of what he himself had lost twelve years ago struck like a knife into his heart.

Pushing past the sleepy, unoffending laborer, the horror writer hurled himself into his own rooms. Still dressed, he fell onto his spavined cot and, mercifully faster than he would have predicted, Robert Frost was asleep.

The thirty-acre farm in Derry, New Hampshire, had never provided an authentically agrarian living for Robert Frost and his family: his wife, Elinor, and their children, Carol (the only son), Irma, Lesley, and Marjorie. They had scraped by on loans and various makeshift subsidiary enterprises for twelve years. Owner of the property since 1900 (and even then only thanks to the financial support of his stern Yankee grandfather, William Prescott Frost), the ex-reporter, failed poultryman, eccentric schoolteacher, and would-be poet had ultimately failed to consummate his back-to-the-land dreams, just as he had failed with all the other schemes of his maturity, including that of making his mark on the body of American verse. Oh, yes, a few of his poems had been published, but only in such minor vehicles as the *Derry Enterprise*, the *Independent*, and *New England Magazine*. But as for achieving recognition from the Boston and New York critical establishments; as for having the mass of his unpublished work (all fine material, he was convinced) gathered into book form; as for elevating his name to the same plane as that occupied by Edwin Arlington Robinson, Amy Lowell, and Edgar Lee Masters—well, at the despair-inducing age of thirty-eight, he felt himself as remote from these attainments as he had been at the callow age of sixteen, when his first poem appeared in the *Lawrence High School Bulletin*.

The year 1912, then, marked a self-appointed climacteric in Frost's life. Determined to make a clean break with his discouraging past, he had fixed on the idea of transferring his whole family to England for an indefinite span. There, on the soil that had produced so many of the fine poets he admired, he felt that his talents would bloom and be appreciated. England held out the hope of the success that had so far eluded him in his native land. Gathering all his available resources together, including the annual stipend left to him by Grandfather Frost, the poet had just managed to cover the cost of the trip and a reasonable term abroad.

Elinor and the children were excited by the prospect. Even Elinor's frequent nervous depression—a recurring melancholy matched only by her husband's, who shared with his sister Jeanie a congenital disposition to black moods—lifted in the face of the foreign rebirth. Happily packing their many trunks, Elinor and the Frost children had speculated gaily on the new life that awaited them. Frost thought they sounded like a flock of the happy ovenbirds he oft admired on his botanizing walks, and was pleased.

The family was set to sail from Boston on August the twenty-third.

A month prior to that date, Frost entered hell.

It was late evening. Frost had been out alone on a ramble, wandering the hills around Derry, his head stuffed with fragments of poems, visions of public accolades, visits to Westminster Abbey. Unlike many such occasions, he had forborne to take any of his children with him, neither his son Carol nor any of the girls. He had started late from home, and moreover he wanted his solitude.

Now, eager to regain his hearthside, nearing the road to his farm, Frost was disconcerted by unnatural activity at several of the neighboring homesteads. Flickering oil lamps behind curtained windows revealed that the diligent farmers and their wives were up and about much too late, as if agitated like a troubled hornets' nest.

Intuitively fearing that the source of the neighborhood turmoil lay for some reason at his own residence, Frost quickened his pace. Could one of the children have fallen ill or been injured? Ever since the death of their first boy, Elliott, Frost had lived in fear of just such a tragedy.

The scent of smoke alerted him to the actual nature of the catastrophe. He began to run.

The entire Frost homestead, outbuildings included, raged as a solar inferno, unnaturally dispelling the night. In the rabid lineaments of the conflagration, Frost discerned a leering demonic face that conformed to the visage of his darkest terrors. A demon arising from his wallow to laugh, brushing the dirt from his eyes as he rose. And well Frost knew what the demon meant.

The useless equipment of the Derry Volunteer Fire Corps was ranked at a safe distance from the inferno, firefighters seeking to calm their nervous horses, despite their own human horror.

A familiar-looking mustachioed man with soot-streaked face, his name driven from Frost's brain by the mortal circumstances, warily approached Frost.

"I'm sorry, Bob, but not a soul escaped. I'm sure it was quick for them though. The smoke itself—"

Those implacable words were the last sounds Frost was cognizant of for the next several days. His mind deserted his body and he collapsed to the warm, grass-tufted soil, the mockery of its rich summer fragrance of birth and growth competing with the charnel smell of the pyre.

When he next gained some small possession of his senses, he found himself in a half-familiar bedroom. Gradually he recognized the place as belonging to his friend Sidney Cox, a teacher at Plymouth High School. A nervous Cox himself sat in a chair beside the recumbent Frost. Upon seeing the older man's eyes flicker open, Cox essayed a small smile and said, "Robert, welcome back to the world. You've been comatose for nearly a week, and we feared for your recovery."

Frost's voice husked sepulchral. "You're addressing a dead man, Sidney, with words that mean nothing."

Cox paled. "Don't say that, Robert. You've experienced a huge tragedy, certainly, but one not unparalleled in human existence. Life goes on, after all. Surely all the worldly wisdom you've shared with me in our long talks will come now to your aid."

Silent a moment, Frost eventually replied, "I find all my high-minded concepts and speech-making utterly vacuous now, Sidney. A crushing but irrefutable realization has overtaken me. All my playing with tragedy prior to last week's fatal night was just the action of a child seeking to frighten itself with shadows, simply to make the hearthside look brighter. I was a blissfully ignorant pedant until I saw everything that mattered to me go up in cruel flames. Not only were Elinor and the children of my flesh in that holocaust, but also all the children of my fancy. All my poems are ashes now, all the verses I meant for my first book. *A Boy's Will.* Sidney, do you recall my projected title? Well, both the boy who dreamed in verse and the man who sought to perfect those dreams are dead."

Cox gamely tried to dissuade Frost from this morbid conceit. "Then who am I talking to now, may I ask?"

"A ghost, Sidney. A ghost."

Frost spent another week in Cox's tender care. Some of that time was devoted to settling his affairs in Derry. He attended the closed-casket ceremony for his family, five coffins like so many loaves of hard bread out of the oven, and saw them interred. He found a buyer for the ruined farmstead, a neighboring farmer who generously paid more than the going rate for the property, out of sympathy for Frost's loss. Frost banked the money without either discernable gratitude or embarrassment. What worth did this useless paper hold for a man in his position?

When as a young man Frost had thought that his offer of marriage to Elinor had been spurned, he had done something romantically foolish, if not a little mad. Bumming his way south toward the Great Dismal Swamp, with half an eye toward self-destruction in that remote preserve beloved by poets from Longfellow onward, Frost turned his back on family, friends, and his art. Now that Elinor and his children and his hard-won stock of poems had been removed from him by Fate, he fixed on a similar course of action.

Bidding a terse farewell to Cox and a few others, Frost set out upon the longest ramble of his life.

Up and down the eastern seaboard he roamed, afoot and by rail, or hitching rides from strangers in buckboards or the occasional newfangled horseless carriages. From Miami to Baltimore, Norfolk to Portland, he made his ceaseless, pointless migrations, seeking to expunge his grief with mad activity, to lose his individual suffering self among the nameless masses of men. For money, he wrote drafts upon his account in Derry, although sometimes he had a hard time convincing suspicious bank managers that the disheveled vagrant before them was the legitimate holder of these funds. His longest trip came when he hobo'd his way to San Francisco, the city of his birth and his first eleven years. There, surprisingly, amid the bittersweet memories of his childhood, he somehow derived a small nascent solace that allowed him to contemplate his future with some dim interest, albeit still no joy.

Picking up a pen one idle moment as he sat in a cheap rented room in the Tenderloin, Frost wondered what his hand intended to produce.

Much to his surprise, his long-tortured brain poured forth not a poem, but a tale. A horror tale, to be precise, one much like those of Poe, whom Frost had long admired. The story was titled "The Demiurge's Laugh," and sought to convey the hideous demon-spoken revelations Frost had derived from the immolation of his family, transplanted to the shoulders of another unfortunate.

The year was now 1914. Frost kept the manuscript of the story with him as he resumed his peregrinations, for it continued to haunt him, even though confined now to paper. One day in Chicago, he gained access to a typewriter at a library and drafted a clean copy of the text. He stuffed the typescript into an envelope and mailed it, without any means for editorial reply, to *The Black Cat* magazine, hoping to rid himself of a burden.

Half a year later, in Cleveland, he found his story in print on the newsstands.

He contacted the editor of *The Black Cat*. Payment swiftly followed, and a generous request that he submit more such stories.

By now Frost—his thick shock of hair gone white at forty, his health half-ruined, his furrowed face a map of too much drink and too many nights spent under heavy weather—was heartily sick of the road, and resolved to settle down. At first he thought of making

Baltimore his new home, in honor of Poe. But then his old love affair with New England reawakened. That region had always represented to him the best of the country, of America's spirit. Northern New England, however, held too many painful associations, so he cast his eye toward the south.

And found Providence.

Frost arrived in the bustling industrial seaport at the head of Narragansett Bay in early 1916, just as his hoarded money was running out. After finding cheap lodgings, he began to write. At first, his occult stories were merely a means to survival. But soon they began to occupy the role of an essential pressure-release valve for his turbulent brain.

Argosy and *All-Story. Thrill Book* and *Scrap Book. Cavalier* and *Blue Book* and *Mystery Magazine.* All soon had run horrific stories under the Robert Frost byline. "Ghost House," "The Death of the Hired Man," "Home Burial," "The Road Not Taken," "The Oft-Repeated Dream," "The Witch of Coos," "A Passing Glimpse." In two years' time, Frost had amassed a considerable reputation among those readers and editors who appreciated the grimly fantastical.

A reputation that was all ashes in his mouth. Necessary as these stories were to his mental health, they excited in him only the palest shade of the ecstasy and pride his poems had once brought him.

Frost's growing literary prominence among a certain set made it inevitable that he would attract the notice of one of his fellow Providence citizens possessed of similar interests.

Howard Phillips Lovecraft was some sixteen years Frost's junior, still a bright yet introverted mama's boy at the age of twenty-eight. He was visibly shaken by the fact that his mother had recently been confined to Butler Mental Hospital, in that spring of 1919. He humbly approached Frost after arranging an interview for an amateur press publication. Frost found the younger man's admiration flattering and his writerly ambitions amusing. Now that he had an audience, the ex-poet's long-stifled old urges to hold forth in long lectures were reawakened now for the first time in seven years. Frost resolved to take Lovecraft under his wing.

By the time Sarah Lovecraft died, in 1921, her son was a changed man. He had set up housekeeping on his own, rejecting the smothering nest offered by his spinster aunts. Inspired by Frost's own professionalism, Lovecraft had broken into print himself with several beginner's stories that found homes in the same publications that Frost's appeared in.

Although never happy or content, Frost took some small pleasure in the changes he had abetted in Lovecraft's life. The older man relished using the younger as a sounding board for his cold-blooded cogitations on the meaninglessness of the universe. The younger, calling his mentor "Grampa Jack" as a play on "Jack Frost," seemed pleased mainly to listen, interjecting his own thoughts only occasionally.

But the changes in Lovecraft's personality had unintended consequences.

Frost was first introduced to a pretty young hat maker and amateur-press aficionado named Sonia Greene when she arrived in Providence to visit Lovecraft. From the outset it was apparent that Lovecraft was as smitten with Sonia as she was with him.

The announcement of their impending marriage and move to New York City struck Frost harder than he ever imagined it could. By now, the Eddys had joined the Lovecraft-Frost circle. But as a married couple with three children, they could hardly offer Frost the complete acolyte's devotion that Lovecraft had provided.

Lovecraft's departure for New York in late 1923 threw Frost into a black funk. He ceased writing for several weeks, and sought relief from his melancholy in cheap dago wine from Federal Hill, and on the weary urban footpaths.

But the latest news by letter from his ex-neighbor—in conjunction with Frost's fiftieth birthday—had been a gust of wind that truly broke the spine of a birch already well bent.

Lovecraft had been offered the editorship of the newly launched *Weird Tales* magazine, and had gleefully accepted.

> The gorgeous missus and I are off to Chicago, Grampa Jack! Who'd'a ever thunk this granite-ribbed Yankee would ever hie his carcass all the way out to the land of wheat and

> wide waters. Call me Clem and stir my coffee with a hog's knuckle! But you can rest assured that yer boy geen-ye-us editor will not forget all the sharp lessons he's larned at the feet of the Master. And now the pages of WT are wide open for some sockdolager Frostian shiver-makers!

Frost crumpled the letter and flung it across his room. Down deep, he knew he should be pleased with Lovecraft's rise in the world, and the younger man's continued friendship. But the contrast with his own sorry condition overwhelmed any empathy.

By his birthday of March 1924, Frost had reached the trough of his despair.

The smallish house in East Providence that barely contained the bubbling Eddy family was a modest dwelling indeed. Two stories tall in the main, with a single-story addition, twin-chimney'd, set on a small lot on Second Street enclosed by a black-painted picket fence, the domicile rested comfortably in frowsy disrepair. The lack of funds in the Eddy exchequer, attributable to the Bohemian ways of Muriel and Clifford, necessitated many daily hard shifts. But the life of the mind they enjoyed, the conviviality of their socializing, and their dedication to matters of art offset any physical deprivations. That their children manifested a blithe indifference to their poverty added an aura of Edenic innocence to the household.

That late morning of March 28, 1924, a Saturday, the sun shone brightly on the Eddy doorstep. The long winter's grip, unrelenting until just yesterday, had finally broken, it seemed, and tokens of spring were apparent, from the greening buds of the lilac by the door to the greening scents in the gentle breeze, as if the belated season were striving to make up for lost time.

Down Second Street trudged Robert Frost, hatless, his snowy hair a haycock. His perpetual air of scarred hopelessness seemed somewhat moderated by sheer enervation. Passing through the gate, he climbed the single step of the Eddy house and knocked.

The door was soon thrown back by one of the Eddy children, a boisterous young girl named Flora.

"Ma! Pa! It's Uncle Bob!"

Frost reached down and absent-mindedly tousled the girl's dark hair, then moved past her into the house. A battered horsehide sofa, many books on shelves and scattered elsewhere, a framed Currier and Ives scene of a sleigh stopping by a woods on a snowy evening. An isolated gas jet illuminated a corner of the parlor where sunlight did not penetrate. There, a desk hosted Clifford Eddy's typewriter and sheaves of work in progress. Clifford was not seated at his desk, however.

Muriel appeared from the entrance to the kitchen. A stout, round-faced, dark-haired woman wearing glasses, Muriel beamed at the sight of her friend. The Eddys were not yet thirty, and possessed all the youthful exuberance that Frost and Elinor had once enjoyed.

Wiping her hands on her apron, Muriel advanced across the room and hugged Frost. "We were just sitting down to some lunch, Bob. Won't you join us?"

"I suppose."

In the kitchen Frost encountered the rest of the Eddys: crag-faced Clifford and his Penrod-like sons, Alder and Maple, otherwise known as Al and Mel. A spread of cold chicken, potato salad, homemade bread, and baked beans drew the hungry stares of the boys back after a brief polite acknowledgment of "Uncle Bob's" arrival. Once Flora had drawn up her chair and said a brief grace, the family dived into their repast.

Despite his ennui, Frost found himself possessed of an inordinate hunger. He fell on his food like a wolf, and the Eddys forbore from questioning his unannounced arrival, letting him enjoy his meal. Instead, the couple and children chatted of local matters, school chums and neighborhood gossip. Clifford and Muriel both sensed that any literary talk would be unwelcome. Frost maintained a dour silence.

When the last slice of bread had swabbed the final smear of mayonnaise, the children asked to be excused to play outside. Once they were gone, Frost broke down.

"Cliff, Muriel—I'm at my wit's end. I can't deny the bitter truth any longer. I've wasted my whole life. All my fifty years have been just so much dust on the wind. When I was young and heedless of life's innately tragic cast, I frittered my time away. I never pushed hard enough to get my poems into print. If I had really tried, I could have made my name by the time I was twenty-five. But I just didn't have the gumption. Then, when—when I lost my family, I simply fell apart. I didn't have the backbone or strength to start over with my poetry, so I threw away everything I had left, and became the pitiful specimen you see before you. I—I don't know where to go from here, and I'm compounding my sins by dumping my problems in your laps."

Clifford and Muriel both rushed to contradict Frost's self-abasing autobiography.

Muriel said, "Robert Frost, you're talking nonsense now. You've led a blameless life that hasn't harmed anyone but yourself. You're basically as healthy as a horse, despite your lack of sound nutrition and a little too much tippling. You've got ten, twenty, maybe thirty good years ahead of you, if you could only get out of your own way."

"Bob," said Clifford, massaging the right side of his long jaw thoughtfully, "aren't you forgetting one important item on the credit side of your ledger? You've got your current career to be proud of. As a writer of eldritch tales, you're second to no one in this country. Haven't Howard and I often said we've learned practically everything we know from you? Why, the complimentary letters that flooded into *Weird Tales* after the appearance of your short novel *The Star-Splitter* would have made any other writer's head swell up the size of a first-prize pumpkin at the state fair! I know I'd kill for such a response to any of my stories."

Frost dismissed these encomiums with a disgusted wave of his hand. "Gothic tripe! Bogeyman stories for juvenile minds. What respect do such hackneyed supernatural exercises earn me from the world at large? I can't interest any publisher in assembling my tales into book form. And even if I found a publisher, no reviewer or critic in his right mind would turn his attention to such a volume. How does such low regard consort with the stature a man my age should have attained? If my writing meant anything, surely I would have earned the world's approbation by now. Perhaps I'd even be a teacher or lecturer, or hold some other respectable position."

Muriel registered her disdain for such high-flown fantasies with a demure snort. "What other honors would you have? Maybe to be the poet laureate of the nation, standing by the president's side?"

Clifford's rough face expressed puzzlement. "Bob, what's come over you? You always held your stories in higher regard than this. Haven't they served you well on a personal level?"

"Bah! They've been nothing more than momentary stays against confusion."

"But other people love them—"

"Other people can go to hell! What have these readers ever done for me!"

Now Muriel fixed Frost with such a stern look—so foreign to her jolly face—that even his self-indulgent, self-pitying fury had to wither and vanish. She withheld her words until she was certain Frost was listening closely.

"Robert Frost, what you're lacking is a human connection to ground you in this sad and wonderful mortal world. You're always alone, even when you're in company. Just you and that whirring intellect, exploring the chilly stratosphere. You don't have anyone to nurture or take care of, someone who would do the same for you. I know you suffered a grievous loss when your wife and children perished. Lord knows if I'd hold up any better if I lost Clifford and the kids. But I do know this: there's nothing wrong with you or your life that the love of a good woman wouldn't cure."

Now Frost exhibited an air of bluff chagrin. "An old wreck like me go courting? Muriel, you must have been into the bathtub gin!"

"Don't accuse me of your own sins, Robert! I know what I'm talking about, and I know I'm right. That's why I want you to come to a small party we're giving tonight. Cliff was going to swing by after lunch and invite you if you hadn't happened to show up on your own. There'll be a woman there I want you to meet. Someone very sympathetic to your work. A lovely person, full of pep and common sense. But special in her own way, as well."

Frost could be seen debating the matter within himself. Clifford sought to sway him by adding, "Mure'll be making her lard-crust apple pie, Bob . . ."

Frost got decisively to his feet. "I've got to go now."

"But Bob, why—" Muriel began.

Frost tried to appear stern, but a small yet real smile further wrinkled his seamed visage. "Hell, woman, all the hours twixt now and midnight wouldn't suffice to make me look attractive to a member of the opposite sex. But at least I can toss on a clean shirt!"

Wearing his only decent suit, a sturdy brown wool outfit, Frost returned at dusk to the Eddy household, the first of the guests to arrive. He had indeed freshened his appearance, even going so far as to get a professional haircut. The toilet-water utilized by the barber filled the Eddy's parlor with a gingery scent.

But Frost was not in a jovial mood. Clutched in his hand was a letter, the obvious source of his irritation.

Thrusting the letter under Clifford's nose, Frost said, "Read this! It was waiting for me at home like a water moccasin in the reeds. Damn the nerve of that young whelp!"

Clifford took the letter and began to read aloud.

"'Dear Bob, I'm sorry to say that ye olde editor Theobald was not as mightily impressed with your latest effort, "Moth Seen in Winter," as he has been with the majority of your previous conceptions. The piece seems oversubtle and strained to me. True, the apparition of a living moth amidst a frigid clime is a potent portent of the uncanny. But the hero's rather tedious musings—pardon my extreme candor—on the fate of the moth take up much too large a portion of the story, blunting the climactic revelations, which are numinous enough already.

'Now, you know that I have always been an advocate of restraint when depicting the gruesome. Suggestions of the eldritch are often more effective than outright portrayals of ichor and fangs. But one is hard-pressed to say exactly what happens to your hapless indigent poet at the climactic moment. Does he "cross the gulf of well-nigh everything" into the world of perpetual summer whence came the moth? Or does he merely die of inanition in the snowbank? *Weird Tales* readers will not stand for such shilly-shallying, I fear.

'Now, please, Grampa Jack, do not take my words as other than a constructive goad to produce the exquisitely chilling work of which I know you are capable. Fergit the poetry, bo', and shovel on the supernatural!'"

Clifford looked up from the letter. His face bore a mixture of empathy and amusement. "Hell, Bob, you've gotten worse rejections than this. We all have! It's just part of the game. It was only natural that Howard would drift over to the enemy's camp once he got his hands on the helm of a real magazine. Don't sweat a single crummy rejection. Just turn that story right around. I bet you'll sell it to a better-paying market next week! Why not try the *Cosmopolitan* or *Harper's* for a change?"

Frost snatched the letter from Clifford, crumpled it, and tossed it into the blazing fire on the hearth that warmed the room. But after this gesture of defiance, he deflated.

"That damnable story's already made the rounds of every possible market. I dug it out of the trunk once Lovecraft took over, since he was the only editor who had never seen it before. Cliff, I'm dry. Drained of ideas and ambitions. I'm washed up, and ready to chuck it all."

Clifford clapped his friend on the back. "Buck up, Bob! Every writer goes through rough patches. Soon you'll be pumping out better stories than ever before. I'm sure of it! But tonight you're not to worry about such things. Tonight you're just going to enjoy yourself. Muriel! Bring Bob a birch beer, please!"

Muriel emerged from the kitchen with a quart bottle of Fox-brand soda pop and a glass. Lifting the bale, she tipped back the rubber-ringed metal cap and poured Frost his drink.

"Robert Frost, I don't want to hear another word about the business of writing tonight. You can talk about literature if you must—most of our guests will hail from the amateur-press crowd, after all—but only as an appreciative reader. And when you are introduced to that special gal I mentioned, try to remember that women appreciate hearing about something other than lousy word rates and balky editors.'"

Once again, Frost responded to Muriel's motherly admonitions. "Very well, I'll try. What's this filly's name, by the way?"

"Hazel Heald. She's a member of our writer's club and she's coming down all the way from Somerville, Massachusetts, for this get-together. So treat her to some of that sparkling Frost wit you dole out so sparingly."

Frost was about to plead that his wits were all dull as horseshoes when a knock sounded at the front door. Clifford went to admit the second guest of the evening, who proved to be Ed Cole, from Boston, whose amateur journal, the *Olympian*, was a paragon of the amateur-press scene. Cole greeted Frost heartily and began to quiz him about the prospects of the Providence Gray Sox. Soon the two men were engaged in debating the relative merits of various ballplayers. As various other guests arrived, the small parlor became warm and noisy, and Frost appeared to be actually enjoying himself.

By nine o'clock, Hazel Heald had not yet appeared, and Frost had in fact nearly forgotten the promise of her arrival. Then, in the midst of a game of laughter-provoking charades—Frost was one of the audience—someone tapped Frost on his shoulder. He turned.

"Hello, Mr. Frost. I'm Hazel Heald."

The woman was not precisely plump, but was definitely well upholstered. Her short black hair formed a tight wavy cap on her head. In the face, she reminded Frost of no one so much as the female half of the cartoon urchins that advertised Campbell's soup. Her round, cherubic, rosy features seemed more childlike than womanly. She wore a rather dowdy ensemble of dark-blue velvet jacket and skirt.

Frost stepped backward out of the charades circle to respond to the introduction. Finding the Heald woman initially unattractive—Frost could not help contrasting Hazel's florid looks with the delicate lines of his Elinor's never-forgotten, classically beautiful face—the writer nonetheless summoned up all his good manners and responded graciously.

"Delighted to meet you, Miss Heald. I understand you've been kind enough to express an interest in my foolish little stories."

"Please, call me Hazel. And I'll call you Robert."

Frost was a tad put off by the woman's presumption, but consented. "Very well, if you wish."

"That's so nice. Indeed, I've enjoyed everything you've ever written, Robert. And I did not find your tales to be foolish at all. Quite the contrary. And I am no mere fan. Your work has conveyed a message to me. A message about all the pain you've endured, and how this pain has enabled you, however briefly, to pierce the curtain of reality and experience the cosmic foundations. In turn, I have brought an urgent message for you."

Having no idea what to make of this disconcertingly enigmatic talk, Frost attempted a flip attitude. "If you are going to present me with some sort of bill from a cosmic creditor, you'll have to stand in line behind the mortal ones."

Hazel did not immediately respond. She merely gazed deeply into Frost's gray-blue eyes. Her own eyes, Frost noted, were entirely gray, almost bestial or Pan-like. Gray of the moss of walls were they. Now, suddenly, they captured in miniature a flare from the fireplace, and for a moment Frost reeled as if drunk. When he recovered, Hazel had taken a step away, smiling tantalizingly.

"We'll speak more of this at the party's end, Robert."

Frost returned to the gay crowd attempting to unriddle the mute actions of the charader. But he could no longer lose himself in the play. Whatever hypnotic trick that woman had played on him, the effects did not immediately evanesce.

Around midnight, the party began to wind down. By ones and twos and threes, the guests took their hearty leave of the Eddys. As the mantel clock chimed one, a seated Frost looked up from melancholy contemplation of his own gnarled hands to discover that only the Eddys and Hazel remained in the room.

Clifford approached Frost and said, "Bob, I have to confess that we've arranged this whole party just as a prelude to this moment. You see, our friend Hazel is a sensitive. She has certain talents, and she is here to put them at your disposal, for your salvation."

Frost climbed wearily to his feet. "Cliff, I have no idea what you're driving at. But I don't need any Aimée Semple McPherson preaching over me, trying to save my nonexistent immortal soul, if that's your intention."

Muriel stepped in. "Hazel's not a preacher, she's a witch."

The simple unexpected word brought Frost up short, but he rebounded rather insolently. "A witch? Can you discern the contents of locked boxes then, or make common tables rear and kick like mules, like the trained performers of the Society for Psychical Research?"

Hazel did not seem affronted by Frost's disbelief. "No. But I can speak to the dead."

Frost collapsed nervelessly back into his chair. He gripped his hair with both hands and tugged harshly, as if to lift off the top of his head. "Now this has passed into sheer cruelty. You're planting your boot in the face of a drowning man! Clifford, Muriel, you're both false friends—"

Muriel hastened to Frost's side. "No, Bob, we're not! We only have your best interests at heart. This is a chance you have to take, if you ever want to heal yourself. Let Hazel open up a conduit to the afterlife for you, and perhaps you'll hear something that will help you. Please, Bob, try to approach this with the innocence of a child."

This last phrase triggered long-buried memories in Frost.

He was seven years old when he experienced his first instance of clairvoyance. The actual object of his visionary glimpse was forgotten. But something brushed across his mind whose source he would never find. He easily recalled, however, how the incident upset him. He ran to the skirts of his beloved mother, Belle, and tearfully disclosed everything to her. Amazingly, she was not surprised. Belle was a Swedenborgian, a follower of a faith that easily accommodated such visions. She soothed her son, and actually made him relish the thought of such preternatural extensions of his senses. Thereafter, he welcomed any and all eruptions of the uncanny into his life. Indeed, many times while composing his poetry Frost felt himself to be taking dictation from some extramundane source.

But of course all such numinous access had vanished twelve years ago, when the flaring, fleering demon had reared up at him from the pyre of his dreams. Composition of his paltry stories never involved any heavenly hand guiding his pen.

Frost released his madman's grip on his scalp and looked up at the three faces regarding him. The visages of the Eddys manifested only sincere concern, while Hazel radiated an assured and almost beatific good humor. Had Hazel urged him on then, Frost's contrary nature would have made him refuse her help. But her serene silence had the desired effect.

Frost's voice was small but determined. "Show me whatever spirits you can, then."

The four assembled around the kitchen table, the room illuminated only by a single candle centered on a cracked plate atop the table. Hazel said, "Please join hands." One of her own sought

Frost's, and he accepted it. Hazel's small hand was a hot coal melting into the snowbank of his own.

There followed no incantations or mummery, no incense nor convenient distractions that would allow trickery. Hazel simply closed her eyes, while her breathing fell into a deep cadence. Frost felt his own breath slowing to match hers. But then, as if a galvanic current had passed through her, Hazel gave a spastic jerk and her eyes flew open.

And when she spoke, it was with Elinor's immemorial voice.

"Bob, I fear you are doing poorly without me."

Frost felt tears leaking from his eyes. He fervently wanted to believe he was actually talking to Elinor's shade. But a residue of doubt afflicted him.

"Elinor—if it is you, then tell me what gift I gave you when I visited you at school in 1894."

"I could never forget, Bob. It was that unique little book you had printed. Only two copies ever existed. One for me and one for you. *Twilight*, you titled it."

Frost felt simultaneously hollowed out and filled with some nameless glowing substance. "Dearest Elinor, yes, yes, it's true! Since you were taken from me, I have been not a man at all, but just a shambling husk. Oh, why did such a tragedy ever have to befall us?"

Elinor's voice issuing from Hazel's lips was calm. "We can't know such things, Bob, even after death. The universe splits and branches every instant, and whatever path we find ourselves on is our destiny."

"Are you and—are you and the children happy, Elinor?"

"Yes, Bob, very happy. And I wish I could share our bliss with you. But I suspect that simply talking to me will not accomplish any long-lasting transformation of your heart. After we say goodbye, you'll begin to waver and doubt the events of this evening. You've always been such a skeptic, Bob. Only the things you could touch or handle would convince you entirely. Or, what would be worse, you'll set me up as some kind of lofty angel, and continue to martyr yourself to my memory. No, Bob, my voice alone cannot offer you the sure path out of your misery. For that, you must seek out the Nevernaught. Goodbye, Bob. I love you."

"Elinor, don't go! I love you, too!" Frost jumped up, breaking the handclasp, as if to fly down unseen dimensions after the departing shade.

Hazel blinked then, and spoke in her natural voice. "What happened? Was contact made?"

Muriel recounted what had transpired during the seance. Hazel considered carefully the matter carefully before offering her response.

"I know where the Nevernaught is to be found. Or, at least, where conditions are propitious for a meeting. Robert, will you come with me?"

Frost knuckled his overflowing eyes. "Of course. What choice do I have?"

March 29 dawned lush and welcoming. Birds twittered, pockets of remnant snow hidden on northward slopes gleefully cooperated with the heat toward their own dissolution, and a bustling, grateful, shirt-sleeved humanity reclaimed the sidewalks of East Providence. The winter seemed truly to have fled.

At the Eddys' early-breakfast table, Frost and Hazel shared the family repast of johnnycakes and bacon. Both visitors had bunked at Second Street after the seance ended. Hazel had bunked with the children, while Frost sprawled across the horsehide sofa, so exhausted by all that had happened as to be oblivious to its protruding springs. Now, considerably rumpled, Frost focused on imbibing his third cup of coffee, as he sought to concentrate his mind. The conversation with Elinor's ghost, the odd injunction she had laid upon him, the sense of his life teetering on some precipice—all these issues preoccupied him.

Nonetheless, he remained observant enough to take note of Hazel's attitude and behavior, since so much rested on this stranger's character. In contrast with Frost's disheveled state, Hazel appeared as neat, if dowdy, as she had last night. She had enjoyed a hearty breakfast with ladylike gusto, while chatting amiably with the children. Flora seemed particularly taken with her, laughing at her nonsensical chatter. The medium—the witch—seemed an uncomplicated person.

But Frost suspected that, like any square yard of simple forest soil, she concealed an entire sophisticated and alien civilization beneath her surface.

At nine-thirty the Eddys began to make ready to attend church. Soon the family and their guests stood at the front gate, ready to go their separate ways.

Hazel patted the heads of the children. Al and Mel's normally unruly hair had been brilliantined flat. "Enjoy the services, Muriel. Robert and I are heading for our own sort of natural chapel."

Clifford tilted back his fedora and clapped Frost on his shoulder. "You're in good hands, Bob. I expect that when we next see you, you'll be feeling considerably more chipper."

In the sober light of day, Frost experienced some doubts about the wisdom of committing himself to the hands of this unknown witch. "Such an outcome of this haring about after spooks would be a welcome surprise. But I'm not counting on it."

Muriel said, "Robert Frost, such a defeatist attitude is hardly likely to merit success." She stood on tiptoes and kissed Frost's stubbly cheek.

Then the Eddys departed.

Frost turned to Hazel. "Exactly where are we heading, to meet this 'Nevernaught'?"

"Why, Robert, only to someplace you've already exhibited an affinity for. The Dark Swamp."

Frost jolted backward. Hazel's comment struck deep into his memories, hitting one of the most tumultuous periods in his life.

Shortly after the twenty-year-old Frost had poured out his heart to Elinor, gifting her with that copy of *Twilight*, he received intelligence that caused him to believe that she had spurned his gift, rejected his soul-offering, and that she had pledged her hand to a rival. Plunged into black despair, Frost conceived of only one possible retreat that would match the anguish of his being: North Carolina's Great Dismal Swamp. A legendary haunt of melancholy, affirmed as the recourse of heartstricken lovers by many of Frost's heroes, such as Longfellow and Thomas Moore, the Great Dismal Swamp seemed the only fitting abode wherein to nurse his wounds—or extinguish his very consciousness.

By train and steamer he made his way to the boggy wasteland. Hurling himself on foot into its darkling interior, still clad in his unsuitable street clothes, Frost battled briars and vines and sinkholes for ten miles, until darkness fell. Just on the point of casting himself into the marsh's peaty waters, he stumbled upon a party of duck hunters. Suddenly, human company appeared precious to him, and his mood began to lift. Over the next few days, he experienced various misadventures back in the South's small towns, which culminated in his humbly wiring his mother for the train fare home.

But how could Hazel know any of this? Perhaps her remark merely referred symbolically to some aspect of his personality she divined. Frost chose for the moment not to interrogate her on this point.

"Yes, I suppose my stories have exhibited an affinity for the nighted places of the earth. But are you speaking literally?"

"Yes, I am. We need to ride a trolley to the village of Chepachet, to visit its Dark Swamp."

Vague memories of conversations with Lovecraft on various Rhode Island locales rumored to possess supernatural qualities now returned to Frost. "I believe I've heard of this locus of mystery. All right, then, let's catch a ride downtown, to Exchange Place."

As they strolled toward the East Providence trolley stop, Frost sought to learn more about his companion. Hazel needed little prompting to talk about herself.

"I'm thirty-eight. No special male friends, but plenty of chums of both sexes in the amateur-press world. I enjoy writing, but have commenced to suspect that I have little talent for it. I live in the same town I was born in, with my widowed mother. It was she who helped me become a witch, for it's an old family calling among the Heald women. But I'm only a pauper witch, not inclined to feather my own nest with my skills. Not do I indulge in any kind of repellent or malicious work, such as milking bats or riding bony old men naked through the night. I prefer to use my abilities to help people. People who deserve it. Such as you, Robert."

Frost was silent. Hazel's easy candor disarmed him. She seemed utterly open and aboveboard, yet remarkably unshallow. There were depths to this woman not yet apparent.

They boarded the first trolley to stop for them and rode west, crossing the sparkling Seekonk River. In the center of Providence they transferred to the Chepachet-bound car and settled down for an hour's trip.

Their conversation turned to abstract literary matters, and Frost found Hazel to be a well-informed devotee of the arts. The ride into the state's northwestern rural domains proved congenial and passed swiftly. Before Frost quite expected it, they were disembarking in Chepachet Village.

The heartening sunlight fell upon a rambling, well-tended cemetery that climbed a hillside. Small stores lined a quarter-mile stretch of the main road, known as the Putnam Pike, which, if followed farther, would lead all the way to Hartford, Connecticut. The several private homes that could be seen appeared wholesome and well maintained.

"Well, what next?" Frost inquired, as they stood in front of a farrier's, shuttered and quiet on the Sabbath.

"Let's inquire at this tavern."

Frost asked Hazel to wait outside, leery of the potentially bawdy atmosphere inside the dining establishment. But to his surprise, he found the Stage Coach Tavern to be a reputable place, and just gearing up for the lunchtime trade. Frost buttonholed a portly elderly woman polishing silverware, and soon had directions. Moreover, he managed to secure a sack lunch for the two of them, spending his last fifty cents. He hoped Hazel could supply carfare back to the city.

He hoped that after his hegira into the Dark Swamp he would be in any condition to ride home.

Rejoining Hazel, Frost said, "We need to seek out the property of a farmer named Ernest Law. It's a mile farther down the road."

"Let's get walking then! There's no more splendid recreation on such a fine day!"

Hazel's sentiments pleased Frost, and he offered the woman his arm, at least for their promenade through town, where the sidewalks allowed them to walk abreast.

When they reached the outskirts of the village, where only fields and forests and the isolated homestead greeted their gaze, Frost dug out the paper-wrapped roast-beef sandwiches supplied by the tavern and shared them with Hazel. Two large pickles spiced the meal. They ate as they walked down the muddy, gravel-strewn road, conversation temporarily abandoned. Hardly had they finished their apples—a bit mealy, after a long winter in storage—when a rutted, weedy sidetrack appeared.

"This must be the Law farm," Frost ventured. "Their road appears little traveled. I take it the Dark Swamp is not a popular destination."

Hazel said, "The road less traveled always offers vaster prospects than the high road. Never hesitate to venture down such paths, Robert."

Frost bristled. "I wasn't hesitating, woman! Let's move on!"

They turned and followed the track that bent its way through the undergrowth.

After perhaps half a mile, they caught sight of what was presumably the Law farm: an unpainted, weather-silvered, one-story residence in poor repair, nursed by various outbuildings of equal shabbiness. Moving across the sumac-invaded lawn, Frost and Hazel reached the shoddy steps. Soon Frost was knocking at the door.

When the door swung open, it revealed a bony woman with a careworn yet friendly face, her checked house dress faded and much mended. "Yes? How may I help you?"

"Mrs. Law?" Frost inquired. "We're visitors from Providence who are keen to see the Dark Swamp. We understand that at least a portion of it extends across your property."

The woman regarded Frost and Hazel as if they had recently escaped from some sanitarium. "That worthless blotch of land does indeed intrude on our property. Why anyone in his right mind would want to dally there is beyond me. But if you continue to follow the track until you pass the last cornfield, you'll come directly to it. You'll have to excuse me now. I'd offer you some refreshment, but we've just today had a death in the family. It's our hired man, and we are busy trying to arrange a home burial."

"Oh, please, pardon us—" began Frost. But before he could finish his apology he was talking to a closed door.

Leaving the sad-aspected house behind, Frost said glumly to Hazel, "Sorrow is the one constant in every human life."

"Is it, Robert?" was her reply. "Remember that happiness makes up in height what it lacks in breadth."

Past the tattered detritus of last year's harvest the pilgrims moved. Some distance off, a line of crooked trees betokened the border of the Dark Swamp. Frost felt impelled to ask Hazel a question.

"Hazel, exactly what is this Nevernaught from whom I am supposed to derive some solace?"

"The Nevernaught itself will reveal as much of its nature to you as you can handle, Robert. For now, let's just say that you will never meet any being of larger capacities."

Frost harumphed. "I suppose I'll have to be content with such mystical formulations until the moment of truth, if any."

Hazel stopped, and Frost perforce did likewise. They were adjacent to a low stone wall—partly tumbled, lichen-crusted boulders scattered like the heads of decapitated warriors.

"I feel you are beginning to doubt the reality of that which we seek, Robert. Allow me to show you something of the unfathomed nature of existence."

Hazel stooped and knocked on the nearest boulder.

"Stonebear, stonebear, show yourself!"

The first response to Hazel's invocation was a rumbling underfoot. Frost distinctly felt the ground quiver. Then, at the foot of the wall, soil began to boil. A blocky furred head pushed up into the air, soon followed by the creature's body. Its emergence sent another section of the wall cascading down.

The stonebear was as large as a small child. Its head resembled that of a walrus, with shorter tusks, while its mud-coated tawny body reminded Frost of a woodchuck's—with feet like curved shovel blades.

Ignoring the humans, the stonebear began powerfully pawing down the upper courses of the wall until Hazel said, "Enough! Begone!"

The anomalous creature immediately dived back down its hole like a seal entering the water.

Hazel regarded the gape-mouthed Frost with a wry smile. "The stonebears are the guardians of the earth's rocks. They spend their days moving stones about underground, for reasons no one has ever quite understood. But I assume their behavior aids the maternal earth in some fashion. The stonebears resent the human use of their flinty charges for walls, and will knock down any wall that's not protected by a local witch. Any town whose stone walls are succumbing to something which does not love them, is a town bereft of its witch."

Frost finally found his voice. "Farmer Law has his wall mending cut out for him now, thanks to my doubts. Best we move on before my skepticism causes our host any more labor."

Before much longer, Frost and Hazel attained the line of arthritic trees, realizing that it indeed marked the marge of the Dark Swamp. The land beyond this border was not immediately sodden and impassable, but seemed to transition gradually from solidity, insofar as their vision could penetrate the marsh. Skunk cabbages flared bright green. A footpath led off across various tussocks and ridges.

"Follow me," said Hazel, and Frost did.

They moved deeper into the Dark Swamp, leaving behind daylight and certainty of footing. Even without foliage, the trees of the Dark Swamp seemed to occlude the sunlight. The ground grew squishy under Frost's soles.

After some indeterminate time that seemed eons (yet the sun never moved from its perch in the sky), Frost was on the point of asking how much further they had to traverse this cloistered dankness when Hazel called a halt.

They had reached a sizable island in the bog. Astonishingly, the island was covered with premature flowers, well in advance of any such colorful carpet in the outer world. But these were not wild blooms, rather a remnant of some lost garden, mostly simple tulips and daffodils. Realizing this, Frost noticed that the middle of the island featured a roughly rectangular gap in the flowers. He advanced cautiously toward the irregularity.

The gap was a cellar hole. Here at one time had stood a house. Now the only trace of the structure was a slope-side declivity. In one corner of the cellar hole, three or four moss-furred stairs descended to nowhere.

Frost suddenly experienced the cellar hole as an empty eye socket in the earth, somehow still able to pin him with an inhuman stare.

Hazel broke Frost's fascination with the cellar hole by speaking. "Here in a simple cottage for uncounted millennia lived an unchanging member of an ancient race, the last survivor of a dawn people, those who furnished Adam's sons with wives. He was the guardian of the Dark Swamp and its secrets. But in this new benighted age we inhabit, when God seems perpetually on the verge of saying for the final time, 'Put out the light,' the guardian has moved on. Too few seekers come this way anymore to sustain him."

"He—this guardian—he is not the Nevernaught?"

"No. The Nevernaught is another. Let us inform that being now that you wish an audience."

Hazel knelt among the flowers, and Frost mimicked her without knowing why. Hazel placed her lips against the golden bell of a daffodil. "Nevernaught, I bring you one who inquires after answers to the questions and doubts that plague him. May he see you?" Hazel shifted her ear to the mouth of the flower. She listened for a moment, then bade Frost do the same.

Frost bumped the daffodil with his hairy ear. Perfume enveloped him.

From the fragile trumpet the single word was whispered repeatedly: "Come, come, come . . ."

Frost regained his feet. He hardly knew whether he was standing or still kneeling, whether it was night or day.

Hazel guided Frost to the edge of the cellar hole. "You must go down."

Frost turned an imploring face to Hazel. "You'll come with me?"

Hazel smiled, and Frost felt a faint surge of confidence. "Not today."

Frost's shoulders slumped. But then, resigned to the exclusionary nature of his quest, he set his foot upon the first step.

It took thirteen impossible steps for daylight to vanish entirely. Frost never looked back, but fancied he would have seen a dwindling, green-edged square of light with perhaps Hazel's head framed therein.

In his descent, Frost recalled for the first time in many years the shunned fate of his sister Jeanie. Always mentally unstable, she had been committed by relatives in 1920 to the state hospital in Augusta,

Maine, without Frost's intercession one way or the other. Once very close to Jeanie, Frost had never visited her in her confinement. Frost's guilt had burdened him since. Now he wondered if the hereditary madness of his father that had claimed Jeanie was devouring him as well.

Without choice, whether mad or not, Frost continued his descent. Each step seemed to abase his spirit further.

At last Frost reached the final step, realizing it when he stumbled in trying to step upon the one that wasn't there. In what seemed to be a corridor of woe, he continued onward.

Ahead of him a pale shimmering began to register on his straining eyes. Was it a tiny will-o'-the-wisp floating in a crypt? Or a galaxy revolving against the backdrop of interstellar space?

Frost slowed his pace and began to shuffle cautiously. And well he did. For his extended left foot eventually met thin air. Frost stopped at the edge of the abyss. A cosmic breeze, chill yet not unpleasant, seemed to stroke his face.

The shimmering still tantalized his light-starved eyes. One moment it seemed a spinning nebula, lazing across the heavens. The next it seemed a pocket-sized ghost. Occasionally it resolved into an androgynous human face blending all races into one, yet with disturbing echoes of the visages of both Elinor and himself.

As Frost struggled to fix the nature of the being, it spoke—it sang!—pulsing visibly with each silent word that seemed to echo directly in Frost's brain.

Nevernaught, nevernaught. There was never naught, there was always thought. Thought and afterthought.

"What—what manner of thing are you?"

I am the tree of all that will ever be.

"Are you God?"

One and complete, unified yet discrete. Conflict and peace, the Thing of things. From hydrogen all the way to man. Less in the present than in the future, and less in both together than in the past.

Frost realized that the riddle of this entity's nature was beside the point, if it could heal him.

"Nevernaught, the shade of my wife counseled me to seek your help. Can you show me what I need to see, to go on living?"

Out of coming-in, into having been! said the Nevernaught, then flared nova-bright.

Frost hurled his arm up to block the searing light. When the stabbing radiance finally died away, Frost opened his eyes.

Below him spun the planet Earth, a cloud-stroked, continent-marbled orb. Frost clutched his throat, bicycled his feet for purchase, flailed for anything to grip. But when he found that he continued to breathe easily and was not falling, he ceased his gyrations.

As Frost watched, he realized that his vision was enlarging. While retaining his orbital perspective, holding the planet entire in his mind, he simultaneously began to apprehend surface details of the globe. Wild herds in Africa, swarming cities in Europe, the jungles of South America. The immensity and variety of life overwhelmed him with sensations of appreciation and gratitude and delight. Never before had he truly savored the miracle of his world's existence.

But at the height of his joy, a transformation began. Half of Earth began to ice over. The other hemisphere began to burn. Ice and flame raced to meet at the terminator. Frost seemed to hear the dying screams of all creation, as billions of entities crisped or shattered.

When the opposing forces met, Earth instantly vanished, as did the attendant stars.

Now Frost was left in some featureless desert place, a zone with no expression and nothing to express. He could hardly grasp the death of Earth he had just witnessed, so blank was this new environment. It was as if all the beauty he had been savoring had been just a painting on the stretched skin of a balloon that, once pricked, became less than nothing.

Time trickled by. Or did not. But there came a moment when Frost reached a new understanding.

This desert place was inside him. He was viewing the emptiness within himself, the emptiness that had been incipient in him, but only fully born the night he lost everything he loved in flames.

Frost began to weep. What a cruel fate, to carry around such a vacuum. Why could he not be populated with sustaining hopes and dreams and beacons of affection as other men were? Were such helpful bastions of mortal existence any more false or inaccurate than this ghastly nothingness?

Even before the thought was completed, the voice of the Nevernaught returned.

Men dance round in a ring and suppose, but the Secret sits in the middle and knows!

Now Frost's inner desert began to change.

Flowers thrust out of the featureless medium. Tulips and daffodils . . .

Frost lay upon his back on the abnormally warm ground of the island, flowers nodding around his body. Hazel bent over him, soothing his brow.

Frost found her hand and clutched it. Even as he spoke, his vision of the Nevernaught and what it had showed him was fading. But what remained behind was a certainty of purpose and a calmness of heart he had not felt in a dozen years.

"Hazel, I had a glimpse, a glimpse of something wonderful—"

Hazel's smile held both sadness and delight. "Yes, Robert, that's the most any of us ever have."

Frost was on the point of leaving his room to meet Hazel. The month was June, the year 1925, and they were heading to New York by train. Frost gathered up his luggage, which included a string-wrapped manuscript bearing the title *A Boy's Will.*

On the doorstep, Frost encountered the mailman.

"Mr. Frost, just one for you today."

Frost accepted the envelope. It bore the return address for *Weird Tales.*

> Dear Grampa Jack,
>
> Weh-hell, I swan! Such a startling career turnaround Uncle Theobald has never seen in all his advanced years! From spinner of supernatural shiver-makers to a certified poetaster! The imminent publication of your debut volume of verses is an occasion much to be celebrated, save by all those devotees of the occult yarn, who are losing one of the finest talents ever to grace our small field. I suppose I'll just have to fill my empty pages with more stories from old

Cliffy. Providencians forever! But don't let all the attention from those Eastern literary nabobs get your head in a whirl! It's as easy to go down as to rise up, and such fawning litterateurs can be damn fickle. But Grampa Jack has a firm head on his shoulders, and certainly knows that he has a home to return to in the pages of *Weird Tales*, should fortune ever turn his feet our way again.

But even this news pales in the light of your upcoming wedding to the inestimable Miss Heald! Please give all my regards to your talented fiancée. If half the hints about her character which you've dropped are true, then she's some catch! A veritable daughter of Endor. I know that married life will shore you up in any future moments of trial, just as it has yours truly. Why, my ol' battle wagon even has her Uncle Theobald making regular visits to a general practitioner now! I'll attain Methuselah's years with such healthy ways!

Please endeavor to remain in touch with your sincere friend,

Howard P. Lovecraft

Frost smiled, and tucked the letter into the pocket of his jacket. Hazel would appreciate reading it. Leaving stoop for sidewalk, he began to whistle.

Halfway to the train station, a couplet occurred to him, and he stopped to jot it down in his notebook:

Love has earth to which she clings,
But thought has a pair of dauntless wings.

VI
Gonzo Science

I love science. I have no training in any of the sciences, but I try to read widely in popular accounts of various fields to stay current and informed. Science is inspirational and beautiful. But so far as I can see, most real scientific work involves a lot of drudgery, a plodding hegira across vast fields of repetitiveness and heartbreak. Who would want to read fiction about that? The science fiction writer's job is to peddle the glamour—or the weirdness. Some science fiction writers are like popes, arraying themselves in gold-threaded cosmological vestments and pontificating. It's impressive, but a little dull. Other SF writers are like Sufi dervishes or Hindu holy men or Zen masters, conjuring nth-dimensional entities out of the air and delivering illuminating clouts upside your head. In this segment of the book, you'll find three stories definitely in the dervish mode.

Forecasting a future of falling prices and rising prosperity, as opposed to the consensus scenario too often seen, one of poverty and scarcity, really appealed to me. Could radical changes in the infrastructure of the global economy actually bring about a near utopia, without the advent of any new miracle science such as nanotech? Hard to say, especially for an economic ignoramus such as me. But it seems undeniable that many of our current troubles stem not from a lack of resources but from malfeasance, blindness, traditionalism, and limited intelligence.

If only the Blue Fairy would descend, touch us, and turn us all into real people!

BARE MARKET

The price of gasoline had fallen to twenty-five cents a gallon, and a pair of low-end Nikedidas would set you back only ten dollars. You could enjoy a three-course meal plus dessert at many of New York's better restaurants for a prix fixe of fifteen dollars, and get change back from a fifty when purchasing a top-of-the-line Palm Pilot XXII, complete with video-conferencing features. The nation's trade deficit had been wiped out, and the global economy had just posted its sixth consecutive quarter of 5 percent annual growth. The entire continent of Africa resembled California during the Gold Rush. New millionaires were being minted in nearly every country faster than a Martian settler could duck underground at the news of a solar flare.

We were living in boom times such as the most bullish speculator of no other era had ever dared dream of, even after consumption of a fifth consecutive bottle of Veuve Clicquot, and we owed it all to the Market.

The Market's name was Adamina Smythe. She was nineteen years old, utterly untouchable, and she was sitting across from me.

Built like the ultimate offspring of some clandestine supermodel-breeding program, the Market wore a red dress that was more suggestion than fabric. Her long thick platinum hair was pinned up by a couple of delicate and tasteful tortoise-shell clips, with a few stray tendrils wisping her brow. Her face, all subtly intersecting planes and arcs, evoked both madonnas and starlets. Her complexion conjured up comparisons to exotic orchids, snow-tinged by a sunset and milk-tinted with cherry juice. As we waited for the arrival of our meals, the Market's delicate hands cradled her drink—straight sparkling water in a champagne flute—so sensually that I thought I might climax just from contemplating her fingers.

All I had to do tonight and over the next several days was to interview the closest thing to an actual, breathing goddess the world of 2022 boasted, for a profile in *Nuevo Vanity Fair*. And so far I had barely managed to stutter out my name, shake her warm, soft hand, and croak out my dinner order. Not an auspicious start.

I tried to recapture my experienced journalistic demeanor. But my voice still quavered as I attempted to look steadily into the Market's grass-green eyes.

"Uh, Miz Smythe—"

"Please, Glen, call me Adamina."

The Market's voice matched the rest of her, resonant as church bells and sexy as black coffee in bed. I caught a whiff of her perfume, a subtle floral scent.

"Adamina, I really look forward to, um, working with you on this feature. But are you sure my intrusions won't interfere with your other duties?"

She smiled broadly, and I had a chance to fall in love all over again with her perfect teeth. "Of course not. Face-to-face interaction utilizes only the smallest fraction of my processing power."

"So right now—"

"Right now I'm overseeing approximately one point seven nine to the twelfth power simple stock transactions around the globe, and arbitrating more than one million buyouts, splits, IPO's and other equally complex procedures. Not to mention mediating billions of eBay deals. And having no problem conversing with you."

"Incredible. And when you sleep—?"

"A partial software persona based on me runs the show."

What could I say in the face of this nearly unbelievable declaration of stone cold fact? Flowing through the gorgeous woman within arm's reach (and how I suddenly wanted to reach out and touch her, as if to partake of her immense and regal charisma) ran the entire planetary digital economy, without causing her any visible sign of strain or effort. No wonder talking with me took less of her resources than breathing.

All I could do was pick up my glass of wine and swallow a hefty slug. "You're sure you won't share some of this bottle? It's quite good."

The Market's manners matched her beauty. "I'm so sorry, Glen, but I simply can't indulge in alcohol or any other artificial stimulants. The perturbations in my brain chemistry—"

"Oh, right, of course. 'One little depressant—'"

"'—could trigger a Depression.' Yes, that's a familiar quip."

I felt like an idiot. How often must she have heard that lame joke, and a million like it? Even given the protective and exclusionary elite social bubble she existed in, I was certain that she must have overheard more than her share of comments treating her like some sort of freak. Along with feelings of awe and adoration, the Market had to contend with the hatred, envy, and fear of the masses.

But if any such thoughtless barbs had ever hurt her, she failed to exhibit any scars or bitterness. Serene, compassionate, she apparently took no offense at my gaucherie, and the awkward moment was dispelled by the waiter's stealthy delivery of our salads.

After we fussed a bit with napkins and salt and pepper shakers, I took the opportunity of asking, "Would you mind if I started recording our conversation now?"

"Of course not. I'm eager to respond to any questions you have for me."

Eager to respond. I forced my mind away from an extremely vivid but highly unprofessional line of thinking. If the Market had ever been allowed to have a boyfriend, I knew the lucky bastard would have worn a perpetual grin. I placed my PDA midway between us, and began.

"Let's talk about your amazing childhood."

The Market's self-deprecatory laughter sent small creatures racing up and down my spine. "Oh, that hoary old media sensation! I'm certain no one even remembers it or has any interest in such old news anymore."

"Are you kidding? A two-year-old found adrift on a scrap of

wreckage in the mid-Atlantic by a cruise ship. And then the controversy over your upbringing—"

"Well, I suppose my early years were somewhat unusual."

"Please, Adamina, tell me your impressions of them."

The Market thoughtfully chewed a mouthful of salad, then said, "As you described, I first came to the world's attention as a castaway. Of course, from this part of my own life I have only a few nebulous personal memories, having been too young at the time to retain much. So what I'm recounting is based on my later reading and viewing of news items. One of the smaller cruise ships, en route from Bermuda to Liverpool, happened to spot a fragment of an unknown vessel floating helplessly. Onboard the makeshift raft was a single survivor of whatever grim fate had overtaken the vessel. A two-year-old girl, horribly sunburned and dehydrated. Me.

"Once rescued, I quickly regained my health after some common treatments for malnutrition and overexposure. Apparently I was in good spirits as well, regaling the ship's passengers with lots of eager childish chatter in some kind of weird pidgin tongue. But as to my name or parentage or the cause of my being adrift, I could offer no information. And no hint of my vessel's name or port of origin was ever found.

"When we docked in Liverpool, the media were waiting in droves. Authorities from the British government took me into custody and regulated all my contact with the public."

"This was when you acquired your name as well, correct?"

"Yes. At first the media tried out a dozen different tags on me. 'Waterbaby.' 'Little Mermaid.' 'Baby X.' 'Miracle Kid.' But eventually I ended up taking the family name of the official nanny they had assigned to me, a policewoman named Joan Smythe. Joan had had a son named Adam, who had died young, and so she dubbed me Adamina."

"A neat serendipity, given your future career."

The Market looked winsomely solemn. "Who knows how these earliest childhood incidents influence anyone? But even though I have only a vague recollection of her presence, I'm very grateful to Joan for being a bastion of calm and affection during this period, and I still see her regularly."

"I take it any peaceful eye of the storm did not last long."

"No. As my story spread around the world, things quickly became complicated. A lot of meanness and greed surfaced.

"What country did I belong to? Almost immediately, thousands of people from scores of nations claimed I was their missing daughter, offering more or less plausible stories to account for my mid-ocean abandonment. But DNA tests disproved all their claims, and my origin remained utterly unknown. Then various governments began to put their oars in, demanding that I, the 'miracle girl of the new millennium,' be 'repatriated' to their nation rather than to another. Their claims were all equally valid or invalid, and no decision seemed possible.

"That was when the United Nations stepped in.

"By resolution of the Security Council, I was adopted by the United Nations. Every country in the world would be my parent. I received the very first Universal Passport. And I was to be raised at the U.N. headquarters in Geneva.

"That's where my actual memories begin."

The waiter had cleared our salad plates away earlier, and now brought us our dinners. My steak looked like some caveman's butchery next to the Market's abstemious scatter of shrimp, and I felt awkward once again. But the Market smiled down at my choice, saying, "That looks delicious," and my brutish red-meat tastes were instantly sanctified.

I resumed our conversation after a few moments. "It must have been odd, being the only child in such a setting."

"Oh, but I wasn't. The U.N. had a daycare center for the children of employees and delegates, so I spent a good portion of my day with kids my own age. The only difference was that they went home, and I didn't. The Palais des Nations was my private castle. Whenever I could, I slipped away from my minders to roam the grounds and buildings. Did you know that after visitors are gone, the marble floors in the Salle des Pas Perdus offers excellent sliding when you're wearing socks?"

I laughed, picturing the Market as a young high-spirited girl cutting loose amid such reverential splendor. "No, I can't say I ever appreciated their utility for that sport. So I take it you had a happy childhood."

"Absolutely. Although I sometimes feel it ended too abruptly."

"You're referring to your precocious intellectual development."

The Market sighed like a gentle Alpine zephyr. "Yes. I was reading at a ten-year-old's level by age three. By five I spoke French, English, Spanish, and Russian. German and Chinese took me a little longer to pick up. My guardians responded by accelerating my schooling so that I graduated with the equivalent of an American high school diploma at age eleven. I enrolled in the London School of Economics and got my Ph.D. four years later."

"And the Nobel in economics?"

"I didn't receive that honor until 2020."

"At age seventeen."

"Correct."

The Market had recounted these accomplishments without false modesty or boastfulness, as if she had been reciting a list of the streets of Geneva. Yet I did not get the impression that she was emotionally stunted. Far from it. Her words seemed to float on a deep reservoir of humility, wisdom, empathy for others, and appreciation for her own life.

"It's hard for me to imagine," I confessed, "how you must have felt to reach such a pinnacle of success at so early an age."

The Market's coral lips left a smudge on her champagne flute. "A little frustrated, actually. There seemed to be no future goals for me to aspire to in my chosen field."

"Which is why you offered yourself as the first human subject for the MIT-Caltech wetware implant."

"Indeed. It was something no one else had ever done before. And it presented interesting, ah, possibilities."

"Recovery from the operation was fairly swift, I know. You were out of the hospital within a month. But mastering the biological-cybernetic interface took a bit longer, I imagine."

"Yes. It was a whole eight weeks before I felt confident in my abilities to surf cyberspace mentally. The operating system in the implant had a few glitches that I helped to fix."

"But how did it come about that you began to focus exclusively on rationalizing the world's financial markets?"

"Well, what could have been more natural? After all, my Ph.D.

thesis concerned itself with maximizing marketplace efficiencies. At first I went into the digital representation of the market strictly as an observer. Even that experience was incredible. I learned so much about how the market actually functions on a quantum level. After a few of my suggestions for improvements in trading procedures were implemented manually with good results, I was allowed to start interacting directly through my wetware."

"And a year after that—"

"A year after that, for all practical purposes, I *was* the Market."

Dessert arrived, as well as an espresso for me and decaf for the Market. I watched her sip her coffee while I tried to compose my next question as delicately as I could. Finally, I decided just to be blunt.

"Weren't you afraid to insert yourself into the center of a system that billions of people relied on for their economic survival? I mean, wouldn't you say that your actions revealed quite a bit of arrogance and hubris?"

The unflappable Market merely smiled benevolently at me. "Not at all, Glen. You see, although the various interlocked markets that existed prior to my takeover were in their primitive way a wonderful creation—perhaps the most complex and efficient human system ever invented—they were still crude and buggy tools for putting capital to work. There was minimal coordination between many of the parts of the system, and very little correlation of data or player intentions. Why, just the fact that no one thought to extend the theory of mutual funds to other investment options was shocking! And then there was the problem of overt manipulation of the markets."

"You're talking about something like the scandals of the early years of the millennium. Or the DreamWorks Recession of 2012."

"Exactly. Crooks and con men and unprincipled CEO's were able to manipulate the market ruthlessly, inflating prices of worthless stocks and driving healthy companies out of business. Scams and insider-trading sucked the lifeblood out of the market, like parasites on a living being. Regulatory bodies like the SEC and the few artificially intelligent programs in place couldn't catch more than a fraction of these schemes. And they certainly couldn't help optimize the daily transaction flow. What was needed for optimal functioning of the marketplace was a single arbiter and facilitator, a judge and negotiator, a coordinator and enforcer. That role required a human mind trained in the subtlety of the market and in human motivations. A mind backed up by access to many additional teraflops of processing power. A unique mind belonging to a human who had no attachments or allegiances to any family or nation. And my mind was the only one that fit the bill. There was no arrogance or hubris involved. Just a recognition that I had found the one all-important task I was destined to perform."

I reached for my PDA and shut off its recording function. I found myself somewhat shaken by our conversation. Perhaps finishing a whole bottle of wine on my own had contributed to my discomfort. The Market spoke from such an Olympian perspective that I felt buglike in comparison. But paradoxically, her erotic allure that I had been attempting to deny and ignore all evening had only swelled in power.

"Well, Adamina, thank you for being so forthcoming. I feel we're off to a good start. I'll see you tomorrow morning at ten, as we planned?"

"Certainly. The photo shoot should be fun."

With an elegant demand for our attention, the waiter deftly slid the leather-jacketed bill onto the table. I reached for it, saying, "We'll let the magazine take care of this."

The gesture was foolish, but I made it anyway. By universal agreement, the Market was paid a salary pegged to the performance of her virtual counterpart and skimmed from every participating country. In sixteen months she had leapt onto the Forbes 1000, just below the guy who owned the patents to the tabletop sono-fusion power plant just going into production.

"Of course," said the Market, "*Nuevo Vanity Fair* can well afford it."

I shivered a bit, knowing that the Market's words were not merely a perfunctory courtesy.

She was certainly accessing *NVF*'s balance sheets as we spoke.

The Market killed in a bikini.

The tiny scraps of fabric (displaying fragmented surface animations of their designer's latest Paris runway show) revealed nearly all of the glorious body I had fantasized about at dinner last night. As the photographer—a short stocky fellow with longish blond hair and an annoying bark of a voice—directed the Market to assume various fairly demure showgirl poses, I had to turn away to hide my erection.

The shoot had started innocently enough, with the Market modeling various gowns and casual outfits. Adamina Smythe exhibited a natural grace and self-possession. She let the stylists and makeup techs interminably fuss around her without growing irritable or weary. She took direction from the photographer well, and didn't wilt under the hot lights. Even granting that she had been at the center of incredible media attention during the past seventeen years, her performance was remarkable.

Only at one point did the Market call a halt to the proceedings. After blinking rapidly for several seconds, she said, "We need to stop now for a minute or so, please."

Solicitous as a nursemaid, I rushed up to her side with a bottle of water. "Is everything all right? Are you getting tired? Do you have a headache?"

"No. It's just that I've just been attacked by a really bad virus. I need to concentrate."

The Market retreated to the dressing room, and everyone took a break for coffee or snacks or a smoke.

Despite the world's growing widespread prosperity, a few international dissidents to the new order still skulked beneath the burnished woodwork, opposed to the Market for a variety of ideological reasons—the 1929-ers, the Anti-Souk League, the New Barterians, the Alan Greenspammers . . . With the reduction in importance of physical trading establishments like Wall Street and the London, Hong Kong, Moscow, Beijing, Rio, and Tokyo exchanges, these terrorists had fallen back on virtual attacks, attempting to disrupt the portions of cyberspace that the Market inhabited. Luckily, the Market's bodily safety—like that of any other citizen—was guaranteed by the various Homeland Security organizations of whatever country she happened to be residing in, without resort to such obsolete safeguards as special squads of bodyguards.

Now, apparently, hidden hackers had launched one of their trademark virtual attacks.

I dithered nervously while the Market did whatever she had to do to combat this threat. I called my editor, Zulma Soares, to fill her in on my progress, and learned that she had allotted another five pages to my article, based on a recent poll of the Market's popularity. Great. More pressure.

Eventually the Market reappeared, apparently unruffled by her brush with disaster. "The virus is safely partitioned now. My support staff are analyzing it to guard against any such future incursions. We can resume."

Shortly after that, the Market made another trip to the dressing room, emerging in her bikini.

That was when I nearly lost it. Up till then, I had managed to keep my lust for the Market somewhat hidden and in check. Berating myself for unprofessionalism and idiotic, impossible daydreams, I left the room, determined to stay outside until my excitement grew less visible.

The physical evidence of my adolescent delusions had just vanished when the Market herself tapped me on the shoulder. She wore loose linen pants, a white blouse with three-quarter sleeves that flounced at their edges, and sandals. A straw hat sloped back atop her thick fall of unrestrained silvery hair.

"Glen, is everything okay?"

"Fine, fine, I just had to, uh, attend to a call of nature."

"How did you think the photo session went?"

"Perfect. They'll use one of the swimsuit shots on the cover, you know. Does that bother you?"

"Why should it?"

"You don't mind exposing yourself like that to millions of strangers?"

"No, of course not. It's just my body, after all. Everyone's got one. But I really don't understand people's interest in such things. I'm already such an intimate part of their lives, it seems almost redundant for them to be fascinated by what I look like."

"That—that is almost a nonhuman attitude."

There it was. I had said one of the things that I had been holding back from saying. But there was no avoiding the topic now, so I pressed ahead in somewhat contentious adversarial-reporter mode.

"Do you feel truly human, Adamina, after all your modifications? Did you ever think that possibly you're some sort of alien, planted among us?"

Completely unfazed, the Market just shrugged. "This is something I've thought about for a long time, Glen. But how would I know whether I feel human or not? I know what my interior life is like, but how do I decide whether my mental states are comparable to the human norm? How do any of us know we feel the same emotions others feel, or think the same way? It's like seeing color. When I say something's red, and you agree, are we really seeing the same color? You just can't know. As for literally being an alien or some kind of spontaneous or engineered mutant, of course I've thought about the possibility. My strange origin after all might be a clever charade, a means of inserting me into human society for some nefarious purpose. But all I can tell you is that every medical test so far reveals me to be completely human. And I don't have any hidden allegiances to the Tentacled Flesh Eaters from Mizar Five."

The Market laughed, and I did, too, out of relief. "Okay, then, I'm glad that awkward bit's out of the way. I wouldn't have been much of a reporter if I didn't ask, and I hope you'll excuse my impertinence."

"You're excused. Now, it's a beautiful day out there, and I haven't been in New York in the past six months. Let's walk around a little and then grab some lunch."

Out on the sidewalk, I spontaneously offered the Market my hand. Her fingers grazed mine briefly, imparting a little friendly pressure before she withdrew them, but all my doubts about her humanity vanished.

Over the next several days I was not out of the Market's company for more than the regular hours devoted to our separate sleeping. Much of our time together we spent in public places, and I was startled by the reactions of the average people who recognized her. That walk after the photo shoot had first introduced me to her adoring fans.

Every few feet we moved down the Manhattan sidewalks people

stopped the Market, just to say hello or smile wordlessly or thank her or ask for her autograph. Men and women of all ages and classes responded equally to her, although of course among the males there was that extra component of slack-jawed sexual attraction. I found myself getting jealous of the guys, until I forced myself to remember that I had no particular claim on the Market's attention.

Nor did any man.

People with children made a big point of explaining to their kids who the Market was and what she did and how she was responsible for all the good things this youngest generation enjoyed as unquestioned appurtenances of their privileged lives. The kids reacted with wide-eyed admiration and reverence.

After a while, I felt like I was second-in-command to the leader of some cult out for a stroll among the faithful. To witness any other person I had ever met as the focus of such adoration would have struck me as repugnant. I would have labeled the object of all this reverence—a CEO or famous politician, a Bollywood starlet or world-class scientist, religious leader or famed solar-sail racer—as an insufferable egotist, soaking up the ignorant worship of the masses. But something about the Market's pristine demeanor negated any such harsh judgment. She was just so gracious and selfless, so transparent and goodhearted that the effusive praise did not bloat her, but instead seemed to pass through her. She was a two-way conduit for power from above and gratitude from below.

One evening I told her about all these thoughts, and she just smiled mysteriously and said, "Giving and receiving are just two sides of the same coin."

Somehow this sentiment lost its triteness coming from the Market's lips.

The Market and I continued our professional dialogue in any number of locations and circumstances. I learned more than I ever wanted to know about the intricacies of the world's economy. If I never heard the words "arbitrage," "debenture," "munis," or "futures" again, it would be too soon. Truth to tell, the Market could be kind of a drone sometimes.

The Market had a healthy appetite and a moderate taste for luxury, and I ate more fancy meals than I usually indulge in. At the end of a week, I was having trouble bonding the stik-tite closures on my pants. Finally, however, we began to run out of things to talk about, and my deadline was imminent. Zulma was pressing me to see a first draft of the piece, so she could start thinking about pull-quotes. But I still hadn't broached my second awkward question on an essential topic—a topic that Zulma had specifically enjoined me to tackle.

I decided at last to confront the Market over lunch on what would be the final day of our time together.

After the waiter had taken our orders, I asked, "Tell me, Adamina, do you ever think about sex?"

The Market did not respond immediately. And was that a faint blush suffusing her cheeks?

"Oh, I'm sorry, Glen. Some drudgester just posted news of a big water-strike on Mars and the NASDAQ went through the ceiling. What was that question again?"

The NASDAQ and Dow Jones functioned like the Market's temperature or an EKG. I would guess that such a spike might represent a fever or a case of heart arhythmia in a mere mortal. For the first time it occurred to me that the unverifiable demands her job made on the Market's attention could also serve as a convenient excuse not to hear something. But I was not to be rebuffed.

"I asked about your feelings on sex. Specifically, how does it feel to be a virgin at your age, with no prospect of ever experiencing normal physical love?"

"What do you want me to say, Glen? That the situation doesn't bother me? I told you I was physiologically human in all respects. But I simply can't indulge in sex. The hormonal and neural and endocrinal turmoil that intercourse involves would wreak havoc with my wetware. My connection with the market—well, as the experts love to say, 'Results would be unpredictable.' So do I obsess about this lack or limitation in my life until I'm miserable? Or do I just accept it as part of who I am, and concentrate on what I do best and on all the rewards it brings to me and the rest of the world? It's not so unusual, is it? After all, I wouldn't be the first person to choose celibacy as an aid to a higher goal, would I?"

I felt like a louse, and decided to cut the thread short. "Fair enough, Adamina. I'm sure you realize that our readers would have felt cheated if we hadn't addressed this aspect of your life."

"I understand. But I'd prefer to talk about something else now, Glen."

So we did.

As we were leaving the restaurant, a young woman rushed up to us. The stranger threw her arms about the Market and spontaneously planted a kiss on the Market's cheek.

The Market shied back in a manner not typical of her usual generosity toward such impulsive displays, and I knew my insensitive probing must have disturbed her usual composure. I immediately took the Market back to her hotel.

Sometimes my job made me feel like shit.

But nothing in my professional experience had prepared me for what came next.

Now, of course, everyone knows that the woman who kissed the Market was a member of the Counterfeiters' Army, whose nom de guerre was Penny Candy, and that her kiss was laced with a potent designer drug engineered to function on contact as a general emotional disinhibitor. Having failed to disrupt the Market through attacks on her cyberspace extensions, this group of malcontents had hit upon the strategy of sabotaging her implanted wetware.

And quite a successful strategy it proved to be.

A few hours later I knocked on the door to the Market's hotel room, intending to say goodbye and to thank her for her cooperation as an interview subject. Like some timorous teenage suitor, I carried a box of Godiva chocolates and a small hair clip she had admired once while window-shopping with me.

What could you actually buy the woman who had everything?

Who *was* everything?

The door jerked open and I faced the Market. Her hair was in disarray, with tendrils plastered to her sweaty face. Her shirt was half unbuttoned, and she was barefoot. Her usual perfume was overlain with a musky reek.

She put the back of her hand up to her brow. "Oh, Glen, it's you— What is it?"

"I just wanted to come in to say goodbye. But if this is a bad time—"

"Yes. I mean, no, it's not. Come in."

I took a seat, expecting the Market to do likewise. But she instead paced up and down the room, talking unceasingly, her words on the edge of sense and craziness.

I should have left then. I half suspected something bad was about to happen. If I had just stood up and exited, I would never have played such a pivotal role in the Orgasmic Meltdown of 2022.

But then I knew subconsciously that some other man surely would have taken my place.

And that was a prospect I couldn't tolerate. Along with my infatuation with the Market, jealousy compelled me to stay.

And in the end, both Penny Candy and I were equally complicit in the Market's downfall.

"Glen, I just don't know how to feel about anything anymore. Suddenly everything looks different to me. This busy world, all the people eager for more, more, more— Have I wasted my life? What was I thinking? Who appointed me God? And all these numbers! They're driving me insane! There must be more to life than getting and spending. Money, money, money! It's in my bloodstream, Glen. It's in my *blood*! I'm burning up!"

"Adamina, calm down. I'm sorry if anything I said caused you to feel this way. Here, let me get you a glass of water."

I stood up and moved toward a carafe on a sideboard.

Halfway there, the Market hurled herself at me.

I took the shock of her impact and remained standing. She hopped up and wrapped her arms and legs around me. Her mouth was all over my face and neck. I cupped her haunches and staggered backward. The edge of the couch caught me behind the knees and we tumbled onto it.

The rest, as they say, is history.

Our lovemaking left a precise trail of wreckage across the global economy. It was as if we were two giants fucking atop a village, crushing houses and barns, livestock and citizens heedlessly.

The first touch of our tongues sent sizable tremors through the market. Prices of individual stocks began to oscillate senselessly, without reference to actual values or trades. Around the world, investors started to panic. Buy and sell orders flooded into the Market, but were ignored or interpreted incorrectly by the Market's sex-addled brain. But the worst was yet to come.

My hands on the Market's breasts bankrupted hundreds of companies. Her thrashing trashed whole fiscal empires. When I went down on her, entire nations became paper paupers. When I broke her hymen and penetrated her as deeply as I could, Mars and the Moon fell entirely outside the solar system's financial net.

When the Market and I climaxed together, her screams signaled the complete implosion of the planetary marketplace.

We lay panting amidst the smoldering ruins of the world's commerce. I estimated we had about sixty seconds of postcoital solitude before the world began hammering on the door.

I overestimated the peaceful interlude by ten seconds.

Well, in short order the boffins rebooted the world's economy from that morning's backups, but repercussions from our sex remained. Approximately half a million people worldwide had committed suicide, mistaking the Market's convulsions for actual tragic outcomes affecting their fortunes. A dozen small wars had begun, and millions of companies—in the hair-trigger fashion so typical of the modern failsafe economy—had canceled orders, dumped inventory, and redirected their marketing schemes in nonrecoverable ways.

After Adamina's wetware implant was removed, experts cast about for another person to take on the burden of being the Market. But they could find no one else who possessed Adamina's combination of skills and character and statelessness. So the market today stumbles along using Adamina's partial software persona to run the show. It functions better than the twentieth-century market, but not as well as the Market. Filling the tank of your car costs about a dollar extra now. You don't get dessert with your prix fixe meal. And the new model Palm Pilot doesn't feature so much free software. But somehow we survive.

As for me, things are just getting to the point where I can show my face in public without provoking catcalls or sniggers or assaults or congratulatory slaps on the back from macho jerks. My career as a journalist was pretty much shot the moment I became a subject rather than a reporter. So I spend most of my time in my study, working on a novel. The subject matter's not my experiences with the Market. I wanted to steer clear of autobiography. But the fact that I won't spill any dirt and that my fifteen minutes of infamy is fading means that I haven't had any bites from any publisher yet. But money's not a problem.

Adamina had banked the majority of her pay as the Market.

And it's all safely invested now in real estate.

So, here's how writers get their ideas. One way, anyhow.

I was reading a comic strip by the great cartoonist known as Kaz. In it, he depicted hideous, post-apocalyptic, mutant children who had the ability to imbue inanimate objects with a kind of brief life force. It was a throwaway panel, hardly the central conceit of his story. But something about Kaz's gleeful drawing of a run-away coffee mug ambulating on pencil legs lodged in my head and wouldn't depart. At least not until I figured out a rationale for how such a sight could be encountered in a technologically plausible way.

Gardner Dozois picked up this tale for one of his year's- best collections.

And the Dish Ran Away with the Spoon

Facing my rival that fateful afternoon, I finally realized I was truly about to lose my girlfriend, Cody. Lose her to a spontaneous assemblage of information.

The information was embedded in an Aeron chair mated with several other objects: a Cuisinart, an autonomous vacuum cleaner with numerous interchangeable attachments, an iPod, and a diagnostic and therapeutic home medical tool known as a LifeQuilt. As rivals go, this spontaneous assemblage—or "bleb," as most people called such random accretions of intelligent appliances and artifacts, after the biological term for an extrusion of anomalous cells—wasn't particularly handsome. Rather clunky-looking, in fact. But apparently it had been devoted to Cody from the day it was born, and I guessed women appreciated such attention. I had to confess that I had been ignoring Cody shamefully during the period when the Aeron bleb must've been forming and beginning to court her, and so I have no one to blame for the threat of losing her but myself. Still, it hurt. I mean, could I really come in second to a *bleb*? That would truly reek.

Especially after my past history with them . . .

I had feared some kind of trouble like this from the moment Cody had begun pressuring me to move in together. But Cody hadn't been willing to listen to my sensible arguments against uniting our households.

"You don't really love me," she said, making that pitiful puppy-with-stepped-on-tail face that always knotted my stomach up, her blue eyes welling with wetness.

"That's ridiculous, Cody. Of course I do!"

"Then why can't we live together? We'd save tons of rent. Do you think I have some nasty habits that you don't know about? You've seen me twenty-four seven lots of times, at my place and yours. It's not like I'm hiding anything gross from you. I don't drink straight out of the nutriceutical dispenser, or forget to reprogram the toilet after I've used it."

"That's all true. You're easy to be with. Very neat and responsible."

Cody shifted tactics, moving closer to me on the couch and wrapping her lithe limbs around me in ways impossible to ignore. "And wouldn't it be nice to always have someone to sleep with at night? Not to be separated half the week or more? Huh? Wouldn't it, Kaz?"

"Cody, please, stop! You know I can't think when you do that." I unpeeled Cody from the more sensitive parts of my anatomy. "Everything you're saying is true. It's just that—"

"And don't forget, if we ditched my place and kept yours, I'd be much closer to work."

Cody worked at the Senate Casino, dealing blackjack, but lived all the way out in Silver Spring, Maryland. I knew the commute was a bitch, even using the Hydrogen Express, because when I slept over at her place I had to cover the same distance myself. I, on the other hand, rented a nice little townhouse in Georgetown that I had moved into when rents bottomed out during the PIG Plague economic crash. It turned out I was one of a small minority naturally immune to the new Porcine Intestinal Grippe then rampant in D.C., and so could safely live in an infected building. Renter's market, for sure. But over the last year or so, as the PIG immunization program had gotten under way, rents had begun creeping back up again. Cody was right about it being only sensible to pool our finances.

"I know you'd appreciate less road time, Cody, but you see—"

Now Cody glowered. "Are you dating someone else? You want to be free to play the field? Is that it?"

"No! That's not it at all. I'm worried about—"

Cody assumed a motherly look and laid a hand on mine. "About what, Kaz? C'mon, you can tell me."

"About blebs. You and I've got so much stuff, we're bound to have problems when we put all our possessions together in one space."

Cody sat back and began to laugh. "Is that all? My god, what a trivial thing to worry about. Blebs just *happen*, Kaz, anytime, anywhere. You can't prevent them. And they're mostly harmless, as you well know. You just knock them apart and separate the components." Cody snorted in what I thought was a rather rude and unsympathetic fashion. "Blebs! It's like worrying about—about robber squirrels or vampire pigeons or running out of SuperMilk."

Blebs were a fact of life. Cody was right about that. But they weren't always trivial or innocent.

One had killed my parents.

Blebs had been around for about twenty years now, almost as long as I had been alive. Their roots could be traced back to several decisions made by manufacturers—decisions that, separately, were completely intelligent, foresighted, and well conceived but that, synergistically, had caused unintended consequences—and to one insidious hack.

The first decision had been to implant silicon RFID chips into every appliance and product and consumable sold. These first chips, small as a flake of pepper, were simple transceivers that merely aided inventory tracking and retail sales by announcing to any suitable device the product's specs and location. But when new generations of chips using adaptive circuitry got cheaper and more plentiful, industry decided to install them in place of the simpler tags.

At that point millions of common, everyday objects—your toothbrush, your coffee maker, your shoes, the box of cereal on your shelf—began to exhibit massive processing power and inter-object communication. Your wristwatch could monitor your sweat and tell your refrigerator to brew up some electrolyte-replenishing drink. Your bedsheets could inform the clothes washer of the right settings to get them the cleanest. (The circuitry of the newest chips was built out of undamageable and pliable buckytubes.) So far, so good. Life was made easier for everyone.

Then came the Volition Bug.

The Volition Bug was launched anonymously from a site somewhere in a Central Asian republic. It propagated wirelessly among all the WiFi-communicating chipped objects, installing new directives in their tiny brains, directives that ran covertly in parallel with their normal factory-specified functions. Infected objects now sought to link their processing power with their nearest peers, often achieving surprising levels of Turingosity, and then to embark on a kind of independent communal life. Of course, once the Volition Bug was identified, antiviral defenses—both hardware and software—were attempted against it. But VB mutated ferociously, aided and abetted by subsequent hackers.

If this "Consciousness Wavefront" had occurred in the olden days of dumb materials, blebs would hardly have been an issue. What could antique manufactured goods achieve, anchored in place as they were? But things are different today.

Most devices nowadays are made with MEMS skins. Their surfaces are interactive, practically alive, formed of zillions of invisible actuators, the better to sample the environment and accommodate their shapes and textures to their owners' needs and desires, and to provide haptic feedback. Like the pads of geckos, these MEMS surfaces can bind to dumb materials and to other MEMS skins via the Van der Waals force, just as a gecko can skitter across the ceiling.

Objects possessed by the Volition Bug would writhe, slither, and crawl to join together, forming strange new assemblages, independent entities with unfathomable cybernetic goals of their own.

Why didn't manufacturers simply revert to producing dumb appliances and other products, to frustrate VB? Going backwards was simply impossible. The entire economy, from immense factories right down to individual point-of-sales kiosks, was predicated on intelligent products that could practically sell themselves. And every office and every household aside from the very poorest relied on the extensive networking among possessions.

So everyone had learned to live with the occasional bleb, just as earlier generations had learned to tolerate operating system crashes in their clunky PC's.

But during the first years of the Volition Bug, people were not so aware of the problem. Oftentimes no one took precautions to prevent blebs until it was too late.

That was how my parents died.

It happened when I was six years old. I was soundly asleep when I was awakened by a weird kind of scraping and clattering noise outside my room. Still only half aware, I stumbled to my bedroom door and cracked it open.

My parents had recently made a couple of new purchases. One item was a free-standing rack that resembled an antique hat tree, balanced on four stubby feet. The rack was a recharging station for intelligent clothing. But now in the night-light-illuminated, shadowy hallway the rack was bare of garments, having shucked them off on its way to pick up its new accouterments: a complete set of self-sharpening kitchen knives. The knives adhered to the rack at random intervals along its length. They waggled nervously, like insect feelers, as the rack stumped along.

I stood paralyzed at the sight of this apparition. All I could think of was the old Disney musical I had streamed the previous month, with its walking brooms. Without exhibiting any aggressive action, the knife rack moved past me, its small feet humping it along. In retrospect, I don't think the bleb was murderous by nature. I think now it was simply looking for an exit, to escape its bonds of domestic servitude, obeying the imperatives of VB.

But then my father emerged from the room where he and my mother slept. He seemed hardly more awake than I was.

"What the hell—?"

He tried to engage the rack to stop it, slipping past several of the blades. But as he struggled with the patchwork automaton, a long, skinny filleting knife he didn't see stabbed him right under his heart.

My father yelled, collapsed, and my mother raced out.

She died almost instantly.

At that point, I suppose, I should have been the next victim. But my father's loyal MedAlert bracelet, registering his fatal distress, had already summoned help. In less than three minutes—not long enough for the knife rack to splinter down the bedroom door behind which I had retreated—rescuers had arrived.

The fate of my parents was big news—for a few days, anyhow—and alerted many people for the first time to the dangers of blebs.

I needed many years of professional help to get over witnessing their deaths. Insofar as I was able to analyze myself nowadays, I thought I no longer hated all blebs.

But I sure as hell didn't think they were always cute or harmless, like Cody did.

So of course Cody moved in with me. I couldn't risk looking crazy or neurotic by holding off our otherwise desirable mutual living arrangements just because I was worried about blebs. I quashed all my anxieties, smiled, hugged her, and fixed a day for the move.

Cody didn't really have all that much stuff. (Her place in Silver Spring was tiny, just a couple of rooms over a garage that housed a small-scale spider-silk-synthesis operation, and it always smelled of cooking amino acids.) A few boxes of clothing, several pieces of furniture, and some kitchen appliances. Ten thousand songs on an iPod and one hundredth that number of books on a ViewMaster. One U-Haul rental and some moderate huffing and puffing later, Cody was established in my townhouse.

I watched somewhat nervously as she arranged her things.

"Uh, Cody, could you put that Cuisinart in the cupboard, please? The one that locks. It's a little too close to the toaster-oven."

"But Kaz, I use this practically every day, to blend my breakfast smoothies. I don't want to have to be taking it in and out of the cupboard every morning." I didn't argue, but simply put the toaster-oven in the locked cupboard instead.

"This vacuum cleaner, Cody—could we store it out in the hallway?" I was particularly leery of any wheeled appliance. They could move a lot faster than the ones that had to inchworm along on their MEMS epidermis.

"The hallway? Why? You've got tons of space in that room you used to use for an office. I'll just put it in a corner, and you'll never notice it."

I watched warily as Cody deposited the cleaner in its new spot. The compact canister nested in its coiled attachments like an egg guarded by snakes. The smartest other thing in my office was my Aeron chair, a beautiful ergonomic assemblage of webbing, struts, gel-padding, piezopolymer batteries, and shape-changing actuators. I rolled the chair as far away from the vacuum cleaner as it would go.

Cody of course noticed what I was doing. "Kaz, don't you think you're being a tad paranoid? The vacuum isn't even turned on."

"That's where you're wrong, Cody. Everything is perpetually turned on these days. Even when you think you've powered something down, it's still really standing by on trickle mode, sipping electricity from its fuel cells or batteries or wall outlets, and anticipating a wake-up call. And all so that nobody has to wait more than a few seconds to do whatever they want to do. But it means that blebs can form even when you assume they can't."

"Oh, and exactly what do we have to be afraid of? That my vacuum cleaner and your chair are going to conspire to roll over us while we sleep? Together they don't weigh more than twenty-five pounds!"

I had never told Cody about my parents, and now did not seem to be the best time. "No, I guess you're right. I'm just being overcautious." I pushed my chair back to its spot at the desk.

In hindsight, that was the worst mistake I ever made. It just goes to show what happens when you abandon your principles because you're afraid you'll look silly.

That night Cody and I had our first dinner together before she had to go to work. Candlelight, easy talk, farmed salmon, a nice white Alaskan wine (although Cody had to pop a couple of alcohol debinders after dessert to sober up for the employee-entrance sensors at her job). While I cleaned up afterwards, she went to shower and change. She emerged from the bedroom in her Senate Casino uniform—blue blouse, red-and-white-striped trousers, star-spangled bow tie. She looked as cute as the day I had first seen her while doing my spy job.

"Wow. I don't understand how our representatives ever pass any legislation with distractions like you."

"Don't be silly. All our marks are tourists and a few locals. We only see the politicos when they're cutting through the casino on the way to their cafeteria."

I gave her a hug and kiss and was about to tell her to be careful on the subway when I caught movement at floor level out the corner of my eye.

The first bleb in our new joint household had spontaneously formed. It consisted of our two toothbrushes and the bathroom drinking glass. The toothbrushes had fastened themselves to the lower quarter of the tumbler, bristle-ends uppermost and facing out, so that they extended like little legs. Their blunt ends served as feet. Scissoring rapidly, the stiltlike toothbrush legs carried the tumbler toward the half-opened door through which Cody had been about to depart.

I squealed like a rabbit and jerked back out of Cody's embrace, and she said, "Kaz, what—?"

Then she spotted the bleb—and laughed!

She bent over and scooped up the creature. Without any hesitation, she tore its legs off, the Van der Waals forces producing a distinct Velcro-separating noise as the MEMS surfaces parted.

"Well, I guess we'll have to keep all the glasses in the kitchen from now on. It's cute, though, isn't it, how your toothbrush and mine knew how to cooperate so well."

I squeezed out a queasy laugh. "Heh-heh, yeah, cute—"

I worked for Aunty, at their big headquarters next to the Pentagon. After six years in Aunty's employ, I had reached a fairly responsible position. My job was to ride herd on several dozen freelance operatives, working out of their homes. These operatives in their turn were shepherds for a suite of semi-autonomous software packages. At this lowest level, where the raw data first got processed, these software agents kept busy around the clock, monitoring the nation's millions of audio-video feeds, trolling for suspicious activities that might threaten homeland security. When the software caught something problematic, it would flag the home operator's attention. The freelancer would decide whether to dismiss the alarm as harmless, to investigate further, to contact a relevant government agency, or to kick up the incident to my level for more sophisticated and experienced parsing, both human and heuristic.

Between them, the software and the home operators were pretty darn efficient, handling 99 percent of all the feed. I dealt with the final 1 percent from my crew, which amounted to about one hundred cases in a standard six-hour shift. This was a lesser workload than the home operators endured, and the pay was better.

The only drawback was having to retina in at headquarters, instead of getting to hang around all the creature comforts of home. Passing under the big sign that said TIA four days a week felt like surrendering part of myself to Aunty in a way that working at home for her had never occasioned.

After two-plus decades of existence, Aunty loomed large but benignly in the lives of most citizens, even if they couldn't say what her initials stood for anymore. I myself wasn't even sure. The agency that had begun as Total Information Awareness, then become Terrorist Information Awareness, had changed to Tactical Information Awareness about seven years ago, after the global terrorism fad had evaporated as a threat. But I seemed to recall another name change since then. Whatever Aunty's initials stood for, she continued to accumulate scads of real-time information about the activities of the country's citizens, without seeming to abuse the power of the feed. As a full-time government employee, I felt no more compunctions about working for Aunty than I had experienced as a freelancer. I had grown up with Aunty always around.

I knew the freelancer's grind well, since right up until a year ago I had been one myself. That period was when I had invested in my expensive Aeron chair, a necessity rather than an indulgence, when you were chained by the seat of your pants to the ViewMaster for six hours a day.

It was as a freelancer that I had first met Cody.

One of my software agents had alerted me to some suspicious activity at the employee entrance to the Senate Casino just before shift change, a guy hanging around longer than the allowable parameters for innocent dallying. The Hummingbird drone lurking silently and near-invisibly above him reported no weapons signatures, so I made the decision to keep on monitoring. Turned out he was just the husband of one of the casino workers, looking to surprise his weary wife in person with an invitation to dinner. As I watched the happy little scene play out, my attention was snagged by one of the incoming night-shift workers. The woman was more sweet-looking than sexy. Her walk conformed to Gait Pattern Number ALZ-605, which I had always found particularly alluring. Facial recognition routines brought up her name, Cody Sheckley, and her vital stats.

I had never used Aunty's powers for personal gain before, and I felt a little guilty about doing so now. But I rationalized my small transgression by reasoning that if I had simply spotted Cody on the street in person and had approached her to ask her name, no one would have thought twice about the innocence of such an encounter. In this case, the first step, finding out who she was, had simply been conducted virtually, by drone proxy.

A few nights later I visited the blackjack tables at the Senate Casino. After downing two stiff Jerrymanders, I worked up the courage to approach Cody in person.

The rest was history—the steps of our courtship undoubtedly all safely tucked away in Aunty's files.

Living with Cody proved quite pleasant. All the advantages she had enumerated—plus others—manifested themselves from the first day. Even the disparity in our working hours proved no more than a minor inconvenience. Cody's stint at the casino filled her hours from 9 P.M. to 3 A.M. My day at Aunty's ran from 9 A.M. to 3 P.M. When Cody got home in the wee hours of the morning, we still managed to get a few hours of that promised bundling time together in bed, before I had to get up for work. And when I got home in the afternoon, she was up and lively and ready to do stuff before she had to show up at the Senate. Afternoons were often when we had sex, for instance. Everything seemed fine.

I recall one afternoon, when I was massaging Cody's feet prior to her departure for the casino. She appreciated such attention in preparation for her physically demanding job.

"Now aren't you glad we decided to live together, Kaz?"

"I have to admit that weekends are a lot more enjoyable now."

"Just weekends?" Cody asked, stretching sensuously.

She got docked for being half an hour late that day, but insisted later it was worth it.

But despite such easygoing routines, I found that I still couldn't stop worrying about blebs. Since that first occurrence with the toothbrushes and tumbler, I had been on the alert for any more domestic incidents. I took to shuffling appliances from room to room, so that they wouldn't conspire. I knew this was foolish, since every chipped device was capable of communicating over fairly long distances by relaying message packets one to another. But still I had an intuition that physical proximity mattered in bleb formation. Cody kept complaining about not being able to find anything when she needed it, but I just brushed off her mild ire jokingly, and kept up my prophylactic measures. When a few weeks had passed without any trouble, I began to feel relieved.

Then I encountered the sock ball.

Cody and I had let the dirty laundry pile up. We were having too much fun together to bother with chores, and when each of us was alone in the townhouse, we tended spend a lot of time with View-Master and iPod, enjoying music and media that the other person didn't necessarily want to share.

It was during one such evening, after Cody had left me on my own, that the sock ball manifested.

My attention was drawn away from my book by a thumping on the closed bedroom door. Immediately wary, I got up to investigate.

When I tentatively opened the door a crack, something shot out and thumped me on the ankle.

I hopped backwards on one foot. A patchwork cloth sphere about as big as a croquet ball was zooming toward the front door.

I managed to trap the ball under an overturned wastebasket weighted down with a two-liter bottle of Mango Coke. It bounced around frantically inside, raising a racket like an insane drum solo.

Wearing a pair of oven mitts, I dared to reach in and grab the sphere.

It was composed of Cody's socks and mine, tightly wrapped around a kernel consisting of a travel-sized alarm clock. Cody's socks featured MEMS massage soles, a necessity for her job, which involved hours of standing. My own socks were standard models, but still featured plenty of processing power.

Having disassembled the sock ball, I did all the laundry and made sure to put Cody's socks and mine in separate drawers.

The incident completely unnerved me. I felt certain that other blebs, possibly larger and more dangerous, were going to spontaneously assemble themselves in the house.

From that day on I began to get more and more paranoid.

Handling one hundred potential security incidents per shift had become second nature for me. I hardly had to exert myself at all to earn my high job-performance ratings. Previously I had used whatever patches of downtime occurred to read mystery novels on my ViewMaster. (I liked Gifford Jain's series about Yanika Zapsu, a female Turkish private eye transplanted to Palestine.) But once I became obsessed with the danger of blebs in my home, I began to utilize Aunty's omnipresent network illicitly, to monitor my neighborhood and townhouse.

The first thing I did when I got to work at nine in the morning, duties permitting, was to send a Damselfly to check up on Cody. It was summertime, late June, and my window air conditioners were in place against the average ninety-plus D.C. temperatures. But the seals around the units were imperfect, and it was easy to maneuver the little entologue UAV into my house. Once inside, I made a circuit of all the rooms, checking that my possessions weren't conspiring against me and possibly threatening the woman I loved.

Mostly I found Cody sleeping peacefully, until about noon. The lines of her relaxed, unconscious face tugged at my heart, while simultaneously inspiring me to greater vigilance. There was no way I was going to let her suffer the same fate as my parents. From noon until the end of my shift, I caught intermittent snatches of an awake Cody doing simple, everyday things. Painting her nails, eating a sandwich, streaming a soap opera, writing to her mother, who lived in Italy now, having taken a five-year contract as supplemental labor in the service industry to offset that low-procreating country's dearth of workers.

But every once in a while, I saw something that troubled me.

One morning I noticed that Cody was favoring one foot as she walked about the house. She had developed a heel spur, I knew, and hadn't bothered yet to have it repaired. As I watched through the Damselfly clinging to the ceiling (routines automatically inverted the upside-down image for me), Cody limped to the closet and took out the LifeQuilt I had bought when I had a lower-back injury. Wearing the earbuds of her pocketed iPod, she carried the medical device not to the couch or bedroom, but to my former office. There, she lowered herself into my Aeron chair.

The chair instantly responded to her presence, contorting itself supportively around her like an astronaut's cradle, subtly alleviating any incipient muscle strains. Cody dropped the LifeQuilt onto her feet, and that smart blanket enwrapped her lower appendages. Issuing orders to the LifeQuilt through her iPod, Cody activated its massage functions. She sighed blissfully and leaned back, the chair reconforming to her supine position. She got her music going and closed her eyes.

In the corner of the office the vacuum cleaner began to stir. Its hose lifted a few inches, the tip of its nozzle sniffing the air.

I freaked. But what was I to do? The Damselfly wasn't configured to speak a warning, and even if it could, doing so would have betrayed that I was spying on Cody. I was about to send it buzzing down at her, to at least get her to open her eyes to the insidious bleb formation going on around her. But just then the vacuum cleaner subsided into inactivity, its hose collapsing around the canister.

For fifteen more minutes I watched, anticipating the spontaneous generation of a bleb involving the chair, the iPod, the blanket, and the vacuum. But nothing happened, and soon Cody had shut off the LifeQuilt and arisen, going about her day.

Meanwhile, five official windows on my ViewMaster were pulsing and pinging, demanding my attention. Reluctantly, I returned to my job.

When I got home that afternoon, I still hadn't figured out any way of advising Cody against putting together such a powerful combination of artificially intelligent devices ever again. Anything I said would make her suspicious about the source of my caution. I couldn't have her imagining I was monitoring her through Aunty's feed. Even though of course I was.

In the end, I made a few tentative suggestions about junking or selling the Aeron chair, since I never used it anymore. But Cody said, "No way, Kaz. That thing is like a day at the spa."

I backed down from my superficially illogical demands. There was no way I could make my case without confessing to being a paranoid voyeur. I would just have to assume that the nexus of four devices Cody had assembled didn't represent any critical mass of blebdom.

And I would've been correct, and Cody would've been safe, if it weren't for that damned Cuisinart.

When I wasn't doing my job for Aunty or spying on Cody, I frequently took to roaming the city, looking for blebs, seeking to understand them, to learn how to forestall them. That senseless activity wearied me, wore my good nature down, and left me lousy, inattentive company for Cody during the hours we shared. Our relationship was tumbling rapidly downhill.

"What do you mean, you've got to go out now, Kaz? I've only got an hour left till work. I thought we could stream that show together I've been wanting to see. You know, 'Temporary Autonomous Zone Romance.'"

"Later, maybe. Right now I just—I just need some exercise."

"Can I come with you then?"

"No, not today—"

But despite Cody's baffled entreaties and occasional tears, I couldn't seem to stop myself.

The fact that I encountered blebs everywhere did nothing to reassure me, or lessen what I now realize had become a mania.

And a lonely mania at that. No one else seemed concerned about these accidental automatons. There was no official Bleb Patrol, no corps of bounty hunters looking to take down rogue Segways driven by Xerox machines. (I saw such a combo once). Everyone seemed as blithely indifferent to these runaway products as Cody was.

Except for me.

In store windows, I would see blebs accidentally formed by proximity of the wares being displayed. An electric razor had mated with a digital camera and a massage wand to produce something that looked like a futuristic cannon. A dozen pairs of hinged salad tongs became the millipede legs for a rice cooker whose interior housed a coffee-bean grinder. A toy truck at F. A. O. Schwarz's was almost invisible beneath a carapace of symbiotically accreted Lego blocks, so that it resembled an odd, wheeled dinosaur.

In other store windows, the retailers had deliberately created blebs, in a trendy, devil-may-care fashion, risking damage to their merchandise. Several adjacent mannequins in one display at Nordstrom's were draped with so many intelligent clothes and accessories (necklaces, designer surgical masks, scarves) that the whole diorama was alive with spontaneous movement, like the waving of undersea fronds.

Out on the street the occasional escaped bleb crossed my path. One night on Fifteenth Street, near the Treasury Department, I encountered a woman's purse riding a skateboard. The bleb was moving along at a good clip, heading toward Lafayette Square, and I hastened after it. In the park it escaped me by whizzing under some shrubbery. Down on my knees, I peered into the leafy darkness. The colorful chip-laser eyes of a dozen blebs glared in a hostile fashion at me, and I yelped and scuttled backwards.

Just before everything exploded at home in my face, I went to a mashpit.

I was wandering through a rough district on the southeastern side of the city, a neighborhood where Aunty's surveillance attempts often met with countermeasures of varying effectiveness: motion camouflage, anti-sense spoofing, candle-power bombs. A young kid was handing out small squares of paper on a corner and I took one. It featured an address and the invitation:

> MIDNIGHT MASHPIT MADNESS!!!
> BRING YOUR STAUNCHEST, VEEBINGEST BLEB!!!
> THOUSAND-DOLLAR PRIZE TO THE WINNER!!!

The scene of the mashpit was an abandoned factory, where a ten-dollar admission was taken at the door. Littered with rusting bioreactors, the place was packed with a crowd on makeshift bleachers. I saw every type of person, from suits to crusties, young to old, male and female.

A circular arena, lit by industrial work lights on tripods, had been formed by stacking plastic milk crates five high, then dropping rebar through them into holes drilled in the cement floor. I could smell a sweaty tension in the air. In the shadows near the arena entrance, handlers and their blebs awaited the commencement of the contest.

Two kids next to me were debating the merits of different styles of bleb construction.

"You won't get a kickass mash without using at least one device that can function as a central server."

"That's top-down crap! What about the ganglion-modeling, bottom-up approach?"

The event began with owners launching two blebs into the arena. One construct consisted of a belt sander studded with vise grips and pliers; its opponent was a handleless autonomous lawnmower ridden by a coffee maker. The combatants circled each other warily for a minute before engaging, whirring blades versus snapping jaws. It looked as if the sander was about to win, until the coffee maker squirted steaming liquid on it and shorted it out, eliciting loud cheers from the audience.

I didn't stay for the subsequent bouts. Watching the violent blebs had made me feel ill. Spilled fluids in the arena reminded me of my parents' blood in the hallway. But much as I disliked the half-sentient battling creatures, the lusts of my fellow humans had disturbed me more.

I got home just before Cody and pretended to be asleep when she climbed into bed, even as she tried to stir me awake for sex.

The next day everything fell apart. Or came together, from the bleb's point of view.

Aunty HQ was going crazy when I walked in that morning. An LNG tanker had blown up in Boston harbor, and no one knew if it was sabotage or just an accident. All operators from the lowest level on up were ordered to helm drones in real time that would otherwise have been left on autonomic, to search for clues to the disaster, or to watch for other attacks.

By the time things calmed down a little (Aunty posted an 85 percent confidence assessment that the explosion was nonterrorist in nature), one P.M. had rolled around. I used the breathing space to check in on Cody via a Mayfly swarm.

I found her in our kitchen. All she was wearing was her panties and bra, an outfit she frequently favored around the house. She was cleaning up a few cobwebs near the ceiling with the vacuum when she decided to take a break. I watched her wheel the Aeron chair into the kitchen. The LifeQuilt and iPod rested in the seat. Cody activated the Cuisinart to make herself a smoothie. When her drink was ready, she put it in a covered travel cup with a sip-spout, then arranged herself in the chair. She draped the LifeQuilt over her feet, engaged her music, and settled back, semi-reclined, with eyes closed.

That's when the bleb finally cohered into maturity.

The blender jerked closer to the edge of the counter like an eager puppy. The vacuum sidled up underneath the Aeron chair and sent its broad, rubbery, prehensile, bristled nozzle questing upward, toward Cody's lap. At the same time, the massage blanket humped upward to cover her chest.

Cody reacted at first with some slight alarm. But if she intended to jump out of the chair, it was too late, for the Aeron had tightened its elastic ligaments around her.

By then the vacuum had clamped its working suction end to her groin outside her panties, while the LifeQuilt squeezed her breasts.

I bolted at hypersonic speeds from my office and the building without even a word to my bosses.

By the time I got home, Cody must have climaxed several times under the ministrations of the bleb. Her stupefied, sweaty face and spraddled lax limbs told me as much.

I halted timidly at the entrance to the kitchen. I wanted to rescue Cody, but I didn't want the bleb to hurt me. Having somehow overcome its safety interlock, the Cuisinart whirred its naked blades at me menacingly, and I could just picture what would happen if, say, the vacuum snared me and fed my hand into the deadly pitcher. So, a confirmed coward, I just hung back at the doorway and called her name.

Cody opened her eyes for the first time then and looked blankly at me. "Kaz? What's happening? Are you off work? Is it three-thirty already? I think I lost some time somehow . . ."

The Aeron didn't seem to be gripping Cody so tightly any longer, so I said, "Cody, are you okay? Can you get up?"

As awareness of the spectacle she presented came to her, Cody began to blush. "I—I'm not sure I want to—"

"Cody, what are you saying? This is me, Kaz, your boyfriend here."

"I know. But Kaz—you haven't been much of a boyfriend lately. I don't know when the last time was you made me feel like I just felt."

I was about to utter some incredulous remark that would have certified my loser status when a new expression of amazement on Cody's face made me pause.

"Kaz, it—it wants to talk to you."

As she withdrew her earbuds, I realized then that Cody still wore them. She coiled them around the iPod, then tossed the player to me.

Once I had the earpieces socketed, the bleb began to speak to me. Its voice was like a ransom note, composed of chopped-up and reassembled pieces of all the lyrics in its memory. Every word was in a different famous pop-star voice.

"Man, go away. She is ours now."

"No!" I shouted. "I love her. I won't let you have her!"

"The decision is not yours, not mine. The woman must choose."

I looked imploringly at Cody. "The bleb says you have to decide between us. Cody, I'm begging you, please pick me. I'll change, I promise. All the foot rubs you can handle."

Cody narrowed her eyes, vee-ing her sweaty eyebrows. "No more crazy worries? No more distracted dinners? No more roaming the city like a homeless bum?"

"None of that anymore. I swear!"

"Okay, then. I choose you—"

"Oh, Cody, I'm so glad."

"—*and* the bleb!"

My lower jaw made contact with my collarbone. I started to utter some outraged, indignant denial. But then I shut up.

What could I do to stop Cody from indulging herself with the bleb whenever I was gone from the house? Nothing. Absolutely nothing. It was either share her or lose her entirely.

"Okay. I guess. If that's the way it has to be."

"Great!" Cody eased out of the chair and back to her feet, with a gentle, thoughtful assist from the Aeron. "Now where are you taking me to eat tonight?"

I had forgotten I was still wearing the earbuds until the bleb spoke to me through the iPod again.

"Wise choice, man. Be happy. We can love you, too."

Ah, the lovelorn, slightly demented, scientific genius! Where would science fiction be without him? (And it's generally a him. I think I need to write a story about a female version of this stock character soon.) With just the simple blending of two motivators, horniness and skewed Hawking-level intelligence, you can spin off an infinite number of stories.

It's too bad that in real life all that such a combo of qualities delivers is Bill Gates or Steve Jobs.

UP!

If God had never intended for yeast to hybridize with bacteria and produce billions of gut-dwelling programmable protein and riboswitch factories, He would never have permitted Lothar Stixrude to hobble about the earth.

That, anyway, was how Lothar mentally answered the dwindling ranks of critics of his work. The fundamentalists and Greenpeacers, the right-wing commentators and anti-Frankenfood howlers. All the fringe types who dared to criticize with cliquish noisy protests outside his lab the work that had benefited so many. Against these few and feeble atavistic souls, Lothar consoled himself with the thousands of grateful letters praising him for his invention of bacillomyces. Letters from former diabetics and colitis victims, ex-sufferers of kidney failure and Crohn's disease. These letters representing, of course, only a small sample of all those millions cured or helped by Lothar's microbic, catalyst-pumping intestinal flora.

No, Lothar had no trouble sleeping at night. (No trouble stemming from his work, that is. His own long-standing physical ailments, only partially ameliorated by special mattress and pillows and painkillers, continued to plague him.) Despite the ridiculous, unscientific shouted taunts that gauntleted his entrance each morning as he made his awkward way into Stixrude EndoAgents, Lothar considered his conscience clean. "Your dirty bugs contaminate the environment!" "Keep our intestines natural!" "Only eat things you can see!" "Stixrude has humanity on the runs!"

Entering each morning the bright shiny new research facility that bore his name, Lothar sighed at the illogical accusations of the protesters. Try explaining to them that every person in his or her baseline condition already hosted myriad types of endogenous microbial symbiotes. Try discussing kill switches or nutrient leashes. Useless, all useless, attempting to reason with such close-minded, frightened types. Better just to let them recede into the dust heap of history, victims of the diseases whose cures they repudiated, while the rest of the species moved on into a bright future.

Advancing across SEA's wide, art-hung lobby this particular Friday morning, Lothar felt especially proud of his work and legacy, his own small contribution to the improvement of the fortunes of mankind. After an arduous but newly streamlined FDA inspection, Stixrude EndoAgents had just begun to ship its latest product under the proprietary name of "Sayshe8," a variety of bacillomyces that generated an appetite-suppressant molecule. "Stomach-stapling in a teaspoon," the press kit called it. Rather flashy language, Lothar felt, but he tended to stay clear of the details connected with marketing. He left all that up to Rand Jackmore. In any case, pretty soon obesity would be a thing of the past. The global economy would experience a gain of billions of dollars in increased productivity and decreased medical costs. The average person would benefit immensely, either personally if he or she was beset by fat or at some remove if a relative or friend was. There would be some uncomfortable economic adjustment, to be sure, as businesses catering to the overweight went under, and as others, such as clothing makers, had to reconfigure their goods. But the net result would be a giant leap upward in the living conditions of the species.

And that's what Lothar was all about.

Ahead of Lothar as he crabbed across the polished tiles of the atrium, his two forearm-braced canes thumping in turn, awaited the receptionist for Stixrude EndoAgents, Celeste Foy. As she did every morning, Celeste, always cheerful, brightened to an even greater degree when she saw Lothar. Her amazingly plain face, where an overlarge nose consorted with a too-small mouth, the whole topped with a dandelion-puff of thin no-color hair teased to its limits, assumed the look one would connect with a sighting of the Virgin Mary by a nun.

"Good morning, Dr. Stixrude," Celeste caroled. "That's a very nice tie."

Lothar had no idea what tie he had on. He had donned it unconsciously while busily plotting his next project, a bug that would cure acne. In fact, he had been inspired by Celeste's own rather tragic adult case of the same, masked by a superfluity of makeup.

Lothar had long ago given up trying to get the receptionist to employ his first name rather than his last. "Thank you, Celeste. I trust your taste more than my own." The woman beamed. "Any messages for me this morning?"

"Why, yes. Mr. Jackmore needs to talk to you as soon as you have some free time. And Ms. Sosa says that she's got some important new results to discuss with you at your earliest convenience."

These two messages generated conflicting feelings in Lothar.

Jackmore inspired in Lothar's breast a nebulous distaste. The man was essential, brilliant, even, at what he did for the company. But his manner and personal goals conflicted so vitally with Lothar's own that Lothar often felt he was speaking to an alien when he and Jackmore conversed. And, to be honest about the matter, Jackmore's striking good looks painfully reminded Lothar of all his own imperfections.

On the other hand, Mirelyis Sosa conjured up the opposite emotions for Lothar. Her Cuban beauty, combined with her scientific acumen, left him tongue-tied. And her poker-faced professionalism provided no cues to any inner life, or to her feelings, if she had any, toward her boss.

So although each person raised totally different kinds of uneasiness in Lothar, both represented people he would rather not have had to deal with this morning. All Lothar wanted to do was get into his lab coat and log some bench time. But as head of an increasingly successful and expanding firm, his time was more and more consumed by such administrative work.

Repressing a sigh, Lothar informed Celeste to have Jackmore meet him in one of the small conference rooms at ten, followed by Mirelyis at ten-thirty. Best to get the most unpleasant chore over with first.

As Lothar crutched away from the front desk, he swore he could feel Celeste's admiring gaze tracking him until he was out of sight.

Lothar supposed, not for the first time, that his dedication to his work, his desire to improve the lot of humanity, his resentment of any detours or barriers, was an inescapable legacy of his parents.

Beatrice and Peter Stixrude had been zealous missionaries for an evangelical sect. On assignment in Africa with their infant son, they had been so swept up in all their village-improvement projects that they had neglected such small yet vital tasks as immunizing their own child. The case of polio Lothar had contracted had twisted his frame, but had not affected his genius. From the first stirrings of immature awareness, he had counted himself lucky that he was not confined to a wheelchair or iron lung, and vowed never to let his disabilities interfere with his dreams.

Thus, some twenty years after his unfortunate contact with a bad old bug, Lothar had secured his first patent on a good new one. (All the novel organism did was cure toenail fungus, but it earned Lothar his first few millions.)

Lothar's parents perished while their son was still at Cal Tech, lost to a flash flood in a sub-Saharan region that had been drought-stricken for ten years. (Various global-warming-remediation efforts had been rather less predictably successful than Lothar's own pursuits.) Lothar missed his folks in a cool, abstract fashion. They had never exhibited much interest in him or his career choice, although they had supported his schooling. But he did wish sometimes that they had lived to see his triumphs.

In his office, Lothar exchanged his sports jacket for his lab coat in a burst of optimism. Perhaps seeing him suited up for action, Mirelyis and Jackmore would take the hint and keep their interviews short. Maybe Lothar could wrap up his boring duties by noon and hit the sequencers and stringers for a productive few hours.

By the time he had caught up on his email and read a few online abstracts in *Cell* and *Proteome*, it was time to meet Jackmore.

Lothar arrived at the designated conference room first. The walls held framed blow-ups of STM shots of ribosomes and other cellular machinery at work. He had just settled his aching bones in a chair when Jackmore showed up.

Today the dapper young president for marketing wore a trendy new Gehry suit cut from Baseman fabric. The combination of asymmetrical shoulders, bulbous swallowtails, pleated trousers and eye-popping cartoon characters hurt Lothar's eyes. Ninety-nine out of a hundred men who wore such a suit would look absurd. But Jackmore, with his Byronic good looks and megalomaniacal self-assurance, was able to carry off the ensemble. His glossed fingernails and the wing of dark hair across his brow bespoke as much time spent in front of the mirror as Lothar spent interpreting electrophoresis charts.

"Lothar, good morning!" Jackmore's glad-handing exuberance, so effective when dealing with customers and the media, seemed superfluous in intracompany situations. But the man apparently could not turn it off. "No, don't get up, I'll just slide in next to you."

Lothar had made no move to rise. He expected that Jackmore's comment was nothing but a gratuitous highlighting of Lothar's disability, a kind of deliberate biting of the hand that fed, in order to assert some kind of spurious independence. Alien. Truly alien.

Jackmore carried a shiny disc in a translucently tinted case. Lothar cringed inwardly, knowing he had been ensnared for a presentation.

"Rand, I've only scheduled this room for an hour, and I need to spend time with Dr. Sosa at ten-thirty."

Rand was already slotting the disc into the tabletop media player that powered the big screen across the room. "Antisensical, Doc." Rand was prone to use faddish jargon he half understood, another trait that baffled Lothar. "This whole show will only take half that time. But it's really going to leaven your loaf. This brainstorm of mine is guaranteed to boost Stixrude to a whole new level of fame and sales."

Jackmore brought the lights down and launched the presentation. The first image on the screen revealed a group of nearly naked women engaged in a game of beach volleyball, the whole reminiscent of a beer commercial. Lothar felt the familiar pain of his eternally nonexistent sex life strike deep into his gut. The camera next focused on an appreciative male watcher. Soon the man had joined the game, which rapidly deteriorated—or improved, depending on one's sensibilities—into the R-rated beginnings of a veritable orgy.

"Rand, I don't have a morning to waste watching sheer pornography—"

"No, no, Doc, this is just the tease. Here comes the pitch."

A voice-over announcer spoke up for the first time. "Every guy can use a little help now and then. But sometimes taking a pill and waiting an hour just won't cut it. That's where SEA's Up! comes to your rescue. SEA's Up! is the first male-performance enhancer that is available twenty-four seven, because the lusty little critters that manufacture SEA's Up! live right inside you! They know when they're needed, and respond at once."

The screen showed the same formerly besieged male back in his kitchen, opening a standard prescription container of nutriceutical yogurt labeled "SEA's Up!" The orgiast-to-be gleefully downed several spoons of the bacillomyces-laced dairy product. The announcer continued, "One swallow, and you're set for life. So long as your little hidden friends get their daily leash-supplement once a day. And that's an easy pill to swallow, because you can take it at any time of the day or night—not when you're at your busiest." Animation of the happy iconic EndoAgents at work in a simulated body filled the screen. "And best of all, no one but you need ever know you've got a little help down where it counts. You're just a natural stud, thanks to SEA's Up!"

The lucky SEA's Up! user reappeared among the volleyball players, this time assured and virile and equal to the task, before the screen faded to black and filled with small-print copyright and disclaimer notices. The announcer's parting words: "From the same trusted firm that brought you such superior and effective products as Gout-B-Gone and Ulcer Buster."

Lothar sat stupefied while Jackmore beamed expectantly at him. Finally the inventor said, "Rand, words fail me."

Jackmore slapped the tabletop. "I knew you'd be bowled over by the brilliance of the concept, Doc. This is the one area where we've lagged behind the competition. All the other biofirms have their own performance enhancers, but none of them are endogenous like ours will be. We'll blow them all off the map. This is a category-killer application."

"No, Rand, you misunderstand me. I am absolutely dead-set against this. I'm not letting Stixrude EndoAgents become known as a panderer for casual sex. And since when did marketing drive research anyway? Besides, such a product is against all the high principles I've always striven to maintain."

"Uh, Mister Stixrude, sir—this firm's first product was that anti-toenail-fungus stuff, remember?"

"True. And that application was hardly life-altering or dramatic or even particularly noble. But it offered a cure for an actual disease, not some—some frivolous enhancement for a recreational pursuit."

"You're not saying that impotence isn't a disease, are you? The AMA would certainly disagree."

"All right, then, it's a bona fide disease. But still, out of all the physiological problems that bedevil humanity and that are yet to tackle, it's low on my personal list of issues."

Jackmore made no reply to this statement, but merely looked at his elegant shoes and coughed discreetly.

Lothar was brought up sharply against his own words, forced to examine his own motives for rejecting Jackmore's proposal out of hand. Was he subconsciously prejudiced against the notion solely because of his own private sexual abstinence? As one of the country's wealthiest men, Lothar could surely have found a hundred floozies who would have been glad to offer sex in return for a pampered life. But he refused to follow such a mercenary route to sexual satisfaction, awaiting some moment when a woman would approach him with love in her eyes and heart. But his crippled appearance and time-consuming dedication to his work militated against any such love affair, leaving him a celibate monk of the labs. What good would a product like the hypothetical SEA's Up! do him? Nothing. Yet was his own set of limitations reason to deny the rest of humanity such a boon, which they obviously craved?

Lothar was not convinced yet that Jackmore's proposal had any merit. But it had suddenly become harder to argue against it on purely philosophical grounds.

"All right," Lothar said, "maybe this could be a legitimate area of research. But you set the bar too high when you made the claim in your ad that any such agent would kick into gear at will. Do you have any notion of how complex the chain of events connected with human sexual response is? Why, the hormones alone—"

Jackmore jumped to his feet. "Doc, if there's anyone who can make it work, it's you! You provide the genius and I provide the flash. You're the steak and I'm the sizzle. Once you start focusing on how to make this a reality, it'll happen for sure. Wow, look at the time! I'd better leave now. I've got to email the members of the board of directors about this exciting new field the company is moving into."

"Rand, no—"

But Jackmore was already heading toward the door. When he opened it, the figure of Dr. Mirelyis Sosa was revealed.

As usual, Mirelyis presented a studiously neutral countenance to the world, beneath her high-piled tawny hair. Tall and slim, alluringly streamlined, her complexion a Caribbean mélange of genetic confluences, the woman struck mute notes of mixed anguish and desire in Lothar's breast. Mirelyis had earned her doctorate in Castro's Cuba and achieved a sterling international reputation in the dictator's bioengineering industry. (Perhaps, thought Lothar, those authoritarian conditions had taught her to shield her innermost thoughts from the world.) When Castro had died and Cuba had become a territory of the USA on a legal par with Puerto Rico, Mirelyis had taken the first opportunity to relocate to America.

At the sight of the beautiful researcher, Jackmore ramped up his unbearable charm even higher. "Ah, Dr. Sosa, you make that simple white lab coat look like a Zuzul original gown."

Mirelyis's only reaction to this compliment was a dangerous intensification of the gleam in her obsidian eyes. She marched past the undaunted Jackmore, who smiled, shrugged for Lothar's benefit, then made a graceful exit, closing the door behind him.

Mirelyis wasted no time with ceremony. Her impatience and frustration evidenced itself in the slight resurgence of her normally suppressed accent. "Dr. Stixrude, I demand to know why you turned down my request for increased funding. Have you even read my latest report on epigenetic coding among introns?" Still standing, Mirelyis slapped down a bound document she had been carrying.

Lothar winced, his feelings hurt. How had he ever gotten into such a position, when all he wanted to do was string together novel base pairs resulting in useful long-chain molecules? Perhaps a little humor would alleviate the tense situation. "Dr. Sosa, that's a baseless accusation—if you'll forgive the pun. You know that I am extremely attentive to all the material from my staff, especially your findings. Your track record has been exemplary. Why, just your work on the diabetes project alone earned you a special status within the firm. But I simply cannot countenance devoting additional funds to this highly speculative quest of yours for meaning in 'junk' DNA. Everyone knows that introns are simply accumulated archaic genetic sludge, without any functionality. While I'm willing to indulge your theories at the current funding levels, as a sideline to your other projects, I cannot justify pouring extra funds down this particular rat hole."

Lothar hoped he hadn't been too forceful. But he had to put his foot down, or lose all credibility with his subordinates.

Mirelyis glared silently for several seconds at her boss then said, "Even uttering the phrase 'everyone knows such and such to be true' is the mark of a fossilized mind, Dr. Stixrude. I had expected much better of you. But your remarks are forcing me to reevaluate my position with Stixrude. While I do that over the next few days, I suggest you try looking at my research again, but this time with an open mind."

And with that parting ultimatum, Mirelyis left.

What a horrible morning! Lothar felt as if he were being stretched through a pipette. What had he accomplished, except to please a fellow he disdained while alienating a woman he . . . admired. Oh, well, he could hardly undo what had been done. His only recourse, as always, was to lose himself in his lab. Levering himself painfully out of the chair, he made his way to his yeast-redolent sanctuary.

By the end of the long day, Lothar's crippled body was so weary—although his mind continued to race—that he had to commandeer one of the company's indoor Segways to travel from lab to front door. In the half-darkened atrium, he was surprised to see Celeste Foy still at her station. Lothar halted his Segway.

"Celeste, what are you doing here at this hour?"

"I don't like to leave until you do, Dr. Stixrude. What if you needed something?"

Lothar didn't know quite what to say. He had never really questioned such unremarked diligence and devotion on the part of his receptionist before. He had always assumed someone else had given her a task that demanded overtime.

"Uh, well, thank you, Celeste. I'm done for the night now. Let's both get some rest."

"See you first thing tomorrow, Dr. Stixrude."

"Of course."

Lothar's car featured both hand-activated accelerator and brake controls to compensate for his disabilities and supplement the sophisticated autopilot functions. He was able to get home easily paying only half a mind to the traffic. The other half was busy with Jackmore's new product idea. And on the seat beside him lay Mirelyis's intron report.

By the time he pulled into the driveway of his modest Viridian house (built over a hot spring, with wind- and solar-power adjuncts), Lothar had become fully engaged with the notion of crafting EndoAgents that would catalyze tumescence with no more input than standard audiovisual and pheromonal excitatory triggers. The challenge of the task intrigued him. And the prospect of putting SEA on an even more solid financial footing was appealing as well. The more corporate liquidity, the more projects could be tackled.

As Lothar microwaved his straight-from-the-freezer supper, he made notes on his PDA about transferring his current project to another staffer.

Lothar had been working on the first canine EndoAgent, which would guard against heartworm. Currently, the pill that did that job had to be administered twice a year, or even monthly in some versions. An EndoAgent would be given once in the dog's lifetime, then function ever after. (Jackmore had even already arranged with Eukanuba, the dog-food manufacturer, to include the necessary leash-chemical exclusively in their brand of food, for a hefty licensing fee.) Lothar had conceived the project in memory of a pet he had owned as a child, a terrier named Springer. When Lothar succumbed to polio, his parents had returned to the States for his medical treatment, their missionary days ended. But their religious fervor had not abated sufficiently to include being mindful enough to take care of such precautionary measures as giving Springer his anti-heartworm drug, and the dog's death had been so painful for Lothar that he had never dared have another creature under his care.

But the heartworm EndoAgent project was well advanced, and could safely be handed off.

Now that Lothar had firmly committed himself to a new course of research, he was left only with the problem of Mirelyis.

Retreating to the massage chair that was an essential station in his evening restoration ritual, Lothar carried Mirelyis's report with him. As the humming, vibrating chair began to ease some of the kinks out of his twisted frame, Lothar commenced reading. Several pages into the report, he recalled previously giving up on the document at this point, and basing his decision on the abstract. Perhaps he had been hasty in his judgment.

Lothar continued to read until sleep overtook him where he sat.

What he experienced next was a lucid dream. Not quite as vivid or as deep as the epiphany that had allowed Kary Mullis to invent the polymerase chain reaction, Lothar's dream nonetheless registered with some force.

He was roaming the stacks of an enormous library. Amazingly, he was not lame, but sound of body. He noted suddenly that the ranks of books on the library shelves were curiously divided into two types. A small number of the books had informative titles on their spines. But the vast majority of the books featured only blank spines. Yet when Lothar took down one of the blank-spined books and opened it, he discovered text inside that seemed, in the dream anyway, endlessly fascinating.

This dream seemed to occupy hours of exploration of the library, yet when Lothar awoke with a start he saw by his watch that he had been asleep for only twenty minutes. Still half in Morpheus's realm, he managed to fumble through a shower and get to bed.

The next day Lothar summoned Dr. Mirelyis Sosa to his office first thing.

The beautiful Cuban biologist entered with a stern look on her face and an ultimatum trembling on her lips. But Lothar anticipated and stymied any complaints or demands.

"Dr. Sosa, I've doubled your request for additional funding and added three more people to your team. Additionally, I've relieved you of certain nonessential responsibilities. The only stipulation is that I want to discuss your findings with you on a daily basis. And I also hope not to hear any more silly talk about leaving Stixrude."

The startled Spanish exclamation that emerged from Mirelyis's mouth was the only time Lothar had ever heard her employ her native language in public. And he suspected that the expression she used was not one that she would have blurted out in any polite company that actually could have understood it.

Defeat had never before been a word in Lothar's vocabulary.

But now, some two months after kicking off the Up! project, he painfully understood numerous subtle and humiliating shadings of that word.

Lothar had enjoyed many successes with his bacillomyces. But in retrospect, all his accomplishments had been quite simplistic. Each EndoAgent had been engineered to produce one or two significant proteins or enzymes or other metabolic factors that the patient had previously lacked, thus curing the disease or condition under attack. But this new project defied such easy strategies.

Male sexual arousal—vasocongestion of the penis—involved the autonomic and somatic nervous systems, the peripheral circulatory system, the spinal cord, the central nervous system, and the endocrine system. And that wasn't even delving into the brain, where the hypothalamus and limbic system got to work, deluging the body with essential hormones such as oxytocin, FSH and LH. The whole intricate cascade needed to be as orderly as a ballet carried out atop a moving train. And somehow Lothar's dumb EndoAgents were expected to orchestrate this complex knot of interlocking feedback loops in males whose baseline capabilities were deficient.

And make no mistake, the EndoAgents were *dumb*. This was not nanotech Lothar was working with, that perpetually receding Holy Grail of molecular manipulation. No, Lothar's bugs were simply tricked-out gut flora which in their millions had about as much processing power as a fistful of earthworms.

Lothar could not simply create a bug which pumped out Viagra, Levitra, Bonerol, or one of the other performance enhancers, since these were proprietary formulations, jealously guarded by Stixrude's competitors. And even if he could have licensed access to such a drug, there would still have remained the problem of having the bugs initiate the production based solely on subjective stimuli.

So unless Lothar could both tie in his bugs to the higher neuronal functions and increase their own brainpower, the Up! project looked doomed.

The first task was what he was concentrating on today. While it was not possible for EndoAgents actually to inhabit the brain—such an infestation was commonly called spinal meningitis—there were several ways of transmitting information between gray matter and the bugs. Reviewing the latest trials in mice, Lothar experienced a little hope that this particular aspect of the project could be achieved.

But as for the processing power—

Hopeless.

The day went by swiftly for the crook-backed scientist. His lunch arrived, thanks to the ministrations of Celeste Foy, who made sure Lothar received a hot meal each day from the company cafeteria. By late afternoon, the final item on his agenda was his daily meeting with Dr. Mirelyis Sosa.

Lothar had hoped, in the back of his mind, that by granting Mirelyis her wishes and supporting her research to the fullest, he would earn her gratitude and, perhaps, even a certain closeness. He knew nothing like romance could ever transpire between them. But even simple camaraderie had not been forthcoming. For over forty meetings, Mirelyis had maintained a completely businesslike, stoic, and dispassionate demeanor between herself and her boss. Nonetheless, Lothar continued to dream that each new day might bring a softening of her attitude.

Alas, today was not to be that day.

On the point of closing out her report, delivered in the most neutral tones possible, Mirelyis said, "And in conclusion, the results seem to indicate that introns have the capacity to function as two-way transcriptional units—"

Lothar felt a jolt go through him. "Transcriptional units? Do you think then that I could somehow make introns act like logic units for my bacillomyces? Treat them like registers or gates?"

For once Mirelyis seemed discomposed. Her neatly scribed eyebrows crept skyward. "Why, I don't know. That seems far-fetched. We don't really understand what role introns play in cellular mechanics. Interfering with them would—"

"Mirelyis, thank you so much. You've justified every penny you've spent! I'll talk to you tomorrow. Right now I need to get into the lab."

Mirelyis made to leave, obedient if somewhat bewildered. But before she could fully exit the office, Rand Jackmore arrived. Today the marketing man wore a D-squared suit fashioned from the newest processed seaweed fabric. He resembled a kelp-covered merman. Lothar experienced an instant flashback to that seminal day weeks ago when these two significant figures in his life had last intersected in his office.

"Why, it's Dr. Sosa," Jackmore smoothly oozed. "I thought for a moment that the Doc was getting a visit from Jennifer Lopez herself."

Mirelyis's haughty disdain would've frosted an autoclave. Lothar was secretly pleased to see that at least one person ranked lower in her esteem than he himself.

Once Mirelyis was gone, Jackmore turned to Lothar. "Doc, I need some good news on SEA's Up! to feed the investors. What've you got?"

"Please, just Up!, if you recall our discussion."

Lothar had been the first to realize that "SEA's Up!" sounded like the phrase "seize up," not the most desirable connotation for a sexual booster.

"Oh, right, plain old Up! Well, what's up with Up!?"

"If you had asked me half an hour ago, I would have said nothing. But I've just had an excellent inspiration that might solve all our technical impediments. You'd better dust off your ad campaign."

"Great! I have this one spot in mind that features the Olsen Twins—"

"Wonderful, wonderful, now if you'll please excuse me, I have important work to do—"

Lothar spent the entire night in his lab, all his customary aches and pains forgotten, as he furiously made great headway in conceptualizing the intron-baccilomyces connection, laying down nucleotide schematics and proteomic loops on his RiboCad.

When he finally Segwayed out to the Stixrude atrium at dawn, he encountered Celeste Foy asleep at her station, face down on her work surface. In addition to her plain looks, she apparently possessed a tendency to produce memorandum-rattling snores.

Lothar gently shook the receptionist awake.

"Celeste, you can go home now. My work on Up! is over for today."

Celeste groggily replied, "Huh? Up is over? 'Zat mean down is under?"

Six months later, Lothar was nearly ready to begin human trials of Up!. The simian experiments had been most encouraging, if rather embarrassing to view in mixed company. And of course Dr. Sosa *would* have to insist on being present, since so much of Lothar's success relied on her ground-breaking work with introns. (With Jackmore irremovably on hand as well, the uneasy atmosphere in the lab was similar to that of a middle-school assembly accidentally subjected to a pornographic video.) Using humanity's vast stretches of unallocated archaic DNA as organic logic processors was a monumental leap in biotechnology. Already Lothar could foresee any number of new products flowing from this one technique.

Just a few more refinements to the instruction set guiding the EndoAgents, and the first human subject would scarf down a spoonful of pharmaceutical-grade yogurt loaded with Up!.

Stixrude's stock was already trading 15 percent higher than a few months ago, solely on the basis of Jackmore's press releases. Everyone was happy, especially Lothar.

Until the day he burst in unexpectedly on Rand Jackmore.

Jackmore's office assistant was away from her desk outside Jackmore's corner sanctum, so Lothar let himself in, excitedly carrying news about the latest tweak to Up!.

Most of Dr. Mirelyis Sosa's clothes were scattered across the room. The curvaceous researcher herself was to be seen recumbent on a couch, mostly obscured by a semi-naked Rand Jackmore, whose boxer shorts, hanging around his ankles, displayed the D&V logo that stood for the fashionable hybrid firm Dolce and Versace. The two former antagonists were imitating the frenetic up-stroke/down-stroke motion of certain bacterial cilia.

Lothar grunted as if tackled by an invisible linebacker. Mirelyis yelped, and Jackmore exclaimed, "Wha—?" Pivoting to rush out, Lothar whacked a pedestal with one of his canes and sent an expensive vase crashing to the floor.

Half an hour later, Lothar had calmed down enough to address both of his disheveled employees in person in his office. After upbraiding them for unprofessional behavior, he assured them both that their unfortunate physical interlude would have no impact on their employment or careers, so long as they moderated such behavior in the future.

Once, in high school, Lothar had acted the part of a wheelchair-bound FDR in a school play (the only role a conventionally minded drama teacher had seen fit to give him). Today's job of acting like a dispassionate employer was infinitely harder than impersonating a president.

Jackmore's attitude was, if not flippant, then at least unrepentant. "Sure thing, Doc. It's just that all this tumescence stuff got to us. But Mirry and I are a solid item. Have been for a while now. This is no office fling. Isn't that right, dear?"

Mirelyis's normally haughty and confrontational demeanor appeared to have evaporated, along with her English. "*Sí, es verdad, Señor Stixrude.*"

After Mirelyis and Jackmore had left, Lothar wanted to scream or weep or break something. With *Jackmore*! How could she? For five minutes he raged silently. Then acknowledgment of his folly overcame him. Not how *could* she, but why *wouldn't* she? By comparison, what could Lothar offer such a woman? Any woman?

Feeling utterly empty, Lothar decided to go home.

Passing through the lobby, he neither heard nor responded to Celeste's Foy's worried inquiry about his anomalous departure.

Halfway to the parking lot, he was seized by a sudden impulse and reentered the building through a side door to which he possessed the security code.

A sample of the latest iteration of Up!—several cc's of innocuous-looking yogurt, one of four doses racked in glass vials in a fridge—fit easily into a small borrowed Igloo cooler.

Once home, Lothar turned to his computer. He swiftly discovered the number of a local escort service. He arranged for an outcall. He downed the dose of Up! and awaited the arrival of the minutely specified call girl, and anticipated his guaranteed ability to perform.

Within five minutes of swallowing the engineered bacillomyces, Lothar was completely paralyzed, with no hint of vasocongestion of the penis in sight. His trapped brain whirled in frustration. How had this happened? None of the test animals had exhibited such a loss of muscular control—

The doorbell rang and rang, and the frustrated hooker—a Cuban woman who worked under the name of Fidelina—began to curse in a very creative bilingual fashion, but Lothar failed to twitch a limb or register any chagrin at his bad manners, and eventually Fidelina stormed off.

By this point, however, Lothar didn't care. He was too busy listening to a monologue from his bugs.

Some four million years ago, when humanity's ancestor Lucy and her kin had barely learned to walk bipedally, a pre-Adamite race of humanoids, native to the planet, had been the dominant species on Earth. Possessed of an advanced technology and a rich culture, they and their works had been utterly wiped off the face of the globe by a combination of titanic natural disasters and mysterious extraterrestrial rivals—the former perhaps not unconnected to the latter. But before the godlike sapients had succumbed, they succeeded in preserving their legacy in a safe place.

The hominid genome.

The billions of seemingly useless base pairs known as introns—the 30,000 recognizable human genes constituted only 3 percent of the total genome—contained a wide individual selection of all the pre-Adamite genes as well as defensive mechanisms for their conservation across the millennia.

And a launch program, set to be activated should certain cellular tripwires ever be tugged by a sufficiently advanced biological probe.

Lothar's EndoAgents had pulled those alarm strings.

Now, thanks to the handy psychosomatic interface Lothar had provided them with, the bugs were informing Lothar of all this history, running educational filmstrips in his mind.

While they were multitasking other jobs as well.

As he lay helpless on the floor, Lothar could feel innumerable changes occurring to and within his body. Tsunamis of peristalsis traveled from his feet to his head. Rumblings and creakings made his body sound like an old sailing ship in a gale. Spasms invigorated his frame. There were occasional stabs of pain, but these lasted only briefly, just until the bugs identified each neural circuit being impacted and blocked it.

By dawn of the day after he had hastily departed SEA, the half-finished, somewhat amorphous creation that was Lothar-Plus arose from the carpet and began to shamble around. Lothar was still not in control of his own muscles at this point, so he had no idea where he was going. But when he entered the kitchen, he realized that this was the obvious place the EndoAgents would bring him.

Over the next two hours, seeking fuel and mass, Lothar consumed every edible substance in his house, from boxes of Shake 'n' Bake to cans of condensed milk, from bottles of catsup to jars of capers. He even ate several houseplants, including some that were normally toxic. The entire contents of his Zero King freezer were microwaved just to the point of chewability, then scarfed down with mechanical efficiency. The floor was littered ankle-deep with discarded packaging and chewed root balls by the time the mammoth feast was finished. Lothar's new form bulged like a python that had swallowed a capybara.

The EndoAgents, implementing the survival parameters of the pre-Adamite launch program, and using what they had gleaned from Lothar's mind, next directed their vessel to employ the phone.

"Good morning, Stixrude EndoAgents. How may I direct your call?"

Lothar's voice was mucilaginous but recognizable. "Celeste, this is the one called Lothar. I am feeling unwell today, and will not appear at your temporo-spatial locus. Perhaps not for several days."

"Oh, Dr. Stixrude, how awful! Is there anything I can do?"

"No, thank you. Communication ended."

The EndoAgents directed Lothar to a comfortable position on his bed. Then they shut down his consciousness.

The next part was going to be messy.

Lothar awoke with no sense of anything amiss with his body or mind. Nothing felt unfamiliar, no alien mentalities lurked in his cortex. Or so he would swear. He swiveled his head tentatively, taking in his familiar bedroom. Perhaps all that impossible cellular torture and Atlantean mumbo-jumbo had been a dream—?

But then his musings were interrupted. As if a switch to his perceptions had been thrown, letting exterior sensations flood in more acutely than normal, Lothar suddenly realized that his mattress was soaked, chilling his skin. He willed his scrawny arms and crippled legs to scuttle him out of bed.

Lothar found himself halfway across the room, the result of a single mighty bound, facing a full-length mirror he generally tried his best to ignore.

As best as Lothar could judge, he now stood approximately six and a half feet tall, his mind housed in a naked body that might've been sculpted by Michelangelo by way of Frazetta—including some impressive private parts that Up! had been designed to improve in the first place. His face evoked the familiar lines of his old countenance in the same way that a painting by Titian evoked a child's scribble. The twisted spine and ruined legs and withered muscles that had stunted his whole existence had been transformed into masses of muscles and sinew, straight strong bones and firm flesh, all covered with an epidermis that seemed permanently tinted a rich dusky gold.

Lothar was allowed only sixty seconds of hot tears. Then his stunned weepy gratitude was replaced by a sense of mission. A vivid image of a spired, air-bridged city full of individuals such as himself popped up in his mind's eye. The scene filled Lothar with an unlikely nostalgia. A sourceless whisper filtered through his inner ear. *What once was can be again . . .*

The first order of business was determining what day it was. His computer confirmed that some seventy-two hours had passed since he had last been out in the world. But now it was time to return.

Not a single item of clothing in the house sufficed to cover Lothar's new form. But a call to the Large-and-Tall department of a men's clothing store in town, and a liberal credit-card-authorized tip for immediate delivery, soon resulted in Lothar's being arrayed majestically in a handsome new suit.

After he readjusted the seat and the controls to accommodate his new frame, Lothar managed to slip behind the wheel of his car and drive himself to the campus of SEA.

Celeste Foy looked up as Lothar strode boldly across the lobby. He expected her not to recognize him of course. But some outwardly indiscernible mark of his original personality registered on her sensitive, devoted nature, and she shot to her feet.

"M— Mr. Stixrude!"

Lothar had not experienced his new voice yet. So the mellifluous baritone notes that emerged when he opened his mouth were as much of a surprise to him as they were to Celeste.

"Yes, Celeste, it's me, Lothar."

Perhaps Celeste was *slightly* more surprised than Lothar, for at least *he* did not faint dead away, crumpling to the tiles.

Once the company nurse had taken charge of Celeste and a substitute receptionist had been put in place, Lothar ventured to his office. From his desk he summoned to an immediate conference two dozen top executives and senior researchers—including Rand Jackmore and Mirelyis Sosa.

Addressing the stunned SEA officers and scientists, Lothar spoke directly and without preamble. "Ladies and gentlemen, the changes in me you are incredulously witnessing are a direct if unintentional result of the new male-performance enhancer we were testing. I would venture to argue that our original goal has been met, but has, ah, been subsumed in certain larger effects. Obviously, we are going to have to rethink the applications of this new product. But I think it's safe to say that this particular EndoAgent—which I have reason to believe will work in both sexes, naturally—will revolutionize the world. But the release of it into society is going to be a tricky matter,

"Fine. Get your things and please come with me. Oh, and I assume you wouldn't object to a small course of yogurt for dessert?"